Good Graces

ALSO BY LESLEY KAGEN

Whistling in the Dark
Land of a Hundred Wonders
Tomorrow River

Good Graces

LESLEY KAGEN

DUTTON

DUTTON
Published by Penguin Group (USA) Inc.
375 Hudson Street, New York, New York 10014, U.S.A.
Penguin Group (Canada), 90 Eglinton Avenue East, Suite 700, Toronto, Ontario M4P 2Y3, Canada
(a division of Pearson Penguin Canada Inc.); Penguin Books Ltd, 80 Strand, London WC2R 0RL,
England; Penguin Ireland, 25 St. Stephen's Green, Dublin 2, Ireland (a division of Penguin Books
Ltd); Penguin Group (Australia), 250 Camberwell Road, Camberwell, Victoria 3124, Australia (a
division of Pearson Australia Group Pty Ltd); Penguin Books India Pvt Ltd, 11 Community Centre,
Panchsheel Park, New Delhi—110 017, India; Penguin Group (NZ), 67 Apollo Drive, Rosedale,
Auckland 0632, New Zealand (a division of Pearson New Zealand Ltd); Penguin Books (South
Africa) (Pty) Ltd, 24 Sturdee Avenue, Rosebank, Johannesburg 2196, South Africa

Penguin Books Ltd, Registered Offices: 80 Strand, London WC2R 0RL, England

Published by Dutton, a member of Penguin Group (USA) Inc.

First printing, September 2011
1 3 5 7 9 10 8 6 4 2

REGISTERED TRADEMARK—MARCA REGISTRADA

LIBRARY OF CONGRESS CATALOGING-IN-PUBLICATION DATA
has been applied for.

ISBN 978-0-525-95238-1

Printed in the United States of America
Set in Sabon Lt. Std.
Designed by Leonard Telesca

PUBLISHER'S NOTE

This book is a work of fiction. Names, characters, places, and incidents either are the product of the
author's imagination or are used fictitiously, and any resemblance to actual persons, living or dead,
business establishments, events, or locales is entirely coincidental.

For my children

Good Graces

Prologue

That summer earned itself a place in the record books that's never been beat. The hardware store sold out of fans by mid-June and the Montgomery twins fainted at the Fourth of July parade. By the time August showed up, we couldn't wait to send it packing.

To this day, my sister insists it was nothing more than the unrelenting heat that drove us to do what we did that summer, but that's just Troo yanking my chain the way she always has. Deep down, she knows as well as I do that it wasn't anything as mundane as the weather. It was the hand of the Almighty that shoved us off the straight-and-narrow path.

Whenever the old neighborhood pals get together, if it's a particularly sticky evening, the way they all were back then, memories get tickled up. Sitting out on one of our back porches in the dwindling light, somebody will inevitably bring up the mysterious disappearance of one of our own that long-ago summer. *Do you think he was murdered? What about kidnapping? He could have just taken off.* Trying to figure out what happened to him has become as much fun for our friends as remembering our games of red light, green light and penny candy from the Five and Dime.

But for the O'Malley sisters, the fate of that certain someone is no more mysterious than the way he broke my front tooth that sultry August night. The two of us know exactly where that devil in the details has been for the past fifty years. He's where we buried him the sweltering summer Troo was ten and I was eleven.

The summer of '60.

Chapter One

Somebody at his funeral called Donny O'Malley *lush*. I couldn't agree more. Daddy was just-picked corn on the cob and a game-saving double play all rolled into one, that's how lush he was.

Someone else at the cemetery said that time heals all wounds. I don't know about that.

Daddy crashed on his way home from a baseball game at Milwaukee County Stadium three years ago. The steering wheel went into his chest. I wasn't in the car that afternoon. I hadn't weeded my garden so he told me I had to stay back on the farm and I told him I hated him and wished for a different daddy. I didn't mean it. I'd just been so looking forward to singing The Land of the Free and the Home of the *Braves*. Eating salty peanuts and the seventh-inning stretch.

When he was in the hospital, Daddy shooed everyone else out of the room and had me lie down with him. "No matter what, you must take care of Troo," he told me. "Keep her safe. You need to promise me that." He had tubes coming out of him and there was a *ping ping*ing noise that reminded me of the *20,000 Leagues Under the Sea* movie. "Tell your sister the crash wasn't her fault. And . . . tell your mother that I forgive her. I'll be watching, Sally. Remember . . . things can happen when you least expect them . . . you . . . you always gotta be prepared. Pay attention to the details. The devil is in the details."

I never forget what he told me or what I promised him, but Daddy is especially on my mind this morning. When it's baseball season, I always remember him better. The other reason I'm thinking about him is because Troo and me just got home from getting our brand-new start-of-the-summer sneakers at Shuster's Shoes on North Avenue. That's the store where Hall Gustafson used to work. He's the man Mother got married to real quick after Daddy died. My sister thinks she accepted his proposal because Hall had a tattoo on his arm that said *Mother*, but I think she did it because Daddy forgot to leave us a nest egg. I watched Mother collapse in our cornfield and beat the dirt with her fists, shouting, "Donny! How could you?" but I forgave him right off. When you're a farmer, it's hard to put something away for a rainy day.

The whole time we were trying on Keds this morning, I kept imagining that slobbering Swede stumbling out from behind the curtain where the shoes are hidden, but that was dumb. Our stepfather doesn't have a job at Shuster's or anyplace else anymore because he got into a fight at Jerbak's Beer 'n Bowl with the owner, who was famous around here for bowling a 300 game but also for being quick with his fists. Hall's in the Big House now. For murdering Mr. Jerbak with a bottle of Old Milwaukee. Sometimes in bed at night when I can't sleep, which is mostly all the time, I think about how good that all worked out and just for a little while it makes me feel like God might know what He's doing. At least part of the time. He did a bad job letting Daddy die, but I admire how the Almighty got rid of Mr. Jerbak and Hall in one fell swoop. That really was killing two dirty birds with one stone.

Troo wasn't thinking about Hall when we were up at the store. Not how he dragged her out of bed and knocked her head against the wall or any of the other rotten stuff he did like sneaking behind Mother's back with a floozy. My sister was having the best time this morning. She's nuts about Shuster's because it's so modern. They've got a Foot-O-Scope machine that's like an X-ray. Troo adores pressing her eyes to the black viewer to see inside her feet, but when I look down at my bones, they remind me of Daddy lying beneath the cemetery dirt.

"Ya know what I been thinkin', Sal?" my sister asks.

We're sitting on the back steps of the house. I'm raring to go, but she's working hard to loop her new shoelaces into bunny ears. Troo was in the crash with Daddy. She played peek-a-boo with him on the way home from the baseball game. Holding her hands over his eyes for longer than she shoulda is what caused the car to go skidding out of control and smash into the old oak tree on Holly Road. She got her arm fractured. It aches before it's going to rain and also made her not very good at tying.

"What?" I ask her.

"It would be a fantastic idea for us to get away from the neighborhood for a while. We should go away to camp this summer," she says, batting her morning-sky blue eyes at me.

My eyes are green and I don't have hair the color of maple leaves in the fall the way Troo does. I have thick blond hair that my mother brushes too hard and puts into a fat braid that goes down my back and deep dimples that I've been told more than a few times are very darling. I've always had long legs, but this past year they grew three and a half inches. My sister thinks I look like a yellow flamingo.

"We need to expand our horizons," Troo says.

Even though we don't look very much alike, we are what people call Irish twins. Troo will turn eleven two months before I turn twelve. I always know what she is *really* thinking and feeling. We have mental telepathy. So that's how come I know my sister isn't telling me the truth about why she wants to go to camp. It's not the neighborhood she wants to get away from. She likes living in the brick house with the fat-leafed ivy growing up the sides and bright red geraniums in the window boxes and lilacs falling over the picket fence like a purple waterfall. It's the *owner* of the house Troo's got problems with. She wants to get away from Dave Rasmussen, who we moved in with at the end of last summer. He is my real father because when Daddy was in the war Mother accidentally had some of the sex with Dave.

For the longest time, I didn't know that Dave was my flesh and blood. When I found out, I didn't think I would get over it, but I mostly have, in my mind anyway. In my heart, Daddy is still my daddy and Dave is Dave. Maybe someday that will change for me, but it *never* will for my sister. Daddy will always be her one and only. He looked at her like she was a slice of banana cream pie. I was his second-favorite, plain old dependable cherry, and that was fine with me. When you got a sister like Troo, you gotta expect these things.

"I don't want to expand anywhere," I tell her. "My horizons are fine."

"Yeah, that's what you think, but Mrs. Kambowski told me

that a person should get out and see the world whenever they can," Troo tells me in her know-it-all voice that is not my favorite. "She said that travel is *très chic*."

"She's wrong." Mrs. Kambowski is the boss of the Finney Library who won't stop teaching my sister these French words no matter how many times I politely ask her to stop. "Ya know as good as me that goin' someplace you've never been before can turn out really bad," I remind Troo. "Remember what happened to Julie Adams in the *Creature from the Black Lagoon* when she went to the Amazon? And what about Sky King? He always gets into trouble when he goes flyin' off into the horizon." Daddy and I never missed that show because he was a pilot, too. "And . . . and what about all the bad stuff that happened to us when we moved from the country to the city?"

"I knew you'd say that," she says with a smile that can bring the dead back to life. She inherited it from Daddy. He gave her her nickname, too. After she got a rusty nail pulled out of her heel and didn't even flinch, he started calling her "a real trouper" and then because that took too long to say we began to call her Trooper and then shortened it even more. Her real name is Margaret. I also call her my Troo genius because she is really smart. She can come up with plans like nobody's business. Like this camp one she's trying to sell to me harder than the Fuller Brush man tries to talk Mother into a new broom even though the old one's still got plenty of bristles. "That's why I was thinkin' we wouldn't go someplace brand-new. We could go to the same camp Mary Lane went to last year. That one up in Rhinelander. She bragged about it so much . . . it's like we've already been there, right?"

"Wrong." Down the block, Bobby Darin is singing on the radio, "Won't you come home Bill Bailey," and that has to be a sign from

God to stay put right where I am. I might not have a lot of belief in Him anymore, but I got enough to pay attention to the details.

Still struggling with the laces, Troo says, "I'm . . . I'm not thinkin' about me."

Yes, she is.

"I looked up what's wrong with you in Mother's medical book. An ocean voyage or a change of scenery is the best cure for people who have lunatic imaginations," she says in her dolly voice, which is so hard not to give in to even if you know she's just putting it on to get what she wants; it's adorable. "Since ya don't like being near water so much anymore, I figure a boat trip is out." When I don't agree, she doesn't give up. She never does. "I bet you'd sleep a lot better breathin' in all that country air."

I doubt it.

Troo hits the hay every night like a bale falling outta our old barn loft. Wrapped in Daddy's sky-blue work shirt that still has the smell of his Aqua Velva hidden under the collar, she holds her baby doll Annie up to her cheek and I feel her sweaty leg pressed up to mine and sometimes I count the freckles on her nose to see if she sprouted any new ones or walk my bare feet against the bedroom wall because it's always cooler on that wall and my thoughts go round and round and I flip over on my tummy and stare at the picture of Daddy that hangs over our bed. He's in a boat holding up a fish. His hair is blown into two horns. Troo says that he looks "devil-may-care" in that picture and maybe he does, but he probably isn't anymore. I didn't do that good a job last summer keeping my sister safe the way he asked me to. It seems like no matter how hard I try to be prepared I'm not ready for the bad when it shows up. Take Bobby Brophy. He was the playground counselor who almost murdered and molested me last summer and I didn't suspect a thing. He hurt my sister, too. Knocked her out cold.

"Hey!" Troo nudges me. "I just remembered. The camp's in a pine forest. That means it'd smell like Christmas every morning and that's your favorite holiday." She brings one sneaker and then the other into my lap and says, "Tie me up."

Oh, how I wish I could. With a strong rope. I would anchor her to me.

"And ya know what the best part of us goin' to camp would be, the real *pièce de résistance*?" she says. "You won't have to visit Doc Keller while we're gone!"

Mother makes me go up to his office on North Avenue once a week so he can give me a dose of cod liver oil and a stern lecture with his breath that smells like old vase water. He warns me each and every time that I better get my imagination under control or else. "An idle mind is the devil's workshop," he says, but Doc couldn't be more wrong. My mind is never idle. Never ever. And it's getting worse. I think all that cod liver oil might be greasing my wheels.

"Whatta ya say, Sal, my gal?" My sister picks up my hand and twines her fingers through mine. She knows I'm a sucker for that. "Ya in?"

"But what about Mother?" I ask. Through the screen door, I can hear the sound of her picking up the house. She's still kinda wobbly. If somebody you know gets sick with a gall bladder that turns into liver problems and then a staph infection like what happened to her last summer, you better start saying your prayers. Doc Keller told all of us that he'd never heard of a person getting over something that fatal. "Who's gonna get her nummy and what if she needs something like—"

Troo hawks and throws a loogie, which is something she has started doing lately when she wants to make a point. "What's-his-name can take care of her."

She means Dave, who bends over backwards for Troo, same as me, so against my better judgment, which I don't hardly have much left of anymore, I end up telling him that night out on the backyard bench that both of us want to go to Camp Towering Pines in the worst possible way. I didn't want to, but I *had* to lie to him. I know my sister. She'd figure out some way to go to that camp without me. There's no telling what kind of trouble she could get into if I wasn't there to stop her. And I made that promise to Daddy that I'll never break. Even if my life depends on it.

Chapter Two

All I keep thinking about on the six-hour bus ride up to Rhine-lander is how hard it is to keep my sister under my thumb in the neighborhood. In a new and different place she could slip through my fingers so easy. This is not even counting that she could drown, get shot through the heart by an archery arrow or, worst of all, the counselors could do something when she least expects it. I asked Dave about them after he pulled some strings to get us into Camp Towering Pines. He told me not to worry, that there would be only girl counselors and, "Maybe getting away for a while will do you some good, kiddo."

At the start of the trip, Troo was by my side counting license plates and singing along with the rest of the kids the *99 Bottles of Beer on the Wall* song, but I didn't open my mouth. I was afraid I might toss my cookies again. I already did once and my sister's mad at me for "stinkin' up the joint," so that's why she moved to the seat behind me and is telling everybody that we got on at different stops.

When the bus pulls into the campground, I turn to tell Troo, "I . . . I changed my mind . . . I'm sorry . . . we gotta go back home right away. I can't . . ." but she's already gone. She rushed right past me outta the bus. Through the window, I can see her bouncing and smiling, looking the happiest I've seen her in over a year.

What choice do I have?

Once the counselors get me and Troo and the rest of the girls lined up in front of the main wigwam, they hold up their palms to each and every one of us, saying "How" over and over and over again when they stick feathers in our hair that still have part of the bird left on 'em. After that, they hand out our Indian maiden names that we are to be known by for the rest of the week. They call me Minihaha. (Mother made me get a haircut from our eight-years-older-than-me half sister, Nell, who, even though she is a graduate of Yvonne's School of Beauty, made my bangs too short because she's a basket case, so even I gotta admit, I look a little funny.)

Troo is to be known as Lovely Princess Floating Gently Down the Stream of Unending Happiness Beneath a Rainbow.

Every day is torture. Every night couldn't be worse.

In the morning, we're supposed to swim in Lake Freezing Cold but I can barely do the dead man's float. When the triangle bell rings at noon, we have to go to the mess hall and eat a lunch of beans and wienies and drink the juice of bugs. After that, we gotta do crafts. Forced to make leather coin purses. There's skeeters the size of dragonflies, an outhouse that anybody could fall into and once the sun sets, those counselors always got a grisly story all warmed up. Their favorite is this one about an escaped lunatic with a hook who goes after couples who are watching the submarine races on Lovers' Lane. After they douse the campfire, one of the counselors always reminds us to pretend we're not kids from the city sleeping in bunk beds in a cabin in the woods of Wisconsin, but real Indian children curled up in teepees on a wide open plain. But even me, who has no problem imagining just about anything, can't feature that. What I *can* picture so clearly is that lunatic with the hook deciding that a pretty little redheaded girl is right up his alley so he rows one-handed from the other side of the lake after midnight, crawls into our cabin, snatches my sister and runs off with her into the woods. The next morning, Lovely Princess would no longer be Floating Gently Down the Stream of Unending Happiness Beneath a Rainbow but found under one of those Christmas trees like a ripped-open present.

That's why I've been spending my nights tossing and turning even worse than I usually do, which I didn't think was humanly possible. Standing watch over my sister is never easy and she hasn't been any help at all. She giggles along with the other girls when they tease me about the dark circles I've got under my eyes. No matter how deep I stick my fingers in my ears, I can hear them calling me "Smudgy" and telling each other how camp is the greatest and that they never want to go home, which makes me feel even more like the odd maiden out because that's *all* I want to do. I miss . . . everything. Troo doesn't. She's been having a gay old time making sit-upons and new friends and practicing her ventriloquist act for The Heap Big Talent Show, which is tonight.

I know that I'm not good at a lot of things, not like Troo is, but I do my best after my sister drags me up on the camp stage and growls into my ear, "You're embarassin' me. Again. Do one of your dumb imitations."

So I try to perform my best Edgar G. Robinson, "You dirty rat," but my tongue gets so twisted up that it comes out sounding like, "You thirty brats," which makes everybody boo, and one kid, who is my sister, throws a stick of beef jerky at me. Of course, after all is said and done, Troo wins the top talent prize, The Golden Tomahawk, hands down. Nobody even cares that her lips moved.

By the time Sunday comes, I am very weak, almost floppy. I got a nose ache from pressing it against the cabin window counting the minutes until Dave's woody station wagon comes roaring up the camp drive to rescue me.

When I finally spot him, I try to yell, "He's here! He's here!" but I hardly have enough air left in me to sigh out to Troo, "We're goin' home."

"You are. I don't got a home anymore," she hollers on her run out the cabin door.

She hides in a tree and refuses to budge, but Dave is brave and tells her that she has until the count of three to get down. That takes a lotta guts on his part because he knows Troo will give him the cold shoulder all the way home. Or maybe that's why he nixed the staying-longer-at-camp idea in the first place. Just to shut her up. I love my sister, I would die for her, but a spade is a spade. Troo is a smart alec, most especially to Dave, who she reminds, "You're not my real father," in case he forgot after she said it a half hour ago.

On the drive home, once Troo falls asleep against my shoulder hugging The Golden Tomahawk, I tap Dave on the shoulder and tell him, "Thank you for sendin' us! That was really something!"

The reason I am not telling him that camp was the fourth-worst experience of my life behind losing Daddy and Mother almost dying and Bobby trying to murder me is because I don't want to hurt his feelings. Dave is a lot like me in the personality department.

That's who I get it from. Not from my mother, who says, "Being sensitive and a dime will get you a cup of coffee."

But when he parks the woody station wagon in front of our house on 52nd Street, since he is a police detective, Dave mighta deduced that I didn't tell him the truth, the whole truth and nothing but about my camping experience. Because after Troo stomps off in a huff, I can't stop myself from leaping out of the car, sinking down on my knees and kissing our front lawn, that's how grateful I am to get back to the city where I know who lives in what house, which shortcuts we shouldn't take and, most important, all the best hiding places.

Chapter Three

The first day back home, my sister and me and one of our best friends, Mary Lane, are having what Troo calls a *rendezvous* at Washington Park, the most important place to everybody in the neighborhood next to Mother of Good Hope Church. The park's got everything.

Like the lagoon.

I used to love standing under the weeping willow and throwing in a hook, but I had to give that up. Instead of whiling away an afternoon dreaming about what I'm gonna catch, all I can think about these days are the innocent little fish swimming below the surface, so overjoyed to see that friendly worm waving in the water that they don't even stop to wonder at their good luck. The lagoon is where the police found the two dead girls with pink undies tied around their necks in pretty bows. First one summer and then the next, Junie Piaskowski and Sara Marie Heinemann were laid out next to the rotting red rowboats you can rent for a dollar and I was almost spread out there, too. I could hear the muddy lagoon water lapping onto the rocks when Bobby Brophy ripped his shirt off over his head.

The park also has a swimming pool. I just about go dead in the water watching Troo climb up those silvery high-dive steps and run to the end of the board screaming, "Geronimo," which she will probably do even louder now after all the practice she got at camp.

The Jack Hoyt Woods are a big relief. When you can't take the sun beating down on you for one more second, you can eat a peanut-butter-and-marshmallow sandwich in a leafy branch or get your an-kles wet when you look for leeches under slimy rocks in the Honey Creek that runs through it.

There's also a band shell, but it's not much good until after it gets dark. That's why it's called *Music Under the Stars*. Once a week you can lie out on a blanket and hear an orchestra perform some-thing like *Rhapsody in Blue* by Mr. George Gershwin (one of Mother and Dave's favorites) and drink cup after cup of Graf's Root Beer (Troo guzzles it) while you search for the Big and Little Dippers in the western sky (Daddy went nuts for them). When the show's all over, everybody in the neighborhood gathers their stuff and walks back home, laughing and calling to each other, or sometimes there's a scuffle because they mighta had too much *Pabst Blue Ribbon Under the Stars*.

And it's not only during the months of June, July and August when this park is the star of the show. When it gets cold and snowy, you can take a leap onto your flying saucer on Statue Hill. Or bundle up and go skating. I feel much better being around the lagoon once it freezes over. I can't do spins or jumps or anything else fancy like that, but I like the feel of the chilly air on my forehead and the blades cutting through the ice sound like I mean business.

But the absolute best part of the park, no matter what time of the year it is, has always been right where we are. The zoo. Sitting on the bench under our favorite climbing tree in front of Sampson the gorilla's enclosure. Daddy and I used to sit at this exact same spot together. He'd point at Sampson and say, "Some people say the lion is the king of the jungle, but I'd have to disagree with them. Just look at him, Sal! He is magnificent!" I would nod my head, but what I was secretly thinking was *No, Daddy, you are the king. Of the land and the sky. It's you who is magnificent.*

That was in the good old days. Before the night Bobby the counselor set me down on the grass near the lagoon. Before I heard Daddy's voice call to me from on high—*Now, Sal, now . . . fly like the wind*—and I ripped down the zoo path and jumped over the black iron fence in front of Sampson's enclosure. When Bobby caught up to me, he gave me the same winning smile I loved when we played chess together at the playground. Only that night he didn't say, "Checkmate. Better luck next time." He ran the tip of his tongue over his top lip so slowly and whispered, "Gotcha," and I was sure that he did. But when he leaped over the fence, the air came off his body and his arms became wings. I waited until the timing was right and I ducked. Bobby flew over my head like Sky King's *Songbird* and crashed down into Sampson's pit. He died, so the only one he's playing chess with now is Lucifer.

The reason we came here today is so I can say one last good-bye to Sampson. On one side of me on the zoo bench this morning is Mary Lane. (We have to call her by her first and last name like that because around here if you just shout out "Mary" you could get trampled to death since it is the most popular name there is due to the Blessed Virgin.) Mary Lane is wearing her usual high-top ten-nis shoes and just like us, shorts and a T-shirt. She smells like stale potato chips. She always does. On my other side is my sister. Troo couldn't care less about saying *au revoir* to Sampson if she tried. She only came along so she can bug Mary Lane. My sister's got on her navy blue *beret*. It's a flat hat perched high on top of her hair, which our beautifying half sister, Nell, has shown her how to put into a French twist.

"Just 'cause they're movin' the zoo doesn't mean ya ain't never gonna see Sampson again," Mary Lane tells me.

She doesn't take up much room on the bench. Even after Doc Sullivan pulled that tapeworm out of her, she is still the skinniest kid you've ever seen. She'd probably go invisible if her zookeeper father didn't give her bananas for free. She is also a peeper. She lights fires, too. And I secretly think that she is the cat burglar that's been prowling around the neighborhood for over two months now. (This is *not* a person who steals pets, which is what most people think until somebody sets them straight. A cat burglar is what you call somebody who gets dressed in black and comes into your house sneaky to steal something precious.) Mary Lane could easily slip through a barely open kitchen window, especially if she smelled a pot roast cooking on the other side, and she spends a ton of time at the zoo so she knows how tigers and leopards move like they're doing you a big favor by setting their feet down and really, she is sort of hard up and doesn't have a very big conscience so it makes sense that she is the one breaking one of the Command-ments and coveting her neighbors' valuables out of their houses. She could hock them at Gerald's Pawnshop on North Avenue to get money for food.

I haven't told my suspicions about Mary Lane to Troo. She

would find some way to use that against her and make fun of my imagination while she was doing it. I know I should, but I haven't told Dave either. He's the cop in charge of hunting the cat burglar down. Mary Lane is one of my two best friends and I'm no stool pigeon, but even if I was, what a waste of time that'd be. Even if Dave caught her and threw her in jail, how would they ever keep her skinny self behind bars?

Mary Lane says, "My dad's been goin' out to the new zoo every day to get things set up for when it opens. He told me that Bluemound Road is pretty far away, but not that far."

Mr. Lane, who works at the zoo feeding the animals and doing other odd jobs, told us that they will all be packed up by tomorrow and then the bulldozers will come and knock down the buildings to put in a new expressway. The birds are already gone. Of course, the swans put up a fuss. They always remind me of Troo. Gorgeous to look at, but what a mouth they got on 'em. While we were away at camp, the chimps got taken away from Monkey Island in black zipper bags after they got sleeping shots. The reptile house has been boarded up for a while, which is no skin offa my nose. Mary Lane kept telling me last summer that Bobby Brophy reminded her of a boa constrictor, which is a kind of snake that can swallow a kid whole. If only I'd listened to her.

"Hey," Mary Lane says, flicking me on the arm. "Ya havin' one a your flights of imagination?"

This is one of the reasons she is my best friend. Mary Lane understands that my mind flies around sometimes without me and *I* understand that she's got a problem with getting her facts straight when she tells a story, so that works out good for both of us.

"Sorry?" I answer.

"I was just sayin' that you'd probably need to take at least three buses to get out to the new zoo to see Sampson."

"Really?" I ask. I'm never sure if what she's telling me is the whole truth or not. You really do have to be careful with her. I used to think she was the biggest, fattest liar around, but she isn't. Not exactly. Mary Lane is what my other best friend, Ethel Jenkins, describes as "a no-tripper." That's what Mississippi folks call somebody who doesn't let the truth trip them up when they're telling you a story.

"Yeah, at least three buses," Mary Lane says, picking at a scab on her knee. "Maybe four, but it could be as many as seven."

"What do ya think?" I ask Troo, who isn't really paying attention. Now that she's done one-upping Mary Lane about getting to go to Camp Towering Pines this summer, going so far as to bring her Golden Tomahawk talent trophy in a shopping bag so she can shove it in our best friend's face, my sister is paging through a book she got yesterday from the Finney Library. She's not actually reading *Around the World in Eighty Days* because according to her, books are for boneheads like me. Troo's looking at the pictures to get the idea of the story so she can tell it to Mrs. Kambowski. You can't hardly go anywhere these days without hearing a joke about how dumb the Polacks are, so that's why there's not a doubt in my mind the librarian will fall for my sister's plan. Troo wants to win the Billy the Bookworm prize this summer in the worst way. She got the free movie passes to the Uptown Theatre last summer even though she didn't really win them fair and square; Mary Lane did. For some dopey reason, Mrs. Kambowski gave my sister the prize anyway.

"What do I think about what?" Troo says, turning the page.

"Could we take three buses or more to visit Sampson out on

Bluemound Road?" I say, trying, but not able, to keep the shakiness out of my voice.

"H-E-double hockey sticks," Troo says, slamming the book down on the bench. "I knew this was gonna happen. I just knew it! You bein' a wet blanket at camp wasn't bad enough, now you're gonna be cryin' and worryin' about that dumb ape . . . and anything else you can dream up for the rest of the summer, aren't you?" Troo laughs mean out of her nose that funny French way she does now. *"Hunh . . . hunh . . . hunh.* You're goin' loonier by the second, Sally."

"Shut your trap, O'Malley," Mary Lane shouts as she springs up off the bench. "Her missin' Sampson is not any loonier than you tellin' everybody to call you *Leeze.*"

Troo made Mary Lane and me go see *An American in Paris* with her during old-timey movie week up at the Uptown Theatre. My sister's French problem got even worse after that. She wants all of us to call her *Leeze* now, which was the name of the girl star in that movie, and if we don't, she'll give you an Indian burn that'll sting for days because that's another thing she perfected at camp.

"Fuck you, Lane," Troo says. She loves all words that begin with the letter *f* but this is her absolute favorite. "You're always stickin' your monkey nose in where it don't belong."

"Oh, yeah?" Mary Lane yells. "If my ma wasn't already married, she . . . she wouldn't be livin' in sin the way yours is, I can tell ya that."

Mary Lane's not the only one, a lotta people in the neighborhood are saying that about Mother because her and Dave are living under the same roof and aren't married. Not yet anyway. They were supposed to get hitched right after high school, but that wedding got called off because *Dave's* mother, who was dying from tuberculosis at the time, thought that *our* mother was just another

Mick in an ankle bracelet and wasn't good enough for her Danish boy. Ignoring the orders of an about-to-die person is the worst thing you can do in life. I should know. Dave *had* to honor his mother's wishes and not just because he didn't want to be haunted; it's the Fourth Commandment. So better late than never. They're planning to say their *I do*'s right after the annulment letter from the Pope comes in the mail. They need the go-ahead from His Holiness because Mother can't get a divorce. Not the way Lutherans do. The only other thing a Catholic woman can do if she doesn't want to be married anymore to a louse like Hall Gustafson is to pray that he gets stabbed in the neck with a fork when he's serving his time.

"Sorry 'bout that livin' in sin crack," Mary Lane leans in and says to me in a much nicer voice. She didn't mean to hurt my feelings, just Troo's. Mary Lane hasn't figured out yet that's impossible. On both counts.

Sampson is getting very riled up. He musta heard Troo calling me names because he's started putting on a show. Beating his chest and waving.

I wave back at him like I always do, only much slower and sadder.

Troo swats my hand down. "How many times do I gotta tell ya? He's not . . . he's just a stupid gorilla shooin' away flies and . . . and don't start up with how he's singin' *Don't Get Around Much Anymore*."

Mary Lane pushes her flat face into my sister's beautiful one and says, "You got the heart of a jackal," and then she shoves Troo, who shoves her back and two pokes later they are rolling around on the grass behind the bench. Mary Lane can pound the snot outta most anybody and Troo likes to fight more than ever, so I can count on these kinds of wrestling matches happening at least once a day.

I normally try to break them up, but I'm too busy being a captive audience. Sampson is singing to me loud and clear.

After she gets Troo to yell "*Oncle*," Mary Lane plops back down next to me and says, "I'm gonna stick around and help my dad. Ya wanna?"

I run my hand across the part of the bench where Daddy rested his strong shoulders.

I've been meaning to ask Mary Lane, *Do you know what they're gonna do with this beat-up bench? If they're just gonna chuck it out, we might have a place in our garden for it*, but the words get stuck in my mouth, which is the first sign that I'm gonna start choke crying and if I do that, my sister's gonna start *hunh . . . hunh . . . hunh*ing again, so as much as I want to spend what little time there is left with my magnificent king, I tell her, "Thanks, but no thanks. I gotta"—I point behind me to my sister—"you know."

Troo has already brushed the grass off her knees, adjusted her beret and is making her way down the path out of the zoo. The shopping bag with the talent trophy is making her lean a little to the right.

Mary Lane cups her hands and shouts, "*Bon voyage, Leeze*," making it sound like the worst kind of insult.

When my sister stops in her tracks, I'm sure she's gonna come barreling back to tackle our best friend around her knobby knees, but what she does instead is reach into the shopping bag and pull out her talent trophy. She lifts the Golden Tomahawk high above her head and with her other hand, she slowly, slowly flips Mary Lane the bird.

Our best friend doesn't go after her, she's not even mad. Mary Lane laughs and says, "What a card," because even though her and Troo throw themselves on the ground faster than you can say Jackie

Robinson, they are alike in more ways than one. "Ya sure ya don't wanna stay and help out? We're gonna load up the rest of the animal food and what not. It'd be a good thing to put in your charitable summer story."

I really, really want to, but my sister is getting smaller on the path by the second. "I can't."

"Suit yourself," Mary Lane says, skipping off toward the cage where they used to keep the grizzly bears.

After I catch up to Troo, I have to remember to tell her that she was right about one thing at least. Sampson's not tapping his foot and singing to me *Don't Get Around Much Anymore* the way he used to. Of course he's not, because that's not true anymore.

I can barely stand to leave him. I get up off the bench on feet that are having a hard time feeling the ground and shuffle down the zoo path. I know I shouldn't, but I can't stop myself from looking back at him one last time.

He's at the edge of the pit, down on one knee, serenading me with Daddy's and my most favorite song of all: *It's one, two, three strikes you're out at the old ball game . . . game . . . game . . . game.*

Chapter Four

"Helen is such a pain . . . Helen is such a pain . . . Helen . . ."
Troo's been singsonging since we left the zoo. She's purposely
stepping on the sidewalk cracks, which you're not supposed to do
unless you want to break your mother's back, but that's the kind of
kid she is. The two of them used to be two peas in a pod, but now
my sister fights with her most of the time and calls her Helen all of
the time. Poor Mother. She only knows the half of it. If she knew
the *whole* truth about Troo's smoking and stealing and swearing
and all the other wild things she does, she would lock her in our
room and throw away the key, which would be so helpful in my
efforts to keep track of her that I am tempted at least once a day to
tattle on her. If I didn't know how much my sister despises squeal-
ers, I would sit Mother down and tell her that Troo is more and more
every day becoming the kid the other mothers in the neighborhood
don't want their kids to play with and honestly, as much as I love

her, I don't blame them. Who wants their nice Catholic daughter playing four-square with a future gun moll?

When the O'Malley sisters were just about to leave through the back door this morning, Dave gave us each a dime and told us to buy ourselves something cold to drink because he thinks this summer might go down in the record books as the hottest ever. That goes to show how thoughtful he is no matter what my sister says about him. (Dave and me have a lot in common, which I've been told is one of the building blocks of any relationship.)

So on our way back home, Troo and me are gonna stop at Fitzpatrick's Drugstore. You can buy Geritol and hot-water bottles there, but the best part is the ice cream cones with jimmies and brown cows and all the other good stuff you can get at the superduper soda fountain.

Just like the sticker on the drugstore door says, it feels better than good to be in this "Cool as an igloo" air and not only because my T-shirt feels wallpapered to me. It's because Henry Fitzpatrick is behind the soda counter, right where he's supposed to be. He's listening to WOKY, singing into a cookie cone and snapping his fingers to *Mack the Knife*, which is kinda funny because Henry has to stay away from sharp objects at all costs. Maybe singing about one is like taking a walk on the wild side for him because he has to lead such a sheltered life. He has a sickness. I thought for the longest time that what he had wrong with him was called *homo*feelya and so did everybody else in the neighborhood, which is why some of the kids nicknamed him Homo Henry. Turns out his sickness is called *hemo*feelya. That means Henry has to be careful. He wishes he could, but he can't come to the playground and play Mumbly Peg with the other boys because if he cuts himself an ambulance has to come before he bleeds all over the place.

"Henry?" I say loud, because he's really wailing into that cookie cone.

"Oh . . . hi, Sally," he says, spinning my way. "I . . . I didn't hear you come in."

"*Bonjour, Onree,*" Troo says, not following me over to the soda fountain. She's taking her sweet time, loitering near the front of the store where they keep the gum and L&M cigarettes.

"*Bonjour, Leeze,*" Henry calls courteously back to my sister, but he only has eyes for me.

His are hazel with lashes that are thick enough to paint a picture. In my book, that more than makes up for what he lacks in the blood department. Another thing that I like about him is that he isn't rowdy like a lot of the other boys. When we went to see *Old Yeller* together at the Uptown, in the part where that rabid wolf bit Yeller and the boy had to take him out back and shoot him? I thought Henry might croak from a broken heart. He loves dogs and wants one of his own so bad, but his parents won't get him one because when he pets them his eyes tear up like crazy. Even though Henry doesn't agree with me, I think not getting a pooch works out for the best. (Under *no* circumstances are boys supposed to bawl. I wouldn't want that *homo* rumor hitting the mill again.)

I give him my deepest dimples smile when I boost myself up onto my favorite stool that gives me the best view of the front of the store so I can keep my eye on Troo in the wide mirror that hangs behind the fountain.

"What's cookin', good lookin'?" I say. It always makes Henry blush when I talk hepcat like that, which makes him look a little more alive, so I try to do it as much as I can. "I'll have my regular chocolate phosphate, please."

"Hi there, Sally. How's your mother feeling?" Mr. Fitzpatrick calls out to me from where he almost always is, on a stool in a window at the back of the store counting pills below the Coca-Cola clock.

He is much nicer than most of the other fathers around here who work at the Feelin' Good Cookie Factory and sing *Danny Boy* or *That's Amore* at the top of their lungs when their beer bottles get empty out on their front steps. Henry's mother is also a very sweet person who does crossword puzzles during Mass. I think she musta lost her faith in God, too, so we'll have a lot to talk about when she comes to our future house for a chicken dinner and a game of Sheepshead every Sunday.

"Hi, Mr. Fitzpatrick," I say back. "Mother is gettin' better by the day. Thank you for askin'."

When he notices my sister messing around up at the front of the store, Mr. Fitzpatrick calls out in a sterner, but still kind way, "Can I help you find something, Margaret?"

Troo shoves her hands into her back shorts pockets. "Oh, no, thank you, sir." She says that real pleasantly but when she sits down at the counter, she bosses Henry, "Gimme whatever Sally's havin'."

"You got it," he says. "Two cp's comin' up on the double!"

(I just adore it when he talks soda fountain lingo like that.)

After Henry gets done stirring the long spoon in the tall glasses and it makes that great clanking sound, he sets our phosphates down in front of us. Mine looks especially scrumptious. Because he is my boyfriend, he gave me extra squirts of chocolate.

He bends across the counter and says quietly, "Have you guys heard about Greasy Al Molinari?"

"For cryin' out loud, Henry," I say. "You know we have."

Henry was there when Greasy Al jumped Troo last summer in front of the drugstore after the Fourth of July celebration. Molinari has a gimpy polio leg, but his arms are the size of a side of beef. That

bully punched my sister and almost broke her nose when he was trying to steal her bike. The only reason she wasn't beaten to a pulp is
because Henry took a gun outta the cash register and waved it in
Greasy Al's pepperoni-smelling face and Mr. Fitzpatrick, who heard
me screaming, came rushing outta the store and called Officer Dave
Rasmussen and he had Molinari sent to reform school.

Dave's always coming up with good ideas like that. He's also the
one who suggested that Troo and me should make a list of ideas on
how to spend our vacation.

My THINGS TO DO THIS SUMMER list is:

1. Never, ever take my eyes off Troo.
2. Practice not blinking.
3. Help Mother.
4. Write my charitable story.
5. Read to Mrs. Galecki on Wednesdays.
6. Visit Granny every Friday.
7. Spend as much time as I can with Henry.
8. Try not to have so many flights of imagination. Pay
   attention to the details!
9. Work harder to keep my sunny side up!

My sister's THINGS TO DO THIS SUMMER list is:

1. Figure out more ways to get back at Molinari.

Troo used to do that by standing in front of Molinari's house and
singing the Banana Boat song, changing the words to: *Daaago . . .*

da . . . da . . . da . . . daaago, but since Greasy Al got shipped off to reform school she can't do that anymore, so she came up with the next best way to torture him. She writes to him every Friday, she hasn't missed once. Her letters always say the same thing. So she doesn't get writer's cramp, Troo uses carbon paper:

> Dear Greasy Al,
>
> I hope you get polio again and somebody kicks the plug out of your iron lung in the middle of the night.
>
> > Fuck you for all eternity.
> >
> > > Troo O'Malley

My sister rips the top off a straw wrapper with her teeth and asks Henry very ho-hum, "What about that *goombah?*" but she can't fool me. She may be acting cool, daddy, cool, but Molinari is the most important subject there is to her.

Henry takes a quick peek to the back of the store and says, "I heard something about him at the game last night." Since there are no pharmacists teams, his father plays catcher on the police base-ball team with a "special dispensation" like you can get up at church when you want to do something that's not allowed by the rules. I wanted to go last night because I knew that Henry would be there, but Troo didn't want to stare at Dave for an hour and a half so we stayed home. "Officer Rasmussen told my pops some-thing about—"

Troo blows the straw wrapper at Henry and hits him in the fore-head. "Don't you mean *Detective* Rasmussen?" she says, snotty that Dave doesn't walk around our neighborhood in a blue uniform anymore wearing badge number 343. He wears shirts open at the neck and sits behind a desk at the police station until something worse than kids ringing doorbells or a dog biting a mailman happens and it makes my sister so mad he got that promotion.

"I . . . I . . . I . . ." Henry stutters when he gets nervous.

"Say it, don't spray it," Troo says, wiping her arms off like he spit on her, which he mighta, just a little. His teeth don't exactly match up in the front.

"I . . . I . . . don't know if I should . . . I . . ."

"C'mon, *Onree*. Cough it up," Troo says.

I give Henry a go-ahead nod because really, whatever he heard at the game, how bad could it be?

Henry takes a shuddering breath, the same kind he takes when he dives into the deep end of the park pool, and says, "I heard Detective Rasmussen tell Pops last night at the game that . . . that Greasy Al . . . escaped!"

"What?!" I have to grab on to the counter so I don't fall off my stool. This is the worst news ever!

Before they shipped him off to Green Bay, Molinari told his brothers, Moochie and Tommy, that he'd get back at Troo someday for getting him sent to reform school and they made sure we heard that, too. Beady-eyed Greasy Al musta been marking on his cell calendar the days until he could come back to the neighborhood to give Troo what he thinks she deserves, but then one of her iron-lung letters came and . . . and he busted out because he couldn't wait a minute longer to get his hands around her neck.

"When?" I ask Henry, barely able.

"Like I told you . . . at . . . at . . . the game."

"No, I don't mean when did you . . . when did Greasy Al escape?" My hands are shaking, but Troo's aren't. I don't think I have ever seen her get *really* scared. She is very much like Doris Day. A *que sera, sera*, whatever will be, will be person.

"I was sittin' a few seats away in the bleachers so I couldn't hear so good," Henry says. "But I . . . I think Officer . . . I mean, Detective Rasmussen, said he got away a few days ago. They're lookin' for him everywhere. He . . . he hit a guard." He turns to my sister. "Remember what . . . what happened last summer. You gotta be careful, Tr . . . *Leeze*."

I press my cheek down on the chilly marble counter. I'm not sure how many miles away Green Bay is. I'm hoping it's too far for Molinari to polio-limp walk all the way back here. Because if he did, I know the first person he would pay a murderous visit to. She's twirling round and round on the stool next to me like she doesn't have a care in the world.

Henry brings his head down to mine and says in a soft voice that he hopes Troo won't hear, "You okay, Peaches 'n Cream?" His breath smells like vanilla and strawberry and chocolate all mixed together because Neapolitan is his favorite ice cream flavor and the name he called me is mine. "Maybe I shouldn'ta told ya."

"A course you shoulda told us and a course she's okay," Troo says with a slap on my back. "She's from fine pheasant stock, isn't that right, Sal."

I am just about to tell Henry that I don't think I *am* fine and the O'Malley sisters are from what Granny calls fine *peasant* stock and to please hand me some ice out of the freezer to run across the back of my neck because I am not a Doris Day *que sera, sera* person. I am much more like Perry Como, a *catch a falling star and put in your pocket, save it for a rainy day* person.

Mr. Fitzpatrick calls from the back of the store, "Henry? Could you come here for a minute, please?"

Henry ducks out from behind the counter, comes to my side and picks up one of my hands in his pale ones that are also trembling. "See ya later?"

That would be so nice. To do what I hoped to do this summer when I wasn't busy minding Troo. I'd love to come back this afternoon and read together on the drugstore step or count Ramblers whizzing past because they're our favorite car and the one we will buy when we're married, but now it looks like I'm going to have to erase *Spend as much time as I can with Henry* off my THINGS TO DO THIS SUMMER list and put on *Keep my eyes open for Greasy Al* instead.

I try never to lie to Henry, so I don't tell him, *I doubt very much if I'll be seeing you again anytime soon because I'm going to be too busy protecting my sister every minute of every day.* I don't want him to get upset because he sometimes gets a nosebleed if he does, so I say to him the same thing I always do after one of our visits, "Thanks for the phosphate. It's the best I ever had."

When Troo doesn't pay Henry a compliment the way she should, I nudge her.

"Thanks for the soda, *Onree*," she says. "It wasn't that bad."

She's got a chocolate mustache, but I don't lick my finger and dab it off the way a good sister should. I have had just about all I can take from Troo O'Malley this morning. (Sorry, Daddy. I know you're watching, but enough is enough.)

Mr. Fitzpatrick calls again from the back of the store, "Son?"

Before Henry disappears all the way down aisle two to see what his dad wants, he stops and blows me a kiss.

"*Awww*, isn't that sweet," my sister says, drippy. "Ya done?" She grabs the soda glass out of my hand and before I can stop her she guzzles down what I got left.

"Troo!" I get her by the shoulders and stare deep into her eyes because you can really tell a lot about a person when you do that. The windows to her soul *are* twinkling, but not in the way regular people's do when they're feeling good about something. Hers have a steely glint. She doesn't care that Molinari is seven years older or weighs a hundred pounds more. She's already thinking about the best way to go about capturing him, I know she is. Greasy Al might want revenge, but so does she, and she won't back down. She doesn't know how. "You're comin' up with one of your plans, aren't you," I say.

"Whatta ya mean?" she says, like she just flew down from heaven, real angelic like that.

"You *know* what I mean, Trooper," I say, slipping off my stool with this certain kind of feeling I've got all the time lately. I can't stop thinking there's something bad waiting for me around the corner with wide-open arms and no matter how many details I pay attention to, no matter how prepared I am, I can't stop it from grabbing me or even worse, Troo.

My sister doesn't snap her dime down on the marble counter the way I just did. She picks up her Golden Tomahawk bag and strolls past me out the drugstore door with a cherry-on-the-top grin. In the back pocket of her shorts, I can see the outline of a pack of L&Ms.

Chapter Five

Just like the park, where the O'Malley sisters are this morning is another important place to be in the neighborhood—Vliet Street School playground. The school is three stories high and made out of brick with a flat roof and a lotta doors, but none of us cares about that. It's the blacktop we're interested in. The heat comes off it in waves. And it's not only the way it looks that reminds me of a bottomless sea. It's the kids. Even if the last thing on your mind is playing a game of Statue Maker or Captain May I you can get lured over here by their happy sounds the same way those sailors did by those singing sirens the nuns taught us about when they covered the importance of resisting temptation. (Those sailors ended up dead, which is a word to the wise.)

The playground is about a block wide, so there is plenty of room to get together all kinds of games. Boys take off their shirts at the basketball court, which I have nothing to do with. Troo does. She likes any games that you play with balls. There are yellow-painted hopscotches and four-squares and flat green wooden benches that you can sit on if you want to play checkers or best of all, braid lanyards underneath the one shade tree, which I warned everybody is going to die soon if they don't stop carving their initials into it. The playground's also got four swings, a shiny slide that can blister the back of your legs in the afternoon if you forget to pull your shorts down far enough, a sandbox and two different kinds of monkey bars. The flat ladder ones that you can swing across jungle-style (Mary Lane's favorite) and the other kind that are twisted metal pretzels that I don't really get what you're supposed to do with.

Just like I adored being at the lagoon, I used to adore being here. Nowadays I leave the house feeling brave, but by the time I get over here my tummy is letting me know it woulda rather stayed right where it was. It's the counselors' shed that Bobby grabbed me out of that's causing all the problems. That shed is like *Hound of the Baskervilles* quicksand to me now. Smooth on the surface, but if you aren't paying attention to the details, if you make one false step, it will suck you under and it only makes it worse if you struggle, so what are you supposed to do?

Thank Jesus, Mary and Joseph that the playground counselors this summer are both girls who aren't murderers and molesters. Barb Kircher is back for more. I'm glad. Barb makes me feel a little less dumb. Like me, she didn't notice last year that Bobby was a bad egg. I think she had a crush on him for a while the same way I did. She is also an expert lanyard maker and I just love those things. The silky colors and the slippery feel of them gliding through my fingers. I've made over fifty of them. I give them to people on their birthdays or any time I think they could use a little pick-me-up.

The other counselor, the new one who is taking Bobby's place, is a girl named Debbie Weatherly, who is a friend of Barb's from their college cheerleading team. Debbie must be the captain because she keeps telling us how she is so, so, so happy to be here! She reminds Mary Lane of that guy on *The Mickey Mouse Club* and I would have to agree with her. Mousketeer Roy, that was his name. (He got me so jumpy that I had to stop watching on Wednesdays, which was Anything Can Happen Day.) The new counselor lurks around in the background the same way he did. She isn't going bald, though. Debbie's got a sleek brunette do that she keeps out of her eyes with a colored headband that she changes every day, so she is very fashionable, but just like Roy, she is on the chunky side and has somewhat of a slack jaw.

The whole Vliet Street gang is here. Troo and me, Willie O'Hara, Mary Lane, Artie Latour and his sister, Wendy Latour, who is the only one of us who is not waiting in line to play tetherball. Wendy is swinging, which is her most favorite thing to do besides wandering off and turning up in the most unexpected places. Once she got found over at the zoo feeding the elephants peanuts way too close for comfort. She showed up in our own bathroom eating a stick of butter when Mother was in the tub. Another time, they found Wendy all the way downtown. This morning, she's swinging, practically naked from the waist up, which she always tries to do because I don't think clothes feel good on her skin. She does have on her training bra. She needs it now because her bosoms are growing up even if she isn't. She is the strongest kid. When we play Red Rover, she can break through our closed-up arms like we're a paper chain and she's a pair of scissors right outta the box. She's also a great hugger and a lot smarter than people give her credit for. She likes me better than she likes Troo and I am just nuts for her, too.

I call over to her, "Hi, Wendy."

She yells back the same way she always does in her voice that sounds a lot like Froggy the Gremlin on the *Andy's Gang* television show, "Thally O'Malley, hi . . . hi . . . hi!"

Wendy isn't a regular kid, she is something called a Mongoloid. With her shiny black hair that is ruler straight, she looks like one of the waitresses over at the Peking Palace where you can get good chop suey on special occasions. Mother told Troo and me that the Chinese are an inscrutable people, which means they're hard to understand, which fits Wendy Latour to a T.

"That's good swingin', Wendy, but maybe you should slow down a little." I point to her head. "Your tiara's slippin'."

It's actually my tiara. Troo calls me a chump, but I don't regret what I did for one second. I knew I was gonna win. The counselors wanted to give me a prize for not getting murdered and molested last summer, but when Barb Kircher was about to announce me as Queen of the Playground at the biggest party we have in the neighborhood at the end of the summer, I looked down at Wendy in a pink party dress, smiling up from the crowd with shiny lips and her Cracker Jack ring on her wedding finger, and I grabbed the microphone and announced, "The Queen this year is . . . Wendy Latour!" The reason I did that is because someday I will grow up and get married to a pale pharmacist, but Wendy . . . one of the worst things about Mongoloids is that they don't live very long, which I try never to think about.

"Hey," I tell Artie Latour, who is her brother and one of the other twelve Latour kids, "Wendy's goin' too high and she's got her blouse off again."

He looks over fast, but he's in the middle of a tetherball game with Willie O'Hara so he doesn't want to stop and take his sister home to their mother so that she can get dressed.

Artie asks outta the side of his mouth, "Could ya do it for me, Sally?"

I say, "Yeah . . . okay," because I'm just waiting to get back in the game, but even if I wasn't, I would help Artie out. I like him. I also feel sorry for him. He is not the best-looking kid. His Adam's apple goes out of whack when he gets jittery, which is a lot because he is really high-strung. He walks with his knees bent and pigeon toes and he's got a harelip and is hard of hearing, too, because his oldest and meanest brother, Reese, who is in the Army now, smacked Artie so hard that his ear swelled up to the size of a fist. That's why he's a half-deaf mess.

Thinking I might not have to go all the way over to the swings because I'm already so sweaty, I stay where I am and shout at Wendy, "Artie says you gotta stop swingin'."

"Flyin'," she hollers back. She is pretending to be the Wicked Witch from *The Wizard of Oz*. This movie made a HUGE impression on her. Ever since she saw it on TV, it has become her favorite. She likes Dorothy and Glenda and the Scarecrow okay, but it's the witch she really loves. "Come. Wish laugh." (I can do a pretty good Wicked Witch imitation. I taught myself how because I knew Wendy'd get a kick out of it.)

By the time I get over there, she is ripping even higher, bouncing in the swing with her head stretched back as far as it'll go. She is a very good pumper for a girl with such stubby legs.

I yell at Wendy, "Slow down. You're gonna go over the top bar like you did last month. Remember what a bad boo-boo ya got on your knees, *my pretty*?" I rub my hands together and throw my head back the way the green witch does. *"Aha . . . hahahaha."*

Troo leaves the line and comes panting up to my side. "You're up next."

"Thally O'Malley . . . me high!"

"Artie," I call to him when I can't get Wendy to listen to me. "Artiiieee!" He lost his tetherball game to Willie, and now he's just standing off to the side of the group looking like someone let the air outta him. "Get over here."

He trudges over, leans against one of the swing poles, but doesn't tell his sister, "If you don't stop, you won't get any tapioca tonight," the way he always does to get her to listen. Instead, he tells me and Troo in a barely there voice, "Did you guys hear about Charlie Fitch?"

The O'Malley sisters say louder than we would for a kid who hears real good, "What about him?"

Charlie Fitch is an orphan and you'd know he was right off. Those kids all got that same look, like if you knocked on them they'd sound hollow. Charlie's also an altar boy so I see him at Mass. He's older than us, the same age as Artie—fourteen. The two of them are best friends. The other thing I know about Charlie besides him having brown hair and one of those dents in his chin is that he wants to be an actor when he grows up. He was Joseph in last year's Nativity play up at church. With that sad-sack look he's got on his face all the time that really seemed believable when him and the Virgin Mary got turned away from the inn and had to go sleep in the manger. (Not with the manager, the way Troo says.) Since both Artie and Charlie are ninety-eight-pound weaklings and not good at rough-and-tumble games, they love playing with their yo-yos when they come to the playground. They know a lot of tricks like walking-the-dog and baby-in-a-cradle and will put on a show. Everybody stops whatever they're doing to watch.

Artie's Adam's apple is going up . . . down . . . up . . . down when he says, "Charlie's gone."

"What do you mean *gone?*" my sister asks, suddenly interested.

"He ran away from St. Jude's when you guys were at camp," Artie says.

I say, "He probably just went out to get a breath of fresh air and fell asleep."

I only said that to make Artie feel better. I'm pretty sure that Charlie's not snoozing under some bushes. He's probably dead. That happens to kids around here. First they disappear and then they're found murdered and molested. On the flip side, trying to be a little sunnier in my personality the way I promised myself I would this summer, Charlie could have left to try his adopting luck somewhere else. He wouldn't be the first kid to run off from St. Jude's. At least once a year one of the older ones makes a break for it by climbing down the fire escape in the middle of the night. I wouldn't want to be stuck in an orphanage named after the patron saint of lost causes either.

Artie says, "Charlie . . . he was about to . . . he was gonna get adopted by the Honeywells."

"Maybe they changed their mind at the last minute and that's why he ran away," I say.

"Or maybe Charlie changed his. Mr. Honeywell's got black hair growin' out of his ears," Troo cracks.

"No . . . it's all my fault," Artie mumbles to himself. "I shoulda listened to what he was tryin' to tell me. I mean, I did, but I didn't believe him and now he's . . ."

I never would have thought that Artie could go more awful-looking than he already is.

"You can tell Charlie you're sorry for not listenin' when he gets back," I say, taking outta my pocket one of the leather coin purses

I was forced to make at camp and sticking it in his hand. I've got eleven of them, so what the heck. "I'm sure he'll turn up real soon and be more than happy to forgive you, right, Troo?"

"Yeah, sure," she says, tossing him a piece of Dubble-Bubble that she always has plenty of in her pocket because she takes other things from the drugstore besides cigarettes and that's one of them.

But nothing we're saying or giving Artie seems to be helping much. Such sadness is shooting out of his eyeballs. The kind that holds you in place, you can barely swallow, that's how bad it gets you around the throat. I know how he's feeling. He's about to start choke-crying.

The only one still moving through the thick, hot air is swinging Wendy and even she's dragging her feet across the blacktop to slow down. "Artie, Artie." She cocks her head to one side and calls to me, "Thad?"

When I nod, she jumps off the swing and lopes over to hug him. Her brother steps away, which is not like him at all. He loves Wendy and she looks up to him like he's all the stars in the sky.

Artie says, "Father Mickey—"

Troo perks up. "What about him?"

My sister worships the ground Father walks on. And so does everybody else. Attendance at church has been way up since he became our new pastor. The ladies of the parish get all dolled up and cram themselves into the front pews at his ten o'clock Sunday Mass, and after church, when he's greeting everybody out on the steps, the mothers bring him plates of devil's food cake and make jokes about that. Even the nuns smile creakily at him when he stops by a classroom to tell us a parable. Father Mickey is not my cup of tea, I don't know why. But I *am* grateful that he's taking time out of his busy life to give Troo extra religious instruction up at the rectory this summer. She's gonna get kicked outta Mother of Good Hope School for her impure behavior if she doesn't get holier by September, so Father better do a good job. I couldn't stand being without her.

Artie says, "Father Mickey told Charlie that he was one of the chosen few and . . ." Whatever he's trying to tell us isn't coming out so he just gives up, stoops to pick up Wendy's yellow blouse where she threw it and says to her, "Tapioca," and this time she listens.

"What are ya waitin' for, Sally?" Mary Lane hollers at me from the tetherball pole line. "The second comin' of Christ? You're up!"

I know I should go after Artie and offer to help him go look for Charlie because that would be the charitable thing to do, but I have been waiting for over a half hour for my ups and just in case I'm right and we find that orphan over in Jack Hoyt woods hanging from a tree by a noose or in an alley strangled with his yo-yo string, I don't want to see another dead kid. I've already gone to one funeral. I didn't even know they made caskets that small.

I tell Troo, "C'mon," but she doesn't. She's watching Wendy and her beloved big brother making their way home hand-in-hand.

When she turns back my way, she's got the kind of look on her face that I can only describe as the same one she gets when she stares at the picture we have of Daddy hanging on the wall in our bedroom. She points over her shoulder and says, "We're not like them anymore. We're not whole. You're only a half sister to me now."

She's been saying this a lot lately. "You know that's not true. We belong a hundred percent to each other forever, no matter who our fathers are. Bein' sisters . . . that doesn't have nothin' to do with how much of the same blood we have."

Troo bumps into me real hard before she runs across the black-top, yelling, "Spilled milk."

I shout after her, "No, it's not. Wait up!" But when I take off after her, I can't stop myself from crying even if it is no use.

Chapter Six

Every night at five thirty, before she calls out, "Supper is served," Mother puts on a freshly ironed Peter Pan–collar blouse and a record on the turntable. The Hi-Fi is her most prized possession. Dave gave it to her for her birthday. It has a diamond needle. She told us she'll cut off Troo's and my hands if we ever touch it and I don't think she's messing around because she doesn't have a very good sense of humor anymore. What she does have is a nice collection of albums and some 45s that she used to like to warble along with. She could've been a professional singer with a big band if she didn't have kids, which is why I think she looks so sad when she listens to the record she made at Beihoff's Music in a soundproof booth. Her favorites are Peggy Lee when it comes to females, and for the men, it's Perry Como, who she thinks is also an excellent dresser. She loves his sweater style. He's the one serenading us tonight. *"Hot diggity dog ziggity boom whatcha do to me."*

Dave and Troo and me are expected to have washed our hands and combed our hair and be seated at the yellow formica kitchen table by the time Mother sets the main course down and we are holding up our end. She is looking especially glamorous tonight. A lot like that movie actress, Maureen O'Hara. Last-of-the-day rays are streaming through the kitchen curtains and hitting her long hair that is bundled up at her neck with a white ribbon that I want to tug on. I'd love to run my hands through her loose red waves, but she doesn't really go in for that sort of thing.

She sits in the chair next to Dave and tells him, "Say grace, please."

Dave clasps his hands together, bows his head, and I think the same thing I think every night at this time when I see the top of his thick blond hair that matches mine. I'm not 100 percent Irish anymore. I got half of Dave's blood in me now and a sneaking suspicion that Danish people are not known for being lucky, only for making delicious sweet rolls.

Dave mumbles, "Bless us, oh Lord, for these gifts which we are about to receive . . ."

Because of mental telepathy, I know exactly what's going on in Troo's mind and it's not how handsome Dave looks in his button-down white shirt. She's thinking about how much she can't stand to be sitting across this table from him and that what we're having for supper tonight is *not* a gift and she'll do whatever she needs *not* to receive it.

". . . through the bounty of Christ our Lord, amen," Dave finishes up.

After we all make the sign of the cross, Mother tells him in a charming voice we don't get to hear very often, "It's so nice to have you home tonight." It really is. Dave's been so busy chasing the cat burglar that he's had to skip suppers with us more than a couple of times every week. "Now . . . who'd like to begin this evening's stimulating conversation?"

Mother has recently started making us talk at the table about important events while we listen to the music and chew with our mouths closed. Dave and her usually chat about what's going on in the neighborhood, but lately they are very keen on discussing what is going on in our nation's capital. Both of them really like John Fitzgerald Kennedy, who is an Irish political man, and more important—a Catholic. Dave and Mother think Mr. Kennedy might become president of the United States if he plays his cards right. I like Ike, so I don't care who the next president is just so long as it isn't that man, Nixon. I saw him give a talk on television. I know from going to the movies that heavy sweating and darting eyes make a person suspicious. That man is a twofer.

"Pass everything," our granny bosses.

Granny doesn't usually eat over unless it's Sunday, but the potluck up at church got cancelled because of the heat making the cafeteria stink even worse than it usually does, so Dave drove over to 59th Street and got her out of her small house where she lives with our brain-damaged uncle who isn't here. Uncle Paulie probably stayed in his bedroom to finish off his newest Popsicle-stick house or he went early to his job setting pins at Jerbak's Beer 'n Bowl, which is at least one thing to be grateful for. He doesn't sing, "Peek-a-boo, Troo, Peek-a-boo, Daddy," every two seconds the way he used to, but just looking at him makes Troo remember the crash. (Our uncle was in the car coming home from the game, too. I think peek-a-boo is the last thing he remembers hearing before he flew outta the windshield.)

Granny's name is Alice. Her and Mother don't get along all that good except at church and on holidays. Granny thinks her daughter is too uppity for a girl that grew up across the street from the Feelin' Good Cookie Factory and will ask her, "When will you learn that you can't make a silk purse out of a sow's ear, Helen?" if she thinks Mother is getting above herself. Granny is largish, especially in her underarm area, which looks like a sheet on a clothesline flapping on a windy day, but her face hardly has any wrinkles considering how old she is—eighty-five. Her hair is Wonder Bread white and she wears it in a page boy. If you ever met her, you would immediately think you'd seen her somewhere before. That's because she looks a lot like George Washington on the dollar bill. Except for her clothes. She used to wear regular dotted Swiss old lady dresses, but lately she's always got on a *muu-muu*. Mother buys them for her out of the Sears and Roebuck catalog. I think the dresses are a bribe so Granny will like her more than she does and Mother may finally be wearing her down because, I'm not kidding, my grandmother goes ape for these flowery dresses. I thought she looked kinda cute in them, too, when I still thought they were spelled *moo-moos* and made by some nice 4-H ladies who could use the extra money because their husbands are farmers and every little bit helps.

It was Mrs. Kambowski who once again wrecked it all.

Dave dropped Granny and me at the Finney Library a few weeks ago so we could get something new to read. She likes books about love and death. All Irish people adore those subjects. And whiskey. I picked up another Nancy Drew story, which I've started loving. (Her father musta told her to pay attention, too, because that girl doesn't seem to miss a thing.)

When we were checking out, Mrs. Kambowski complimented Granny on her *ensemble* and then, because she can *never* leave well enough alone and just *has* to teach you something every time she runs into you, the head librarian said, "Do you know that your grand-mama's dress comes all the way from the Hawaiian Islands, Sally?"

I told her, "No," a little snippy because her always teaching my sister French gets my Irish up.

"*Muu-muu* means *amputated* in their language," Mrs. Kambowski told us.

Granny said, "You learn something new every day," but I said, "Am . . . pu . . . ta . . . ted?" and felt pretty queasy. "Doesn't that mean not having an arm or a leg?"

Mrs. Kambowski said, "A gold star for you, Sally."

So that means the purple-and-pink parrot one Granny's got on tonight was probably made by some of the most famous armless and legless people there are—lepers, who live with the most famous of all Hawaiians, Father Damien, on an island called Molokai. We learn all about lepers at school. This is a big subject. How those poor people gotta walk around and yell, "Unclean" if they still got legs. Since they can't work in a store or some kind of factory because they are so contagious, lepers must earn money by sewing *muu-muus* for Sears and Roebuck. That's why I'm relieved Granny is sitting on the other end of the table tonight. Part of those lepers could have fallen off into her dress and I don't need that disease to hop out of a hem and onto me. I got enough on my hands keeping Troo safe. And getting this supper down.

I am sorry to have to say this, but my mother is the worst cook in the neighborhood, maybe on the whole west side or the world. They don't even ask her to contribute to the Pagan Baby Cake Walks at school anymore because the last time she did three people had to get their stomachs pumped out at St. Joe's. That was the only good thing about her being in the hospital almost all of last summer. We didn't have to eat her cooking. She made us SOS tonight. Shit on a Shingle. (Help us, o mighty God.)

Granny reaches across the table and scoops a heaping ladle of the slop onto her plate. Her eyes are always bigger than her stomach. She has a medical condition called a thyroid so her peepers look like two ping-pong balls.

"Did you hear about the boy who ran away from the orphanage?" Granny asks, starting off tonight's stimulating dinner conversation.

I *cough . . . cough . . . cough* and say, "That's . . . they're talkin' about Charlie Fitch. Did you hear *why* he ran away?" I am hoping it's for some reason other than Artie Latour not listening to him. I'd love to be the one to tell him his best friend's leaving wasn't his fault.

Granny says, "All Sister Jean told me at morning Mass is that the boy took off in the middle of the night. Hand me the succotash, Sally."

That's okay. She may not have the scoop now, but she will hear some more about Charlie's taking off sooner or later. Our granny *always* finds out what's going on in the neighborhood, the really secret stuff. Like how Mrs. Delancey who owns the grocery store down the block from her, the one our half sister Nell's apartment is over, used to work in a nightclub dancing with snakes. Granny drinks six bottles of Coca-Cola a day that she gets free from Mrs. Delancey to keep her mouth shut.

I lift another forkful to my mouth and *cough* some more into my napkin.

Dave says, "Gosh, Sally, you're doing a lot of that tonight. Are you feeling all right?"

"Did you catch a cold?" Troo asks, seeing an opening. "A fever?

Let me check." When she reaches to put her hand to my forehead, she accidentally on purpose brushes her spoon down to the linoleum.

This was another one of her Troo genius plans. Coming up with this coughing-into-my-napkin trick and her dropping-the-spoon trick to avoid having to eat Mother's food. Thank goodness for our little collie, Lizzie. She's lying openmouthed at our feet like she got invited to an all-you-can-eat dog buffet the same way she does every night except for the ones Dave cooks.

Mother says to me, "You don't look flushed."

"I'm fine. It's just that . . ." She has no idea how disgusting her food is. She thinks she's the next Betty Crocker. I want to tell her the truth because how is she ever going to improve if somebody doesn't, but I don't think that would go over so big. I look over at Granny, who you can usually depend on to point out Mother's faults, but her mouth is full, so I say, "I'm only coughing 'cause . . . I can't swallow the SOS down fast enough."

When Mother smiles, I swear to Mary, the kitchen goes three shades lighter. "I'm so glad you're enjoying it, Sally, but remember what I told you the last time. The proper name for this dish is chipped beef on toast points."

"Six a one, half dozen of another," Granny says, throwing in under her breath, "A sow's ear."

Dave stays out of it, but gives me a wink when I look his way. I really would like to question him while I have him. He's been so busy working day and night that I haven't had the chance to ask him the number one question that's been burning itself into my mind. I've been hoping what Henry told us at the drugstore was wrong. It gets awfully loud at the baseball games. He coulda misheard what Dave told his dad.

"Is it true that Greasy Al escaped from reform school?" I ask.

Dave stops buttering his bread in midair and looks over at Mother. When she nods, he says, "Girls, I have been meaning to talk to the both of you. Especially you, Sally. I don't want you to get yourself in a tizzy over—"

"He means he doesn't want you to be a fruitcake in the imagination department," Troo butts in.

I'm surprised that Mother doesn't say anything about her minding her p's and q's, but she doesn't, and I know why when I look down at my sister's plate. You can see her reflection in it. When we were busy talking about my coughing, Troo musta slipped it under the table and Lizzy chowed down.

Troo purses her lips and kisses her fingers the way French people in the movies do after they get done eating. "My compliments to the chef. Supper was *magnifique*."

Mother says, "Why thank you, Troo."

"No, no . . . *merci beaucoup* to you, Helen." Mother is lapping it up. I've noticed that when it comes to compliments of any kind, there is no bottom to her bowl. Troo musta noticed that, too. "I'm goin' over to the playground. See ya tomorrow . . . I mean Friday, Granny."

Granny says back like she always does, "Not unless I see you first, you little banshee."

So I'm left to push the SOS around on my plate while Dave and Mother talk some more about Mr. Kennedy and his wife, Jackie, who dresses so stylishly, and Granny tells us that Uncle Paulie has been keeping very odd hours, and then the three of them go into other neighborhood news until everyone is done eating except for me. (I was so thankful that Granny didn't bring up the annulment-letter-from-the-Pope problem. She likes Dave a lot, but she is one of the main people who thinks that Mother is living in sin.)

After removing Mr. Como from the Hi-Fi and reapplying her

lipstick, Mother comes back into the kitchen. "I know that you're savoring every single bite, Sally, but you need to finish up by the time I get back from taking your grandmother home. Dave and I have plans tonight." This means she wants to play footsie with him. "Ready?" she says, guiding Granny toward the front door so she can drive her back to her tiny bungalow.

"Sally?" Dave says, once they're gone.

He's got a grave look on his face. He musta noticed me and Troo feeding Lizzy the SOS under the table. After all, he is a detective. He won't shout at me the way Mother would. Dave has only been a father for a little while so he's still learning how to be mean. What he'll do is clear his throat and give me a calm sermon about the nature of good and evil. Since he's a police officer *and* the treasurer of the Men's Club up at church, knowing the difference between right and wrong are the subjects dearest to his heart.

Or maybe not. In the movies, cops smack you with a rubber hose when they want you to tell the truth, which I'm sure Dave wouldn't do, but things can happen when you least expect them. I didn't think Hall Gustafson would throw Nell down on our kitchen floor last summer or that Bobby would try to kill me either. And I was so sure that Dave was the one who was murdering and molesting little girls in the neighborhood. I used to think I was a good judge of people, but I'm not. I am unreliable. I can't count on myself anymore.

"Do you have something you want to tell me?" Dave asks, steepling his fingers below his chin.

I'm going to beat him to the punch. I'm going to confess. "I'm really sorry," I blurt out. "I won't ever do it again, I promise, and I'll make Troo swear, too."

Dave leans in and he smells good. He slaps on Old Spice when he's done shaving. He points down at my SOS that now looks exactly like the fake vomit they sell at the toy store. His lips, which aren't poofy like Mother's and Troo's but on the thin side like mine, are curled into a smile. "Between you and me, I can barely get it down myself. Got my fill of it in the Army," he says, putting my plate down in front of Lizzy, whose tummy is just bulging. "Now that we got that settled, I'd like to further answer the question you asked me earlier about the Molinari boy." He leans back in his chair and stretches his long legs out in front of him. "Yes, he escaped from the reform school last week."

"But how . . . he could . . . what if they don't catch him and he comes back here and does something bad to . . ." There are so many ways that Greasy Al could hurt Troo. I try my best to keep my eyes on her at all times, but she is so good at outfoxing me.

"I know this might be hard for you to understand, Sally, but it's not like Alfred's a hardened criminal. Sure, he's gotten himself into a few fixes, but he's just a boy not much older than you." Dave runs his hand over his mouth. He does that when he is trying to come up with a good explanation about why I shouldn't be afraid of something. "When Alfred got polio . . . his family didn't . . . the Molinaris are a tough bunch."

No kidding.

"He's not a lost cause," Dave adds on. "All the boy needs is someone to care about him."

Poor man. If that's what he thinks, that all Molinari needs is some TLC to set him straight, he's wrong. I heard that his father used to hit him with fists. And I've seen with my own two eyes that even his own mother doesn't love Greasy Al. She's the hostess at Ristorante Molinari where Dave takes us to eat sometimes because Mother adores their butter-drenched bread. Before Greasy Al got sent to reform school, on the nights he used to work at the family restaurant being a busboy, Mrs. Molinari would yell at him from her podium up front, "Hey, Chester, clean up . . . table six," because her boy walks like that guy in *Gunsmoke*. Everybody in the dining room would crack up, no one louder than her. And Troo.

"Sally?" Dave says from a distant land where I bet things look clearer to him than they do to me. "Please, don't."

I'm so glad Mother's not here to see me blubber. She'd run a pretend bow over a pretend violin and sing *Cry Me a River*.

Dave stacks his big hands on top of mine. "There's nothing to worry about. You're safe now."

That's the same thing Mother and him always say when I wake up screaming after one of my nightmares. Bobby is still alive when I bolt up in bed. I can smell his leather belt and hear him whispering how much he loves me and that he's going to make me his bride. Or sometimes it's Daddy who comes to me bloody in my dreams holding Sampson by the hand, telling me with a rotted mouth to fly like the wind. By the time Mother rounds the corner to our room and Dave comes pounding down from upstairs, my sister is already up on her knees, yelling, "Sally, wake up!" doing her darndest to hold my still running legs down on the sheet soaked with my sweat.

I know that Dave and Mother mean well, but they can never, will never, understand what I'm feeling twenty thousand leagues deep. Only my sister does.

Chapter Seven

Troo snuck off and stuck me with the supper dishes again. By the time I get over to the playground, she's already made her way through the line of kids waiting to take their turn at the pole, which has become the biggest challenge. Last year it was dodgeball and before that it was box hockey, but this summer, everybody has gone cuckoo for tetherball. Anyone who can runs over here straight after supper because if you're the last one serving when they turn off the lights for the night, the counselors will congratulate you and give you a box of free Wheaties, which is the Breakfast of Champions and very popular.

My sister is squaring off against beefy Willie O'Hara. Just like us, Willie isn't from around here originally. He moved to Vliet Street from Brooklyn, New York, with his mother the same summer we did because his father ran off with his hubba-hubba secretary. Mrs. O'Hara has relatives around here who are helping her get back on her feet. Willie used to be Troo's boyfriend, but he's moved on to greener pastures.

Trotting over to stand with the rest of the kids who are watching the game, I shout, "Go, Troo, go!" and wish that Debbie the counselor would quit hovering over us and do a somersault or the splits or something else really cheerful to distract Troo. My sister looks like she is about to charge at Willie and take a big bite out of him. That's what he looks like with his bright red hair and chubby tummy. A juicy burger with ketchup.

"Why's she got her undies in a bundle?" Mary Lane, who left the front of the line and came back to keep me company, says over my shoulder. "Molinari?"

I'm pretending that I am so interested in watching the game that I don't hear her.

"Hey. Helen Keller." She stabs me in the back with a bony finger. "I know ya know that Greasy Al broke out of reform school. Troo just told me."

If only that juvenile delinquent would've stayed put like he was supposed to. I already started writing a letter to that school with some reform ideas of my own:

Dear Mr. Warden,

Have you ever heard of gun towers? Guard dogs? The gas chamber?

Mary Lane says, "I bet you're havin' a conniption."

I *am*. And not just about Greasy Al escaping.

The day we got back from camp, even though I have lost almost all of my faith, I right away went up to church and lit candles. I prayed for the kind of summer days where you can stick your nose into a peony bush and breathe so deep that everything goes pink. Or spend a whole morning reading under a shady tree or making lanyard after lanyard at the playground. But here we are only three weeks into summer and there's a convict on the loose and a cat burglar and Troo is acting like a wilder animal and Sampson is gone and Mother is sulky and we've got a runaway kid.

What is God thinking? Hasn't He ever heard of good news?

Before Mary Lane can start in on how Molinari is going to make mincemeat out of Troo when he catches her, I'm gonna ask her if she heard any details about Charlie Fitch's disappearance. She has to know more than me. She's a peeper who lives two houses down from the Honeywells. I'd like to help out. It bothers me to see Artie looking like the Lone Ranger without his Tonto.

"You got any idea why Charlie Fitch ran off?" I ask her.

"Uh-uh."

"Do you think Mr. and Mrs. Honeywell coulda changed their minds about takin' him in and that was more than he could stand?" That's still the only reason I can think of why he'd run away right before he was going to get adopted. Our Brownie troop went up to the orphanage at Christmas and brought those poor kids bars of soap and holy cards wrapped with red curly ribbon. Their eyes lit up over those crummy presents, that's how desperate they are for someone to take them home.

Mary Lane says, "The last time I peeped on 'em the Honeywells seemed all set. They fixed up their spare room and it looked really good with pennants on the wall and two new yo-yos were sitting on the madras bedspread." She shrugs. "I guess it's possible they coulda found out between then and now that Fitch was bad news. Ya never know what you're gettin' with an orphan." She hitches up her shorts because they're always falling down. "There was that kid who was livin' up there for a while before he got adopted. Teddy Jaeger? He picked his boogers and ate 'em. I know mosta them kids are nice at St. Jude's and all that, but there *could* be a few bad apples just like everywhere else in the neighborhood."

I would have to agree with her. Teddy Jaeger *was* a booger-eating orphan and there are a few people around here that *are* rotten to the core. The entire Molinari family, for instance.

Mary Lane says, "Maybe right before the Honeywells were headin' over to St. Jude's to bring Charlie home somebody knocked on their door and told 'em something terrible about him."

"Like what?" I ask.

"Like . . . like he was the long-lost son of Ed Gein or something."

"Ed who?" I ask, not recognizing the name. "What block does he live on?"

"*Gein*," Mary Lane says. "He's not from around here. He killed a buncha women around the state capitol and took 'em home and hung 'em upside down in his living room like they were deer until all the blood drained outta them. Then he peeled off their skin and made lampshades out of it and a little suit he wore around the house and he was a grave robber, too. The cops found shriveled heads at his house and skulls on his bedpost and . . ."

This is one of her no-tripper stories. Next she'll go on about how Charlie didn't run away from the orphanage. That he was kidnapped by gypsies. Somehow she'll work wienies into the story. I don't know why, but a lot of Mary Lane's stories are about gypsy kidnappings and wienies and my tummy already is not feeling so great.

I turn back to the game, put two fingers in my mouth and whistle good and loud. Dave taught me how. "You got him where you want him, Troo." She is punching the tetherball two-fisted and springing for it when it comes whipping back. Even with all her sweat and wild hair she is a beautiful kid.

Mary Lane must be thinking the same thing that I am because she props her chin on my shoulder and says, "Too bad Molinari's gonna rearrange her face when he shows up."

"But . . . how would he get back here?" I ask. I've given this a lot of thought in the middle of the night. "Ya know, his polio leg."

Mary Lane pulls out one of the bananas she's always got in her shorts pocket and says, "Well, he for sure couldn't walk all the way here. Green Bay is really far away. My father took me to a Packers game up there once and we had to stop three times on the way so I could go to the bathroom."

That's such a relief to hear. That makes me breathe a lot easier.

"But you know what *could* happen?" Mary Lane says, after taking a big banana bite. "A Good Samaritan could see that greaseball hunch limpin' along the highway and offer him a ride."

"But—"

"Go, O'Malley," and "Ya sissy, O'Hara. Ya can't beat a girl?" the kids watching shout.

The tetherball rope is wound around the pole close to the top and Troo's got her victory smile on.

Needing to get Mary Lane off the subject of Greasy Al before she tells me something else I don't want to hear, I make a *whew* sound and brag to her, "Looks like she's got it in the bag. Thank God." Her and just about everybody in the neighborhood knows what a sore loser my sister is. She hates ties, too.

Mary Lane chuckles. "'Member how my dad had to break up her and Artie at the Fourth picnic last year?"

Of course I do. Troo tied with Artie Latour for best costume. He grabbed the genuine Davy Crockett cap off the prize table before she could so the two of them got into one of those roll-around-on-the-ground wrestling matches. After he pried them apart, Mr. Lane, who was one of the judges, awarded Troo the cap. Artie has tried plenty of times to get it back, but she tells him she lost it, which is not the truth. It's under our mattress. See, it's not about the cap for my sister or even winning. It's about having something somebody else wants with all their heart that is the real prize for Troo.

Mary Lane licks her fingers clean and shoves the banana peel back into her pocket. "What're ya doin' for the parade this year?" she asks. "Are ya just gonna watch or are ya gonna find something to decorate?"

Before I can answer, the new counselor, perky Debbie Weatherly, juts her head in between us and says, "Were you girls just talking about the Fourth?" She knows darn well we were. She's been buzzing around us like we're daisies and she's a bee. Like we're Mouseketeers and she's Roy. "Did you hear that we're having a party the day before the parade and there's going to be plenty of decorating and it's all free!"

"Free?" Mary Lane says with a lot of suspicion, but because I'm her best friend, I can also hear the hope in her voice. I don't know why, but her family seems poorer than the rest of ours. "Ya givin' away bikes, too?"

The counselor slaps the top of her legs and yips, "Free bikes? *Ha . . . ha . . . ha.* You slay me."

Peppy Debbie doesn't know how close to the truth that is. You don't ever want to be the one crossing Mary Lane. While I like her for her patience with my flights of imagination and her love of animals and we both watch the same television shows, the part of her that makes her Troo's best friend is what *they* have in common—a love of revenge.

Mary Lane shoots back at Debbie, "For your information, I don't need a bike. I was just makin' sure ya weren't givin' any away. I'd have to tell my butler to build another room onto the mansion to keep it in if you were." (By butler, she means her father, whose middle name really *is* Butler so she uses that one a lot. And by mansion, she means the drafty old Lane house, which *is* on the largish side, but needs a ton of repairs.)

Debbie's face goes blank. I've seen this happen before. Mary Lane's no-tripper stories can hypnotize you if you're not used to them. People's eyes go glassy, and if they have a slack jaw like Debbie does, it will go as unhinged as the Latours' back gate.

"You New York turd," my sister yells from behind me. "Quit hittin' so high over my head!"

The tide has turned at the tetherball pole. Willie's got my sister right where he wants her and it's making her foot-stomping mad. It's never a good idea for Troo to get so worked up. I'll have to rub her back for over an hour tonight and she'll make me sneak into the kitchen to get cookies out of the jar and will eat them on my side of the bed if I don't do something. I step up to her side and start helping her out against big-boned Willie.

Between hits, O'Hara shouts, "Two against one! Do something, Debbie!"

A gasp goes through the line of kids. What I'm doing is against playground rules, but what Willie just said is worse. He knows better than to ask an outsider for help.

Snapping out of the trance that Mary Lane's story put her in, Debbie is about step in and referee. But when she comes marching toward Troo and me, Mary Lane takes the banana peel out of her pocket, tosses it on the ground and up, up Debbie goes. She doesn't fall down, but her arms are flapping like mad when she stumbles back to Mary Lane and asks, "Why . . . what did you do that for?" like she can't imagine, and really, she can't. I don't think she understands us Westsiders. We aren't like the rich people who live on the opposite side of the city like she does. We can get especially hard to deal with during the summer when we get even hotter under our collars. We don't have Lake Michigan to cool us off the way Eastsiders do.

"I'm tellin' ya for the last time," Mary Lane warns Debbie. "Keep your stuck-up nose outta our business. We don't need your help. We fight our own battles around here."

Willie O'Hara hollers again, "But . . . they're cheatin'!" and smashes the tetherball with all he's got.

No matter how hard we're hitting, the O'Malley sisters are just not strong enough to keep the ball from winding up to the top of the pole with a mean sounding *snap!*

So fast, the crowd of kids goes quiet. They know the same way I do that something bad is about to happen. Like in a gunfight in an OK Corral movie, they're watching and waiting the way the townspeople do to see whose side they should jump over to, except for Mary Lane who is rubbing her hands together, getting fired up to pound the daylights out of whoever she thinks needs it the most. She's eyeballing Debbie.

Troo breaks the silence by saying, "Just so you know, O'Hara, I let you win . . . ya fat cow." She spins toward the rest of the gang. "And you . . . all of ya . . . you're not fit to lick my boots. You're nothin' but . . . cookie factory riffraff."

Now, if we really *were* in the Old West, these kids would already be throwing bottles at my sister from a saloon window or from the alley next to the blacksmith's barn and, honestly, as much as I adore her, I might pick up a rusty horseshoe and toss it at her, too—when she wasn't looking, of course.

My sister gets a kick out of my imitations every so often and it's all I can think to do before a rumble starts. These factory kids know how to fight.

I lower my voice as far as I can, and say just like John Wayne does to his sidekick when they're in trouble, "I got your backside, Troo."

Mary Lane and a couple of the other kids in the crowd chuckle, but my sister doesn't. She shoves her *beret* to the back of her head and tells me very ornery, "What did ya say?"

She's got excellent hearing, so I don't get what she means at first, but then I do. I waddle around the pole the way Mr. Wayne would, like he's wearing a diaper that needs changing. "I mean . . . I got your *derriere, Leeze*."

For the longest time, all I can hear is my fast breathing and my heart knocking against my ribs, but then my sister starts *hunh . . . hunh . . . hunh*ing and yells, "Fuck all a ya and . . ." She elbows me.

"And . . . and the horses you rode in on," I say the way she taught me, and then I loop my arm through hers and we mosey toward the playground gates, and ya know, just for that second, that precious moment in time, everything is coming up roses.

Chapter Eight

Mother called to me from the backyard this morning and told me to run up to the Five and Dime and get her a Snirkle bar. She has a gigantic sweet tooth. It seems like a lot of us in the neighborhood do. I think it's because those chocolate chip cookies bake night and day over at the Feelin' Good factory so that smell is part of our every breath and we want more, more, more! That's why the O'Malley sisters are skipping down the street where we used to live before we moved in with Dave. Vliet Street is the way we always go to North Avenue because a lot of stuff that happened on this block was bad, but some of it was good, so it's sorta like walking down Memory Lane if it had a bunch of potholes.

Right after we moved here, Mother would play the name game with me and Troo so we could learn about all the different kinds of people who live in the city. "You can know just about all there is about a person when you hear their last name, so be sure to ask it" is what she told us. Wops, who have mostly vowels in their names, are loud but great cooks. And the Polacks have names that end in *ski* and brains that run on the small side, but noses that run larger than normal. I'm not sure where bohunks come from but they are thick-ankled and wear *babushkas*. And if someone has *man* in their last name they are probably a German who loves *kielbasa* and polka music. (I could never tell Mother that the name game is right some of the times, but not always. I am friends with a Kraut who loves music by a man named Mozart much more than she likes Lawrence Welk.)

The people who live in them might look different, but most of the houses on the block are the same shape and size and made out of wood or brick and always two stories high, maybe three. They're enough alike anyway that you might head into the wrong front door if you have too much to drink late at night. That happened to Mr. Fred Latour. He accidentally got into bed with Mrs. O'Hara, who lives next door to him. That was a laugh riot. Mrs. O'Hara started calling him Fred La*mour* until his wife made her stop. (*Lamour* is French for love bucket.)

Something like that would never happen to me. Even if I gouged my eyes out of my head the way St. Lucy did, if somebody led me past any of these houses at suppertime, I could tell you who lives there without second-guessing.

The Fazios' smells like this spice called garlic they use on just about everything and the Latours' like cheesy casseroles made with condensed milk. The O'Haras' reeks of cabbage and sometimes liver and onions if they're celebrating something. If you walk past the Goldmans' at six o'clock, the aroma of sauerkraut and *schnitzel* will be drifting out of their kitchen window along with their Germanese and violin music.

Troo's a little in front of me bouncing a red rubber ball that she "borrowed" from the playground shed. She's warming up to play that *a* my name is *Annie* and I come from *Alabama* with a carload of *Apples* game. When she gets to the letter *f*, her name will be *Fifi* and she comes from where else but *France*. I refuse to repeat what she will have a carload of.

When we pass the Osgoods' house, the flag flying off the front porch reminds me to ask Troo, "What are you gonna do for the Fourth? Are you gettin' ready to decorate? Is that why you're comin' with me? To get some Kleenex to make your flowers?"

If my sister does not end up being a ventriloquist or a drummer in a band like Sal Mineo or the fat lady in a traveling freak show, all ideas that she has from time to time, she could become a Kleenex flower maker. That's how good she is at folding the tissues, sliding a bobby pin down the middle and separating the layers until they spring alive and look like real carnations, which was Daddy's favorite that covered his casket.

When Troo keeps bouncing, I keep asking, "Are you gonna wear a costume again?" Last summer, besides covering her bike in flowers, she dressed herself up like the Statue of Liberty because that was a gift to America from France. "Or are ya just gonna do up your bike?" I don't have a Schwinn. Even if I did, I don't think I would fancy it up for the Fourth. What if I accidentally won the decorating contest? Having the feeling of that silky blue ribbon sliding across my neck is just not worth Troo tricking me with some of that gum that turns your teeth black or licking my Jell-O when my back's turned. "What's your plan?"

"You writin' a book?" Troo asks snotty.

"No, I'm just tryin' to—"

"What I'm doin' is for me to know and for you to find out," she says with a flip of her ponytail. "But I'll tell ya one thing, I'm gonna win that decoratin' prize this year hands down. No ties. And I'm gonna be Queen of the Playground again, the same way I was the first year we moved here." She starts up the game for real very loudly. "*A* my name is *Annie* and I come from . . ."

"Whatever you're doin', you better get busy. Time's runnin' out," I tell her when we come to the front of the Kenfields' house.

When we first moved into the city, it was into the house next door to them. Late at night horrible sounds would come out of a bedroom that was across from mine and Troo's. I thought the place was haunted and I guess in a way it was. Mr. Kenfield would moan into his daughter's pillow that probably still had the smell of his precious girl's perfume hidden in the seams the same way that Daddy's blue shirt still has Aqua Velva. After he was cried dry, he would go sit on the front porch of this house and smoke his Pall Malls, rocking until the church bells rang twelve midnight. After Mother went into the hospital, some nights after Troo would fall asleep and I was sure that Hall had passed out, I'd slip outta our bed and go sit with our neighbor. We didn't talk so much. We held hands and listened to the creaky sound the porch swing made. I'd like to do that again, but I'm not sure Mr. Kenfield would. Sometime between last summer and this one, he got a reputation for being the neighborhood crank.

"*C* my name is *Carol* and I come from *California* with a carload of *candy*," Troo sings.

"Wait a sec," I tell her when she dribbles past our old duplex. There's a Yellow Taxi parked out front of 5081 Vliet Street, which is something you don't ever see around here. This is the closest I've ever come to one. The trunk is open and there are some suitcases jammed in. "Something's goin' on at the Goldmans'."

Troo doesn't glance up. She just keeps on singing in her high soprano voice that she inherited from Mother, "*D* my name is *Denise* and I come from . . . come from . . . damn it all, Sally, look what you made me do? Now I can't think of a place that starts with *D*." She spikes the ball. If you mess up you gotta start over and even hell-with-the-rules Troo O'Malley plays by that one. "Who gives a crap about the Goldmans anyway?"

"I do," I say, feeling bad again about letting our old landlady down. I promised Mrs. Goldman I would stay her friend even after we moved out of this house, but I haven't.

She is standing on her front porch in a crisp blue shirt and a pleated black skirt, her special sturdy shoes in size 10 peeking out from beneath the hem. Her dark curls used to be braided and wound around her head but now her hair looks pixie cute. She is instructing a man in a T-shirt with rolled-up sleeves, "Careful vis it. Careful."

I wait until the man passes me by carrying a big black trunk and grunting something under his breath to call out to her, *"Yavol!"*

Mrs. Goldman brings her hands up to her cheeks and says, *"Liebchen!"*

Her calling me sweetheart in her language is making me feel even worse about not showing up the way I told her I would, but she looks happy to see me, so I race up the house steps two at a time and wrap my arms around her spongy waist.

"Mein Gott, how you've grown," she *ho . . . ho . . . ho*s. "Your legs—"

"I know, I know," I say, looking the long way down.

"And vere is your sister the Trooper?"

Everyone always asks me that if they come across me when I'm alone because they're used to seeing the O'Malleys roaming the neighborhood's nooks and crannies together.

"She's right down there. See? Hey, Troo!" I excitedly point to Mrs. Goldman like we've been searching for her for months. "Look who I found!"

"Top o' the morning," our old landlady yells down to the curb. (I taught her that.)

Troo gives her a blank-eyed stare. My sister is still holding it against our old landlady for liking me better than she likes her, and also for not letting our dog Butchy live with us so he had to stay in the country with peeing Jerry Amberson, who lived on the farm next to ours and would hose you down with his wiener for no reason. Dave drove out and got Butchy back for Troo last summer, which I thought was so nice, but Butchy didn't. That dog couldn't get used to living in the city. He broke through two chains and ripped Mimi Latour's pants right off her body when she tried to pet him, so he had to go back to live with the Ambersons, which made Troo hate Dave even more and call him an Indian giver.

There are also some other people in the neighborhood that have grudges against our old landlords; my sister isn't the only one. Even though we come from diffcrent countries and like different food, there is one special thing that holds us together. We're all Catholics. The Goldmans aren't. They are Jewish, and everybody seems ticked off at them in general for killing Christ, but I think that's unfair. That'd be like blaming me for the Great Potato Famine starving all those people or Eric the Red pillaging all those towns.

"How did your schooling go this year, *Liebchen*?" she asks.

Mrs. Goldman was a teacher at a college before she came to this country. So she's smart. She knows that bad things can happen when you least expect them. Her daughter got taken away by these people called the Nazis and they never brought her back again. Her name was Gretchen. She died taking a shower, which broke my heart, but didn't shock me. (If you watch Mr. Wizard as much as I do, you learn that many accidents take place in the bathroom.)

"Sixth grade wasn't too bad," I tell her. "I got all As except for a D in arithmetic. I don't really have a head for those problems. I'm not good at them."

"You are good enough," she says, patting me on the head. "And vhat about your sister? How is she doing in her studies?"

"She's . . ." I don't want to tell Mrs. Goldman that Troo might be getting kicked out of Mother of Good Hope School for her impure behavior. "She's doin' great in gym class."

Mrs. Goldman is gazing down at the curb at my sister's back. "Are you keeping the vatchful eye on her?"

"Tryin' to." Troo cannot stay still for long. She is throwing at car tires when they pass by, timing it so the ball bounces back to her.

"That is good," Mrs. Goldman says. "And how is your *mutter* feeling these days?"

I picture her this morning in the shade of the garden with her TV tray in front of her and our collie licking her toes. "I wouldn't say that she's a hundred percent in the pink yet, but she's better. She does jigsaw puzzles to pass the time until her legs get built back up."

Mrs. Goldman says, "It makes me glad to hear that Helen is on the mend. I like those puzzles, too."

"Really?" I get a bright idea. I'm gonna bring some of Mother's old ones over to Mrs. Goldman to make up for being such a bad friend to her. There's a bunch of those kitties playing with yarn puzzles gathering dust on the shelf in our front closet. "Do you like cats? 'Cause if you do, I might have a big surprise in store for you."

Mrs. Goldman says in a more serious voice, "I like the *katze* but am not much for surprises . . . but for this . . . the one you have given me today, I am so very glad. So happy that you have come to see me. I have missed your curious mind." She picks up my hands in hers. She has numbers tattooed on her arm. "Your coming to see me today . . . it is kismet."

I never heard that word before. "Kismet?"

"*Schicksal*," she says. "Fate. You understand the meaning of this?"

"Ohhh, yeah, sure," I say, glad. I don't like it when I don't get what somebody is talking about. They could be saying something important that I should be paying attention to and it's flying right over my head. "They teach us all about fate in Catechism class. It means that God's got everything already planned out for us. That our life is in His hands."

I think if that really is true, then God must have the worst case of butterfingers. There is no other explanation why He would let Bobby Brophy lick the inside of my ear. And make Daddy crash on the way home from a baseball game. And take Mrs. Goldman's little daughter away from her. I know He's supposed to work in mysterious ways, but I don't think that's mysterious. He's being a bully and I know all about them.

The grunting man who was lugging the trunk down to the taxicab comes halfway back up the steps, mops his forehead with the bottom of his T-shirt and says to Mrs. Goldman, "That all of it?" and you can tell he sure as heck hopes it is. He's the color of boiled rhubarb.

Mrs. Goldman says, "Thank you. That is it. Vee vill be right there."

I got so caught up in becoming friends with her again that I put what she's doing out of my mind. "You're leavin'," I say, feeling the bottom drop out of my heart.

"*Ja*. Mr. Goldman and I are taking of a trip," she says. "To Rhein-land."

"Rhinelander?" I say, completely astounded. That's the home of Camp Towering Pines. "Troo and me just got back from there!"

For a person who doesn't like surprises, my old friend is in for one of the worst of her life. I'm about to warn her when she says, "I think perhaps you misunderstand me, *Liebchen*. Otto and I are returning to the Motherland. To Germany."

"*Oooh*." Otto has been the man of her dreams for over forty years. I've heard him speaking from behind the curtains lots of times, but I have never actually laid eyes on him. Troo thinks he doesn't come out of the house much because he's a hunchback, but I think it's because he's shy about his English not being so good.

"My brother . . . he is ill and vee are going back to run Hans's clock shop for him until he is feeling better."

She's got a bellowing grandfather clock and some silly cuckoos and there's another that chimes like the bells at church. I could really count on those clocks to get me through the night when we lived upstairs. Now I know where they came from.

"I'm so sorry your brother's sick," I say. It is my responsibility as a Catholic to try to make her feel better even if I can't count it as a charitable work. Doing a good deed for a Jew is frowned upon. I don't think it's an actual sin to do something nice for them, but it could be. "Is there anything I can do to help you? I'm really good at packing. I watched Mother get ready for the hospital. She put tissue paper between the layers so her clothes didn't get wrinkled and sprinkled perfume on them so she'd smell good and not like shots when she came home."

"*Nein*, thank you for the kindness offer, but the packing it is finished. But there *is* something that occurred to me the moment you appeared on this porch, *Liebchen*." She raises her finger straight above her head. "Vere you familiar vith the Peterson family that vas renting of the upstairs?"

"Not really." We heard they didn't have any kids so nobody really bothered with them.

"The husband lost his job at the cookie factory. It is empty now."

Lots of times it felt that way when we were living there so I don't look up at the second-story windows.

"I entrusted this job to Officer Rasmussen, but he is very busy with being a detective and his new family." Mrs. Goldman winks at me and it is so adorable because she is not very good at it. "I know what good attention you pay. Do you think you could assist your father? Keep your eye on the house while vee are gone?"

She's right. This *is* fate. And such a great way to make everything up to her. "Sure I could help watch the house. Don't worry about a thing. What about the garden?"

When I still lived here, me and Mrs. Goldman planted tiny seeds together in the backyard and soon juicy red tomatoes rounded on the vines and carrot tops pushed up so determined, which has always made me wonder how something so delicate could at the same time be so strong. We also put in purple pansies and yellow daisies. Daddy only grew crops but Mrs. Goldman thinks that while having good things to eat is important, something lovely to look at fills you up in a different kind of way. She also taught me on those early mornings that people are a lot like a garden. Not everybody is beautiful or scrumptious. There are some weeds that you've gotta watch out for that would be happy to choke the life out of you and she was right.

"Do you want me to pull out the dandelions?" I ask her. "What about the caterpillars? Should I pick them off the vines?"

"*Ach*. I'm afraid there is no garden this summer." She shows me her knobby knuckles. They've gotten worse than they were.

"Sally!" Troo shouts the way she does when she wants me to be at her beck and call.

Mrs. Goldman says, "Before you go . . . the key to the house." She rummages around her skirt pocket until she finds what she's looking for. "It opens both doors up and down. In case of the emergency." She sets the key in the palm of my hand. "Vhen vee get back from our trip, I vill pay you five dollars for your hard vork."

"No joke?" I know I should tell her, *Oh no, thank you, I'm happy to do this favor for you without getting paid to make up for letting you down*, but I have been saving up for bus fare to go see Sampson at the new zoo. I went over to the old one yesterday to see what was left.

Troo was getting punished for lipping back, so she had to stay in her room and write a hundred times on a piece of paper, *I am not the Queen of Sheba*, and Mary Lane was nowhere to be found, so that's the reason I went all by myself.

Three yellow bulldozers were lined up, getting ready to wreck everything, but Daddy's and my bench was still there. It's old and pretty heavy. I wanted to drag it back to our house a little at a time every day, but I didn't feel strong enough to get it more than a few feet. The whole time, I kept looking over at Sampson's enclosure expecting to see him waving or hear him singing, but all that was left were the orange rocks and his favorite blue ball floating in the murky pool.

The money I would get from Mrs. Goldman to watch over her

house could buy me a bus pass. I tell her, so she knows how much Sampson and me would appreciate it, "Five whole bucks? Thank you! That's a mint!"

She pulls me close and gives me one of her good *schnitzel*-smelling hugs. "What a special girl you are," she says, somewhat proud, but also somewhat something else. Sad?

Troo yells something, but I can't make it out. I back out of Mrs. Goldman's arms even though I don't want to and shout down to the curb, "What?"

My sister makes this obnoxious sound like I'm a contestant on *Beat the Clock* and my time is up.

"Marta," Mr. Goldman calls to his wife from behind the drawn curtains. "Vee must go. The meter it is running."

"Well, I guess we both gotta hit the trail," I say. "You have a safe trip. I'll say a rosary for your brother to get better fast and come look at the house every day. Remember to check the stove and unplug your iron before you go." Mother always makes sure she does that before she leaves the house. "And . . ." I don't think Mrs. Goldman has any fancy jewelry that could get stolen, she never wears any, but she could have some guns from the war or a shoebox full of cash hidden away, which are some of the things that have already gotten taken out of people's houses, according to Dave. Of course, everybody is talking about the burglaries and how worried they are that they could be the next to get hit, but since Mrs. Goldman doesn't go to Mass or the baseball games or bowling, she might not have heard the scuttlebutt. "There's been a cat burglar prowlin' around the neighborhood. Lock up extra tight."

"This is good advice." When she says that, she is not looking at me. She is watching Troo bounce her ball up the block very ferociously. "All of us must vork hard to keep vhat is valuable to us safe. Promise me you vill keep a good vatch, *Liebchen.*"

"You can count on me." I don't say *this time*, but that's what I'm thinking. "See ya when ya get back. A lot more often. *Aufedersein,*" I say, hurrying off the porch to catch up with my still-buzzing sister.

Chapter Nine

The sign hanging above the store says in peeling white letters:

KENFIELD'S FIVE AND DIME . . . WE HAVE WHAT YOU NEED!

That's not tooting their own horn. They really do.

The floors are a yellow color and the aisles are close together but packed high with bottles of bubble bath and sewing needles and erasers and, well, just about everything under the sun. There's pets, too. Chatty budgies and whisker-twitching mice and lovebirds that have to be kept in different cages because they don't actually get along that well and all sorts of different kinds of fish. This is where Dave bought me the aquarium that's on top of the dresser in our bedroom. The pet aisle reminds me of living out on the farm, but the rest of the Five and Dime smells like popcorn. There is a machine up front that pumps it out all day long. You can get a small bag for two cents and a bigger bag with butter for a nickel and the salt is free.

The best part of the store, though, has gotta be the candy case. It's the first thing you see when you come in and it's even better now that it's been new and improved! My favorite used to be pink and green Buttons, but I got sick from swallowing too much paper, so I switched over to Oh Henry! bars in honor of you know who. Troo's favorite used to be licorice, but now she goes silly for those lips made out of wax because she has gotten very interested in kissing recently. The Frenchy way, less lips, more tongue, which I tried to explain to her is just asking for trench mouth, but would she listen?

Our old Vliet Street neighbor, Mrs. Kenfield, lifts up her head to greet whoever just walked into her store, but when she sees that it's Troo and me, she mutters, "The O'Malley sisters," like somebody just asked her to name the last two kids in the world she'd like to have come through her doors this morning. She goes back to spritzing Windex on the counter and rubbing it off with a blue rag until the smudges disappear, maybe wishing she could do the same to me, and for sure Troo. "How's your mother?"

Of course, Mrs. Kenfield sees her at choir practice and up at the Kroger when she goes on Wednesdays, which is the day they hand out extra S&H Green Stamps, but just like Mrs. Goldman and Mr. Fitzpatrick, whenever anybody in the neighborhood runs into Troo and me they automatically ask how our mother's doing because they really can't believe she's not dead and sometimes I can't either. That's why I kneel next to her bed in the middle of the night and watch her chest go up and down. I set my head against hers on the pillow and breathe in her leftover powder and perfume, just for a little while, just to make sure.

"Mother's feelin' better and better," I tell Mrs. Kenfield as Troo disappears down aisle two. What is she doing? Kleenex for flowers is in aisle four. "Gettin' stronger and stronger by the minute."

Mrs. Kenfield says, "Glad to hear Helen's on the mend," but she doesn't sound it and I don't blame her. I don't care what the Bible says about loving your neighbors more than you love yourself. I think it's hard to even *like* people when your own family is going belly-up the way ours was last summer. You can't help but wish you had what they had.

The reason she's so grumpy is because her husband, Mr. Chuck Kenfield, is going down the drain. His daughter, Dottie, the one he used to wail over and maybe still does, had some of the sex when she was still in high school. She got pregnant so he had to send her away to a special home in Chicago to live with some other girls who did the same thing. What Dottie was supposed to do was have her baby and leave it there for somebody who was married to come by and pick it up so she could go back to her regular life, but that's not what happened. Grown-ups gossip about this after Mass all the time. Dottie's disappearance is still piping hot news because she snuck out of the Chicago hospital when the nurses weren't looking, so now it's both her *and* the baby that're missing. I heard she had a little girl.

The reason Dottie had to go away like that to Chicago is because around here it's a mortal sin to do what she did. I think the Kenfields just should've packed up and moved to another neighborhood. Or maybe Dottie could've done what Nell did when she got knocked up last summer by Eddie Callahan. Get married when nobody is paying attention. When the baby came out of the oven in April instead of June, Dottie could tell nosy buttinskis that her kid is just a real go-getter. "Early bird gets the worm!" is what Nell chirped to visitors until Troo told her to shut the hell up.

Missing Dottie, that's why Mr. Kenfield has become so sloshy that Mrs. Kenfield has to run the Five and Dime all by herself now. You can tell that being on her feet all day is hard on her. She has gotten very close veins in her legs. She doesn't complain out loud, of course not. The Kenfields are English. They are a people who like to keep a stiff upper lip, which means they don't like to show you any of what they are feeling. I see them in the movies. They usually wear clothes that are clean and full of starch, but I'm positive this is the same shirtwaist Mrs. Kenfield had on the last time we were up here and the part in her hair looks like a dandruff plantation and she's got pimples on her chin that she put some Clearasil on and forgot to wash off this morning.

I'm about to ask the same exact question I always do when I come up here. Even though her husband and me don't spend a lotta time together the way we used to, outta sight does not mean outta mind for me. I still think of him often as my good friend. "How has Mr. Kenfield been?"

Wiping the glass counter even harder, Mrs. Kenfield says, "I'll tell him that you asked after him, Sally." That's what she always says.

"Oh, don't bother," I say, coming up with something else I can put in my charitable summer story. "I've been plannin' to stop by one of these nights so we can talk on the porch swing like we did last—"

"Don't you dare!" Mrs. Kenfield practically bites my head off. "You remind him of . . . I mean . . ." She swallows and says quieter, "That wouldn't be a good idea. Chuck . . . Mr. Kenfield has been feeling under the weather. I wouldn't want you to catch what he's got."

I would have to agree with her.

"Hellooo!"

A new customer breezes into the Five and Dime on shiny red high-heeled shoes, seamed nylons, a skirt higher than her knees and a blouse that looks like it got shrunk in the wash. It's Mrs. Callahan, Mother's best friend since they were little and living across the street from the Feelin' Good Cookie Factory. She won't ask me how Mother is feeling because she already knows. They chat every night on the telephone for hours. She didn't use to be, but Mrs. Callahan is related to us now. She is the mother of Eddie Callahan, who got Nell in the family way. (When I heard the two of them groaning in her bedroom on Vliet Street last summer, my half sister told me that they were doing their Royal Canadian Air Force exercises, but my niece is living proof those two were touching a lot more than their toes.)

Mrs. Callahan parks herself in front of the small fan that's whirring on the Five and Dime's front counter.

"Where's your sister?" she asks. She likes Troo better than she likes me. They play rummy for pennies.

"She's ah—"

"Hi, Aunt Betty," Troo calls from somewhere in the back of the store, not even trying to be secretive.

"What's the score, Eleanor?" Aunt Betty shouts back friendly, but to me she says real urgent, "Forget whatever it was the two of you were doin' next Friday night. Eddie's gonna take Nell to the drive-in and I told them I would watch the baby, but . . ." She really has to work on improving her aim. Her cherry smile would be nice if she didn't draw so much outta the lines. "Detective Riordan just asked me out to dinner at Frenchy's!"

"That's great!" I say, because Aunt Betty really does need another husband. Her original one got flattened by a cookie press four years ago. I heard her complaining to Mother not long ago, "I despise the smell of those goddamn cookies. It's bad enough we've had to breathe it in since the day we were born . . . I can't stand it for one more minute, Helen. I gotta get outta there. I need a new man. Pronto."

I don't blame her for hating it up at the factory where she has to work in the packaging area to make ends meet. Those cookies don't make her *Feel Good the Way a Cookie Should*, the way they're supposed to. Those cookies killed her husband.

I ask her, "What time do you want us to go over to the apartment on Friday?" I was planning to work on my charitable summer story, but I guess that's gonna have to wait.

"Seven thirty. Bring your pj's and your church clothes. By the time the movies are over, it'll be too late for Eddie to drive you home."

She means he will be too shnockered to drive us home. Him and Nell like to swig beer at that passion pit.

"Wait . . . maybe you better come a little earlier," Aunt Betty adds on. "I just remembered they're not going to the 41 Twin like they usually do. They're drivin' out to the one on Bluemound Road to see the Hitchcock movie everybody's talkin' about."

This has gotta be another sign from God! The new zoo is on Bluemound Road. Maybe right next door to the drive-in. If I could talk Nell and Eddie into letting Troo and me come along to the movies with the baby in her basket, I might get a glimpse of Sampson.

Troo calls to me from the back of the store, "Floor it," which means she's gotten whatever she came for.

Aunt Betty reminds me, "Tie a string around your finger, Sally. Next Friday. Seven thirty." Then she says to Mrs. Kenfield, "Did that new Max Factor rouge—?"

"Excuse me, I'm sorry to interrupt, but I need some of those wax lips really bad." I point to the third row in the new and improved candy case. "The red ones."

Troo musta been watching, waiting for me to distract Mrs. Kenfield because that's when she makes her getaway. I hear the back door of the dime store that lets out into the alley slam shut. That would be my job normally, to make sure it doesn't.

Mrs. Kenfield hands me the wax lips with a dirty look on her face. "That'll be four cents. I'll add whatever your sister stole and settle up later with Detective Rasmussen."

"Ya gotta give it to her," Mrs. Betty Callahan snorts. "The kid's got moxie."

Mrs. Kenfield puffs out her cheeks and says, "Honestly, Betty. Don't encourage them. I plan to speak to Father Mickey about Margaret's stealing soon as I get the chance."

I beg, "No . . . please, please don't do that. Father Mickey will tell Mother and she has enough on her mind with gettin' better from her sickness and waitin' for her letter from the Pope and . . . I think Troo took some pencils and paper so she could start writing her 'How I Spent My Charitable Summer' story and that's a good cause, right? I'll pay you back."

Mrs. Kenfield waves me off because unlike Aunt Betty, she *is* very religious. She wears a girdle to keep her wiggle in check and doesn't go to church only on Sundays. Even during snowstorms, she's up there. All Mother of Good Hope kids have to go to Mass every morning when we're in school, so I've seen her kneeling, always in the same pew. The one that's closest to the St. Christopher statue. He's the saint that keeps people safe when they're traveling.

"And don't think you're getting off scot-free either, Sally," Mrs. Kenfield adds on. "I'll see that Father Mickey knows the part you play in these little escapades."

The second his name is mentioned, Aunt Betty gets that same goofy look on her face that all the girls and women get when the subject of Father Mickey comes up. "Michael Patrick Gillespie," she sighs like Sandra Dee. "You're only a coupla years older than me, Joyce. You knew Mickey back in high school, didn't you?"

"From what I heard, not nearly as well as you did, Betty," she says, looking down her long nose at her.

Aunty Betty throws her head back and laughs. Ladies are always whispering behind their hands about her being "a hot patootie," so she's used to it. I really admire how she takes those snippy comments as compliments about how good-looking she is. That is making the best of a bad situation.

Aunt Betty says with a fond-memory voice, "I remember this one time Helen and I came across Mickey and Paulie down at Honey Creek—"

"Paulie? Our Uncle Paulie?" I'm shocked. "I didn't know that he knew Father in the olden days."

Mrs. Callahan brings her hand to her bosoms and says, "They were best friends. Those two boys gave your granny her gray hair."

I already know that our uncle was hell on wheels because Ethel Jenkins told me all about him last summer, but this is the first time I heard that Father Mickey was a troublemaker from around here.

"When did Father Mickey move away?" I ask.

Mrs. Callahan closes her eyes. She always does that when she tries to come up with an answer to a question. I can do a pretty good imitation of her if I borrow some of Mother's blue eye shadow. "Well, let me see . . . after he was ordained, Mickey was assigned to St. Stan's and then some small town in Illinois and soon after that the church sent him all the way to the jungles of the Congo to do some missionary work with the little Pygmy people. That's when I stopped gettin' postcards from him, 'til he showed up here again."

Sounds to me like she's been keeping close track of him.

"You want to know something else, Sally?" she says. I really don't think I do, but there is no stopping her when she gets this naughty smile on her face. She reminds me a lot of this kid from Vliet Street, Fast Susie Fazio, when it comes to spreading hair-raising facts. "I wouldn't say that Mickey had what's known as a true calling to the priesthood."

I know what she means by that. They're always trying to convince girls to be nuns and boys to be priests up at school. To keep their ears open for a call from Jesus.

I say, "Kenny Schultz was told to join up in a dream. He went to St. Nazianz seminary right after high school."

"Yeah, that's how it goes for most boys, but M.P.G. . . . well, he wasn't most boys." I must look like I lost track of the conversation. "That was Mickey's nickname back then. Ya know, his initials? M.P.G. Miles per gallon?" She rumble laughs deep in her throat. "That boy could give a girl the ride of her life and . . . hey, don't take my word for it. Ask your mother," she says, with a wink.

"That's quite enough, Betty!" Mrs. Kenfield smacks her hand

down on the glass case. Then to me, she says, "Make no mistake about it, I'm reporting you and your sister to Father the first chance I get."

"Oh, for chrissakes." Mrs. Callahan throws up her hands. "The kid's not responsible for her sister, isn't that right, Sally?"

"I . . . I . . ." Don't agree with her. And neither did Daddy.

"I am my brother's keeper," Mrs. Kenfield says, holding her teeth closed so tight that I can't believe the words got through them. "I believe the Lord would have the same apply to sisters."

"Oh, you do, do you? You got a direct line to Him now?" Aunt Betty says, losing her cool. "Outta anybody in the neighborhood . . . you should know ya can't take heat for whatever foolishness somebody in your family is doin', Joyce. Get off your sanctimonious horse. You used to be the life of the party. When'd ya get that goddamn stick up your butt?"

Not waiting to hear Mrs. Kenfield's answer, which I was interested in because I would like to avoid that sort of thing happening to me, Mrs. Callahan spins toward me and says, "I'll tell ya what I'm gonna do, Sally. I'm gonna give you an advance on your babysittin' money and a few pennies more for what I lost to Troo playing rummy a coupla nights ago." She snaps open her shiny black pocketbook. On the bottom, I can see the peppermint schnapps she keeps in there. She tells people it's just to freshen her breath. She sets the bottle carefully on the top of the candy counter, slips out her coin purse, which is one of the leather ones Troo made at camp, and slaps down two quarters. Looking her right in the eye, Aunt Betty flicks them with her pointy red fingernail too hard toward Mrs. Kenfield, who doesn't put up her hands to block them. The coins go tumbling down to the floor. One of them rolls away for a long, long time. "And *that* should cover whatever Troo took." Aunt

Betty sets her jaw the same jutting way my sister does when she won't back down, and starts unscrewing the schnapps cap. After she's taken three deep swallows, she dabs at her mouth and giggles. "Care for a nip, Joycie?" she says, thrusting the bottle across the counter. Mrs. Kenfield's arm stays as frozen in place as her face, which looks like an ice-skating rink, cold and flat like that. "Not right now? Well, maybe you'd like to take some home to holier-than-thou Chuck. I'm sure he'd have no problem finishin' it off."

It goes midnight-in-a-cemetery quiet. The parakeets stop chirping and even the corn has stopped popping. All I want to do is get out of there and catch up with Troo and be on our merry way, but then I remember why I got sent up here in the first place. Mother'll blame a flight of imagination if I forget to pick up her afternoon "nummy," which she takes very seriously and goes even grumpier without. I've had my fill of cod liver oil this week.

"I . . . I'm sorry . . . Mrs. Kenfield . . . I . . . ah . . . forget something." She doesn't notice that I'm talking to her so I reach up to tap her on the shoulder, but then I'm not sure that's a good idea, so I ring the bell next to the cash register instead. "I'll take one of Mother's usual please, if you don't mind and that's all right with you."

The owner of the Five and Dime doesn't take her eyes off Mrs. Callahan when she grabs the candy out of the case and pitches the Snirkle at me.

"Thank you, Mrs. Kenfield. You, too, Aunt Betty," I say, fast as I can. "If I don't see her first, tell Nell we'll be there next Friday night to sit for the baby. I hope you have a nice time eatin' and dancin' with Detective Riordan," and then I scramble out of the store.

Heading back down North Avenue toward Troo, who I can see

a few blocks down bouncing her ball again, I'm feeling sorry for Mrs. Kenfield. First she had problems with her daughter and then her husband starts falling down a lot and now she's gotta run the Five and Dime looking like a rag picker with a stick up her butt.

I guess, just like Granny says, when it rains, it pours.

Mrs. Kenfield really could use an umbrella.

Chapter Ten

It's not just Troo and me, *all* the kids who go to Mother of Good Hope School have to write charitable stories over the summer. If you don't show up with it the first day of school you'll be punished by Sister Raphael, who is the principal but is also in charge of good deeds. She's also the nun who wants to kick my sister out of school for more than one reason. Since Troo was in her office at least once a week for doing one bad thing or another, Sister told me she's thinking of having the chair in the corner of her office engraved permanently with Troo's name. (If she bothered to look at the back, she could save a few bucks. Troo stole a penknife outta the Five and Dime last summer.)

The last straw happened at recess two weeks before school let out.

Jimmy "B.O." Montanazza was hanging off one end of the monkey bars. My sister was sitting on top. She musta been holding her breath because B.O. can't even play hide-and-seek, that's how easy he is to track down. His pits just reek. I couldn't hear what exactly Troo asked him; I was playing double Dutch at the time, but I heard B.O.'s answer cut through the sound of the slapping ropes because like all the Italians, he talks so darn loud. "Take it from me, O'Malley, sex is like a hot dog. It's all about the weiner and the bun," B.O. said. Troo started hooting like a maniac. Sister Imelda didn't. She dragged the both of them off the bars straight into the principal's office. I had to take the note home because Sister Raphael didn't trust Troo to deliver it to Mother:

> *Dear Mrs. Gustafson,*
>
> *Once again, Margaret is suffering from impure thoughts. She will not be allowed back next year if she continues down the path she is heading. Perhaps your current living arrangements are a contributing factor.*
>
> > *May God have mercy on your soul,*
>
> > *Sister Raphael, S.D.S.*

My sister's dirty mind doesn't have a thing to do with where Mother lives. Troo is being influenced by a bad element. The Italians. These are a people who are interested in getting as much of the sex as they can. Look at Gina Lolloabridgida. Her bosoms . . . they're the size of watermelons. Same goes for Annette Funicello. I don't think it's my imagination that Mousekeeter Lonnie couldn't keep his eyes off her chest.

And then there's Fast Susie Fazio, who might be the worst Italian of all. She's three years older than me and knows all there is to know about first base and second base and sliding into home. Thanks to her, I couldn't listen to a Braves game for over a month after she told me and Troo how babies are made during one of our sleepovers.

This is why I try to avoid going anywhere near her house, but when the noon whistle goes off at the Feelin' Good factory, I call back to Troo, "We were supposed to be there fifteen minutes ago. Hurry up." We don't have any choice now but to cut through the Fazios' yard to get to Mrs. Galecki's place. I'm already late and Ethel keeps to a schedule. She likes me to read to Mrs. Galecki right after she feeds her an early lunch but before she takes a long afternoon nap. Troo is dragging her feet on purpose. She knows how much I hate being tardy.

Like always, Italian opera music is coming from outta the Fazios'. Fast Susie's grandma is singing along to Rickie Caruso while she's cooking, which is pretty much all she does besides casting spells on people. She is a Strega Nana . . . an Italian witch! But an excellent cook for such a small person.

The reason I know that is because it was another one of Troo's genius plans last summer that we should just show up over here around suppertime because nobody was feeding us at home. Hall was spending day and night up at Jerbak's Beer 'n Bowl and Nell quit taking care of us the way Mother told her she was supposed to so she could have more time to exercise with Eddie.

Even though we pulled chairs up to their kitchen table at least once a week, I still don't know the names of all the Fazio kids because there's ten of them. I do know Fast Susie's oldest brother,

Johnny, everybody does. He's a singer in a band called the Do Wops. They'll play at the Fourth of July celebration at the park and the crowning of the King and Queen of the Playground Festival the same way they do every summer.

Fast Susie's mother likes to be called Jane; I don't know why. Her real name is Angelica. Every afternoon, Jane lies in her robe on the davenport in the living room and watches "her shows," which I have seen with her a few times when Troo wants to spend time yakking with Fast Susie and I don't. The one called *Guiding Light* reminds me of our neighborhood because so many things go wrong . . . *zip* . . . *bang* . . . *boom*. And *Queen for a Day* I like because after those down-on-their-luck women are done telling the host, Jack Bailey, how crummy their lives are, I feel really grateful that we have our own washing machine.

As far as Fast Susie's father goes, I have only seen him at supper a few times and Mass every so often because he's got an important job. His name is Tony. He sells silverware, which he must do really well because he wears shoes made outta alligators and suits made outta sharkskin. Mr. Fazio works with a man called Frankie the Knife.

When we come into her backyard, Fast Susie says, "O'Malleys!" This is almost where she always is during the summer, lying on a greasy white sheet. Next to her, there is a bottle of baby oil with iodine in it. She slathers it all over her arms and legs, the whole hairy mess.

My sister plops down next to her and says with a load of admiration, "Zowie." Troo isn't talking about the two-piece bathing suit Fast Susie's barely got on. She's impressed by her bosoms. She is *very* interested in them in general and can't wait until hers come in. Every morning she stands in front of the mirror on the back of our bedroom door to check to see if they've grown during the night.

Fast Susie beams down at the polka-dotted suit top that's standing out about a foot from her body. "It's like that song. An itsy bitsy teenie weenie," she says, bouncing.

She inherited her bosoms from her grandmother the same way I inherited my long legs from Dave. Back in the old days Nana's musta looked like freshly filled water balloons, too, but now she has to strap them down with a belt when she's cooking so they don't accidentally dangle into a pot of spaghetti and I hope the same thing happens to Fast Susie. She's mean to me. She thinks I'm not cool. Not the way Troo is.

Fast Susie says, "Funny you two should show up. A little birdie told me something that might interest the both of ya."

For once, I think I know which little birdie she's talking about, so I say, "If it's about Greasy Al escapin' from reform school, Henry Fitzpatrick already told us." Even though it's the worst news, I'm proud of him. It really is something if you hear neighborhood gossip before Fast Susie does. Mother calls her the Hedda Hopper of Vliet Street.

Fast Susie pops up and says, "*Fitzpatrick* told you? That . . . that Casper Milquetoast?"

I take a step back from her waving arms. You gotta watch out for her all the time, but especially when she gets mad because the Fazios aren't only Italians, they're a special type called *Sicilians*, who are a people from the south side of Italy who are famous for paying you back for anything mean you've ever done to them even if they die trying. In their language, this is called having a *vendetta*.

Fast Susie says, "Ya better watch out, Troo. When Greasy Al shows up, you're *morto*."

She runs her pointer finger across her throat and makes this awful gagging sound.

I gasp, but my sister says, "I'm shakin' in my boots," only she isn't. Her sides are splitting. "Greasy Al can sit on a screwdriver and rotate."

I don't like where this is heading. "Ethel's waitin', Troo." All I want to do is go see my good friend and read to Mrs. Galecki. We are in the middle of the best Nancy Drew and if I never hear the words *Molinari* and *morto* again in my entire life, that would be fine by me.

"Did that little soda jerk also tell ya that one of the orphan kids ran away?" Fast Susie asks me, taking another stab at breaking news.

"No, it wasn't Henry. I heard that from . . ." I almost tell her that it was Artie Latour who told us that Charlie ran off, but that might make her have a *vendetta* for Artie, which is the last thing in the world that kid needs. Troo is still too busy staring at Fast Susie's bosoms to notice much of anything else, so I know she won't disagree with me when I say, "Nope. Haven't heard a thing about any orphan runnin' away."

"I didn't think so," Fast Susie says, unclenching her fists, feeling better now that she's finally got a scoop. "Charlie Fitch took off from St. Jude's in the middle of the night."

"No kiddin'," I say, doing my best to act amazed. "Do you know why? I mean, did ya hear if it was something that Artie Latour did that caused him to run away?"

"Naw," she says. "Fartie didn't have nothin' to do with it." After Artie Latour eats certain kinds of foods . . . he toots. A ton. That's why Fast Susie and some of the other kids have started calling him that nickname, which may not be charitable, but is unfortunately correct. "Fitch ran off 'cause he got caught stealin' money outta the poor box at church."

"He did?" I say, dumbfounded. Even though I didn't know Charlie all that well, I was positive he was a good kid. Even after Mary Lane told me that no-tripper story about how he might be the kind of orphan that kills people and strings them up in his living room to drip-dry. Now here's Fast Susie telling us Charlie's a thief. How am I ever going to protect Troo when I can't tell the good guys from the bad ones?

I ask, "How . . . who caught him stealin'?"

Fast Susie picks her suit out of her crotch and says with a smile, "Father Mickey."

I say, "Oh," and look over at Troo to see what she thinks about all this because she's *always* interested in any news about our pastor, but she's still staring at those Italian cantaloupe bosoms.

"Hey . . . I just thoughta something. You two . . . wanna stay over one a these nights?" Fast Susie says, all of a sudden like we're her best friends. (That's the other thing you have to watch out for in Italians. They can turn on a dime.)

"Ah . . . thanks. I can't. I'm . . . ah, busy," I tell her.

Troo, finally breaking free of the spell Fast Susie's chest has put on her, says, "I want to!"

I knew she'd say that because Fast Susie is her idol, but I despise staying overnight at the Fazios'. We have to sleep in her spooky attic, which is bad enough, but then Fast Susie will tell us a bedtime story she knows will scare the underpants offa me. Like the one she told us the last time we stayed over, the one about Count Dracula. How after he sucked everybody dry in his Transylvania neighborhood, he'd turn into a bat and fly off to somebody else's neighborhood to quench his blood thirstiness. A neighborhood just like ours. All I could picture was Henry sleeping in his bed on 49th Street with the window open. He would be like finding a pot at the end of the rainbow for the Count. That vampire would lick his bat lips and open up my boyfriend's hemofeelya neck like he was the drink spigot at the soda fountain. The time we stayed over and Fast Susie told us about Frankenstein stealing body parts was bad, too. I had to go home in the middle of the night because I couldn't stand hearing that story for a minute longer. I should've waited until the sun came up because that was the first time Bobby came after me. I didn't know it was him. I couldn't see his face in the dark, only his pink-and-green argyle socks from under the Kenfields' bushes where I hid.

"Aw, c'mon, ya gotta stay over, Sally," Fast Susie says. "I wanna tell you all about this movie Tommy took me to see last week." She's going steady with Tommy Molinari, who is one of Greasy Al's brothers, but is mostly known as The Mangling Meatball. "You'd love *Psycho*. It's all about this square who takes extra good care of his mother!"

Troo, really keyed up now, says, "Can we eat over, too?" She adores all of Nana Fazio's cooking, but especially her *cannolis*, which are these creamy little rolled-up sandwiches.

I check Daddy's watch on my wrist for the third time. "Troo, I'm goin'." I nudge her with my foot. "Did you hear me?"

She nudges me back in the ankle much harder and shouts, "Do I look deaf?" She reaches into her shorts and slides a pack of L&M's out of her pocket.

I say, "You know where I am if you change your mind," and then I run out of that backyard because when her and Fast Susie light up those cigarettes and start puffing away, Nana Fazio starts shouting some crazy-sounding Italian curse out of the kitchen window and Fast Susie yells something back that sounds like "Basta or pasta" and Troo begins her French *hunh . . . hunh*ing and more than anything, all I want to do is be with somebody who speaks my own language.

Chapter Eleven

W here ya been, Miss Sally? I was gettin' ready to send a posse out for ya," Ethel says when I come barging through Mrs. Galecki's back door.

My other best friend is standing at the sink barefoot to give her bunions some breathing room while she's popping the tops off juicy red strawberries and running them under cool tap water, never hot. That would suck the sweetness right out of them. There's an angel food cake baking in the oven. She makes one every week around this time. Later on, she'll whip a bowl of cream 'til, as she says, "It's cryin' for mercy." Strawberry shortcake is Mrs. Galecki's favorite dessert. Because she's so long in the tooth, she gets to have it whenever she wants.

Ethel's wearing her white nurse dress that she's always got on when she's working. It sets off her skin that is almost the exact same color of chocolate pudding after you pour milk over it and mix it all together. Ethel is tall and solid, like the Kelvinator. Once she knows you some and likes you more, she'll let you pat the top of her hair. It feels like a new mattress because it's got a lotta bounce to it. Though she says a lady never tells her age, I know that she is thirty-six years old because I always give her a green lanyard on her birthday, which falls on St. Patrick's Day.

Ethel has been taking care of Mrs. Galecki for . . . I'm not sure how long. Mrs. Galecki's husband died in a war so she lived alone in the house next door to Dave's until she got a bum ticker. That's when Mrs. Galecki's son, Gary, who lives in California, hired Ethel to come and take care of her. Ethel has nursing experience and is also a great baker. Mrs. Galecki needs medicine and appreciates a flaky crust, so they scratch each other's backs.

I say, "Sorry I'm late," and slide out the three-step ladder she keeps next to the sink for me. This is almost always where I get situated when we have what Ethel calls a rockin' chair visit minus the rockin' chair.

"Apology accepted." Ethel wipes her wet hands on the yellow dish towel and says, "Peanut 'n marshmella?" That's Troo's and my favorite sandwich in the world.

"No, thank you." My stomach is still not calmed down from what Mother served us last night at supper. She called it jellied moose. "But I'd love some Ovaltine." That's Troo's and my favorite drink in the world.

Ethel says, "Sure 'nuff," and gets up on her toes and gets down my favorite lilac metal glass off of the top shelf of the cupboard and takes out two of her famous Mississippi blond brownies from the cookie jar in case I change my mind about eating something, which

I already have once I get a load of the melt-in-your-mouth buttery squares on the clean white plate.

"Where's your sister?" Ethel asks in that accent of hers that sounds less like talking and more like crooning. If Frank Sinatra came from Calhoun County he would sound just like her. He wouldn't be so skinny either.

I say, "Troo's over at the Fazios' talkin' to Fast Susie."

"That's fine, long as she ain't listenin' to her." Ethel shakes her head. "That Fazio girl had one good idea it'd die from loneliness."

She said that to make me feel better because she knows how much Fast Susie razzes me. It's Ethel's way of sticking up for me. That's the kind of person she is. True blue. And not only to me. She takes such good care of Mrs. Galecki and that's why she deserves exactly what's coming to her. When Mrs. Galecki passes away, Ethel is going to get a bunch of money from her Last Will and Testament. Ethel doesn't know that though. The reason I don't tell her is because she loves a good surprise, and second off, Mr. Gary Galecki made Troo and me promise not to tell a soul when he let that inheritance secret slip because he had too many Tom Collins cocktails on his screened porch last summer during his yearly visit. Mr. Gary adores Ethel and he doesn't need any of his mother's money. Just like Dave, Mr. Gary has a thick wallet. He's in the movie business. I want Ethel to open a bakery with that money she gets, but one of her dreams for the future is to open a school for Negro kids, so that's what she'll probably do. She should call the place Miss Ethel's School of Manners and Everyday Advice. She's smart at those things and a lot of others. She studies both the morning and evening newspapers and never misses the *Reader's Digest*.

I ask, "How's Mrs. G been feelin'?"

Ethel sighs hard enough to flutter the curtain above the window-sill where Mrs. Galecki's medicines, over ten bottles, are lined up.

She says, "Her gut's still actin' up. Gotta go pick up some more Pepto. That's what Mr. Lou recommended for this sorta thing."

My future father-in-law and Ethel Jenkins are friendly because she has to go to the drugstore all the time to get the pills Mrs. Galecki needs to take every day to keep her going, which Ethel doesn't mind because Henry's father acts toward her the same way he acts toward everybody else. Gentlemanly. Not like the vegetable man at the Kroger. He treats Ethel like she's week-old cabbage.

"Would you say hello to Henry for me when you go?" I miss him and our visits. Next time I know that Troo can't get into anything she shouldn't, when she's locked in our room for disobeying Mother again, that's where I'm heading. "Please tell him I'll get over there really soon to count Ramblers."

"Will do," Ethel says, stirring my Ovaltine. She is such a great cook. Gets all that malty grit to dissolve just perfect so there's only smoothness going down your throat. "Ya heard anything more 'bout the orphan boy that disappeared?"

That's the way it is in the neighborhood. It's like living with a hundred Chet Brinkleys. No matter where you go—the park, the playground, Mass, the Five and Dime, the library—you can't get away from the hottest subject. Even if the last thing you want to do is think about it anymore, rotsa ruck. Everybody'll be flapping their lips about Charlie's running away from us and Greasy Al running toward us—well, limping toward us—until another disaster happens, which could be at any minute. When we lived in the country, all I ever had to pay attention to was not getting too close to the chickens, who have the worst personalities, but here in the city . . . it's the people you gotta watch out for in more ways than one. They can egg your worry on and even if you are doing your absolute best to keep it under control, they won't let you with all their jibber jabber.

"Thank you," I say, when Ethel sets down the lilac glass that's sweating as bad as the both of us. "All I heard about Charlie is that he's still missin'." I pull up the neck of my T-shirt to dry myself off and Ethel uses her arm on her forehead because she's already got her hands full. She's taken the blue bowl of strawberries to the counter and is holding a small sharp knife to slice them up real thinly between her fingers.

"Miss Bertha's friends with Sister Jean from the orphanage," Ethel says. "She come over for a visit and was real broke up. Told us that boy was really something. And how the Honeywells are so disappointed to have lost him. Father Mickey is tryin' to put some men together to go lookin' for him."

I don't tell her that Father Mickey probably doesn't give a hoot about some orphan kid, he just wants the poor-box money back. The church loves moo-la-la. If it isn't paper drives, it's fish fries or Bingo. They're always asking to give until it hurts. Especially lately. Father Mickey says we need to build more classrooms onto the school. All the money that gets taken in will go to finishing the new wing, but even if that's a good cause, I notice people's pinched faces when they drop dollars into the collection plate on Sunday. They have to work hard for their money, almost all of them at the cookie factory.

Ethel says, "That Father Mickey sure is something. Easy on the eyes, too." Music is coming out of her bedroom. I can't barely hear it, but her body is having no trouble keeping the beat. It's swaying. "Ya know what I been thinkin', Miss Sally?"

"What, Ethel?" I say, snitching a berry out of the bowl.

"I been thinkin' I'm gonna switch myself over to the Catholics."

"Oooh . . . nooo . . . nooo . . . I wouldn't do that if I were you,"

I say, in the same no-nonsense voice she uses on me when I come up with an idea that she thinks stinks. "That . . . that would be like takin' that shiny orange dress of yours and tradin' it in for a . . . burlap sack."

Mother lets Ethel take me down to her church on 4th and Walnut Street sometimes. It's in an old store that has the sign: JOE KOOL'S SMALL AND LARGE APPLIANCES FOR THE DISCRIMINATING hanging above the door. The basement windows of the church are stained, not with glass, but who cares? The whole congregation dances and shouts even when the Reverend Joe Willow is sermonizing. I have already decided that when I grow up, that's what I'm gonna be. A Baptist. Mary Lane said she'd do it with me. I'm sure more for her hungry tummy than her hungry soul. She went down there with me and Ethel a coupla times so she knows all about the fried chicken and colored greens they put out after the service.

"You've got the wrong idea about our church," I tell Ethel. "You've only been up there for funerals. You don't know how bad it can get."

"*Mmmm . . . hmmm.*" In southern, that means, Go on, tell me more.

"You gotta starve yourself for hours before you receive Holy Communion." Ethel would especially not like that part. She adores a big country breakfast with ham first thing every morning. She wouldn't like the taste of the body and blood of Christ. He's really bland. (I'm too nervous to bring this up to anybody who might know the answer, but isn't swallowing down Jesus kinda like being a cannibal?) "And the nuns, they got ways of torturin' people that are worse than the Red Chinese."

"That's nothin' but your big 'magination talkin'," Ethel says with a snort.

"No, it's not! Swear to God. The sisters tied Mary Lane down and dripped holy water on her forehead after they caught her peepin' on them."

"Sounds to me like that girl was spinnin' one of her no-tripper tales," she says, still slicing away at those berries, making them not too thin so they fall apart, but not too thick either. "I only know the one nun. Sister Jean seems real nice."

"She's only bein' nice to you because ya aren't a Catholic." Ethel doesn't understand how those crabby penguins work. "You can't believe how bossy they are. They're the brides of Christ so that makes them almost as powerful as priests," I say, hoping that I'm getting through to her. "If you join up, you'll be under all a their thumbs. Even in your dreams they can come after you."

"Well, I sure wouldn't like that." No, she wouldn't. She needs her beauty sleep and takes pride in her freedom. "Here I been thinkin' that was a place of worship all these years. That only goes to show ya how wrong a body can be about something, don't it? Thank you kindly for the warnin', Miss Sally." Ethel's teeth are enormously white. She sucks on lemons to make them that way. She shouldn't be smiling, though. I'm not kidding around. "But I'd be keepin' my voice down 'bout that church stuff if'n I was you," she says.

As usual, the smartest woman I know is right. Catholics are not supposed to even *think* something bad about the church, so saying it out loud has gotta be worse.

Ethel lifts her chin and nods it at the window. "Ya wouldn't want Father Mickey to hear ya."

I jump up off the stepladder and almost knock it over. "Father's right outside?"

"He's out back with Miz G. Surprised ya didn't see them when ya got here."

Shame on me. I was in such a hurry to escape from Fast Susie that I wasn't paying attention to the details. I creep over and inch back the white kitchen curtain. Just like Ethel said, there's Mrs. G in her wheelchair under the crab apple tree and Father Mickey's by her side. "What's he doin' here?"

"He's been comin' to give Miss Bertha comfort and the Holy Communion you was tellin' me 'bout. Too hard for her to get up to church much as she'd like." Ethel cracks opens the oven door to check on her cake. "Father's also been kind enough to watch over her while I run out to do my errands."

Seeing handsome Father Mickey has made me come up with an even better reason to keep Ethel from turning her back on the Baptists and joining forces with the Romans. "If you changed over to Mother of Good Hope, you'd never get to see Ray Buck." That's her boyfriend, who is a bus driver. They spend every Sunday together, which is Ethel's day off.

"Don't see that as a problem," Ethel says. "Ray Buck could join up, too."

I'm not gonna be the one to tell her that I don't think that would be allowed. I'm sure they only let Ethel go up to church because she has been in the neighborhood for so long. Ray Buck doesn't live around here. He lives in the Core with the rest of the Negroes. Ethel might think that Father Mickey's the best thing since the invention of aluminum foil, but I got news for her.

Before I can stop myself, "I don't like him" just dribbles out.

"Whaaat?" Ethel says, wiggling the cake out of the oven into her dish-toweled hands. It's perfectly browned on top, just how she expects it to be. "Since when don't ya like Ray Buck?"

"What're you talkin' about? I adore Ray Buck."

(More than she'll ever know.)

"Is this heat gettin' to me or is my imagination gettin' more het up than yours?" Ethel says. "I swear ya just told me ya didn't like him."

"I . . . I didn't mean Ray Buck."

Ethel sets the angel food cake down on the top of the tall green bottle she uses to cool it off. "Who *did* ya mean then?"

It's too late now. I am putty in her hands. "Father Mickey," I say, getting right up close to her so there's no chance he could hear me with his all-powerful priest ears.

"For heaven's sakes, what could be wrong with . . . wait a Tallahassee minute." When she turns her head my way, her warm cheek is pressed almost on top of mine. I can smell the violety toilet water behind her ears. "This is soundin' awful familiar to me," she says with suspicious eyebrows. "You're not gettin' a bee in your bonnet over Father Mickey the same way ya did with Mr. Dave last summer, are ya?"

No matter how hard Ethel tried to convince me that I was wrong about him, I was sure that Dave was the murderer and molester. So I could have a bee in my bonnet and not even know it. I can't seem to get a grip on these sorts of things.

"I don't think so," I say.

"I should hope not," Ethel says, getting back to sprinkling powdered sugar over those berries and mixing it in with a wooden spoon. "It takes a lot to dedicate your life to our Savior. Ya need to respect that." She's shown me pictures of her brother named Gaston, who is a preacher back home in a country church, so I knew she might take that the wrong way. That's why I haven't told her how I felt about Father Mickey before now. "Sacrificin' the pleasures of life for the ways of the Lord ain't easy."

"I know, Ethel, I know. That's really nice of people to dedicate their lives to God. That's why I am gonna try my hardest not to feel that way about Father from here on out."

When she doesn't say anything reassuring back the way she usually would, I slip my arm around her waist. "Are ya mad at me? For not likin' Father?"

"Your feelin's is your feelin's. I'm just ponderin' the why of 'em. Last summer, it was Mr. Dave that got ya all worked up and now it's the priest." She holds out a spoonful of sweetened strawberries for me to taste. "Maybe ya got something against men in uniforms. Had me a dog like that once. Wouldn't let the ice man get within ten feet a the house."

I don't know the reason I don't like Father Mickey, but I don't think it's because of the way he dresses, which is your basic black. He hasn't done anything wrong to me, just the opposite. He always admires my long legs and asks if I'd like to sign up for the girls' basketball team when I pass him in the hallways at school. And he's being extra, extra kind to Troo. I don't know. Maybe I don't like all of the time him and her are spending together. Mother is jealous of all the time Dave is spending with *his* partner, so maybe it's like that.

"You sure you're not mad at me?" I ask Ethel because she hasn't said anything for a minute or so and is mixing the berries more than she should. They're starting to look floppy.

Ethel sets down the spoon and says reluctantly, because she is not a complainer by nature, "It's not you, honey. I got a few other things that's makin' my mind distracted."

Since she's my sounding board, I always try to repay the favor if something is bothering her. "Like what?"

"I can't hardly put my finger on it . . . but . . . something strange is goin' on round here. Miss Bertha, she had me call up Mr. Cooper to come over last week." He is the man Mr. Gary Galecki picked out to make sure his mother's bills are paid. He also signs Ethel's paycheck that comes in the mail every Friday from his office called Cooper, Cooper and Barrow. I've only met him once. He was carrying a briefcase and didn't say hello back to me. "After Mr. Cooper arrived," Ethel says, "Bertha shushed me away and the two of them and Father Mickey got settled in the parlor and had a nice long visit. Usually I'm included. Can't figure out why I weren't."

I bring my hand up to my chest, roll my eyes and do my imitation of her. "Lord, I can't imagine." That's a very Mississippi thing to say when you're stumped. "Maybe Mr. Cooper's fixin' to fire ya." I'm trying to make her laugh because that is so silly. She will never get let go from this job. Nobody could take better care of Mrs. Galecki than she does.

When all Ethel gives me back is a small smile as she slides the bowl of strawberries into the fridge, I tell her in my regular voice, "Don't feel bad." Long as she's in there, she takes a breath of that cool air and paddles some down the front of her dress. "I got worries, too." I've found when somebody tells you something that's bothering them they appreciate it if you tell them something's bothering you, too. That way it doesn't seem like you think that you're better than they are. "I can't stop thinkin' about Greasy Al and how he's gonna—"

"*Whoa* up." She closes the fridge door and flips up both of her pink palms. "Like I told ya before on this subject, ya gotta think a something else ya really like when that boy comes to mind."

What she really told me was, "When I'm 'bout to blow a fuse, I think about dancin'. And Ray Buck. You could think about Henry . . . or you could read or pray."

I tried doing what she wanted me to do, I really did. The second

I started thinking about Greasy Al, I tried to switch gears and think about my future husband. Or driving around the countryside with Nancy Drew in her blue coupe. But somewhere down the road, Molinari would flag us down and ask us for a ride back to 52nd Street so he could murder my sister. I also tried praying to Daddy, but all that did was make me feel like if I didn't work harder at keeping Troo safe, how disappointed he was gonna be when we met again in heaven.

Ethel runs her big cool hand down my arm and says, "All right then. Think we 'bout wore this conversation out, don't you? Time for storytellin'." She steps into the back hallway and opens the milk chute, which is where I keep my book so I don't forget and leave it at home.

"Are you gonna come out, too?" I ask when she hands over *The Hidden Window Mystery*.

This is the third Nancy Drew that I've read to them and, by far, our favorite. There's a colored woman in this story. Lovable old Beulah who serves corn pudding and *strawberry shortcake*. Just like my Ethel! The story also takes place in the South so that's gotta give her a home, sweet home feeling.

"Ya know, sittin' down in the shade and listenin' to ya read sounds mighty nice," Ethel says. "Don't think the sheets are gonna dry on the line today anyways. Too hot and wet." She does her slidey walk to the kitchen window that makes me think she's hearing *Waltzing Matilda* in her head. She calls out, "Y'all 'bout done out there, Father?"

I couldn't hear his answer, but Ethel turns back and gives me a look that says whatever it is you are thinkin' at the present moment, it'd be a mighty good idea to keep it to yourself and get your behind outta that door.

"What a delightful surprise," Father Mickey says when we join him and Mrs. Galecki under the crab apple tree. He is a different kind of Irish than our family is. He is *black* Irish, which doesn't mean he's a Negro born in Killarney the way people might think. It means that Father has hair the color of a funeral, not a stop sign. Most Irish people have bad tempers, but black Irish people are famous for having the worst. "Hello, Sally. Haven't seen you since school let out."

"Good afternoon, Father . . . I . . . I came over to read to Mrs. Galecki." I hold up the book so he doesn't think I'm lying.

"Ah, yes. Your sister tells me you're quite the reader."

"Don't you mean she tells you that I'm a bonehead?"

When Father Mickey smiles grandly, I can see what everybody goes silly over.

"That's a beautiful watch you've got there." He taps his finger on the face. "A Timex, isn't it?"

"It was my daddy's," I say, forgetting that pride is a sin. Father musta forgot that, too, because the watch he has on is *very* fancy. "Mother got it made small for me."

Father says with a twinkle in his eye, "Helen's always been a very considerate person."

I wouldn't use that word to describe Mother in a million years. I guess he must be referring to the way she used to be back in the olden days. Before Daddy died. Before she got married to Hall. Before she got sick.

"Is there anything I could offer ya before ya go, Father?" Ethel with the perfect manners asks. "A glass a fresh-squeezed lemonade should set ya right."

"I cannot imagine anything I'd enjoy more, but I'm afraid I've got another parishioner to attend to." He lifts up my wrist and taps my watch. His fingers are soft and his nails are shiny like they've been painted with something. "Takes a lickin' and keeps on tickin'," he says, not to me, but Mrs. Galecki. "Just like you, Bertha."

Mrs. Galecki's head bobs up and down, but that doesn't mean she is agreeing with him. She's got some palsy.

Father slips his golden chalice that he brought the Holy Communion in over from the church into a black velvet bag and says, "Tell your sister to come a little earlier Tuesday night, Sally. We have a lot to discuss."

That's the day Troo goes up to church for her extra religious instruction. If she doesn't get holier soon, she's gonna end up going to Vliet Street School. I will miss walking up to Mother of Good Hope with her and eating lunch together and even ringing doorbells on our way home, but most of all, how will I ever keep watch over my sister if we're not going to the same school? The thought of her being out of my sight that many hours of the day makes me want to curl up. The only one that could prevent that from happening is Father Mickey.

He tells Ethel, "Tomorrow, same time," and heads toward the front of the house, but stops at the bushes that run alongside it. When he trots back and lays the pale pink flower in Mrs. Galecki's lap, he says, "A rose by any other name."

Now, if you weren't me, you would be thinking to yourself, *Boy, how did this neighborhood get so lucky? This priest is really something! He can even make the same quote that Donny O'Malley would make when he'd stuff fallen petals into his daughters' pillowcases so they would be guaranteed sweet dreams.* But on this hot, hot day, all I can think of as Father Mickey leaves to minister to another one of his flock is how much he reminds me of the black ice we get on the streets during winter. It's slick. And invisible to the naked eye.

What's wrong with me?

Ethel places the rose Father picked off the bush gently into Mrs. Galecki's high hair and says, "Don't that look nice. Miss Sally's gonna read to us now, Bertha."

Her patient doesn't answer. She's fallen back to sleep again. She does that. I can be right in the middle of a sentence and *kablooie*— she's dead to the world. That's okay. I decided a long time ago that reading still counts as a charitable work even if she can't hear it. I open the book and bring my face down to the pages and breathe. Books do not have the reputation of smelling nice, but they do. Not as good as mimeograph, but still very good.

"The name of this chapter is 'An Angry Suspect,' " I say, kicking off my sneakers and getting comfy in the backyard chair. " 'Bess was so startled to hear the name of the man for whom the girls were searching that she—' "

"Bertha? Bertha?" Ethel shrieks. She pops up and presses her ear down to her boss's lilac blouse. I am not worried. This happens all the time. At least once a week, Ethel is sure that Mrs. G has sucked in her last breath.

While Ethel's still down on her chest, Mrs. Galecki's eyes fly open and she says in the meanest voice, "What're you doing? Trying to steal my locket like everything else?"

That completely flabbergasts me. How dare she say something so cruel about the woman who gives her bubble baths and wipes the drool off her mouth and sometimes her heinie?

Before I can suggest to Mrs. Galecki that she should count her blessings, Ethel lifts her head off her chest and says back so kindly, "Locket's safe, Miss Bertha." My good friend stands and pulls me a few steps away. "She's been gettin' more and more confused the last coupla weeks. This mornin' she went yelly about how her emerald necklace was missin'."

I don't understand why this is bothering her so much. Being a nurse, Ethel should know the same way I do that old ladies' brains can really go to pot when their arteries get hard. Our other granny changed her name from Margie O'Malley to Marie Antoinette on her eighty-sixth birthday.

"Where did ya end up findin' it?" I ask.

"Tha's the funny thing. I looked and looked for that necklace, but it weren't in the hatbox under the bed where it usually is or nowheres else. Bertha didn't come right out and say so, but . . ." Ethel shrugs. "I think she's believin' I'm the cat burglar who's been sneakin' around."

I know I shouldn't, but I can't help it. I burst out laughing. Ethel is way too big to sneak around anywhere. When she's somewhere, you know it.

I remind her, "Once somebody's mind takes a turn around the bend like that, not only do their memories get backed up, but they can start sayin' strange things." What I'm trying to tell her as politely as I can is that Mrs. Galecki's brain has gone as stiff as her hair. "Granny Marie Antoinette used to misplace stuff all the time and then blame her husband, Louie, for stealin' it. Her husband's name was Alvin."

Ethel looks at me and, for the first time ever since I have known her, she doesn't have anything to say. Her eyes that are usually gentle brown pools look stirred up when she returns to Mrs. Galecki's side and places her strong hands on the chair that she starts pushing carefully toward the back door of the house so her patient, who is snoozing again, doesn't get a bumpy ride. "She was real attached to that necklace," Ethel tells me. "Her husband gave it to her the night 'fore he went off to the war."

I lay one of my hands on top of hers. "Don't you worry. It'll turn up." I scurry over to open the screen door so Ethel can push the wheelchair past me. "I'll help ya look the next time I'm over," I say once she's inside. "You know how great I am at findin' things."

Out of the dark hallway of the house, my beacon of light, my Land Ho! my Ethel says, "That'd be fine, Miss Sally," but she doesn't sound like she means it. She sounds like the wind has gone outta her sails.

Chapter Twelve

"Now I lay me down to sleep, I pray the Lord my soul to keep. If I should die before I wake, I pray the Lord my soul to take," Troo and me mumble by the side of our bed. I've been meaning to talk to her about saying something else before we turn in. That prayer does not help me keep my sunny side up at all.

Troo rolls onto the sheet and reaches for Daddy's sky-blue work shirt that I used to keep under my pillow when we lived on Vliet Street. After we moved over to Dave's, I knew she needed it more than me, so I slipped it under hers.

Once I'm over on to my side of the bed that's closest to the wall, my sister leans over to give me a butterfly kiss on my cheek. That's what Daddy always did when he tucked us in. "Night, Sal, my gal," she says. "We're gonna win the pennant this year."

I flutter-kiss her back and say, "Night, Trooper. Lew Burdette has a hell of an arm," and just like everything else Daddy said, he was right. The Braves beat the Yanks in the World Series two months after he got buried. Mr. Burdette pitched three times and won them all. That's what I was told anyway. I bought a bag of salty peanuts and tried to listen to the games, but just couldn't.

Troo rolls away from me and I get ready to do what I do every night. We used to take turns, but she gave up rubbing my back for Lent and didn't start up again the way she was supposed to after the Resurrection. That's fine. I don't mind. She may have Daddy's shirt in one hand and her Annie doll in the other, but I got her to soothe me. She feels like a baby blanket. Especially around her edges, which are usually satiny. But in this kind of heat that is making the O'Malley sisters feel like cookies baking away at the Feelin' Good factory, I gotta sprinkle some of the powder I keep on the windowsill over Troo's back. My hand won't glide if I don't.

Her snoring tonight is reminding me so much of the Hiawatha train that chugged down the tracks that ran behind our farm. Between that good sound and the steamy night and how tired I've gotten from chasing her, I can feel myself falling into dreamland face first, which is not like me at all.

When I wake up in the dark, I feel dopey and confused. That's why I don't right away shake Troo awake when I hear the clawing noise. I tell myself it must be left over from a nightmare. Bobby Brophy's long fingernails made that kind of raking noise across his shorts zipper after he set me down in the lagoon grass. But once I hold my breath and listen, no matter how hard I try to convince myself, I know the sound isn't part of a bad dream that's going to fade away. That awful noise is in the here and now. And so is the putrid smell. Both of them are coming from right outside our bedroom window.

My heart is galloping, but I can't move my arms or legs, and my mouth won't make words. It feels like I'm being held down to the sheet by the rough hands of an invisible bully. It's not until the clawing sound finally goes away, taking some of my scared away with it, that I can reach for my sister and say into her ear, "Wake up! Wake up!"

Troo answers back, thick and groggy, "What?"

I lift my nose into the air and say, "Do you smell that?" When she doesn't say she does, I tell her louder, "Breathe in, breathe in," and give a little jab to her ribs to wake her up even more.

Troo bats my arm away and says, "I don't smell nothin' 'cept for the cookies. And you. Did you wet the bed again?" She slides her hand sleepily down the sheet to check.

"No . . . I . . . there was a clawin' sound on the screen and the smell of . . ." I think again and realize it wasn't exactly the smell of pepperoni I breathed in, but close enough. Maybe it was some other kind of Italian sausage. "I'm sure it was Greasy Al tryin' to get in here. I gotta go wake up Mother and tell her to go get Dave and his gun outta bed right away!"

I try to hop over her, but Troo wraps both of her arms around me and says, "Don't you dare. She'll get mad and tomorrow she'll be worse crabby than she usually is. It was just your dumb imagination." She pushs me off and starts her *choo . . . choo* snoring again in no time.

The longer I lie here and think about it, the more I know Troo is right. If I wake Mother up, she won't rush upstairs to knock on Dave's door and tell him to go after Greasy Al. Just like my sister, my mother will think it's my imagination, she always does no matter what I tell her, but she especially won't believe me in the middle of the night.

What I need is some kinda proof that Greasy Al was about to break in and murder Troo.

I slide on my tummy to the end of the bed, tiptoe through the kitchen and out the back door. I'm trembling so hard that I can barely keep a hold of my under-the-covers reading flashlight when I take baby steps around the corner of the house. I need to make sure. I promised to keep Troo safe.

The bedroom window screen *does* look like somebody used their fingernails on it, but that's not enough to convince Dave to call in the troops. I search harder. Lift up branches and run my hands over the grass, but I don't come up with a pizza cutter or anything else sharp that Greasy Al coulda used to slice open our screen and Troo's neck.

When I inch back around the corner of the house, worried that Molinari could still be lurking around, that's when I see my sister. She's not out here looking for me. She didn't even notice I wasn't lying next to her anymore. Sometimes in the night, she starts missing Daddy too much and thinks too long about how he'd still be here if she hadn't accidentally killed him, so she'll come out to the glider in the backyard and smoke a cigarette and rock really fast. I can't let her know that I'm watching. I want to rush over and tell her that accidents happen, but the last time I tried that she shoved me down on the ground and kicked me. She didn't mean to hurt me. She just can't stand it if anybody sees her not pretending to be brave, not whistling in the dark. But tonight, Troo isn't gliding and puffing away like usual. She's lying on her tummy next to the vegetable garden, breathing in the dirt smell that Daddy always had on his overalls after a hard day in the field. I can hear some cursing mixed in with her crying. I want so bad to put my arms around her, but she'd hate it if I did. All I can do is slink back to our room on still shaky legs and wait.

By the time Troo comes back to bed, I think hours musta gone by. I wasn't worried because I was sure she fell asleep out in the yard the way she does sometimes. But when she spoons me, she smells like something else besides baby powder and grass. I can't put my finger on it. I know I've smelled it before, I just can't remember where or when. It has a rusty odor.

I bolt up and ask her where she went, but she laughs and says, "What are you talkin' about, numnuts? I been here the whole time. Go back to sleep."

I wouldn't even if I could. I'm sure that after she cried herself out in the backyard over Daddy's being gone, she decided to believe me about pepperoni-reeking Greasy Al being outside our bedroom window. I bet she flew into the night, tryin' to sniff him out. She might even try again. That's why I'm gonna stay on my toes until I hear Mother wake up with the clanking of the milkman's bottles to put on her face.

At the breakfast table, freshly shaved and smelling like starch, Dave tells me over crispy bacon and scrambled eggs, "Good news, Sally! Alfred Molinari was spotted in a park yesterday afternoon by the Racine police."

"I . . ." I desperately want to tell my father that those cops should get their eyes tested. Let him know that if I hadn't woken up last night, Molinari would've slid over our windowsill, stuffed Troo under his arm and took off to someplace where he could torture her in private before I was able to scream bloody murder. But in this sunny kitchen with the smell of just-cut grass coming through the window and the birds singing their hearts out and coffee percolating, I keep my lips zipped. Troo'd never talk to me again if I give Dave a clue to Molinari's recent whereabouts. My sister doesn't want Detective Rasmussen to be the one to catch Greasy Al. *She* needs to be the one who hangs him by his thumbs.

Dave flaps open the *Milwaukee Sentinel* and sticks his nose in the sports section, his favorite part. "Big game tonight," he says.

He doesn't mean that the Braves are playing out at County Stadium. He's talking about the one that's going to happen over at the playground later on. The one game of the summer that nobody in the neighborhood misses.

Mother, who looks lovely in a creamy blouse, lights up a cigarette and says, "We'll be there rootin' for you, right, girls?"

The urge to tell Dave about Greasy Al paying us a visit last night is so powerful, but I can't face the rest of my life with my sister not speaking to me, I just can't. So I tell him, "Wouldn't miss it for the world. Go get 'em, tiger."

Troo doesn't wish him good luck. She gives Dave a dirty look, stabs her fork down at her plate and doesn't even thank him for making her *French* toast.

Chapter Thirteen

I will always love baseball the same way Daddy did. Unfortunately, coming to these games puts me in a pickle. I spend most of every inning thinking about how much he would love being here on a hot summer night and how bad I miss feeling his hairy arm pressed against mine, the look of his chipped-tooth smile after a really great play and how he'd jump to his feet and shout, "That's showin' 'em who's boss!"

How do you make yourself forget?

It's the Policemen (The Clobbering Coppers) versus the Feelin' Good Cookie men (Chips Off the Old Block) under the playground's big lights tonight. I'm sitting high up so I can get a bird's-eye view, but not of the action out on the diamond. I'm memorizing the faces of the people coming and going. I'm looking for Greasy Al. It would be so simple for him to blend into this crowd and bide his time, especially if he was wearing a disguise like a black beard or something. After the ninth inning, he could stream out the gates with everybody else and hurry to hide between houses to follow a little girl named Troo O'Malley home. When I least expected it, that's when he'd reach out from behind a tree and grab her. I gotta keep my eyes peeled and this is no easy job.

The bleachers around the diamond are always packed when these two teams go at each other. The last time they played it got kinda heated up and nobody talked to anybody for about a week. Mr. Jessup, who is the regular ump, is pretty strict. He got on everybody's nerves so bad reciting the rules of the game that one of the factory men yelled out from the crowd, "Shut up already with the sermon on the mound," and then somebody else offered Dave ten dollars to shoot Mr. Jessup and it went downhill from there.

That's why Father Mickey is behind home plate tonight. Nobody would dare question his infallible calls. Troo is chatting up a storm with him. Usually she doesn't like people to fidget with her, so I'm shocked when Father licks his finger and rubs it across a smudge on her cheek and she doesn't seem to mind at all. Her religious instruction must be going really, really well, so that's at least one thing I can like about him.

Wendy Latour comes skipping through the playground gates with the rhinestone tiara on her head and when she spots me, she spreads her legs and shouts out the same way she always does, "Thally O'Malley, hi, hi, hi!" After she throws me lots of See the USA in your Chevrolet Dinah Shore kisses, she tries to crawl up the bleachers to give me one of her enormous hugs, but she steps on somebody's hand so Artie has to pull her back. He is really taking Charlie Fitch's running away to heart. He looks like the "Wreck of the Hesperus," which I have never actually seen but sounds pretty bad. All wrecks are.

Mary Lane's mother musta given her a Toni Home Permanent Wave and left it in too long. She looks like she got struck by lightning. She is strolling alongside Fire Chief Bailey's son, Skip, probably asking him about different and better ways to start fires. She set one last night at the empty television repair store on Lisbon Street. It's not seeing a place burn down that she likes so much. It's the trucks that come to put out the fire that she adores. She would like to drive a hook and ladder someday, but that will never happen because they're called fire*men* and not fire*women*, but that's one of the other reasons I like her so much. She holds on to her dreams even if they're bound to go up in smoke.

I can see Willie O'Hara playing rock, paper, scissors with Debbie, the peppy counselor, and Fast Susie Fazio is leaning against one of the swing poles. She's flirting with her boyfriend, The Mangling Meatball. Her long black hair is swishing back and forth across her bosoms that are pushing at the seams of her white blouse like they're trying to make a break for it.

When Father Mickey shouts out, "Play ball," I make sure to watch that Troo comes right over to sit behind me in the bleachers in the spot I saved for her. She's kicking me in the back every two seconds, so that's good. There's no sign of Greasy Al, but at least I know where she is.

The police team moves ahead of the factory guys in the second inning. Mother claps and so do I when Dave makes a double play, stretching off third base to catch the ball that was fired at him by shortstop Detective Riordan, who is the man that Aunt Betty Callahan is currently going gaga over. (She mighta had a few too many breath-freshening nips of her peppermint schnapps before the game. Her old friend Father Mickey has to call a time-out when she wobbles out on the blacktop in her red high heels to give Detective Riordan a smooch after that double play.)

Our half sister Nell has come to the game to cheer for her husband, who lost his job at Fillard's Service Station and is now working up at the factory. Nell nodded our way, but didn't come over to sit with us. She found a spot in the bleachers on the first-base side for her and Peggy Sure. That's the name of her baby. She was supposed to be called Peggy *Sue* after the Buddy Holly song, but the lady in the office at St. Joe's who fills out the birth certificates, Mrs. Sladky, wrote the name down wrong in ink. Troo thinks Mrs. Sladky played a prank because Peggy Sure was born on April 1, but my sister's wrong. (The woman doesn't have a funny bone in her body. Believe me. She was my Brownie leader. That battle-ax only took the job because she likes to boss children around with scissors in her hand.)

During the fourth inning, I cross over to the factory bleachers and squeeze in next to Nell because she looks like she could use a friend and Daddy always told me, "Be nice to her, Sal. She is not the worst big sister in the world. There might be two or three worse."

Nell doesn't even say hello before she hands me a diaper, two pins and the baby. "I'm sick of changin' her," she says. "You do it."

Things aren't going too great for Nell these days.

Her and Eddie moved in above Delancey's Grocery Store on 59th Street after they got married so Troo and me stop by to see her every Friday afternoon when we're done washing out socks at Granny's. Spending time with our half sister is something I bribed Troo to do so we can add visiting the infirmed to our "How I Spent My Charitable Summer" stories. She hasn't stopped holding it against me for a second.

When the two of us climbed up the steps to Nell's apartment last week, Troo groused the same way she always does, "I can't believe I let you talk me into this. Comin' over here is worse than bein' one a them martyrs they're always tellin' us about at school. At least St. Joan of Arc burned up quick."

We'd brought along our sleepover clothes the way Aunt Betty told us to. I'd planned out a whole speech begging Eddie and Nell to take Troo and me with them to the Bluemound Drive-in. If they said yes, I was gonna ask if we could stop for a few minutes at the new zoo so I could check to make sure Sampson was doing okay without me.

The apartment door was partly open so we could see Nell and the baby sitting on the davenport. I thought at first that I got the wrong Friday because Nell didn't look ready for a hot date. Of course, her hair that's the color of a brown paper bag looked good combed back into a DA, but she was wearing a nightie that was stained brown and snot was pouring out of her ski jump nose.

Troo took one look at her and said, "Holy God in heaven."

Nell cried out, "Eddie . . . we aren't goin' to the movies . . . he's been eatin' every night at the Milky Way . . . and . . . I think he's been feelin' up Melinda Urbanski . . . there was glitter under his fingernails . . . and . . ." Nell yanked her nightie up past her bosoms and moaned, "Eddie doesn't call them my thirty-six *dee*lightfuls anymore. He calls them . . . *sob* . . . *sob* . . . *sob* . . . my old *longies*."

Eddie Callahan is a big fat drip, but I understand why he's going up to the drive-in for supper. Nell learned to cook from Mother and the Milky Way . . . Our Food is Out of This World has the best grub with nifty outer space names like the Giant Galaxy Burger and Uranus Fries brought to you by girls with classy chassis who wear silvery skirts, and on their heads, glittery antennae bob back and forth when they glide on their roller skates between the cars to loud rock 'n' roll music. And since I heard that *large*, not *long* bosoms are a very big deal to boys, Nell's probably right about her husband feeling up Melinda the skating waitress. Even *I* noticed that her chest is high and mighty. (If Eddie's so nuts about outer space bosoms, I think he could give Nell a *little* credit. At least part of hers look like flying saucers.)

When Troo and me got back home from the apartment, I ran straight into Mother's bedroom and told her how awful Nell looked and how she suspected Eddie was being moony over an outer space skank. Mother was perched at her dressing table, brushing her glimmering hair with her golden brush. I thought she'd be understanding and so sympathetic because the same thing happened to her. Hall Gustafson stepped out with a cocktail waitress at the Beer 'n Bowl when Mother was supposed to be dying up at St. Joe's. But Mother didn't take her eyes off the mirror when she said, "Your sister made her bed, Sally, now she's got to lie in it. Let this be a lesson to you."

The cop side goes up on their feet when Mr. Kollasch hits a high fly ball that sails over Eddie's head in right field.

"Where do you think Dottie is right this minute?" Nell asks me, not even noticing that her husband let a run get driven in. "Out dancin' in a new dress with her hair done up in a bow?"

Nell and Dottie Kenfield were in the same class in high school together so they knew each other, but didn't have much in common back then. Dottie was on the honor roll, and Nell . . . like Troo says, most of her brain is in her bra. Nell only started bringing up Dottie all the time after she heard that she escaped from the hospital with her baby in Chicago. She's sure that Dottie's living the high life in some fancy supper club and wishes she could be, too.

"How am I supposed to know where Dottie is?" I feel sorry for Nell, but I am getting as tired as Troo is of her asking us what we think has become of Dottie, so I answer her the same way she does minus her special *f* word. "Do I look like a map?"

"Ya know, being a mother isn't all it's cracked up to be," Nell spits back. "Tell your sister that. I see those looks she's been givin' me."

Just like her, I can easily see Troo sticking out in the crowd. There's other redheads in the neighborhood, but none like my sister. She's giving Nell dagger eyes. She's never liked her and she hates it when I go outta my way to be nice to her. She's also giving me the c'mere finger.

"Well, nice chattin' with you. I gotta go," I say, kissing freshly diapered Peggy Sure on her nose and handing her back to Nell, who takes all that pinkness back into her arms like she's a piece of Dubble-Bubble I clawed out from underneath the bleachers.

"Oh, where oh where has my little Dot gone, oh where oh where could she be?" Nell starts singing, *not* to Peggy Sure.

She's been acting like this since she got home from St. Joe's with her bundle of joy. I think she caught a disease in the hospital that is making bats fly out of her belfry. That is not just my opinion, I know something about this. Troo reminds me all the time that people who have big imaginations can go off their rockers the same way Virginia Cunningham did in *The Snake Pit* movie, so I have memorized the signs to watch out for:

1. Talking to objects or singing to yourself.
2. Not brushing your teeth regularly.
3. Smiling or laughing at times or places when you're not supposed to.

It wouldn't surprise me one bit if somebody told me tomorrow that they saw Nell running down the street chortling at dead birds on the sidewalk with her tan teeth. Mark my words, one of these days the men in the white jackets will be coming to move her out of her apartment and over to the county loony bin.

Stepping over feet on my way back to my bleacher seat, I catch a glimpse of Mr. Kenfield. He hasn't come across the street to cheer with the rest of us, but is watching the game from his porch swing. The tip of his cigarette is glowing in the dark. I'd like to head over there to have a visit with him after the ninth inning the way I woulda last summer, but I just don't know anymore if my old friend would be happy to have me rocking next to him. He told me once during one of our visits that he loved children and wished he coulda had a whole houseful, but I think he mighta changed his mind. I heard he's been chasing kids outta his yard.

His wife, Mrs. Kenfield, is sitting ramrod straight on the other side of Mother, who looks particularly pretty tonight in gold hoop earrings and a sleeveless white blouse that shows off her summer brown-sugar skin. I can hear the two of them talking, but not what they're saying. I scoot closer, afraid that Mrs. Kenfield might be ratting Troo out for stealing from the Five and Dime, but the only thing I catch her saying is ". . . so upsetting about Charlie Fitch. I asked Father Mickey to say a novena for Lorraine and Ted. To lose that boy . . ."

I could tell she was trying to hold back tears. And not just for the Honeywells. Mrs. Kenfield had to be thinking about what *she's* lost. She must miss her disappeared daughter and her granddaughter, and her husband, who is still here, but not really, not the way he used to be anyway, which in some ways I think has gotta be worse.

Seeing that awful lonely look on Mrs. Kenfield's face makes me want to go sit next to Henry in the worst way. He's two rows in front of me in the bleachers, keeping his mother company. Maybe he's not so special to a girl like my sister, but there's something about the way he listens to me without rolling his eyes and sometimes when he looks at me in a certain kind of way, I wish Henry could bottle himself. I would buy him by the case.

Troo uses her mental telepathy on me and says, "Well, lookee-lookee. *Onree* got a fancy new haircut."

She's right. Since I saw him last, he got it cut short and is making it stand up straight from his skull with butch wax. I already adore it and I'm sure that my sister does, too. She likes all things modern.

"I love him . . . I mean . . . *it.* The flattop," I tell her, hoping I can find some time soon to meet him at the drugstore and run my hand across the top. It's gotta tickle.

"Ya know what I think . . . *Peaches 'n Cream?*" Troo leans down and says with so much snide. "I think he looks like the Kenfields' hedge. *Hunh . . . hunh . . . hunh.*"

Hearing her wild French laugh makes me remember that I forgot to do what I was supposed to be doing. I got caught up thinking about Daddy and Nell and Peggy Sure and Mother and Dave's third base playing and the Kenfields and adorable Henry that I forgot to pay attention to the details. During my flight of imagination, I betcha any money Greasy Al slunk right past me.

Chapter Fourteen

The smell of the chocolate chip cookies baking in the big ovens on 49th Street got stronger during the top of the seventh inning. It was like the cookies were giving the men a *two four six eight who do we appreciate* cheer. I thought that might make the Feelin' Good men get a second wind, but that's not what happened. Living up to their name, the cops clobbered the factory team, 10–3.

Snatches of different songs are coming out of the cars driving past us with all their windows open or, if they are lucky enough to own a convertible, with the top down. No crickets yet, but the fireflies are out. Troo loves fireflies. They flock to her. I think because they start with the letter *f*.

Strolling up Vliet Street on our way home after the game, we pass by the factory men who gave it their all out on the diamond. They're on the front steps of their houses drinking cold beer in their undershirts, hoping to catch a breeze. They tip their hats to

Dave and say, "Good game," and he says back, "Thought you had us there in the fourth. Better luck next time."

Dr. Heitz, who doesn't play ball because he is a dentist, smiles at me when we pass him changing a tire on his car. He likes kids so much. He goes to the Saturday matinees at the Uptown and will give you a free box of Milk Duds if you sit on his lap to watch the movie. I think it's his way of apologizing for having to drill you.

Dave and I are walking slightly ahead of Troo, who is kicking a rock that is coming dangerously close to my father's ankle. Mother and Nell and Peggy Sure are behind her on the sidewalk. The reason Nell is with us and not with Eddie the way a wife is supposed to be is because after the game he was nowhere to be found, which means he probably headed up to the Milky Way. (Dave tried to have a man-to-man with Eddie about being a better husband and father, but that talk didn't make a dent in that moron's thick skull.)

I decided the walk home would be the perfect time to get more information out of my father. I have had hardly any time with him. He's been so busy trying to catch the cat burglar. "Can I ask you a coupla questions?" I say.

"Shoot," he says, which is cop talk for, go right ahead.

"How did Molinari get out of the reform school anyway? Did the guard doze off?" That's what happens most of the time in movies when a criminal breaks out of jail. That, or a ripe-looking Italian girl shows up with a bottle of wine in a low-cut blouse with a black cinch belt.

Dave looks down at me with so much kindness. "We'll apprehend Alfred eventually, Sally. Don't worry. He can run, but he can't hide."

"Well, actually, he *can't* run," Troo butts in from behind. She pretends to ignore everything that Dave says and does, but she watches him, waits for him to make one wrong move. "If you were such a good detective, you'd know that." She swings her leg back and kicks the rock hard. It bounces off the heel of Dave's shoe. "By the way, did you catch the cat burglar yet?"

Dave heard Troo's sassy remark just fine, but he doesn't blow his stack the way Mother would've if she'd heard Troo smarting off like that. Dave keeps his steady green eyes on mine and tells me, "Rest easy. Law officers from Milwaukee and all points south are aware of the situation."

"But just *knowin'* that Molinari's escaped isn't enough," I say. "Did they issue an All Points Bulletin? Do they have tommy guns? Are they—"

Mother, who's closer than I thought, tugs down hard on my braid. "Simmer down, Sally!" She bustles to Dave's side and says in an even more fed-up way, "Maybe next time you'll listen to me. Filling up her mind with talk of your cases and . . . and all those criminal television shows the two of you watch . . . see what you've done?"

Dave gives Mother an *I'm sorry* look and I do, too. Not only do I not want to cause any more problems between them, I can't have her yell at me for the rest of the night and then not talk to me for three days. That's the worst punishment there is, to feel invisible like that, so I swallow back the questions I have about Charlie Fitch, too. The next time Dave and me work in the garden together, that's when I'll ask him. It's important to find Charlie even if he's dead, not only for Mr. and Mrs. Honeywell's sake, but for Artie Latour's. When we walked past his house, he was standing out on his porch yo-yoing, but you could tell his heart wasn't in it.

When we make the turn onto Lloyd Street, three houses down, we come to the Molinaris'.

Their place is not rising out of a swamp with moss hanging all over it the way you'd expect. The house has got fresh white siding with a mowed lawn and two robins are splashing around in the birdbath that's set in a yellow petunia flower bed. Sure, the place looks nice on the outside, but so did Bobby Brophy. Who knows what evil deeds those Italians are up to in their rumpus room. Or their garage. That's where Greasy Al's brothers, The Mangling Meatball and Moochie, have a bench they lie down on to lift barbells under a pinup picture of Jane Russell lounging in a haystack. Those boys have bulging muscles and switchblades that they're not shy about flicking open to remind you who's boss around here. There are all sorts of sharp tools hanging on the walls of that garage that a convict could use to cut off his ball and chain.

Because I'm walking with my head turned back to my sister to make sure she doesn't run off, I don't even notice that we've made it to the front of our house until I bump into the back of Dave.

Mother flips up the baby's buggy top and says to Nell, "Well, you better get a move on. It's late."

Nell whines, "But . . . I'm so tired . . . it's six blocks. Could I get a ride back to the apartment? Please, Mother."

"Absolutely not. You need the exercise. Your rear end, it's . . ." Mother widens her arms out as far as they go. "How do you ever expect to get your figure back?"

"Helen, it'll only take a few minutes, let me . . . ," Dave tries to say, but before he can get the rest of it outta his mouth Mother gives him her do-you-smell-dog-poop look and that's that.

I can't take this anymore. "Hold on, Nell. I'll get Lizzie on her leash and walk you back at least part a the way."

Troo says, "I'll go with." Not for Nell's sake. Or mine. She adores Peggy Sure. When she thinks you aren't looking, she smothers her tummy in raspberries. But baby love is not all she's got on her mind tonight. Troo's gonna ditch me on the way back so she can go look for Molinari. Walking past their house riled up her revenge feelings.

Mother tells us, "You two'll do no such thing." She runs her hand across Nell's hair like she understands how cruddy things are for her being married to outer-space-skank-loving Eddie Callahan for the rest of her life, the same way things were bad for Mother when she was married, and still is, to waitress-loving Hall Gustafson. But when Nell's pointy chin starts trembling and she tries to put her head down on Mother's shoulder, Mother steps out of reach and says, "Powder your nose. Pull yourself up by your bootstraps, for godsakes."

When Troo opens her mouth to point out to Mother that Nell has on flats, the phone starts *bring . . . bring*ing from inside the house. It's the station house calling for Dave. It always is this late at night.

Dave says sheepishly to Mother, "I'm sorry. I've got to get that," and takes our front steps three at a time.

I'm right behind him, thinking to myself another reason why I need to make Troo buckle under immediately. She's gotta be prepared for when we get old like Nell. When Mother pushes you outta her nest, you better have your wings in good working order, sister.

Chapter Fifteen

The inside of the house is quiet, except for Lizzie, who is bouncing up to my chin, looking for a biscuit. When Granny says, "Hope springs eternal," she must have our little collie in mind.

I'm always happy to see our furniture waiting for us with open arms. It's nicer than what we ever had before. It's double-stuffed checkered and it matches, even the hassock in front of the davenport that Dave and me can put our feet up on when we watch TV. His sink in next to mine and look good. We got the same-shaped toes.

It still smells in here like the pigs-in-the-blanket Dave made us for supper. I never saw any father do this before. Not even Daddy. I like to watch Dave in front of the stove stirring the same way I used to like to watch Daddy shave in front of the sink or tinker with the tractor. Dave tells me he enjoys cooking and I would like to send out a special thank-you to St. Theresa the Little Flower for prayers granted. (Mother made us something yesterday called *slum-goodie*, which had hamburger and tomatoes and some secret ingredient that must have something to do with the *slum* part of its name because it had absolutely nothing to do with the *goodie* part.)

Dave is dashing through the living room toward the black telephone that sits in an alcove in the hallway like one of the shrines up at church. I'm hoping with all I got that somebody in the neighborhood saw Molinari lurking outside his garage and they called the station and now the cops over on Burleigh Street are ringing Dave up so he can help capture Greasy Al, who they have trapped in a dragnet.

"Rasmussen," he says into the horn. "Yes, sir. When? Uh-huh. Uh-huh. I'll get right on it, Captain."

After Dave drops the phone back down in the cradle, I ask, "Is it Molinari? Did they catch him?"

He shakes his head and runs his fingers through his usually light blond hair that has gone knotty pine–colored from his baseball sweat. "When we were at the game, somebody broke into the Livingstons' house."

"Oh, no. What . . . what got stolen?" I ask.

"They haven't had a chance to go through the whole house yet to check what's missing, but so far, Tom's rodeo belt buckle is gone along with their best silver. I need to get over there."

I know that Greasy Al isn't the regular cat burglar because things were getting stolen before he escaped from reform school, but it could be him just this one time. It's been weeks since he has been on the run and his stomach should be growling. He can't just show up at his family's restaurant or the Milky Way in his striped prison suit. Yes. That makes perfect sense. Greasy Al burgled some food *and* the Livingstons' silver because even *he* isn't uncivilized enough to eat raw meat with his bare hands.

"You should check the freezer in their basement," I tell Dave when I'm done thinking it through. Mr. Livingston is our butcher. His daughter, Kit, is in my grade at school. She brought a hunk of beef for show-and-tell. When she was done explaining to the class that her father is originally from Montana and that's why he knows how to cut up cows, she told us they had a whole freezer full of T-bones in their basement. "There's probably a few steaks missin'."

Dave's pale eyebrows shoot up straight as exclamation points. "Sally . . . that's . . . why would somebody take—are you okay?"

I should tell him right this minute about my suspicisons about Greasy Al. And Mary Lane, who I'm sure has been doing the burglaries this whole time. It's got to be one of the two of them who broke into the Livingstons'. At the game tonight, Mary Lane was looking extra skinny. She mighta slipped away during the seventh-inning stretch for a late-night snack. But Dave's unbuttoning his baseball shirt in a hurry and heading into the bathroom, just missing Mother, who walks past me on her way to the kitchen. If she hears me telling Dave anything having to do with police business of any kind she'll get mad all over again.

She calls out to him, "I'll make us some popcorn and pour us a couple of beers. I thought we could watch Jack Parr. I kid you not. *Hardy . . . har . . . har.* Who was on the phone by the way?"

Dave sticks his head out of the bathroom, sighs and shrugs, and I do the same back to him. She knows darn well he can't stay to cuddle up with her while they watch *The Tonight Show.* He's gotta leave and do his detecting job. Mother's trying to make him feel like he is letting her down. Again. This is something that she is astoundingly good at. She could be the Eighth Wonder of the

World when it comes to letting you know how much you disappoint her.

"There's been another burglary," Dave says, down in the mouth. "That was the station calling."

Mother says like this is the first time the thought has crossed her mind, "The station?"

"I'm sorry. I know you made plans, but I've got a responsibility to—"

"But you promised," Mother says. "You told me that . . ."

Dave must apologize to her five times a day and I don't want to hear him doing it one more time. She was so happy when they first got together again and moved into this house with the white shutters and window boxes that my father keeps filled with red geraniums because that's her favorite flower, but nowadays, most of the time all Mother does is complain. Especially about him working such long hours since he really doesn't need to have a job at all. You wouldn't know it because he doesn't drive a Lincoln Continental or swing a gold watch on a chain, but Dave is filthy rich. He won't get his money stolen by the cat burglar though, because it's not here in the house. He keeps it in something called a trust fund, which I really like the sound of.

After I found out that Dave was my father, I had so many questions. Especially about my other grandparents that I never met. I went straight to Granny's little house. I knew she wouldn't get worked up the way Mother would if I wanted answers and I was right. When I asked her to fill me in, Granny didn't even mention how curiosity killed the cat. She arranged melba toast on a plate and poured me a cuppa out of her copper kettle that she brought all the way from the old country. (A cuppa is what she calls a cup of tea chock-full of milk and sugar.)

"So, Sally m'girl, you want to know more about the other half of your family?" Granny asked, across from me at the kitchen table. "The Danish side?"

"Yes, please," I said, sipping and nibbling, wondering like I always do why the dickens she loves melba toast so much. It tastes like shingles.

Warming up to the idea since she's got the gift of gab, Granny said, "You wouldn't have liked your other grandmother. Before she died from tuberculosis, Gertie was very vain about her legs, which were nice, but not that nice." Granny's eyes went even more bulgy than usual. "But your grandfather, Ernie, now there was a horse of a different color. The man had a heart of gold and the Midas touch. He got a lotta *dough* for the cookie factory when it sold," she told me, which was a pretty funny, so I laughed, too.

What am I thinking? What am I doing?

Troo.

Where is she? I didn't see her follow Mother back into the house. Maybe she's in our bedroom.

"You in here?" I whisper-call. Except for Daddy looking down on me from the wall and baby doll Annie's legs sticking out from under her pillow, it's empty.

I take a couple of steps backward into Mother's bedroom. My sister likes to come in here, but usually when our mother isn't home. Troo'll sit at the dressing table and dab perfume behind her ears and smooth on lipstick, smacking her poofy lips in the mirror when she's got it just right. She also loves to snoop. She's always looking through my "How I Spent My Charitable Summer" notebook and under Granny's bed and over at Nell's, she'll rifle through the closets. She especially likes rooting around in Mother's drawers. I'm not sure what she's looking for.

Back in the hall, I call out, not too loud, "Stop messin' around." I'm getting frantic, but if Mother hears me, she'll shout that upper-class people do not raise their voices indoors.

Going through the dining room on my way to the front door, I'm thinking Troo might be out on the porch steps shouting rude stuff at the neighbors when they go by after the game, which is something she really likes to do, but out of the corner of my eye I see her. The floor in here doesn't have the luxurious gold shag carpeting like the rest of the house does. When you press your cheek down on the wood it's almost as cool as the linoleum in the kitchen, but Troo's not doing that tonight. She's on her back. Dead Junie Piaskowski in a golden frame is hanging on the dining room wall right above her. A little light that Dave never turns off shines down on the picture. Junie was his niece who I only knew a little before Bobby Brophy got his hands on her. She's wearing her Holy Communion dress in the picture. The rosary draped over her praying hands was supposed to keep her safe.

Junie's mother and father are living out of the neighborhood now in Appleton. Even though they aren't trying to sell their house anymore the way they were right after Junie got murdered, I don't think they're ever coming back. Dave told me they will, but it's been almost two years. It just about kills me when I see the look in his eye when he goes over to their place to mow the lawn in the summer and shovel the walk in the winter. I feel even worse awful when his eyes go to the little birdhouse that he and Junie made together that's still hanging from the rain gutter. She loved birds, especially bluebirds. She called them happiness with wings. That's another one of the things I really like about Dave. He doesn't let bygones be bygones, same as me.

"So?" my sister says. Even though she's got her eyes closed, she can hear my footsteps on the loose board in front of the hutch where Mother keeps her fancy dishes displayed. "Whatta ya think of *my* imitation?"

I study her. "Who're you supposed to be?"

"Your dead cousin."

"Troo! For godsakes."

I know what she's doing. She's trying to rattle my cage, but I will not fall for that.

I ask, "How about playin' Battleship?" She loves that game. She always beats me at it. Because of our mental telepathy, my mind tells her mind where I've hidden all my ships, but I don't understand why it's never vicey versa. "I'll go get the paper and pencils. Meet you in the livin' room."

I offer my hand to her, but she says, "Scram. I'm busy workin' on my revenge plan."

Just like I knew she would be after we walked past Molinaris' house. This is one of those times in life when it doesn't feel so great to be right.

"Please, please, don't do that . . . you gotta leave him to . . ." I almost slip and say, *Dave*, but bringing his name into this wouldn't be smart. She'll batten down her hatches. I gotta try another tactic. "I don't know why you'd wanna waste your precious time. Greasy Al is probably halfway to . . . to . . ." I can't think of any place where he'd run that isn't where Troo is.

"Nice try," she says. "And for your information, I don't *wanna* go after him, I *gotta* go after him. And not just to settle the score the way you're thinkin'."

I look at the picture of Junie. From up in heaven, she knows all about somebody going after somebody.

"Then why?" I ask.

"I need a dummy for my ventriloquist show."

Is she telling me that after she catches Greasy Al she's going to ask him to sit on her lap? No, that can't be right.

"Whatta ya mean?" I ask.

"Mary Lane told me the cops give big rewards for catchin' wanted people. If I could capture Molinari, I . . . I could use that money to buy a professional dummy like the one Edgar Bergen's got."

"*Ohhh* . . . that kind of dummy. Like what's his name . . . Charlie McCarthy."

Troo nods with brimming eyes that I'm never supposed to notice. "They got one for sale called Jerry Mahoney up at the toy store. It's got a cute suit and a bow tie and . . . it's *crème de la crème*, Sal." Her bottom lip is quivering. "They're addin' something new onto the Queen of the Playground competition this year and I gotta be ready."

"What something new?"

I haven't heard anything about that. Every year since we've been here it's been just the announcing of the winner and then they go up on the stage to get the tiara placed on their head and we get to stay up late and stuff ourselves with the food the mothers bring and dance to the Do Wops 'til our heels blister.

Troo says, "I told the counselors they should put a talent part in this summer like we had up at camp and Debbie thought that was a fantastic idea. So unless ya can do ventriloquism or sing as good as me or . . ."

She knows that I can't throw my voice, and songs sound good in my brain, but by the time they come out of my mouth they go flat. I tried tap lessons at Marsha's Dance and Baton Studio on North Avenue. I loved the shoes with cleats, but I couldn't get the hang of the shuffle-ball-change. I wasn't a terrible twirler, but not good enough to stand out from the pack. If I'm going to have a chance to win the tiara this year, I need to make a talent splash. Maybe I could do some magic tricks. Find a book at the library that would teach me how to pull a rabbit out of a hat. Or practice some new imitations before the Queen of the Playground party.

"And . . . and I'm gonna win the Fourth of July contest, too," Troo says. "Just you wait and see."

I'm having a hard time stopping myself from kneeling down to wipe her tears off the same way I do when she's sleeping. When she wakes up in the morning, she'd feel the dried saltiness on her cheeks if I didn't use my pillowcase to blot her cheeks. It's so important to her to win. To be the best. No ties. She wasn't always like this. Not this bad anyway. She'd fall down and pretend she'd sprained her ankle during a race that I was gonna win by a mile or get hiccups if we were having a hold-your-breath competition. Little things, ya know. They got much bigger after Daddy died. Everything became a contest.

"A course you're gonna win for decorating, Trooper. Not a doubt in my mind," I say, not believing it for a minute.

Usually by this time our bedroom would look like the cemetery, blanketed with carnations. Not the real ones, the Kleenex kind. Her blue bike should already have a bunch of those fluffy flowers taped to the handlebars and fenders, but when I checked today to see how it was coming along, I found it leaning against the side of the garage looking not ready at all.

In the hallway, I can hear Dave still trying to smooth things over with Mother. He calls to her, "I'll be home as soon as I can. It shouldn't take long. Riordan's already over there."

Mother slams a pot down on the counter.

Needing to cheer Troo up, I tell her, "If you don't want to play

Battleship, let's play War." She'll kill me at that, too. Any kind of game that has fighting in it is something she's great at. "I'll get the cards. You wait for me here, okay?"

I'm sure she's going to be contrary like she always is when something isn't her idea, but she says, "Okay, but only if ya kiss me first. I need to practice." She opens up one of her hands to reveal a pair of those red wax lips I get for her at the Five and Dime. She slips in the lips and closes her eyes. In her mind, she's smooching with somebody better than her sister. Somebody named Rhett Butler. She adored *Gone with the Wind* when we saw it at the Uptown Theatre during old-timey movie week. We cracked open our piggy bank and went four times so that's how come I can do an imitation of Rhett that is "damn" good if I do say so myself.

"Fine," I tell her. "I'll kiss ya, but keep your tongue to yourself. No pullin' any of that Frenchie stuff."

"You gotta say the words, too," she answers, muffled by the lips.

Troo is asking me to repeat what Rhett says to Scarlett O'Hara when he comes to visit her at her magnificent house. That's my sister's favorite part of the movie. She swooned all four times we saw it.

I kneel over her, lower my voice and do the accent that Rhett has, which is a little like Ethel's, but not quite as much. "'You should be kissed, and often, Scarlett. By someone who knows how.'"

When I'm done pressing down, Troo slips the lips outta her mouth and says, "Don't you think Father Mickey looks a lot like Clark Gable?"

Father Mickey? How the heck did he get into this?

He wears his hair slicked and parted so he does kinda look like Clark Gable without a mustache. Father Mickey also has those kinda eyes that look like half-raised window shades and . . . well, I'll be a monkey's uncle. I know what's going on here. Troo's got a fat crush on Father! She's been bitten by the same lovebug everybody else has around here!

I snatch the wax lips out of her hand and scold her, "You better get to confession soon as you can. You've been playin' too much rummy with Mrs. Callahan. You're gettin' hotter to trot than she is!"

Chapter Sixteen

Tonight the old Vliet Street gang is gathered out front of Willie's house the way we usually are if there isn't something else big going on in the neighborhood. The O'Haras have the most steps and they live across from the playground, so if we don't get a big enough group together for a decent game of red light, green light or kick the can, we can cross the street and play tetherball. I never like going over to the playground once it gets dark, so I'm hoping more kids show up before the sun goes all the way down.

"Good evenin', ladies and germs," chubby Willie O'Hara says to us in his Brooklyn accent. When he grows up he wants to be something called a stand-up comic, which is a person who doesn't sit down and tells jokes for a living. Like Henny Youngman. Willie needs to practice all the time if he wants to get on the *Ed Sullivan Show* someday. "A funny thing happened to me on the way to the steps tonight. I thought of a really good joke," he says.

This is the way he always starts out. I don't know where Willie gets them, but he always has a new one all warmed up for us.

"What does it say on the bottom of a Polish Coke bottle?" Willie says.

"What?" we ask like we're half of the choir at Mother of Good Hope, which we are.

"Open other end," Willie says.

Everybody laughs louder than the kid sitting next to them.

Maybe that's what I could do for the talent part of The Queen of the Playground contest. Being funny always goes over good around here. I would have to ask Willie to teach me a coupla new jokes, though, because everybody already knows what's black and white and red all over. (A nun with a bloody nose.)

Troo's not supposed to be lying out on the step in front of me with her feet up on the iron railing. She snuck out of our bedroom, where she is supposed to be right this minute saying a rosary on her knees. Mother found a pack of squishy cigarettes in Troo's shorts when she was doing the wash after supper. She came up the basement steps, yelling, "Margaret O'Malley! Goddamn it all!" Once she got a hold of her, she slapped Troo on the back and sent her to our room. My sister's French laughing did not help matters and neither did her teasing Mother the way she does at least once a day about not getting her annulment letter yet. "Love and marriage, love and marriage, go together like a horse and carriage? Uh-oh. Looks like your horse fell down and broke its leg, Helen. Ya know what they do when that happens, right? *Bang . . . bang*."

I'm smooshed between Artie and Wendy Latour on the steps. Because there are thirteen of them, the Latour kids always outnumber us no matter what we're doing. Artie lacks luster. Wendy is her normal smiley self. She has her tiara pinned in her hair that is freshly washed and almost looks waxed, it's so shiny. If Wendy wasn't a Mongoloid she could be a Breck girl. Mimi Latour, who is planning on being another kind of sister when she grows up, is two steps down, right below Troo. They're in the same grade together, one back from me.

There is plenty of room on the step, but Mary Lane is crowding Mimi. She's trying to talk her into giving her some of her grape Popsicle. She's always asking you for some of whatever you got.

She tells Mimi, "They don't let greedy girls into the convent, ya know. That's their number one rule. They even got a sign posted out front that says no selfish brats allowed. You better gimme some of that before it's too late."

I'm watching Mimi struggling to crack the melting Popsicle in two, when Artie Latour taps my shoulder and points up the block. Uncle Paulie is coming toward us on his way to work at at the Beer 'n Bowl. His head is down like it always is and he's whistling *Pop Goes the Weasel*, which is his all-time favorite song.

My sister gets the oddest look on her face when she sees our uncle coming our way. She looks sorta . . . guilty? She must be feeling bad about making him a half-wit, but she's never seemed remorseful before. I always thought she knew that in a funny kinda way she saved him.

When he gets in front of where we're hanging out, Uncle Paulie stops and stares with his mouth open. He's wearing blue jeans and a white shirt that's got *Jerbak's* embroidered above the pocket in gold. He's got a load of freckles on his pretzel-skinny arms, but he's not bad-looking elsewhere. You can tell he's related to us. To Troo anyway. His hair is thick red, but our uncle's starts back farther so you can also tell he is related to Peggy Sure, who also has one heck of a forehead.

Mary Lane, who can pick a Popsicle clean faster than a piranha fish, hands over the leftover stick to him and says, "Don't spend it all in one place," when my uncle shoves it in with the other ones that are making his back pocket bulge.

Troo says, "*Bone sware*, Uncle Paulie."

That's a new one on me. Maybe where she's been sneaking off to is the library to move herself up on the Bookworm ladder and get extra instruction from Mrs. Kambowski in the language of love. I've already lost track of her two times this week during the day and once in the middle of the night. (Sorry, Daddy. I'm trying my hardest, but as you know, your Trooper can be so darn slippery.)

"*Ooo la la, Leeze*," our uncle says back to Troo and that's just great, real great. Now I have to say, "Hi," not because I want to, I just don't want him to get mad at me.

Even though Uncle Paulie does not seem like the same rancid person he used to be before the accident, somewhere inside of him he still could be. He used to be a bookie. (This is not somebody who works at the Finney Library. This is somebody who gambles for a living and wants as many people as he can get to do it, too.) Ethel told me that in the old days my uncle had the worst temper. He wasn't a nice brother to Mother, and Granny went meek around him. He hurt other people, too. He broke a man's leg in half when the guy didn't vigorously pay what he owed on a gambling bet. Then he took advantage of the man's wife all the way down to the skin. He was gonna go to jail for doing that, but his brain getting damaged in the crash saved the day. So that's why, if ya ask me, our uncle owes a big *merci beaucoup* to *Mademoiselle* Troo for playing peek-a-boo with Daddy on the way home from the game.

Wendy Latour announces loud in her froggy voice, "You in gutter, Paulie."

"Wendy!" I'm shocked. I can't ever remember her saying something mean like that. "That's not a nice thing to tell somebody when they're down on their luck," I say, shaking my finger at her. "Say you're sorry."

"Thorry, Thally, thorry, thorry, thorry."

Artie leans in close to me. "Just so ya know, she wasn't being rude. My mom's been takin' her up to the bowling alley every Monday afternoon. Mom thinks if your uncle can do that job settin' pins then maybe Wendy can someday, too. He's been showin' her the ropes."

Uncle Paulie grins at Wendy and says, "Balls, balls, gutter balls," and walks off toward North Avenue to punch his time clock.

He'll be up at Jerbak's late. 'Til after three in the morning if business is hopping. I've heard him when I'm lying awake in bed waiting for the dawn to come. As a shortcut, Uncle Paulie takes the alley behind our house back to Granny's. *Pop Goes the Weasel* sure sounds a lot different when you listen to it in the dead of night. Maybe I was wrong about Greasy Al. It coulda been our uncle who scratched on our bedroom window that night smelling like pepperoni. They serve pizza at the bowling alley and sometimes Uncle Paulie does some really creepy things. (I saw him bury something in Granny's backyard once. I'm dying to know what, but I'm too much of a coward to go dig it up.)

"So . . . what yous wanna do?" Willie O'Hara asks us.

Troo grumbles, "Put you on a slow boat to China."

She's got a bone to pick with him because Mimi Latour is his girlfriend now instead of her. I know this is another not-charitable way to feel, but I would have to agree with Willie's choice this time around. Mimi is *much* easier to work with. She reminds me of a piece of Play-Doh. Troo is more like a stone. A boulder. The Rocky Mountains.

O'Hara tries again. "Ya wanna play kick the can?"

Troo throws down a loogie that lands an inch away from Willie's sneaker. "Red light, green light."

All of us know that unless she gets her way, she will make sure we have a cruddy game of kick the can, so we all just say, "Red light, green light's good."

Willie asks, "My way or yours?"

A coupla summers ago we let him show us how they play this game in Brooklyn, where they call it Ghost in the Graveyard. In his version, instead of us hiding and the ghost looking for us, the ghost hides and we go looking for him. I like Willie's way more, so I speak up and say, "Vliet Street rules" because I know Troo will be her stubborn self and say, "Naw, let's play the Flatbush rules," and she doesn't let me down.

"Okay, Ghooost in the Graveyard it is," I say, doing my spooky imitation to get everybody in the mood. "The steps are the entrance to the cemetery like alwaaays."

A coupla other kids have wandered over from the playground the way I wished they would. I don't know all their names except for the boy with ringworm. Everybody calls him Yul now. His real name is Peter Von Knappen. He was my boyfriend before I liked Henry, so I hope his hair grows back someday.

Willie O'Hara throws his heftiness around and says, "Guess I'll be it."

Troo hops up off the step and goes toe-to-toe with him, or as close as she can get. "Guess again, lard butt. I challenge you."

After Willie told that great Polack joke, I was pretty sure she would challenge him. Like a lotta other things that go on around here, this never happened when we lived out in the country. By the time we'd walk over to somebody else's farm, we'd be too worn out to see who can jump from the top of the silo without breaking their leg or try to milk a cow blindfolded, but these challenges happen all the time in the neighborhood. One kid goes up against another kid to determine who's the best at something. Anything. You can get challenged to steal pumpkins in October out of old man Moriarity's garden or to say the Stations of the Cross in under half an hour. Sometimes the challenges can even be death defying. Like who can run in front of a car without getting hit or hold your breath and then blow on your thumbs until you faint and smash your head on the sidewalk. One time Timmy Maddox challenged Howie Teske to play something he called Rushing Roulette with his father's gun and ended up getting shot in the elbow.

Even talent can be challenged. Like when they have battles of the bands up in the gym.

That's what this one is. Comedian versus ventriloquist.

Willie fires the first shot. "So . . . ya heard the one about the Polack and the ventriloquist, O'Malley?"

Troo shakes her head and doesn't put up a fuss. She knows the rules. If you don't play along, the other kid automatically wins. Period.

Willie says, "Well . . . there's this ventriloquist who tells a Polack joke during his supper club show. After he's done for the night, a big drunk Polack comes up to the stage and tells him, 'Ya know, I'm sick and tired of these jokes. I'm gonna knock the shit outta ya.' The ventriloquist says, 'I'm sorry, sir, it was all in good fun.' And then the Polack says back to him, 'I wasn't talkin' to you, mister. I was talkin' to the little asshole on your knee.' "

It takes a couple of seconds for all of us to get that one, but when we do, we start chuckling like crazy. Even Troo.

She says, "Fine, you win," and doesn't even try to beat him. She couldn't even if she wanted to. She's laughing too hard to keep her lips closed.

"You're a handful, O'Malley," Willie tells her.

My sister grabs one of the jelly rolls hanging over his shorts and says, "Takes one to know one, O'Hara."

"Go on, be the ghost, ya little pisser," Willie says gruff, but he's smiling.

His mean-sounding accent hurts my ears and he's got pimples on his forehead that he insists on showing you on a daily basis, but being a bossy gentleman is also part of Willie's personality. Most of the time I like the way he takes the bull by the horns, but not tonight. I don't want Troo to be the ghost and run off into the dark without me. I want her to be by my side. Permanently attached. (I'm asking for a pair of handcuffs this Christmas just like Dave's got.)

Willie and all the rest of us turn our backs and start counting, "One o'clock, two o'clock, three o'clock . . ."

I cover my eyes, but don't join in because I can barely swallow my own spit. There is just no telling with Troo. What if she's pulling a switcheroo? What if she runs right over to the Molinaris' to search for Greasy Al? I turn and peek between my fingers. She's not heading that way. She's sprinting toward the Latours' backyard, so that's good. That means she's gonna hide in their bomb shelter if it's unlocked. It's supposed to be off-limits, but Troo doesn't care. When she rises outta the ground and grabs you by the ankle, it's like a buried body resurrecting out of a grave and she adores that. Scaring the ever-loving heck out of people is one of her hobbies.

"Thick o'clock, tree o'clock, leben o'clock," Wendy Latour says next to me. She's got her pudgy hands over her face, but her fingers are as wide open as her eyes.

Once we get to twelve o'clock we're supposed to go walking around in the dark chanting, "Midnight, midnight, hope we don't see a ghost tonight."

We'll go between houses and into the alley and yards. When we get close to where Troo is hiding she'll jump out, or if she's hiding in the bomb shelter, she'll rise up and chase you. If you make it back to the graveyard—the O'Haras' steps—you're safe to live another day, but if Troo catches you, you gotta be the ghost the next time around.

"Ten o'clock, eleven o'clock . . . midnight!" Willie shouts. "Ready or not, here we come."

Everybody dashes off in different directions except for Wendy and Artie.

"Thally, me go you? Paulie not gutter ball. Thorry," droopy-eyed Wendy says, wrapping her strong arms around me.

"Sure, a course ya can come with me," I say. "Just like always."

I feel like such a pill for yelling at the sweetest kid in the world. She's a hunk of burnin' love, that's what our Wendy is. And so protective of me, which is a quality I really like. When Buddy Dietrich tried to steal my transistor radio over at the playground, Wendy picked him up and tossed him into the sandbox like he was a used toothpick. If this bowling job doesn't work out for her, I'm going to suggest to Mrs. Latour that Wendy try becoming a strong girl in the freak show at the State Fair.

"Okay, you can let go of me now, " I tell her. "I'm not kiddin'. I can't breathe."

"Thorry, thorry," she says, letting her arms drop down to her sides.

"Just hold my hand, okay?" When she puts hers in mine, I can feel that she's not wearing that plastic ring on her wedding finger anymore. It musta broke. I'm gonna have to start eating Cracker Jack again to see if I can find her another one.

Artie is still on the step looking lost, so I say to him, "C'mon," and then tell the both of them, "I gotta do something real quick before we go lookin' for Troo. I promised Mrs. Goldman that I'd check on her house while they're gone and I forgot today."

I already decided that cutting through people's backyards would be the fastest way to go. I don't want to waste time saying hello to our neighbors who are out on their front steps trying to catch a breeze on this muggy night. I take off and Artie comes right after me, but Wendy, who broke outta my grip, is lagging behind because she has the goofiest way of running. We make our way through the Sheldons' and the Mahlbergs' and the other backyards without any problems except for a near beheading from Mrs. Frame's clothesline.

When we get to the edge of the Kenfields' property, I stop. I haven't gotten this close a look at their place for a while. It's not so dark that I can't see the house needs paint and the grass is ankle-high. The garbage cans out by the alley are lying on their sides and a tiger cat is picking through what's spilled. It really does look like a ghost house now, the way Fast Susie used to tell me it was. Mr. Kenfield used to take pride in his property. Mother told me he cut his lawn with scissors. Before his daughter, Dottie, disappeared, he loved it when kids played catch back here and would sometimes grab his glove and join in, but I heard if your ball wanders back here now, he goes crazier than Lizzie Borden.

I kiss Daddy's watch for luck and point across the yard that seems wider now than center field. "I don't have to go all the way over to the Goldmans'. If we make it to the other side, I can just look through the hedge." It's gotten overgrown like the rest of the yard and doesn't look at all like Henry's new haircut. "Ready?" Both of them nod even though only one of them knows what the Sam Hill I'm talking about. "You gotta keep up with us, Wendy," I say, scared about what might happen if she doesn't. "No dawdlin'."

"Yeth, Thally O'Malley. No dawdlin'."

When I make a dash for it, I can hear Artie panting right behind me, but I realize too late that there's not a peep coming from where Wendy's supposed to be. When I turn around to see what happened to her, she's in the middle of the Kenfields' yard, hopping from foot to foot.

"Wendy . . . c'mon." I wave my arm and whisper-yell.

She looks up at me and then back down at the grass and then back at me and starts yelling, "Thnake . . . thnake!" really, really, loud.

Keeping my eye on the house, I hurry to her. "No . . . no . . . *shhh . . . shhh . . . shhh.* It's not a snake. See? It's not movin'." I kick at the garden hose that shoulda been wound up nice and neat next to the house and push Wendy fast back to the hedge where Artie is crouching at the exact same time that the back porch light flicks on.

Mr. Kenfield comes banging out the door, weaving in his boxer shorts. He doesn't have on a shirt or shoes, just a beer can in his hand. I don't think he can see us because the porch light reaches only so far and I bet his eyes are blurry from drinking, but when he cocks his head at the hedge, I'm sure it's because he must hear my heart beating.

"Who's out there?" he says, slurry. "I . . . iden . . . identi . . . who's there?"

I press my hand even harder over Wendy's mouth so she can't jump up and holler, "Thee the U Eth A in your Thevrolet."

"Dottie?" Mr. Kenfield calls out again, not mad-sounding this time. More like the way you would call out if you were lost in the woods and given up all hope of ever being rescued, but then you spotted a plane flying overhead. "That you, sweetheart?" he says, coming down the steps on legs that look delicate.

Since we spent so many nights together in the olden days, I'm not hard on him like the other kids are. I don't fill a grocery bag up with Lizzie's poop and set it on fire on his steps. I don't call him names like Loopy Lou or In the Can Kenfield behind his back either. I am just about to call out, *It's not Dottie, sir. It's your old friend Sally O'Malley. Sorry for bothering you,* but his wife doesn't give me the chance.

She shouts from inside the house, "Chuck? What're you doin' out there? The show's back on."

He looks around his yard one more time, squinting especially hard into the hedge shadows where we're hiding. "Goddamn kids," he says, throwing down the beer can and going back into the house hunched over. He forgot to switch off the porch light. Two moths are circling it.

I take my hand off Wendy's mouth and wipe it on my shorts. She licked me. She always does that. She thinks I taste good.

Artie whispers, "Geeze, that was close."

To the bone. I especially understand how Mr. Kenfield is feeling and Troo does, too. It's so hard to lose someone you love. Our hearts growl for Daddy the same way our tummies do when we're hungry. It must be even worse for Mr. Kenfield. I know my daddy's gone forever in the deep blue of the western sky. I'll never hear the sound of his voice again or feel his late-day whiskers on my cheek or spend time after supper curled up on his lap listening to his happy shouts when Hank Aaron hits a homer on the radio. But Mr. Kenfield's daughter is not dead. She's out there somewhere. I bet if my old neighbor had it to do all over again, he wouldn't have sent Dottie away to the unwed mothers' home the way the church told him to do. He doesn't even go to Mass anymore.

"We gotta get back," I tell Artie, when I hear screams coming from up the block. "Sounds like Troo's tagged someone."

I spring up to peek at the Goldmans' house to check to make sure everything's okay, but he yanks me back down before I can see a thing.

"What're you doin'?" I say, jerking my arm away.

"I . . . I'm sorry. It's just that . . . I need to tell you something in the worst way," Artie says. "I already tried once, but you didn't answer me."

He did not. I haven't hardly seen him at the playground or anywhere else. He's been acting too pooped to participate ever since Charlie Fitch disappeared. "What do ya mean you tried to tell me something in the worst way? When?"

"On Mimi's birthday. We had beans and wienies for supper and . . . and my brothers kicked me outta our room because . . . ya know."

I do. Beans are the musical fruit. The more you eat, the more you toot. Our cabin at camp smelled worse than the outhouse.

"Didn't you hear me scratchin' on your screen?" Artie asks.

It takes me a second to put together what he's telling me, but then that night comes whipping back. "That was *you*?!" I give him a two-handed shove. "Ya scared the bejesus outta me!" The clawing on the screen. And that awful smell floating into our bedroom window.

It wasn't pepperoni-reeking Greasy Al coming after Troo the way I thought it was. It was Fartie Latour leaving his calling card! "What's wrong with talkin' to me durin' the day like normal?"

"I . . . I needed to talk to you in private," he says. "I thought that'd be a good time to tell you what I gotta tell you without Troo hearin'. I know ya don't sleep so good."

Everybody around here knows that about me. After one of Troo and my overnights at the Fazios', Fast Susie spread around that I scream in my sleep.

I peek around Artie at Wendy. Nothing we're saying seems to be bothering her in the least. She's squatting next to her brother, happily sucking on a cherry Life Saver and waiting for the skeeter she swatted to fly away again. I don't think she really gets death. Sometimes I think being a Mongoloid is not such a bad deal.

"Why can't you tell me whatever it is in front of my sister?" I ask, less mad and more curious.

Troo and Artie were an item once, but that ended when she wrestled the coonskin cap away from him last Fourth of July. Maybe he's decided to forgive her and wants my opinion on how to get her to like him again in the same lovey-dovey way.

Artie says, "Because Troo likes Father Mickey so much and . . . I know she's been goin' up to church a lot to see him and . . ."

Just like I thought. He wants to be Troo's boyfriend again and he's jealous of all the time she's been spending with Father Mickey. Artie's in the clutches of the green-eyed monster.

"You got it all wrong," I say. "Troo only likes Father because he's givin' her extra religious instruction. The nuns won't let her back in school if she doesn't." But then I remember how she has that little crush on him. I don't mention that. Artie's having a hard enough time as it is. "We can talk about this some more later, okay?" More squealing comes from up the block. "We gotta go now. They can't start another game without us."

Artie sets his sweaty hand on my arm, gently this time. "Father Mickey . . . he's the reason Charlie ran away."

"I already know that," I say. "Fast Susie told us that Father caught Charlie stealin' from the poor box. Now let's get outta here before Mr. Kenfield comes out again."

"It's not what it sounds like! Charlie . . . he had to take that money . . . Father Mickey is up to no good and . . ." Artie's Adam's apple takes the long trip down his throat and shoots back up again. "And it wasn't only Charlie. . . . the other altar boys are bein' forced to . . . Father is making them do something bad."

What a load of malarkey. I may not like Father Mickey much, but everybody knows how he is especially kind to his altar boys. He took them all to Wisconsin Dells to feed the deer and ride the Ducks and they stayed overnight at a motel and went to breakfast at Paul Bunyan's restaurant. He does other extra good things for those boys, too. Has them over to the rectory for special sleepovers and he coaches the boys' basketball team after school.

"You gotta believe me," Artie says, almost in tears. "Father's committin' some bad sins and he's gonna commit more unless we do something to—"

"Cut it out!" I say, pressing my hands against my ears. Artie needs to keep his opinions about Father Mickey to himself the same way I have, except for accidentally telling Ethel how I feel. What he just told me is much more serious than just not liking Father. He's being a heretic. "You're gettin' mushy feelings for Troo again and you're jealous about how much time her and Father are spendin' together and . . . and on top of all that, your best friend is probably d—" I cut myself off before I can tell him that Charlie's never coming back. I'm sure that orphan's dead. "Doc Keller told me that your brain can play tricks on you when you lose people you love. I lost my daddy and when Mother was in the hospital I thought she was gonna die . . . so I'm sorry to be the one to have to tell you this, but your imagination is runnin' away with you the same way mine does." Artie has no idea what kinda problems he's in for once this starts happening. "Tell ya what. I'll bring you some cod liver oil, okay? Maybe we can nip this in the bud."

"Thanks for nothin', O'Malley." Artie stumbles up to his feet. "If anybody was gonna believe me around here, I figured it'd be you," he says, charging off into the darkness.

Wendy looks up when her brother disappears down the alley. "Arthie?" she says. "Me . . . go?"

"No, you stay here with me, okay?" I'm afraid she's gonna cause a commotion if she chases after him, so I give her another cherry Life Saver to keep her busy and part the thick hedge the best I can. All I need to do is take a quick look at Mrs. Goldman's house so this whole time won't be spent for nothing.

My eyes start at the front of the Goldmans' house and move backward past the living room and dining room windows. It looks like nobody is home the way it's supposed to, but when I look to where I know the kitchen is, the stove light is on. Mrs. Goldman musta forgot to turn it off after she was baking some of her excellent brown sugar cookies to take to her sick brother in Germany. I've been checking the house only during the day, so that's why I haven't noticed it before now. Tomorrow I'm gonna have to use the key she gave me in case of an emergency to go switch it off. Electricity is expensive.

"C'mon. This way," I say, tugging on Wendy's T-shirt sleeve and pointing. We're gonna go back through the Kenfields' side yard because I don't want Wendy to forget I told her the hose isn't a snake, which she will. I have to remind her to be sneaky every single time we play Captain May I or else she'll just run up and shove the Captain down. "Watch me." I get up on my toes and show her how to crouch over to make herself smaller.

When we creep past the Kenfields' living room window, I can't stop myself from looking in. I'm not a peeper like Mary Lane. I don't get real close and watch for an hour. I just like to see people when they're in their houses at night, drying their supper dishes or working at their sewing machines or playing a game of Pinochle. Even some teasing is fine. Seeing them gives me hope that no matter what horrible stuff happens to a person, life just keeps going on.

I can see perfectly the Kenfields sitting on their davenport. No lamps are switched on, but the televison is throwing light on their faces and on the wall above them where a picture of a beautiful girl with brunette hair takes my breath away. The picture used to hang up in her bedroom that I could see from my room when we still lived next door. Dottie's got on her mint-colored senior dance dress and her hair is swirled up on top of her head like a Carvel cone and there's a ruby going-steady ring around her neck. I have been thinking for a long time that whoever she had some of the sex with musta given her that red ring.

Because the Kenfields' windows are open like everybody else's on the block are I can hear Perry Mason shouting out of the TV, "Objection, objection, Your Honor!" But even louder than that lawyer, I can hear Mr. Kenfield making the same sound I used to hear when I'd stay awake in my old bed and listen for Dottie's ghost. That horrible moaning sound.

When I say to Wendy, "Let's go," and we head off down the block, I vow to myself not to peek in on people for a while, especially never again on the Kenfields. What I saw in there, Mr. Kenfield's head in his wife's lap . . . her patting him while their missing daughter looks down on them . . . that is not life going on no matter what. That is life spinning its wheels.

Chapter Seventeen

There's a spot in our backyard where you can sit and breathe in all the good. We've got a glider and a shiny new bench back here that I'm hoping to replace with the old one that's in front of Sampson's cage if I can figure out a way to ask Dave that won't hurt his sensitive feelings. In June, the peony flowers smell great. So do the two purple lilac trees and red and white roses. The vegetable garden is planted with radishes and carrots and cucumbers and something new Dave put in this year. He planted four rows of corn along the fence. I think he did that for me and Troo, like a tribute to Daddy. Dave doesn't understand that when the O'Malley sisters hear the rustle of stalks coming through our bedroom window on a breezy August night, it will make me tear up and even though Troo will call me a crybaby, she'll feel Daddy's goneness, too. She'll go out to that corn in the middle of the night to run the silky tassles across her lips. They were always her and Daddy's favorite part.

Every branch of the garden bushes and tendril of the vines fills me with the most peaceful feeling, better even than Midnight Mass on Christmas Eve. But the part that soothes me the most is the teepee. It looks just like a real one, only smaller, and instead of buffalo fur or cattle skin, we've got green beans racing up the poles. There's room inside for two. (I was worried that after my horrible camp experience that I wouldn't feel the same way about the teepee this summer, but thank goodness, I still adore it.)

Troo came out with me tonight because a storm is coming. She won't leave my side when there's one rolling in. I told her she could French inhale to steady her nerves. I just had to get out of the house. Troo likes listening to them fight, but I couldn't take hearing Mother snip little pieces off of Dave for one more minute. There's been another burglary. This time the cat snuck into the Holzhauers', who live on 53rd.

I say to Troo after we crawl in, "I've been meanin' to tell you. Artie Latour likes you again. A lot."

"Oh, yeah?" she says. When she reaches into her back pocket, I can smell Mother's Midnight in Paris perfume. Troo's got on her red lipstick, too, and around her wrist there's the charm bracelet that Daddy gave Mother for their second wedding anniversary. Mother is too upset with Dave to notice that Troo's been in her things and my sister knows that. "Too bad for Fartie. I got other fish to fry."

I don't ask her who that fish might be because she would never tell me. Poor Artie. I think of him pining away for Troo and his yo-yoing friend, Charlie Fitch, and what bad condition he is in overall. The bible says, *Suffer, you little children*, but how much more can one kid take? I left a baby jar of cod liver oil on the Latours' porch last night with Artie's name on it. I haven't blabbed to anybody what he told me about Father Mickey committing a bad sin.

Not even Troo. That wouldn't be right. Ethel taught me that. "You should never repeat what a body tells ya when they're barin' their heart and soul," she said. "That's the worst kind of betrayal there is. That's takin' advantage of them when they're already down."

"How's it goin' with Father Mickey?" I ask Troo. Since it's Tuesday, she had her religious instruction tonight. She never complains about having to go up there right after supper, so I thought she might be ditching the meetings. That's why I secretly followed her last week. Other than stopping to throw an egg at the Heckes' front window, she went straight to the rectory. I was impressed. It's not like her to be so obedient. She must want to go back to Mother of Good Hope School in September as much as I want her to, which really does my heart good. "Does he make you study the same borin' catechism we learn in school or do you talk about more interestin' stuff?"

Troo smiles like our old barn cat would when he was lapping up a puddle of spilled cream. "He . . . ah . . . more interestin' stuff," she says, lighting a match to use on her cigarette, but blowing it out when Mother comes slamming outta the back door.

"Maybe I should start breakin' into people's houses," Mother rants. "It's the only way I'm going to get to spend any time with you." And then she goes on a rip about how long it's taking to get permission from the Pope so they can get married and how she can't wait forever and how she wants Dave to buy her things. Not later. Now! These fights are like listening to the Moriaritys' dog barking over and over. "When are you going to get me my own car?" Mother wants to drive downtown to the museum and buy her clothes at Chapman's, not Gimbels. She wants to "Soak up some culture and look good doing it." And especially she wants to get away from the neighborhood "riffraff." Everybody is talking behind her back about how she's living in sin. Even though she'll tell you she couldn't care less what people say about her, she does.

Dave is trying to calm her down in his always-cool Danish way. "I know I haven't been around much lately, Lennie, but I think . . . that might change soon."

She doesn't tonight because we're being secretive, but Troo usually laughs when she hears him call her that. Lennie was Mother's nickname when they were the prom king and queen. (When Mother showed us the pictures of them on their matching thrones in the high school gym, Troo whispered to me, "Just like I thought. She's *always* been a royal pain in the ass.")

"We got a break in the case," Dave tells Mother, but he doesn't sound happy like the television detectives do when that happens to them and I wonder why.

Mother answers snippy, "Oh, really," because even though this is great news, once she gets this worked up she can't just shrug it off. Her mad clings to her worse than a slip when it comes outta our new dryer.

Their voices have gotten closer-sounding, so I know they moved over to the shiny new bench.

Dave says, "We found footprints under the bushes at the Holzhauers' place and they don't belong to either Bill or Heidi."

"Can you . . . will you be able to tell who's stealing . . . how does that work?" Mother doesn't know anything about detecting. She doesn't like to talk to Dave about his work the way I do and her favorite show on television isn't *77 Sunset Strip* the way it is ours. She likes *This Is Your Life* and just like Mrs. Fazio, *Queen for a Day* is also one of her favorites. "Can you tell who's doing the burglaries by looking at the footprints?"

"No. Not until we catch a suspect to compare them to," Dave answers.

"So what did you mean about getting a break in the case?" Mother asks.

"I meant that we've narrowed the suspect pool down. I think . . . we think . . . we're pretty sure a kid is doing the burglaries."

My throat goes skinny and Troo starts licking her lips.

Mother says, "A kid?" All the hope that she was feeling about getting to spend more time with Dave is replaced by a sore-loser laugh. "Who came up with *that* dumb idea? No, don't tell me. It had to be that weasel Joe Riordan."

She's not thrilled that Detective Riordan has been romancing her best friend, Mrs. "Aunt Betty" Callahan. Detective Riordan has the reputation as a love-'em-and-leave-'em type. I would have to agree with Mother on this. I'd say I don't like Detective Riordan about the same as I don't like Father Mickey and it's not just because he is such a Romeo. Detective Riordan splashes on too much of a cologne called English Leather and once when I caught him staring at Nell's bosoms, his eyes looked like two sewer-hole covers and oh, I don't know. Maybe Ethel is right. Maybe I do have a problem with men in uniforms. But if that was true, then I woulda immediately started liking Dave's partner a lot more when he became a regular-clothes detective and I still think he stinks.

Mother asks, "What would a kid do with the paintings and silver and . . . that doesn't make sense. Joe Riordan wants that sergeant's job. He's trying to make you look bad." I notice that Mother doesn't doubt for a second that kids would do something so terrible. She just can't figure out what we'd do with the loot. "Did it ever cross your mind that the burglar could be a small-footed man? It . . . it could be Paulie."

That's not nice to think your own brother could be guilty of burglary, but they have never gotten along. Even before his brain got damaged, she never liked him, but other than that, she's right. My uncle's feet are not much bigger than mine and Granny did mention during the SOS supper that he's been keeping odd hours.

Troo mouths to me in a very exaggerated way at the *exact* same time Mother says to Dave, "Or . . . it could be Harvey Charles."

Mother can't stand Mr. Charles, who is the Tick Tock Club's manager. He fired her when she worked there as a singing hostess before she met Daddy. She blames everything on him.

"Harvey's got those teeny feet to match his teeny mind and . . . and something else that is probably very teeny, too."

"Len . . ." Dave sounds like he's working hard not to smile, which is smart of him. Mother might tell him to wipe that smirk off his face or she'll wipe it off for him. "A small-footed adult is a good theory, but Paulie's much too damaged to pull off something like this. And as far as Harvey goes . . . have you ever seen him wearing a pair of Converse?"

Of course she hasn't. Only kids wear those. I don't have any, but Troo's got some white ones and . . . and sweet baby Jesus in heaven, that's the only kind of shoes Mary Lane wears! It'll be just a matter of time now before the cops figure out that it's one of our best friends who is breaking into those houses. I gotta tell Mary Lane to stop being a cat burglar immediately, before Dave and the other cops start going door-to-door asking to look at kids' shoes like . . . like some kinda crime-busting Prince Charmings.

"I have to go. They're waiting for me. I'm sorry," Dave says to Mother. "I tell you what . . . how about this weekend we look at a car? Flip Johnson's got his red Studebaker for sale and it's a beaut."

When I can't hear their voices anymore, I peek through the

green beans. I thought Mother mighta coldcocked Dave because I know she really wants a Pontiac, but they're kissing. When they finally come apart, he puts his arm around her small waist and they go back into the house, so for now they have come to a meeting of Mother's mind.

I should turn Mary Lane in to Dave right this minute. If I do that, Mother will stop acting like a fire-breathing dragon toward him because he won't have to spend all his nights looking for the cat burglar instead of massaging her feet, and next to keeping Troo safe, I want more than anything to see in their eyes that melting look of love. But how can I hand my other best friend to him on a platter?

What I need is some good advice and nobody is better at giving it than the smartest woman I know, Ethel Jenkins. She is out on her screened-in porch next door soaking her "dogs" in the white pan. I know that she's off duty because I'm not hearing the bouncy rhythm-and-blues music Ethel listens to when she's tending to Mrs. Galecki. After she's done for the day, after the sun goes down, my good friend listens to broken-heart songs that have the sweetest, saddest sounding horn called a saxophone in them and sometimes a singer named Billie Holiday.

But if I'm going to hop over there, I need to be quick about it. The sky is getting noisier than Jerbak's Beer 'n Bowl on a Saturday night. Not right above us, but it's coming our way.

My sister blows a smoke ring at me. "Doesn't seem like things are goin' so swell for Helen and Dave. If she gets worked up enough, she might even call off the weddin'. Gee, that'd be too bad," she says, not meaning it.

Troo hasn't thought this out. It really would be too bad. Mother doesn't have any money of her own. What would we do? We couldn't go live with Granny. There's not enough room in her little bungalow house. Her bigness and Uncle Paulie's weirdness take up a lotta space. Mother would have to get a job at the cookie factory to put a roof over our heads the way Aunt Betty had to.

From over the fence, Ethel's voice comes pouring thick and sweet. "That you O'Malley sisters ponderin' the questions of the universe in that bean teepee?"

She knows it is. Who else would it be? Ethel's just using her fine southern manners. I open up my mouth to ask how her evening has been going and tell her that I'll be right over for some good advice and how I'll help her look some more for Mrs. Galecki's lost jewelry that hasn't turned up yet, but Troo shakes her head and scowls. She loves Ethel as much as I do and would normally be halfway over there by now, but that's the kind of mood she is in tonight and most nights, come to think of it. If I say black, she'll say white. If I say go, she'll say no.

"I got a little something-something waitin' on you," Ethel drawls out. That means she's got something good to eat.

When the first lightning flashes, I can see Troo even more perfectly. She's got the L&M dangling from her lips so she can use her hand to rub her bad arm that got hurt in the crash. What I should do is take her back into the house, get under the bed and plug her ears with cotton balls like I usually do when a storm kicks up, but I don't.

I shout back to Ethel, "Be there in two shakes."

The heck with Troo. If she wants to stay in here smoking and gloating over how Mother and Dave are barely getting along instead of stretching out in Mrs. Galecki's porch with our other best friend eating a little something-something, then let her. Mother made us *sweetbreads* for supper tonight and they didn't taste like cinnamon toast the way I thought they would. I'm so darn hungry. My stomach feels like a wishing well.

I've crawled almost all the way outta the teepee when Mother yells out the back window with all she's got, "Girls? You out there? Get in this house. It's about to pour."

Dang.

I call back across the yard, "Ethel?"

"Ya girls listen to your mama. I'll see y'all on Wednesday. Lessin' Miss Troo stunts her growth from smokin' them weeds and shrinks herself to the size of a gnat, then a course it'll just be you I'll be seein', Miss Sally."

That's a good one. That makes me laugh. "Sweet dreams, Ethel. Watch out for those bedbugs," I say, feeling a splotch of rain landing on my bare arm when I turn toward the house.

I call back to her, "Trooper?"

I wait, but nothing comes outta the teepee but a wisp rising through the top like a smoke signal. I know I should go back in there, snub out that cigarette and drag my sister into the house, but I am just so tired of her digging in her heels. All I'm ever trying to do is honor my promise to Daddy to keep her safe and all she's ever trying to do is run me ragged. I wish . . . I wish the teepee would get struck by lightning and those sparks would come flying down the poles and flow through Troo just enough to make her go woozy for the rest of the summer. I would prop her up on the backyard bench and always know where she was. She could do some jigsaw puzzles with Mother. They could be two peas in the pod again the way they used to be instead of . . .

(Sorry again, Daddy. *Mea, mea culpa.*)

Chapter Eighteen

Troo and me are at another best place in the neighborhood this morning. The Finney Library. Mary Lane and my sister come up here every Monday so they can check to see how the Billy the Bookworm contest is going. I tag along so I can pick up a new Nancy Drew to read to Mrs. Galecki and to make sure the two of them don't kill each other. I'm also here because I need to talk to Mary Lane about a couple of important things I have on my mind. We didn't get to see her all last week because she was up at the new zoo helping out. At least once every summer the rhino steps on her dad's foot, so she helps him hobble around like his own personal cane.

"Can you believe the nerve of this kid?" my sister says, jabbing at the Bookworm chart the second we come through the library doors. She wants to win the prize in the worst way because she really adores going to the movies and, of course, ending up on top of the chart is another something she can lord over our other best friend. "Look at how high Lane's worm has crawled! She's gotta be cheatin'." If we weren't in the library, she would hawk a loogie. She still might. "I'm gonna go tell Kambowski on her."

When Troo storms off to complain to the head librarian at the front desk, I go looking for Mary Lane. I find her right away browsing down one of the aisles and pull her into the lavatory with me.

"Don't ever let your mother give you a home permanent again," I tell her once we get in there. "You look like the Bride of Frankenstein."

"Cool," Mary Lane says, turning toward the mirror above the sink and making the same face the actress in the movie did right after she got electrified back to life. Head cocked to the left and then to the right, glaring at the doctor with the kind of look that says, *What the heck did you do to me, you mad scientist you?*

"And you gotta stop stealin' immediately," I say. "I'm not jokin'. Dave is hot on your trail for being the cat burglar. I'll help you get rid of the evidence." I've given this a lot of thought. "We're gonna tie a rock around your All Stars and throw them into the lagoon. Then we'll go to all the houses you stole from in the middle of the night. We'll put their precious things on their front porches, the ones you haven't already taken to the pawnshop. I'll make apology notes by cuttin' words out of a magazine so no one will recognize my handwritin'. The way they do in movies, ya know, like a ransom note only in reverse."

When I get done with my spiel, Mary Lane laughs and says, "You been eatin' too many nuts, O'Malley. They musta gone to your brain. You ever seen me steal?" She has a book called *Blaze and the Forest Fire* and another one called *The Terrible Tale of Mata Hari* in her arms, so just for a second I believe her, because I mean,

I never *have* seen her steal and there are only so many hours in the day and she's already pretty busy with her other two hobbies.

"You *sure* you're not the cat?" I ask.

Mary Lane sets her books down and boosts herself up onto the counter next to the sink. "I think I'd know if I was breakin' into people's houses, don't you?" She answers so *la de da* that it makes me go back to thinking she's lying after all. If somebody accused me of a crime that I didn't do, I'd get my feelings hurt, but Mary Lane, all she says is, "Boy . . . do I got some juicy news for you."

I head into the stall, hardly listening to her because I don't like tinkling anywhere except at home, but I gotta go really, really bad.

Mary Lane says, "This week on *Hawaiian Eye* Cricket got herself in a real fix, but then she got outta it." She loves that show. I used to, too, but every time I try to watch it lately all I can think about is finding a leper eyeball in the pocket of one of Granny's *muu-muus*. Mary Lane keeps me up to date. "And a man at the new zoo has been showin' me how to drive the train they got out there, which is not that hard, so I'm thinkin' if bein' a fireman doesn't work out I'm gonna be a conductor *aaa*nd . . . you're never gonna guess who I peeped on," she says on the other side of the toilet door that has telephone numbers and other stuff scribbled over it. Like who's available if you're looking for a good time. (Fast Susie Fazio.)

I rip the toilet paper off the roll and carefully lay it down, making sure all of the black is covered in a crisscross pattern. Troo told me you could get pregnant if you let your private parts touch the seat. She's sure that's what musta happened to Dottie Kenfield and even though I don't agree with her—I think whoever gave Dottie that ruby ring is the culprit—I can see why that makes sense to my sister. It's nearly impossible to keep a piece of juicy news quiet around here and nobody has said a word to me or anybody else I know about who the father of Dottie's baby is so it's not out of the realm of possibility that she had an Immaculate Conception caused by a toilet seat. Nothing in heaven and earth is impossible. It happened to the Virgin Mother, it could happen to Dottie Kenfield.

"I was over at the old bottling plant on Burleigh Street the other night," Mary Lane says. "Scoutin' it out."

Scouting it out is the same as saying that she is planning to set that abandoned building on fire the same way she did the tire store on North Avenue last summer. And the old TV repair shop a few weeks ago. She could never put that in her summer story, but I think it's kinda charitable when she burns those buildings down. They're such eyesores. They put up a spiffy appliance shop where the tire store used to be. Maybe they'll open a new dress store where the bottling plant was. Something really fancy. Mother would like that.

"Geeze, O'Malley. What'd ya drink this mornin'?" Mary Lane says. "*P*eewaukee Lake?"

After I flush, I come out and turn on the sink water. I don't look so good in the mirror. Sometimes I barely recognize myself anymore. The dark half moons under my eyes look permanent and my hair is so bleached out from all the time I've been spending under this hot summer sun, it's almost white.

"So who did you peep on?" I say, acting interested because that's the polite thing to do.

"Father Mickey!" Mary Lane says, thrilled and wiggly.

I don't know why she's so excited. You'd think this would be getting old to her by now. Her favorite people to peep on are nuns and priests. Last summer, she caught our ex-pastor, Father Jim, dancing around the rectory in a white dress and high heels to *Some Enchanted Evening.*

"Father Mickey was at the abandoned bottlin' plant last night?" I ask, drying off my hands on the towel thingie.

"Yup," Mary Lane says. "He was in a black car talkin' with you're-never-gonna-believe-who."

There is an excellent chance of that.

"Who?" I ask.

"Mr. Tony Fazio!"

What would the two of them be doing at that old plant together? That doesn't sound right. Mary Lane must be winding up to tell me one of her famous no-tripper stories.

"Did you hear what they were talkin' about?" I am trying not to sound like a doubting Thomas, but not doing such a good job.

"I couldn't make out all the words, but Mr. Fazio was yellin' at Father something about bein' overdue and then Father started yellin' back at him," she says.

Yeah, this is one of her stories for sure. Nobody would yell at a priest. And I have never seen Mr. Fazio at the library, so what does he care if Father is late getting a book back.

Just to be polite, I'm about to ask Mary Lane to tell me what else she mighta heard Mr. Fazio and Father discussing when my sister comes barging through the lavatory door shouting, "Where is that fuzzy-haired drip?" Spotting her, Troo shoves past me and yanks Mary Lane off the sink counter. "You're gonna beat me on the Bookworm!"

Mary Lane pinches Troo hard on the nose and yells back, "Tough titty, kitty," and their yelling echoes off all that green tile so loud that Mrs. Kambowski comes rushing in.

"What in God's name is going on in here?" the head librarian asks. She gets the both of them by the scruff of their necks and gives them a good shake.

Mary Lane mumbles something, and Troo acts contrite and tells the librarian, "*Pardonnez-moi*," but the second we get through the library's front doors, she throws herself on top of Mary Lane piggyback-style and they end up wrestling around on the grass like they always do until I can't take it anymore and pull Troo off.

"Let go a me!" She shoves me down to the ground next to Mary Lane, screws up her face and screams like a she-cat, "Fuck the both of ya," then she hops on her bike and takes off without me on the handlebars.

Mary Lane and me watch Troo darting in and out of cars down Sherman Boulevard with held breaths. After my sister turns toward the park and we can't see her anymore, Mary Lane rubs her leg where Troo kicked her. She's not laughing like she usually would after one of their wrestling matches. She's got a hurt look on her face and question marks in her eyes. She's wondering why my sister has been acting even wilder than she usually does.

I *could* tell Mary Lane that Troo is acting worse because we're half sisters now instead of whole ones or because Dave and Mother want to get married or because she's having a hard time finding Greasy Al or maybe it's because she's falling behind on the Bookworm chart, but I don't think that's all there is to it. I think it's more than that. Something else is making my sister go around the bend.

Mary Lane helps me up off the grass and says, "What's her problem?"

I wish I knew. I'd give anything for the answer to that sixty-four-thousand-dollar question.

Chapter Nineteen

How I Spent My Charitable Summer
By Sally Elizabeth O'Malley

I went to Granny's every Friday and washed out Uncle Paulie's socks, which might not sound like such a sacrifice, but believe me it is. His socks smell like old bowling shoes from not just one person's feet, but from a lot of persons' feet, which made me think of Mary Magdalene drying Jesus's toes off with her hair. That was so nice of her because from walking barefoot in Galilee and around lost sheep, the Son of God's feet had to be really raunchy. Or maybe they weren't because He also spent a lot of time walking on water. And I was really charitable to Wendy Latour. I have done so much wicked-witch laughing for her that I lost my voice for a week. I was also kind to her brother, Artie. When his best friend disappeared, I gave him one of my leather coin purses that I made eleven of at camp because that is the number of Apostles minus Judas, who I want nothing to do with. I'd also like to mention here for your holy consideration that my sister, Margaret, also gave Artie a piece of gum and hasn't missed one of her religious visits with Father Mickey. I helped Mother clean behind the stove, painted her toenails and got her nummies. She has not gotten boils yet for living in sin with Dave Rasmussen the way you told me she would. ~~I also checked on Mr. and Mrs. Goldman's house the way I told her I would while she is in Rhineland taking care of her brother who is sick.~~

That's where I left off after Troo and me got back from listening to *Music Under the Stars* over at the park with Mother tonight. I'll get extra credit points for using Mary Magdalene's hair and Jesus's feet and the Apostles. The reason I crossed out that part about keeping an eye on the Goldmans' house is because even though I *am* doing that, they *are* Jewish. Sister Raphael would take off my extra points to even the murdering Jesus score.

When I used the key Mrs. Goldman gave me to go into their house yesterday to turn off the light I saw glowing on the stove and bring her the kitty puzzles, I wound all her clocks, too. A clock that isn't ticking is as sad as dead flowers. Normally I don't like being anywhere without Troo, but it felt kinda nice to be alone for a change. I opened a window because it was such a hotbox in there and sat down on Mrs. Goldman's davenport and started thinking about how sad it was that she couldn't plant a garden this summer and how charitable it would be for me to go up to the Five and Dime tomorrow and get some seeds and stick them in for her. When she came back home from her trip, that'd be one surprise she would really like. She'd see her blooming backyard and wrap me in her arms and say, "Oh, *Liebchen*. What a special girl you are. *Danke schoen!*" And the next thing I knew her cuckoo clock woke me up. I don't know why, but I felt like I got my hand caught in the brown-sugar cookie jar. I dashed out the door and didn't stop running until I got home.

When I can't sleep at night, when my mind goes from one thing to another and back again, sometimes I can stop it for a little while by using some of Ethel's good advice. I read. Or write. That's what I wanted to do tonight, add something else onto the charitable summer story under the covers after I got Troo to sleep, but that's not gonna happen. My sister's up to something.

"Harder," she says from her side of the bed. "Over to the left more, between my shoulder blades." The pages of my notebook that I set on top of our dresser are getting flapped by the fan while I rub her back. They grab her attention. "You're workin' on your story already?"

"I thought I better before—"

"You're such a brownnose." I can't see her face, but I know that she's sneering. (She usually waits until the night before school starts and copies off my story.)

I say, "Maybe you could try to start a little earl—"

"Holy cow, I'm beat," she says, pulling her back away from my fingers and punching her pillow. "You better turn in, too. Tomorrow is a big day."

One of the biggest. When we wake up, it will be the Fourth of July.

After we do our butterfly kissing and mentioning of Lew Burdette having a hell of an arm, my sister right away starts breathing slow. She's trying to fool me, but I can hear her fast-licking her lips the way she does when she gets nervous or excited. That can only mean one thing. Even though she's stretched out like a cartoon cat, she's planning on sneaking out of our bed. For a kid that prides herself on her trickiness, she's gonna have to try harder. She didn't even put on her nightie after our bath. She slipped on the same pair of shorts she had on all day and her sneakers are waiting for her next to the bedroom door.

I am going to bide my time by watching what's going on in the aquarium Dave bought me until she tries to make her move. I adore the angelfish with the feathering fins that glides through the water not paying attention to the littler fish. If they had noses they would be stuck up in the air and if they had shoulders, they would wear a ritzy fox fur draped over them. They remind me of Mother. There is a pirate ship sunk on the bottom of the tank and next to the anchor is a treasure chest mostly buried in the pink gravel. That reminds me of Troo. The skeleton with the Jolly Roger hat reminds me of Nell. Same smile. I called her on the telephone after supper. I didn't talk. I just breathed heavy so she would think that at least somebody thought she was still lush enough to make a dirty phone call to. Nell cried into the phone, "Eddie? Is that you? Please come home."

That didn't work out exactly the way I planned it, so that's why I'm extra determined that I will not fail Troo. I've got important work to do. I'm being a lifeguard.

My sister slowly opens one of her eyes to see if I fell asleep.

"You can stop pretendin' now," I tell her.

She giggles and props her head up on her hand. Her hair is waving down the sides of her face like the red velvet curtain over at the Uptown Theatre. She picks up a piece of my hair and twirls it around her finger. That's another thing she does to help her fall asleep.

I don't ask where she was planning on running off to because she would never answer that. I ask her something else that's really been bugging me. "Tell me how come you didn't decorate anything this year for the Fourth contest."

If she wants to win the blue ribbon so bad, what is she thinking? Those Kleenex flowers aren't gonna get folded and stuck on the Schwinn all by themselves. We spent the whole afternoon at the playground-decorating party that Debbie told us about. Troo had every chance in the world to bring her bike over, but she sat next to me with our backs pressing against the school bricks and didn't lift a finger. Mary Lane didn't either. She never even showed up. Dollars to donuts, she skipped the party because she didn't want to give counselor Debbie Weatherly the satisfaction of knowing that she doesn't have eight bikes after all, not even one.

Using her mental telepathy on me, Troo asks, "You told Mary Lane about the cops knowin' the cat burglar is a kid, right?" You'd have to have known her her whole life to tell, but she's worried. I know my sister can really go after Mary Lane, but that doesn't mean she isn't one of her best friends. That's just how those two are together. Pick. Pick. Pick. "I'm sure it's her, aren't you?"

I *was* positive, but ever since I told Mary Lane in the library lavatory that she better quit leading a life of crime and she acted like I was two Hail Marys short of a rosary, I just don't know what to think anymore.

I say, "She told me she wasn't the cat, but I still mostly think she is. I'm gonna remind her again at the park tomorrow to knock it off.

She missed the playground party but she wouldn't miss the picnic, right?"

Troo doesn't say, *Are ya kiddin' me? Mary Lane wouldn't miss all that free food if the world was coming to an end.* She flips over without a word. I rub her neck between my fingers until I'm sure she really *is* asleep. How I can tell is by hearing her *choo-choo* snoring and her sucking the two middle fingers of her right hand that she quit last summer but for some reason has started up again.

I check Daddy's Timex at ten after ten, so that means I've got at least seven more hours to keep watch over Troo. I'm gonna pass the time by making shadow puppets. I can do a bird and another kind of bird and a bunny, and when I get done with that, I'll put my feet up on the wall and I'll imagine myself walking to see Sampson at his new home. Maybe I'll go out to the bean teepee once I'm sure that Mother and Dave have gone to bed, which won't be long now. I heard the front door open and shut, which means that Dave is back from work, and from out in the living room I can hear muffled talking. I hope Mother doesn't start complaining again because hearing her going after Dave is bad enough during the day, but at night, the hot words that come pouring out of her mouth make my sweaty skin go clammy. I know that her wanting Dave to buy her so many things is not the only reason she gets after him. Mother has never completely forgotten about him jilting her way back when his mother told him to. You know what they say about forgiveness? Mother and Troo are not at all divine at it. They can't help it. It's their 100 percent Irish blood. Same goes for Granny. She held a grudge against a boy in the old country for ten years because he made fun of the sack dress she wore to school. (She won't tell me what she did to even the score, only that the kid was known from that day on as Toothless Tom.)

I would adore seeing Dave even if it's just for a minute. It's been a tough day guarding Troo and the sight of my father makes me feel better, so I scootch down to the end of the bed. When I open our bedroom door a crack, I have a straight shot into the living room, but it isn't Dave next to Mother on the davenport. This man's hair isn't light, it's dark. All of him is black, even his shoes. It's Father Mickey! I can't hear what they're saying because my ears feel like Niagara Falls is rushing through them, but I'm thinking that Mrs. Kenfield told Father about Troo stealing out of the Five and Dime and now he's come to tell Mother. But why does he have a letter in his hand? He wouldn't write it down if he was here to tattle on Troo, he would just . . . oh. That letter . . . it's gotta be the annulment from the Pope that Mother's been waiting for!

Father Mickey is tilting forward, offering it to Mother, but when she's just about got it, he snatches it away.

"Knock it off, Mick," she says, loudly. "Get it over with."

She must be so scared that it says:

> *Dear Helen,*
>
> *So sorry to hear that your husband Hall Gustafson is a beer-bottle killer, but I don't think it would be a good idea to give you an annulment at this time. Try again later.*
>
> *Holiest regards,*
>
> *Pope John the twenty-third*

Father Mickey mumbles something and Mother shakes her head so he unfolds the letter and reads it out loud. When he's done, a beaming smile comes onto her face and that is such a rare thing to see that I gasp and hope they don't hear me. Father puts his arms around her and moves closer. Mother stops him with a hand to his chest and starts to cry, and that is such another rare thing. This is not sadness breaking loose from my mother's heart. This is the kind of crying you do after you think that you're for-sure dead, but then somebody brings you back to life. The kind of sobbing that Lazurus probably did on Jesus's shoulder. The same way I cried that night at the zoo when Daddy told me to fly like the wind away from Bobby.

Mother takes in a breath and presses her Matador Red lips to the white sheet of paper from the Pope that has just told her probably in Italian and maybe some Latin:

> *Dear Helen,*
>
> > *Greetings from the Vatican!*
> >
> > *I have granted you an annulment so anytime you want to, you can start picking the flowers out for your wedding.*
>
> > > *Dominus vobiscum*
> >
> > > *Your friend in Christ, the Pope*

Mother has asked and she has received. His Holiness has decreed that she is no longer married to that murdering Swede and, matter of fact, never has been. Granny told me that an annulment in the Catholic Church isn't like a divorce a Lutheran gets. An annulment erases everything like it never even happened. It's like getting matrimonial amnesia.

After closing the bedroom door and slipping back into bed next to Troo, I'm feeling relieved that she didn't slip out the bedroom window when I was watching the goings-on in the living room and that the fighting between Dave and Mother is finally gonna stop, but that's not the only thing I'm feeling. *Never a rose without a prick* is what Granny would say if she was here right now. I would have to agree with her. Tomorrow morning when my sleeping beauty sister finds out that the Pope has given two thumbs-up to Dave and Mother's wedding plans, she's gonna erupt like Mount Vesuvius all over the place.

And it's not only for Troo that I'm feeling the worst kind of worry there is. I haven't told Dave out loud because I can hardly believe it myself, but I think I am beginning to love him at least half as much as I loved Daddy. I don't think I can stand to lose both of them, which I probably will. I have been worried about this almost from the first day I found out he was my real father and that Mother wanted to marry him. On a picture-perfect afternoon in the not-too-distant future, they will stand toe-to-toe at the altar to commit the holy sacrament of marriage. The groom in his best blue suit and wing-tip shoes will slip that gold band on his bride-to-be's finger and say:

> I, David,
> Take you, Helen,
> To be my wife,
> To have and to hold,
> From this day forward,
> As long as we both shall live.

It's the last line of that vow that's been tying my tummy into a knot.

Isn't Dave concerned the same way I've been that if he marries

Helen Riley Durand O'Malley Gustafson, he could be taking his life into his own hands? He's a detective, for goodness sakes. He should've noticed by now what terrible fatal luck Mother has in the husband department. First off, Nell's father died smelling ammonia. Then Daddy was killed in the car crash. And Hall will probably get electrocuted in the chair.

People are always saying that bad things happen in threes, but what if they're wrong? What if bad things happen in fours?

Chapter Twenty

The Fourth of July is served up sizzling hot on a blue plate, sunny-side up.

Mother has been cracking "Independence Day" jokes all through breakfast. Troo is next to me at the table in her usual spot, plucking the streusel topping off the cream-filled coffee cake we get from Meurer's Bakery on special occasions. My sister doesn't suspect a thing. My leg is bouncing under the table and sweat is trickling down my sides. I can't take this. Troo never thought that Mother and Dave would ever *really* get hitched, not in her heart of hearts. She is usually very good at getting her way and has done everything she can to throw a monkey wrench into the wedding works. I should've rolled over in bed this morning and whispered the news so she'd be prepared. This . . . just sitting by . . . this is like twirling your thumbs when the fatted calf gets led to slaughter.

Dave, who is dressed this morning in a red checkered shirt, takes a sip of his Sanka, checks the cat clock over the sink and says, "Gosh, it's almost seven. I've got to get over to the park. Do you have something you'd like to tell the girls before we head over, dear?"

Mother plays along. She gives him a what-in-the-world-are-you-talking-about look and says, "Gee, I don't think so." She's got on a scoop-neck navy blue top and a gold ribbon in her hair that makes her seem ready to set sail. "Oh, wait a sec."

This is it. This is the moment I've been dreading. I prayed last night that Mother wouldn't spring this life-changing news on my sister like she's about to. That she would take her to Daddy's grave late in the afternoon. Troo is always more willing to listen there. Mother could bring carnations for him and they could sit in the grass next to his headstone. She could tell her daughter how Daddy would want her to be happy. He forgave her for doing what she did with Dave, and so Troo should, too. And when the sky started turning the color of raspberries and oranges, my sister's most favorite time of day, Mother could pick Troo's hands up in hers, kiss her fingertips and tell her in her kindest of all voices how Dave and her are getting married.

But once again, God turns a deaf ear to me because Mother didn't do any of that.

She says cutely, "How silly of me. I'm getting as absentminded as Bertha Galecki. Thank you for reminding me, honey, there *is* a *little* something I wanted to bring up to the girls." She reaches down into the front pocket of her white capris and when she draws her hand out from under the table she's got on a ring and it's not little. It's by far the fanciest, shiniest diamond I have ever seen.

"Surprise! Father Mickey brought over the annulment papers

last night! We're getting married at the end of September after it cools off. I'm going to wear a tailored suit from Marshall Field's and we'll have a reception party and take our honeymoon in Miami Beach," Mother says, like she can see it all now. "Lying on the sand under a starry night, those warm waves rolling over us . . ." She puts her head down on Dave's shoulder. "We'll be like Deborah Kerr and Burt Lancaster in *From Here to Eternity*!"

"No, you won't! You will not!" Troo shoves her chair back so hard that it wenches my arm that I was using to hold her in place. This reminds me so much of the night out on the farm when Mother told us she was going to marry Hall. "You can't! He said . . . he promised me that if—"

Mother thinks she's being funny, but what she's really doing is throwing a humble pie into my sister's face when she starts humming the "Love and Marriage" song. The one that Troo's been taunting her with every chance she gets.

"Trooper . . . you know what we can do . . . we can . . ." I'm trying to think of something to tell her, to give her, anything that is gonna make this all better, but she sweeps her breakfast off the table and barges out the screen door.

"Wait up!" I yell, but Dave stops me on my way to catch up with her.

"Let her be, Sally. She needs to blow off some steam," he says, bending down and picking up the plate pieces.

"But . . . she's gonna . . ." I don't know what she's gonna do exactly, but it won't be good, it never is.

Dave says, "You can catch up with her at the park. She just needs a little time to take this all in."

My neck skin crawls at the sound of his always-cool Danish

voice, his everything-is-going-to-be-okay-just-you-wait-and-see way of looking at everything. His green eyes. My green eyes. His long legs like mine. Dave being sensitive just like me. That was so nice for a while. It made me feel like I belonged, that I was a pea in his pod, but all of a sudden, I don't care about any of that. I want to shake Dave and shout, *Stop bein' such a cold fish! Be fiery for once! Bring Troo back!*

"Wait'll they get a load a this at the park today," Mother says, holding up the ring so she can admire it from a distance. The sunlight coming through the kitchen window catches the diamond and a hundred tiny squares of dancing light surround us. It is just blinding.

This has gotta be the biggest Fourth party ever.

The grassy part of the park is jammed with kids of all sizes and ages. Everybody's got a bike or coaster wagon or a baby carriage decorated to the nines. After the contests are over there will be games, and then everybody in the neighborhood will sit down together at picnic tables to eat hamburgers and hot dogs, kielbasa sausage, bratwurst and Dixie cups of ice cream and as much free lemonade as they want.

Dave brought along a folding chair for Mother and set it at the edge of Jack Hoyt Woods next to Mrs. Callahan, who saved her a spot.

Dave pins on his judge's badge and disappears into the crowd after giving me a chuck on the chin and Mother a kiss on the cheek. I would usually stick close to her, make sure that she had one of my lanyards around her neck so she could whistle for me to get her whatever she needs, but I'm not ready to forgive her yet for what she did to Troo. So I leave her there basking in the shade with her best friend, who right away starts salivating over the diamond engagement ring and says, "Jesus H. Christ . . . it's . . . it's the size of . . . you must give one helluva—"

Mother scolds, "Betty!" but she laughs louder than I have heard since Daddy was alive.

I've worked my way over to the edge of the crowd of jammed-together kids. I'm jumping up and down on my tiptoes, but I can't see Troo, who I can usually spot easy because of her hair.

I would love to see Henry, too, but my boyfriend can't come to the festivities because he could get stuck in the eye with a flag on a stick, which really happened once. Henry started bleeding and went white, and then a little blue around the mouth. The nurses at St. Joe's gave him a special decorating badge before they sent him home with some extra blood. So he can't come for the decorating and eating part of the party, but he can see the fireworks from the safety of the drugstore stoop. I'll stop by on our way home and we can talk about our favorites.

Thank goodness, there's Ethel. She really sticks out because she is so big and brown. She's not with the other grown-ups, who are lounging around the refreshment booths. She's up on the hill, looking down at where the zoo used to be. I'm dreading seeing what she's seeing, but I really need to talk to the smartest woman I know. I also might be able to see Troo from up there. I know her. My sister wouldn't skip one of the biggest bashes of the year even if she is, as Ethel would say, "fit to be tied" over the annulment news.

Ethel's not in her white nursing dress. She's got on a skirt of some kind of print I've never seen before. It's many shades of green and very jungly. On her top half, she's wearing a pale pink blouse that sets off her skin below her broad-brimmed hat that's got fruit hanging off it. She looks scrumptious. I bet her boyfriend, who is standing next to her, would love to take a bite outta her. His entire name is Raymond Buckland Johnson, but he lets Troo and me call him Ray Buck the same way Ethel does. He is almost too handsome to look at without blinders. His hair doesn't have coiled bounce the way Ethel's does. He wears it parted on the side, slicked with something that looks like it's never gonna dry out called pomade, which is the colored version of Brylcreem. Ray Buck is the snappiest dresser. Crackling crisp, always. Today he's got on a snowy white shirt and matching pants and loafers that are a cool blue. Ray Buck goes over the moon for shoes. He doesn't get them at Shuster's, though. Negroes have their own shoe shops in the Core.

"Happy Fourth!" I shout to them when I'm a few feet away.

Ethel spins around at the sound of my voice and says, "Well, look who we got here, Ray Buck." She plants her hands on my shoulders and doesn't seem surprised to run into me even though she is pretending she is. "Don't you look like a breath a mountain air this mornin', Miss Sally?"

She expects me to answer, "How kind of you to say so," which I do, even though I probably look more like a breath of midnight in the swamp in my seen-better-days cutoff shorts and wrinkly yellow T-shirt. In all the excitement, Mother didn't remember to braid my hair so it's loose and snarled up. Ethel is just being polite, as always. When she opens up her school with her secret inheritance that she's gonna get from Mrs. Galecki's Last Will and Testament, by the time she's through with them, the children who are lucky enough to attend will be able to beat out Miss Emily Post when it comes to manners.

"How do, Miss Sally," Ray Buck says with a little bow and I go swoozy. If Ethel didn't adore him and I hadn't already promised to marry Henry Fitzpatrick, I would ask this bus driver to wait for me even though that is dreaming a dream that can never come true. Negroes cannot marry white people, but if they could, I would be the first in line. Ray Buck is from the South the same way Ethel is, but not from Mississippi. She calls him her "Georgia Peach," and I would have to agree with her. He just oozes with juice. If Troo can have a crush on Rhett Butler and Father Mickey, I can have one on Ray Buck. Not only is he good-looking, he tickles my funny bone. When he stands sideways, because he is a little hunched over on top, he looks like a question mark, which makes him look curious all the time and that cracks me up.

I got a new vocabulary word I have been waiting to use on them. "You look *ravishing* this morning, Ethel. Simply *ravishing*. You, too, Ray Buck."

Ethel's lemony grin doesn't cheer me up like it normally does because even though I told them not to, my eyes have moved down to where the zoo used to be. The bulldozers and the men that run them have this special day off, too. The only things I still recognize in the mess of broken-up white concrete and black iron bars is the moat around Monkey Island and our favorite climbing tree that hasn't gotten knocked down yet. Daddy's and my bench should be sitting below the tree, but it's not. I should've rescued it. Now it's gone forever, too.

I ask Ethel, "Remember how last Fourth of July everybody went over to visit Sampson?" He was the best part of the zoo, not only for me and Daddy. Everybody thought he was the cat's meow.

Ethel takes a frilly hankie from between her bosoms, dabs at her broad face and says to Ray Buck, "I swear this humidity's thick enough to slice and serve. Would ya mind fetchin' us something cool to drink, sugar?" She waits until her beau heads down the hill toward the booths and then she says to me, "I hiked up here thinkin' you might show up thinkin' about that gorilla."

"Oh, Ethel." *Could there be a better best friend than you?* For a woman with bunions, it is no easy feat getting up this steep hill.

"Just 'cause they moved him, it's not the end of the line," Ethel says. "You can always go visit him at the new place."

"That's what everybody keeps tellin' me, but . . . I don't think it'll be the same. Do you?"

"Hardly nuthin' is, honey."

"He's gonna forget about me," I say.

"Oh, ya couldn't be more wrong 'bout that." She's fanning herself with one of the newspapers that she almost always has in her hand. She thinks it's important to know the goings-on not just in the neighborhood, but in the whole world. "I read in the *Reader's Digest* just last month how gorillas got longer memories than elephants."

I hope she is not making that up. She mostly tells me the truth, but she'll stretch it to keep my feelings from getting hurt.

"Ya know what I been thinkin' we could do?" Ethel says. "We could ask Ray Buck what buses to take and we could go see Sampson on a pretty Sunday. Ya know, to put your mind at ease."

"That would be very nice," I say, thinking I'm not sure that anything, not even seeing Sampson, could put my running-at-full-throttle mind at ease and I'm pretty sure she knows that. Her brain hasn't exactly been just cruising along lately either.

Yesterday I was kneelin' in our room, saying my rosary, begging the Virgin for help in taming Troo. Even though I don't hardly believe in God anymore, I will always have a special place in my heart for His mother and a rosary is almost nothing but Hail Marys. Through my window, I heard Ethel telling Mother over the fence that Mrs. Galecki won't stop accusing her of stealing and no matter how much Pepto she gives her, her stomach won't stop bothering her. "I tell ya, Miss Helen, don't know whether to wind a watch or bark at the moon," is what my good friend said.

Dave, who is the chief cook and bottle washer when it comes to the Fourth of July party, cuts the music off from somewhere down below, and says out of the loudspeaker, "Welcome, one and all! Father Mickey will open up today's festivities with a prayer."

There is a screeching sound like there always is, and then, "Bless us, o Lord, on this day that brings us all together to celebrate the birth of this fine nation." Father pauses the way Willie O'Hara does right before he gives you the punch line of one of his jokes. "If you could turn the sun down a notch, that would be greatly appreciated."

Everybody chuckles. Everybody except me. I wish I knew what it was about Father that makes my tummy feel like somebody threw a baseball at it. He's charming to everybody, but especially it seems to our family. He's always friendly to me, he spent hours instructing my sister and he burned the midnight oil to make Mother and Dave's dreams come true.

"The annulment letter came," I tell Ethel.

"Know all 'bout that. Your mama come over first thing this mornin' to tell me." They're friends, too. Not as good as me and Ethel are, but they get along just fine. "There's nothin' like a weddin' party to liven things up, don'tcha think?"

"No, ma'am, I don't." The one where Hall and Mother got married at the courthouse was on Beggar's Night so there were ghosts hangin' everywhere. Nell and Eddie's wedding almost gave me whiplash it went by so fast. But worst of all was what Bobby had in mind for our ceremony. "Ya know." Ethel knows all about how

Bobby told me on his way over to the lagoon that night that he was going to make me his bride. She's the only one who will let me talk about what happened. Everybody else tells me to put it out of my mind, go back to sleep, let bygones be bygones, get control of my imagination, which I would really love to do, but no matter how hard I try to forget, it seems like that night at the lagoon is engraved in my memory.

Ethel runs her chocolate pudding hand down my arm and says, "Well, this here weddin' is gonna be different. This'll be a fine celebration. Gonna hafta get me a new pair of dancin' shoes."

I didn't hear Mother say so, but I bet the party afterwards will be at Volpano's Supper Club since it is the ultimate around here. The popular Mill Combo will play, so I could dance with Ray Buck, but what about Troo? Now that she knows what her future holds, what does she have to look forward to? Her life is all downhill from here on out. It's not only the annulment news. She really was counting on winning that blue decorating ribbon and she didn't even bring her bike over this morning. I checked after she ran off.

Dave gets back on and announces, "Children under twelve, you're up next. Meet under the oak tree with the red ribbon near the picnic tables."

"Here ya go, ladies," Ray Buck says, coming back up the hill with our drinks. Gosh, he smells like he just stepped out of a tray of ice cubes. "How about after y'all drink that down we move over to the lagoon? I'll row the both of ya 'round for a bit."

Ethel gives me a wondering look. She knows I don't go to the lagoon anymore or too close to the rowboats, but she doesn't want to be rude and not ask me to join them. It would also be safer to take me since the boat is really gonna sag on her side and I could add a little more balance. I'm gonna save her the trouble of inviting me, even though I really would like to watch Ray Buck row us. He may be thin, but his chest and arms are muscular, which for some reason is something I really like to look at.

"You two have a good time," I tell them. "Thank you for askin' me, but I gotta go be with Troo."

"And where *is* your sister?" Ethel says, not letting me off that easy. She hasn't said anything, but she knows that Troo did not take the annulment news well. She doesn't miss much. "I know what a momentous day this is for your sister. I'd like to wish her good luck."

"Twelve and unders. Last call," Dave says over the loud speaker.

"Troo's . . . ah . . ." My eyes look the hardest they can down at the crowd. At first I don't, but then, over near the judging area, just for a second, I get a glimpse of Troo's hair. "Right there," I say, moving my arm to where Dave told the twelve-and-under kids to gather to compete for the blue decorating ribbon. There's gotta be at least forty or more kids. Why's my sister hanging out where everybody's waiting to be judged? That is so heartbreaking.

Ethel puts her hand to her forehead like an explorer. When she sees Troo, she says, "Lord. What in tarnation does that child got on? Is she blinkin'?"

What in tarnation *does* she got on? I'm not as tall as Ethel so I can't really make out all of it, but Troo definitely *is* blinking. I gotta get down there.

"Ask for boat number six. It's the one that's rotted out the least. I'll meet ya at the fireworks, same place as always," I shout back to Ethel and Ray Buck.

Barreling down the hill toward my sister, I'm remembering how she was the Statue of Liberty last year and how we ran into Greasy Al and he took out his switchblade and cut off all the flowers she had taped onto her bike and squished her crown between his fingers. I haven't forgotten him for one minute. Just because he hasn't shown up yet doesn't mean he's not going to.

"Excuse me, pardon me . . ." I've got my arms out in front of me, swimming through the kids. I'm trying to get to Troo, who I've lost sight of now that I'm on flat ground. She's been swallowed up again. Ahead of me, I can see Mary Lane floating through the crowd so easily because she can get through tight spaces that normal-sized children can't. "Mary!" I shout. About twenty kids turn to look at me because I forgot to add on her last name. "Mary *Lane*!"

She looks to the left and to the right.

"Behind you!"

When she gets a bead on me, she stops and waits.

I shove closer until I get right up next to her. She's got the Stars and Stripes tied around her neck with a jump rope.

Mary Lane says, "I been lookin' all over the place for you. Ya like my costume?" She tries to spin around to show it off, but there's not enough room with the crush of kids, even for her. "I'm a flagpole."

I don't know what to say to that, except, "You sure are."

"Wish it'd get windier," she says, trying to fluff the flag up. "Looks a lot better when it's wavin'."

"You seen her?" She knows who I mean.

"Attention please!" Dave says. "I've got a couple of contest winners to announce! Drumroll, Maestro." Even though I can't see them either, I know he's talking to the drummer of the Do Wops, Johnny Fazio's band. They'll play later on when we eat, and after it gets dark, they'll serenade us while we wait for the fireworks to start. "The winner of the baby carriage contest is Mrs. Walker. Top-notch decorating, Donna."

I already knew that Nell's name was not gonna be announced. I took some supplies yesterday over to the apartment. I was gonna help her decorate the baby's buggy. After I cleared the stack of old TV dinners off her kitchen table and set down what I brought, Nell asked, "What's this for?"

"The Fourth!" I said.

She blew her nose into one of the Kleenex flowers it took me most of the morning to make. "The fourth what?"

Dave announces, "The winner of the three-to-eight-year-old category is . . . Jimmy Latour. Nice job on those spokes, Jimmy."

I spot Artie clapping for his brother. I'm so surprised to see him out and about and he's even got on a costume. Artie'll compete in the *over*-twelve category. After kids turn thirteen around here, something weird happens to them and they think dressing up for the Fourth party is not cool, so hardly none of them enter. Artie is the exception. Since he was the only one that entered last year, he had to go against the younger kids, but this year it looks like he's got a little competition from a couple of other boys whose costumes aren't nearly as nice as his. He's got on the same getup he had on last year and looks thrilled to pieces. And a lot like Daniel Boone from the television show because both of them are lanky and have those enormous Adam's apples and . . . is that a coonskin cap he's got on his head?

"Artie!" I holler. "Over here!"

He doesn't see or hear me, he's too wrapped up in looking at the same thing everybody else is. I can't see who all the kids have made a circle around until Mary Lane says, "Move," and jabs someone with her elbow that's like a stiletto and a hole opens up.

All I can say is, "Sweet Jesus," and I can tell that's what everybody else is thinking, too.

My Troo is in the center of the cirle wearing the most fantastic costume I have ever seen! It's made of hundreds of Popsicle sticks all glued together. Like a sandwich board, they're hanging down the front and back of her and there's twinkling white lights running up the edges, and right around her middle, she's written out on the sticks in red and blue poster paint:

AN AMERICAN IN PARIS

That's the name of the movie we saw during old-timey week at the Uptown Theatre that Troo loved so much. My sister has turned herself into a living, breathing Eiffel Tower!

Dave, who has to do double duty as a judge, steps into the admiring circle. He takes his time, but when he's done judging Troo, he says real loud—maybe even my sister can hear the pride in his voice— "I think all of us can agree hands down that we've never seen anything quite like . . ." He sweeps his hand toward her. "The blue ribbon for the under-twelves this year goes to . . . Miss Margaret . . . sometimes known as Troo . . . also called *Leeze* . . . O'Malley! Let's hear it for her, gang!"

Troo starts *hunh . . . hunh . . . hunh*ing and everyone's clapping and Wendy Latour's throwing Dinah Shore kisses and Artie shoots off his cap gun and Mary Lane is chimp-grinning and man, oh, man, excuse my French, but what a fucking genius my sister is!

Chapter Twenty-one

The heat usually dies down around this time of night, but I guess it's making a day of it same as me and Troo and everybody else who's spread out at the lagoon waiting for the sky to go a smidgeon darker so the fireworks can get shot off from the island in the middle.

My breathing is coming a little faster than it normally does, but I'm not feeling as jumpy as I usually do being this close to the murky water. It was right over there where Bobby set me down. My loved ones being close by helps. Troo is lying next to me and Ethel and Ray Buck are two blankets over. I've already said a prayer for Junie, my little cousin, who would also be cuddled up with us along with her mother and father if she wasn't rotting away in the cemetery in her little white coffin. I bet Dave is thinking about his dead niece, too. All the blue today had to remind him of Junie since that was her favorite color. Can you see fireworks from heaven?

Mother and Dave are perched in folding chairs behind us, getting along better than the lovebirds in the pet aisle at the Five and Dime.

The ladies in the neighborhood were swarming all over Mother for most of the day. They wanted to get a close-up look at her engagement ring. Most of them told her congratulations, but I heard one lady grumble, "And not a moment too soon, if you ask me. I was afraid to let my husband leave the house without me. The woman's a Jezebel."

I don't know where Uncle Paulie disappeared to but wherever he is, he's busy. The Fourth party is *the* biggest day of the year for him. All the Popsicle sticks lying around on the grass are like manna raining down from heaven for my uncle. Granny isn't here. Even though she likes fireworks, she never comes to the celebration anymore because she got sick of people telling her how she should win a prize for looking so much like George Washington. Nell, she's not here either because she doesn't even know what month it is. But her nincompoop of a husband showed up. I saw Eddie earlier over where they were selling beer. He was hanging out with Tommy "The Mangling Meatball" Molinari, who musta challenged him to a chugging contest because the both of them were blotto. I stuck around for a while to see if Greasy Al might show, but all that ended up happening was Eddie and Tommy weaved down to the Honey Creek and tinkled into it.

Father Mickey is visiting with his parishioners around the shadowy lagoon, stopping to ask about how things are going up at the Feelin' Good factory or with their kids. When he comes by Dave and Mother they treat him like a king, can't thank him enough for getting them the annulment. They also talk about the cat burglar. Everybody has been. The Montgomerys got hit yesterday and lost a boatload of money that Mr. Montgomery, who doesn't believe in banks, kept in a coffee can under the sink. Nothing else was taken. Dave told me that houses are usually ripped apart when a thief searches for hidden treasures, but our cat just zeroes in on the good stuff like he's got a treasure map or something. *X* marks the spot.

Father Mickey stops to say hello to the O'Malley sisters, too. I say, "Hi," back, but Troo doesn't. She doesn't even say thank-you when he compliments her on her winning costume.

I know why. She's holding him responsible for getting Dave and Mother permission to get married. I bet Troo has already added Father Mickey's name on the top of what she calls her "Shit List," which is already over a foot long.

This is another one of those times when I think God really does have a plan because Father Mickey getting the annulment letter worked out really good for Troo in the long run. I'm almost positive she's moved her crushing feelings off the priest and back to her old flame, Artie Latour, because he was definitely wearing the coonskin cap. It was flat as Troo's beret from being under our mattress for so long, but it still looked good. Artie was also Troo's partner in the egg-on-a-spoon and three-legged races and they dangled their feet in the Honey Creek during the afternoon, talking, talking, talking. When I took three Dreamsicles down and tried to join in with them, they told me, "Thanks," but they clammed up about whatever it was they were chatting about.

My sister and me are lying on our stomachs, which we barely can do because of all the apple pie we ate. She's tuckered out after her big winning day. I adore her all the time, but a little bit more when she gets sleepy like this. That's when she's more like olden-days Troo. Still whistling in the dark, but not as as loud. Her blue decorating ribbon and two more for winning the games are hanging off her neck, swinging like the pendulum on Mrs. Goldman's grandfather clock. That reminds me. I've gotta get over there soon to check on her house. I've been slacking.

I look over to where Troo set her Eiffel Tower costume against a tree. It's still blinking.

"How'd ya get the lights to stay on like that?" I ask.

"Batteries," she says. She doesn't smell like an Evening in Paris. She smells sticky with everything we ate today, mostly sweet. "Uncle Paulie was in charge of that part."

"No kiddin'." For a man who once went to work with his boxer shorts on the outside of his pants, that is a smart invention. "Did he figure out how to get all those sticks to stay together like that, too?" I say, wondering if someone's brain can grow back. Some worms can do that if you split them in two.

Troo says, "Remember the day we went up to the Five and Dime and ran into Aunt Betty?"

She means the time Mother sent me up there to get her a Snirkle and Troo went skulking around the aisles and I found out from Aunt Betty that Father Mickey was originally from the neighborhood, but what does that have to do with . . . "*Ohhhh*, I get it. You took some glue and that's what's keepin' them together."

She says, "Yup. Once we got the sticks stuck together and they got all dried out and could stand on their own, I painted the movie title on the front." She musta been asked this question by everybody and their brother today because the words roll outta her mouth like a multiplication table.

A couple of blankets down I can hear Mrs. Latour telling her daughter to pipe down. Wendy won't stop yelling, "Thally, Thally, me thee you, Thally." I know if I tell her I see her, too, she's gonna come crawling over everybody asking me to witch laugh and as much as I like her, I need to talk to my sister, so I act like I don't hear her, which is impossible. Just like her mother, who has to call a dozen kids to supper every night, Wendy's got a set of lungs on her.

"Where did you do all the work on it?" I ask Troo about her costume.

"Granny's garage."

I give her a gentle noogie in the arm. "So *that's* where you've been disappearin' to, you little banshee."

Her keeping something this big from me makes me wonder what else she's been up to that I don't know about. She hasn't been giving me the slip just during the day. She disappeared in the middle of the night those coupla times. She couldn't have gone over to Granny's garage to work on the costume then because Uncle Paulie is up at Jerbak's setting pins in the wee hours. I want to ask her again where she snuck off to, but the timing isn't right. I don't want to rain on her parade.

Troo rests her head against mine. "I couldn't tell you about the costume. I . . . I wanted to surprise everybody," she says. She really does love a good bushwhack. Next to scaring people, that's her favorite.

"So, you must like him a lot better now," I say, rolling over onto my side so I can get a better look at her.

"Who?"

"Uncle Paulie." I sure would if I were her. That costume is going to go down in neighborhood history.

"He's all right." Troo plucks a fat blade of grass, positions it between her thumbs and makes that kazoo sound you can get out of it sometimes. "He's better than he used to be. Don't ya think?"

I say, "Sure," but I'm not. That *was* nice of him to help Troo out with her costume, but I haven't forgotten what Ethel told me about Paulie Riley in the old days being "nastier than chicken poop on a pump handle." And also how Granny says, "A leopard can't change his spots," or maybe she says, "A leper can't change his spots," oh, I don't know. She's got so many of those darn sayings and most of them don't even make sense. Who would want to skin a cat in the first place?

I look back to check on Mother and Dave, but they aren't paying us a bit of attention. They're tapping their feet to the sounds of the Do Wops who are playing *Be Bop A Lula Be My Baby*.

I pick up Troo's hand and twine her fingers in mine. "I need to talk to you about what you did."

"Whatta ya mean?" she says, clamping down.

"Givin' Artie the coonskin cap back. You can definitely write that in your 'How I Spent My Charitable Summer' story."

"Oh, that," she says, going limp again. "You bonehead."

From out on the lagoon island, there's a high whistle and a *boom . . . deboom. . . . boom* and after the explosion, the first firework rains down red. From around the lagoon, our neighbors say all together, "*Aaaa*," the same way we all say, "*Aaaa*men" together at Mass at the end of a prayer.

"Just so ya know, I've been keepin' a coupla other secrets from you, too," Troo says.

"What kind a other secrets?" I ask her even though I'm sure she's about to fess up about how she slipped outta our bed and wandered the neighborhood looking for Greasy Al, which is great because now I won't have to pry it outta her.

Troo sneaks a peek at Dave and Mother to make sure they aren't listening, which they aren't. They're locking lips. "Father Mickey is doin' something with the altar boys that he shouldn't be doin'."

Shoot. Shoot. Shoot.

Down at the creek today when they were gabbing away, I was afraid Artie was telling Troo the same thing he told me that night in the Kenfields' backyard about Father Mickey commiting a bad sin with the altar boys.

I tell her, "I know you're happy that ya got back together with Artie, but . . . but you can't listen to what he's saying about Father." I'd like to wring Latour's scrawny neck right about now and that's not like me at all. "He's not thinkin' straight lately because he's upset about Charlie Fitch vanishin' and he was jealous about you spendin' so much time with Father Mickey. Artie's imagination, I'm sorry to have to be the one to tell you this, has taken a long walk off a short pier."

Another firework goes off, but I don't look up. I've still got my head turned to Troo. That's when I see him out of the corner of my eye. About ten feet behind and to the left of us, Father Mickey is leaning against a tree pretending to listen to one of his parishioners, but he's not. He's watching us, staring straight at Troo and me.

My sister says, "I know ya left Artie a jar of cod liver oil on his porch, but he doesn't need it. He's not imaginin' anything. He's not a fanatic like you. What he told ya about Father Mickey bein' up to no good is the truth. I got proof." Troo must feel the priest's eyes screwing into the back of her neck the same way I can because she scootches up closer to me, slides her hand down to the front of her shorts and takes something out that she keeps balled up in her grubby hand. "If I show ya this," she whispers, "ya gotta promise ya won't tell a soul and especially *not* Dave."

Since I take them so to heart, I don't ever promise anybody anything if I don't know what I'm getting myself into. Except for my sister.

"Promise."

She wiggles even closer, her warm skeeter-bit arm presses against mine. When she opens her hand, Mrs. Galecki's missing emerald necklace is lying in her palm, just glimmering.

Chapter Twenty-two

For the past two weeks, things couldn't *be* more topsy-turvy around here.

Me and my sister are doing the dishes together, trying to guess what mystery food Mother made us tonight. When she placed it down on the table, she said, "Ta-*daaa*" and called it "Brains a la King," but she had to be kidding around. That's how good of a mood she's been in. She sings along in her warbly voice when a tune she likes comes on the radio and she hasn't done that for the longest time. Her newest favorite, she goes giddy when she hears it, is *Puppy Love.* She stops whatever she's doing and makes Lizzie get up on her hind feet so they can dance around the kitchen. She's not doing her puzzles in the backyard on the TV tray anymore. Mother has been spending most of her day cutting pictures out of magazines and driving around in her new red Studebaker. She looks mouthwatering in that car. After tying a chiffon scarf around her hair and knotting it in back, off she goes to expand her horizons. She's in her bedroom right this minute getting ready to go pick up Aunt Betty. They're driving downtown to Chapman's, which is the fancy store Mother's been wanting to shop at for the longest time.

"That Helen," Troo says, handing me a sorta rinsed-off plate outta the dishpan. "Brains a la King. What a kidder," she says, not doing her *hunh*ing but her regular old Chopstick laugh that sounds just like when she plays it on the piano. *Ha . . . ha . . . ha . . . ha . . . ha . . . ha.*

Just like Mother, Troo's mood has been fabulous, too, these last couple of weeks. She had the gall to say to me yesterday when we were taking out the garbage, "Boy, I feel happy! You should try it sometime, Sal."

My sister wants us all to believe that she's turned over a new leaf since the Fourth of July. She's not making me call her *Leeze* anymore. And when Dave and Mother discuss the wedding, which is going to take place on September 24th, Troo doesn't look like she's about to burst a blood vessel. She's doing her chores before she's asked and once this week—this was really awful—she rubbed my back when I got done rubbing hers. Even worse than this Shirley Temple mood she's been in, my sister has this annoying smile plastered on her face all the time. Even when she's sleeping, she's dreaming about something that makes her look like a cat that ate a canary and two of its cousins.

Her acting so cheerful is terrible, but what's driving me most up the wall is that no matter how much I badger her, she won't cough up how she got her hands on Mrs. Galecki's green necklace. I've tried about a hundred times to get it out of her, but each and every time she reminds me of the promise I made her at the lagoon on fireworks night not to tell a soul, especially *not* Dave. And then she says mysteriously, "Soon *aaalll* will be revealed," sounding very much like the fortune-teller up at the State Fair.

I think my sister snuck next door and took Mrs. Galecki's necklace, but I don't know why she would do something like that. Since she is so light-fingered in general, it even crossed my mind that Troo could be the cat burglar. So I looked and looked, but did not find a candelabra or any other stolen loot stashed around our bedroom. That's why I'm still 99.9 percent positive it's Mary Lane who's been taking stuff out of people's houses. It's gotta be.

Even though Troo's not acting like it on the outside, of course she can't fool me. She's still spitting mad at Father Mickey for getting Mother the annulment. She hasn't asked me to smooch her with the red wax lips and doesn't swoon anymore when she hears Father's name. And she has stopped going up to the rectory for her extra religious instruction. Mother and Dave haven't noticed that she's been skipping. Their spirits are too high to pay much attention to Troo and me these days. Both of them are on cloud nine.

And so are a lotta other people in the neighborhood. The burglaries have stopped. The cops are still looking, but the high-top footprints they found outside the Holzhauers' house ended up belonging to Hank Holzhauer, the kid who lives there, so that was a dead end. Since no more valuables are being stolen on a weekly basis, the search for the cat seems to have taken a backseat. (That talk I gave to Mary Lane in the library lavatory musta done some good.)

So leaving to go look for the burglar is not why Dave told Mother he was going to skip supper tonight and grab something up at the Milky Way, the lucky dog. He went over to the house of his sister, Betsy, and her husband, whose name is Richie Piaskowski, to take the sheets off their furniture and spruce the place up a bit. They're coming for a visit and Dave hopes he can convince them to stay longer than a week at their house on 56th Street across from the church where their daughter, Junie, had her funeral. I can see her grave when I go to sit next to Daddy's at Holy Cross Cemetery every Saturday. How they could bear leaving their girl beneath that mound of dirt, I don't know. Dave takes his niece a bouquet on all the holidays except at Christmas, when he brings her a wreath trimmed with angel hair and blue bulbs to decorate her gravestone, but that's not the same. I could never move away from Daddy, not even for a little while, but I am not going to throw stones at their house. They're my aunt Betsy and uncle Richie now and they could be Troo's, too, if she'd let them, which she won't because they're related to Dave. (Since their last name ends in *ski*, after meeting them she'll right off the bat tell a *huge* Polack joke. I'm gonna have to take them around a corner and explain that they shouldn't take it personally.)

Well, my sister can stand next to me here at the kitchen sink and tap-dance all she wants, but I know her. Below all her bubbliness, she's coming up with another one of her Troo genius revenge plans because she had to give up on the capturing Greasy Al one. Of course, she's disappointed that she can't use the reward money to buy the Jerry Mahoney ventriloquist doll, but Troo's not stupid. She figured out that if Molinari *was* coming back, he woulda showed up by now. I would have to agree with her. I think he escaped for good, too. Maybe to Brooklyn, where Willie O'Hara used to live. He told me that city has loads of Italians and pizza parlors. Molinari could blend right in like a greasy chameleon. Dave has not recently mentioned to me a thing about his "imminent capture," so that's another reason I believe that dago is gone forever.

After I set the white plate carefully in the drying rack, my sister tells me, "After we're done here we gotta go straight over to the Latours. I got a surprise for you."

"I can't," I say, rubbing off the bowl she hands me with the green checked dish towel. "I told Dave I'd water the garden and after I'm done doin' that I'm gonna work on my charitable summer story and some other stuff."

Troo and Artie are still back together. Them spending so much time by themselves hasn't been all bad. Even if Artie's imagination has gotten the best of him, I know I can count on him to keep her out of trouble. Not having to watch her every second has let me take a breather. I paid Henry a couple of visits, and I found the time to work on a new imitation. I can do a *Wizard of Oz* munchkin now. I haven't tried it out on Wendy Latour yet, but I think she'll go bonkers when she hears me singing the *We Represent the Lolly-pop Guild* song at the talent contest next month. That's the only idea I had that worked out. I checked out a magic book from the library, but none of my shirts have sleeves long enough to hide a rabbit. I also asked Willie to loan me some of his jokes, but he told me he couldn't share his "material," so I guess he changed his mind about being a comedian and is now going to be a tailor when he grows up.

I tell Troo, "I also gotta go over to the Goldmans' to check on the house." I look above the sink, where I taped Mrs. Goldman's post-card that came all the way from the Alps. The snowy mountains look very refreshing when Troo and me are slaving over a hot sink.

On the back of the card is the sweetest note that also lifts my spirits:

> *Dearest Liebchen,*
>
> *Hans is feeling better. Please to say hello to your sister for me.*
>
> *Sincerely, your friend,*
>
> *Mrs. Marta Goldman*

> *P.S. We will be home in the middle of September.*

It's too bad that she won't be back for the end-of-the-summer party, but I'm glad she has not been killed by an avalanche. When she gets home, Mrs. Goldman is gonna give me that five dollars for keeping my eye on her house. The first thing I'm going to do is rush up to the toy store and put that ventriloquist doll on layaway for Troo. I'm also going to take the bus to the new zoo to see Sampson on some pretty Sunday with Ethel. Mary Lane took that picture of him the way she promised she would with her Brownie camera, but it's not taped up next to the postcard from Mrs. Goldman. I got it under my pillow, the same way Troo keeps Daddy's sky-blue shirt under hers. Like everybody else around here, even Sampson seems thrilled with himself in that snapshot. He's got a smile on his face and one of his long arms looped around a tire that hangs from the ceiling looking like he just came back from a night on the town.

Up to her elbows in bubbles, my sister bosses, "You're not gonna water the garden or work on your charitable story or go over to the Goldmans' or . . . or anything else boneheaded." She unplunges her hands from the dishwater and gets me by the wrist. "I been plannin' this for weeks. You, Mary Lane and Artie and me are havin' an important powwow over at the Latours tonight."

I say, "Okay, okay," because Troo looks like she means Indian burn business and it's such a relief to see her being her old ornery self. "But I gotta water the garden real quick. The corn . . . I promised Dad . . . Dave, that I would."

"Girls?" Mother says, making a sweeping entrance into the kitchen that reminds me so much of Loretta Young on her television show. She's wearing seamed nylons on her legs, which are making a strong recovery, and a shirtwaist dress the same color as a plum with a flipped-up collar and a wide white belt and high heels that match. She smells different, but still divine. She's started wearing a perfume called Chanel No. 5 that also comes from France, but I think is a cut above Evening in Paris. That's how she acts anyway when she dabs it on. She jiggles the car keys our way. "I'll be back late. Dave should be home from his sister's around ten."

Soon as we hear her heels clicking on the dining room floor, Troo bends back and calls, "No hurry, Helen, dear. Take your time. Say hi to Aunt Betty for me and have oodles of fun!"

My sister telling her to have oodles of anything should've made an alarm bell go off in our mother's head no matter how excited she is about shopping for her wedding, but she doesn't miss a step.

When the front screen door slams shut and we hear the Studebacker's engine start up, Troo wipes her hands down the front of her shorts and says, "You finish up. I'll meet ya over at the Latours'."

"Are we gonna play a new game?" I ask, trying to figure out what "surprise" she has in store for us tonight.

"No, we're gonna . . ." She stops on the porch step, looks back at me very crafty and says, "Yeah. I got a new game to show ya," and off she goes into the night, laughing. Not her airy Chopsticks tinkle or even a deep French *hunh . . . hunh . . . hunh*. That laugh is badder sounding than the time she stabbed Jeffie Lewis in the arm with a pencil after he called her "Clarabelle Hair" one too many times. It is even more wicked than the one Troo gave after she tricked Mimi Latour into petting ankle-biting Butchy when she found out that Willie liked Mimi more than he liked her. The laugh might be even more devilish than the one my sister did when she came up with a way to capture Bobby over at the playground shed and that was the worst one ever.

That laugh—the one that is still echoing around our empty house and filling my heart with the worst kind of scared—*that* is my sister's revenge laugh.

Whatever genius plan she's been brewing for the past couple of weeks, I knew it would bubble up to the surface eventually and I was right. Tonight at the Latours' is when *aaalll* will be revealed. Somebody who has done my sister wrong but good is about to get theirs and even though I can't be sure, I think I know who Troo's got in mind. God help us all.

Chapter Twenty-three

I'm not going over to the Latours' the way Troo told me to. I don't want to hear her plan. I'm afraid to hear her plan. That's why I'm running over to the Piaskowskis' as fast as I can. Dave's still over there getting his sister's house up to snuff for her return.

One part of me wants to rush in the front door of the house and tell Dave that he has got to drop whatever he's doing because Troo is right this minute preparing to seek revenge, but the other part of me knows if I rat Troo out, she'll never forgive me. Ever. Even after she's dead. And I couldn't really blame her. It's bad enough to rat out your sister, but to tattle to Dave, the man who took Daddy's place? I can't even begin to think what she'd do to me. But what about keeping her safe the way I promised Daddy I would?

I'm still going back and forth, listening to an angel on one shoulder and the devil on the other, not sure which is which, when

I come round the corner of 56th and Lloyd and one of the other places where everyone in the neighborhood spends so much of their time looms over me.

Mother of Good Hope Church.

Next to Gesu, which is downtown and so fancy that it makes you feel sorry for people who aren't Catholics, our church is one of the most beautiful ones in all of Milwaukee. It's got two spires, a bell that peals every hour and lots of windows with stained-glass pictures of sheep and saints and the inside is gorgeous, too. There's row after row of pews with red leather kneelers. The confessionals are made out of cherry-colored wood. They're where you have to go and tell on yourself at least once a week if you're me, more if you're Troo. The altar up front is white marble and there's lots of gold dripping off everything and Jesus is hanging on the cross, blood oozing down his forehead from his crown of thorns. Votive candles are always flickering with ten-cents-a-pop prayers in front of statues that have got these special kinds of eyes. Like the ones in the stuffed deer head that hangs behind Jerbak's bar, those eyes follow you around no matter what direction you go in like it's all your fault they're dead. The exception to that rule is the Blessed Virgin Mary. Her eyes are chipped and she's got outstretched blue arms that, if nobody is around, you can climb between and breathe in the incense that sticks to her cloak, especially around her neck.

Behind the church is the school that's two stories high and made of red bricks, same as Vliet Street School. Father Mickey kept telling everybody that we'd outgrown it and needed more classrooms so that's why there's a giant hole next to the cafeteria that has DANGER signs hanging off the rope around it, which is just asking for trouble. That hole is like putting a chocolate cake with chocolate frosting in front of kids and telling them hands off. Denny Desmond already broke his collarbone. He fell in after B.O. Montanazza challenged him to walk the plank across the hole on the first day of summer vacation.

They're going to get busy building the rest of the school as soon as Father Mickey has taken in enough money from his parishioners, which he'll hand over to Mr. Tony Fazio, who I recently found out in a rude way from Fast Susie isn't exactly a silverware salesman like I've been thinking this whole time. Mr. Fazio owns the construction company that's building the new classrooms. His business partner, Mr. Frankie "The Knife" DeNuzio, will be helping him. (Fast Susie also told me in a very cutting tone that Mr. DeNuzio is also known by another nickname, "Mr. Thanksgiving," because, "Frankie is the best there is at carvin'.")

On the opposite side of the playground is a spooky-looking old house where the nuns live, and according to Mary Lane, torture children with dripping holy water.

Father Mickey and Father Louie live together, too, in a one-story house called a rectory that's behind the school. Father Louie's practically an antique, but very sweet in his personality. He plays Santa at our church Christmas party, that's how jolly and red he is, especially in his nose. He's not here right now. He's been taking the summer off to go on a special retreat someplace really dry and won't be back until school starts, so that's why Father Mickey has been living alone the past couple of months.

I've never been in the rectory, but Troo has. That's where she gets her extra religious instruction. She told me the priests have got a living room with two davenports and an office with pictures on the wall of their boss on earth, the Pope. And they have a bathroom with a tub and both the priests have crosses hanging over their beds with palm fronds the same way Troo and me do. That seemed so funny to me. How those priests are pretending to live like any Tom, Dick or Harry, when they're not. They don't resemble normal people at all. They're above and beyond.

I'm still staring up at the church, trying to decide whether or not I should go tell Dave about Troo's revenge plan, when Mary Lane comes peeling around the corner, head down, legs pumping a mile a minute and skids right into me.

"For crissakes," she says, grabbing me up off the grass and dragging me into the familiar bushes in front of the Kohls' house. We hide in them all the time after we go out ringing doorbells or when the Molinari brothers chase us. One of Troo's old Dubble-Bubble wrappers is caught in the bottom of a branch. Mary Lane's got her black high-tops on like always. And her Brownie camera is hanging off her neck. That's kinda unusual. It's her most prized possession. She won it in a church raffle and hardly ever takes it outta the house. She shoves me into a squat, not giving me enough time to put up a fight, which I would lose anyway.

"What're ya doin' here?" she says. "You're supposed to be over at the Latours'."

"I was on my way to the Piaskowskis'. Dave's over there and I . . . I . . . what are *you* doin' here?" Troo told me that Mary Lane was going to be at the powwow tonight. "And who are we hidin' from?"

"Father Mickey . . . he's after me," Mary Lane says, wiping her leaky nose off with her finger and running it down her tan shorts. Her bare legs look like two soda straws. "For an old guy . . . he's pretty quick, almost fast as you."

It takes me less than a breath to figure out what's going on. Mary Lane's not here scouting out the school, thinking about setting it on fire even though she's threatened to a couple of times. That's just big talk. She wouldn't really do that. I don't think. Our little cat burglar musta been up here doing what movie thiefs always do before they break into a place. They don't just dive right in to commit a crime. They come the night before to have a look around to see if there's a mean dog or a night watchman.

I point at the rectory and ask her, "Were you casin' the joint and Father saw you?"

"What?" Mary Lane says with a look on her face that reminds me so much of a monkey that's gotten a peanut stolen out of its hand by another monkey, real astonished like that. "Didn't Troo fill you in? Didn't she tell ya about—"

"Over here," someone shouts from across the street. I can't hear the rest of what the person says, only that he sounds furious and out of breath.

"That's him. He's comin'," Mary Lane says, spreading apart a couple of bushy branches. "Look."

Father Mickey is ripping across the school playground, hollering at two boys who are working hard to keep up with him. When he comes to a stop across the street from us, he checks up the block one way, then the other, and now he's staring where we're crouched and he's so close. That look on his face . . . it's the same look Bobby Brophy used to get when we'd play chess together at the playground, when he was planning his next capturing move that I never saw coming. I can't help it, I groan.

Mary Lane slaps her hand over my mouth and whispers, "Shut your trap. He's got really good hearin'. You recognize the boys?"

I couldn't at first, but now that they've caught up, I can see that it's Larry Montgomery and Hank Holzhauer. If Mary Lane wasn't cat-burglaring around, then there's only one other reason I can think of why she'd be getting chased by Father and the boys.

I take her fingers off my mouth and say, "I know what you did. You peeped in on one of their overnight parties." The altar boys brag about how they bring sleeping bags over to the rectory and stay up to all hours of the night snacking and playing games, and it drives Mary Lane right up a wall that there aren't any altar girls. "What were they doin'? Playin' checkers and eatin' jujubes?" (Her favorites.)

I'm waiting for her to launch into some no-tripper story about how they were doing something else that priests and altar boys would never do. There would be kidnapping gypsies involved and maybe that man, Ed Gein, she told me about would stop by with a blood-dripping woman, but she doesn't. She says, "They were sittin' around in the livin' room with all the shades drawn. I could barely see 'em."

"Oh, they musta been watchin' a movie and needed it dark." I know all about that. I am the visual-aids girl in our classroom.

Mary Lane says, "The only thing they were watchin' was Father Mickey shakin' his fist at 'em."

That doesn't sound anything like the kind of fun sleepovers I heard they have.

From across the street, Father says, "Did either of you get a good look at her?"

None of the boys answer him.

"Hank?" The priest is singling Holzhauer out because he is the head altar boy.

"No, Father."

When the church bell starts ringing, Father Mickey checks his fancy watch and says, "It's getting late. I have an appointment. Go back to the rectory and tell the boys I want to see them at the same time tomorrow night."

Hank and Larry say, "Yes, Father," and scoot after him across the playground the same way they follow him down the Communion rail with their golden skillets in case he should accidentally drop the Host.

I wait until I can't see them anymore before I begin belly-crawling out of the bushes, but Mary Lane's got another idea. She grabs me by my braid and reels me back.

"Seein' that Troo hasn't gotten ya up to speed yet, I guess I will," she says with a first-place smirk. The two of them. Always trying to one-up each other. "Whatta ya think of when you hear those two boys' names?"

Oh, this is such bad timing. Not the time to play the name game at all. But Mary Lane, just like me, has a lot of stick-to-it-iveness. She's never going to let go of me until I answer, so I tell her, "Hank is really superstitious. He's always throwin' salt over his shoulder at lunch and knockin' on Woody Anderson's head for luck and Larry is the captain of the basketball team."

"Not their first names, their last," she says impatiently.

"Ah . . . Holzhauer is a Kraut and Montgomery . . . I don't know what he is. Can we go now?" I gotta get back to doing what I was doing before Mary Lane ambushed me. Trying to decide what to do about Troo. Should I or shouldn't I tell Dave that she's coming up with a scary revenge plan?

"Holzhauer and Montgomery." Mary Lane gets me by the shoulders, brings her face in real close to mine. I can smell her banana breath when she slowly says, "Montgomery and Holzhauer. Conner.

Livingston. Jenkins. Put on your thinkin' cap, Sal. What do those names have in common besides all of them bein' altar boys?"

The split second after I say, "I don't know," that's when it comes to me. "Holzhauer and Montgomery, all the others . . . those families have all gotten robbed!"

Mary Lane rocks back on her heels and says, "Give the little lady a cigar," but when I don't say anything else, she blows up. "Don't you get it? The altar boys . . . they're the cats. They've been takin' stuff from their own houses!"

"I . . . I . . . what?!"

That can't be right. Sure those boys are rowdy and full of themselves, but they'd never do something like that. Mary Lane has really gone off the deep end. It must be the heat. Or maybe the Toni Permanent fried her brain along with her hair.

I say, "But why . . . why would the boys steal their own stuff?"

Mary Lane says, "It's not their idea. Troo told me they're stealin' against their will. Somebody's makin' 'em and then takin' the loot. Who do ya think that could be?"

She knows who it is, I can tell by the teasy look on her face. It's got to be one of the bad apples we got around here. They're the only ones who could bully those altar boys into doing something so against their religion.

"The Molinaris?" I ask.

"Nope."

"The Twomy brothers?"

"Uh-uh."

There are more, but those are the worst of the batch. "I give."

Mary Lane gets the gummiest smile. "Father Mickey! He's makin' the boys steal."

I can hear the *wump* my jaw makes when it drops.

"Yeah, yeah," she says, using her pointer finger to close up my mouth. "I don't blame ya for not believin' me. I didn't believe Troo when she told me either."

As much I'd like to think that I was right about Father Mickey being slippery, him being the ringleader of a gang of thieving altar boys . . . that can't be the truth. Any kind of stealing is against the Eighth Commandment. And taking things from his own parishioners, the neighborhood people who trust and love him, put him up on a pedestal like he is God's gift, and using innocent boys to do it, that wouldn't be just sinful, that . . . that would be . . . evil.

Mary Lane says, "I knew they were gonna have one of their parties tonight 'cause I heard Hank tellin' a kid at the playground this afternoon, so I came up here to eyeball it for myself. To see if Troo was bein' honest or just screwin' around."

I'm not sure if Mary Lane is telling me the truth or not, but I'm not going to automatically think she's lying the way I did last summer. I learned my lesson. She tried to warn me about Bobby and I didn't believe her.

"Could . . . did you see anything besides Father shakin' his fist at the boys?" I ask.

"Not right away 'cause of those pulled-down shades, but then I looked around and found a higher window that was a little more open and I dragged over a concrete block they got in the pile for the new wing," Mary Lane says, like this is all in a day's work. "After I got up, I could see every one of them boys in the livin' room, not just Hank and Larry. Billy Maertz was cryin'. He was hugging that silver bowling trophy that belongs to his dad. Father Mickey ripped it right outta his arms." Mary Lane looks down at a scratch on her arm and licks off the blood. Taps the top of her Brownie. "I woulda had a picture of all of 'em, but I slipped off the block. Father heard me fall into the bushes."

Artie Latour tried to tell me how Father was doing something bad with the altar boys. I was sure he was just being jealous about the priest spending so much time with Troo. And when Troo told me the priest wasn't a good egg at the Fourth fireworks, I thought that was nothing but sour grapes over him getting the annulment for Mother. Could I have been right about Father all along? That he is slick and dangerous as black ice? I can't believe that wasn't my imagination. Maybe that cod liver oil really *is* doing its job.

Or maybe not.

I say, "Wait a minute." I think I mighta found a hole in her story. "Why would the boys go through all the trouble of climbing through their house windows? They coulda just taken the stuff when their parents weren't payin' attention."

Mary Lane looks at me like I'm thicker than the Yellow Pages. "Father had to make it look like a real cat burglar was doin' the jobs so the cops would waste all their time searchin' for somebody who doesn't even exist. You know . . . it's like a whatchamacallit . . . a . . ."

I don't know what it's called either, but they do that sort of thing in movies all the time. Try to trick you into thinking it's somebody else doing dirty deeds even though it's always the butler, so I guess that adds up. But the longer I squat in these bushes thinking about all this, something else doesn't. When we watch our detective shows together, Dave tells me that there's always got to be something called a motive when there's a crime. Even if we don't understand how some people's diabolical minds work, there is a reason someone stops listening to their conscience.

"But *why* would Father make the boys steal and hand him the loot?" I ask.

Mary Lane shrugs and says, "People who steal usually do it 'cause they need dough really bad, right?" Troo doesn't. She gets a nice allowance from Dave and still takes whatever she wants without paying. "In *Hawaiian Eye* there was this guy who stole from a savings and loan because he—"

"But Father doesn't need money," I say. "Priests take a vow of poverty!"

Everything him and Father Louie need is provided for them by the church. I know that because Dave is the treasurer of the Mother of Good Hope Men's Club. I think most of the checks are written by the Pope or his helpers, but not all of them. Dave puts on his reading glasses and spends one night a month going over the church expenses at our kitchen table trying to find some leftover money to put toward the new wing on the school.

Mary Lane pulls out her bottom lip, which is what she does when she thinks. "Maybe Father needs extra cash 'cause he's gotten himself in deep with Mr. Fazio. He owes him. Yeah, that's gotta be it. I *told* you I saw 'em in that car the night I was scoutin' out the old bottling plant! Mr. Fazio was yellin' at Father about being overdue."

When she mentioned that to me in the library lavatory, I thought she was telling me a no-tripper story about Mr. Fazio hollering at Father about returning a late book, but what if I was wrong?

"Let me get this straight." I try to gather up my thoughts, which are flying away like dandelion fluff on a windy day. "You're tellin' me that you think Father Mickey owes Mr. Fazio's construction company for buildin' the new wing onto the school and . . . and he's late paying him and that's why Father made the boys steal so he can use the extra money he's gonna get from selling the burglary stuff to pay off Mr. Fazio?"

"Good one, Sal," Mary Lane snorts.

"Whatta ya mean?"

She looks at me with squinty pity. "You really don't know?"

"What?"

"Mr. Fazio and Mr. DeNuzio are gangsters."

Oh, for cripes sake. I can't believe I almost fell for all of this. I don't know anything about Mr. Frankie the Knife/Mr. Thanksgiving, but Mr. Fazio . . . he's Fast Susie's dad. He lives two blocks away from us in the nicest house on Vliet Street.

"Mr. Fazio and Mr DeNuzio are *not* gangsters," I tell Mary Lane. "Gangsters don't live in Milwaukee, they live in Chicago. Like Al Capone in *The Untouchables*." Dave and me never miss that show so I'm sorta an expert of Italian bad guys.

Mary Lane says, "Yeah, well, I guess some of them decided to move up here."

I doubt it. Those gangsters seem pretty smart about the law. Crossing state lines makes anything you do a Federal offense, which Dave told me is much, much worse than a local offense.

Mary Lane says, "Mr. Fazio and his partner . . . everybody in the neighborhood knows they're not *only* construction men. They take bets on the ponies in a parlor somewhere and . . . and if you welsh and don't pay them back what you owe, they'll make you a cement overcoat and drop you into Lake Michigan." I must have the most disbelieving look on my face because she throws her hands up in air. "Ask anybody! You could ask your uncle if he was right in the head. He used to work for Mr. Fazio as a bookie. Ask your granny. She knows everything that goes on around here. She'll tell you how much gamblin' trouble your uncle and his best friend, Father Mickey, got into in the olden days."

Mary Lane admires Granny's ability to know everything that goes on in the neighborhood to the nth degree. She wouldn't bring her into this if she wasn't sure of her information.

"For cryin' out loud . . . ask your sister!" Mary Lane says, at the end of her rope with me.

Why am I always the last to know?

I must look like I finally believe her because Mary Lane springs up outta the bushes and says, "Let's beat it over to the Latours'." I have never seen her so excited except on trick-or-treat night. "Now that I know she wasn't ribbin' me about Father Mickey and the altar boys, I can't wait to hear the rest of Troo's plan."

I'm not going anywhere. My legs feel like rubber bands and my tummy is all balled up. I'm snuffing, swallowing, doing everything I can not to break into tears. I promised to keep my sister safe and now she's in the worst kind of trouble. I feel like I'm standing on the shore watching her go under for a third time. I gotta do something to save her, only I don't know how to swim.

I can't go running to Mother to ask her to rescue Troo. She would tan my sister's hide with her golden hairbrush and tell her, "You made your bed, now lie in it." Granny is out of the question, she's got enough troubles of her own. My other hope would be Nell, but she's barely keeping her own head above the water. For sure, I can't go to Dave. He's a policeman sworn to uphold the law no matter what. The only other person I can think of asking for a helping hand is Ethel. Maybe she could figure a way to get Troo outta this jam.

With all my heart, I don't want to believe that Troo is guilty of stealing from our neighbors the same way she does from the drugstore and the Five and Dime. But there are those middle-of-the-nights when she snuck out of our bed. And Mrs. Galecki's emerald necklace that's hidden in the toe of one of her Wigwam socks. There is just no getting around this. How could my sister tell Mary Lane about Father Mickey and the altar boys unless she was part of his gang of cat thieves?

Chapter Twenty-four

My sister gave me the cold shoulder all day. That's how she always acts when I don't do what she tells me to do, which was show up at the powwow she had planned over at the Latours' last night where she was gonna reveal her revenge plan. I could just kick myself. That's what I shoulda done. Hearing what Troo's got up her sleeve would've been awful, but thanks to Mary Lane, now I know something even worse. Something that could get Troo sent to reform school if she gets caught. Getting revenge is not against the law. Not like stealing from your neighbors is.

I *was* going to talk to her about what she's been up to with Father Mickey and the altar boys after we turned in tonight, but then I decided keeping my sister's criminal life to myself is the smart way to go. What would be the point? After I accuse Troo and she finally admits to being one of the cats, she'll cuddle up and talk to me in her purring dolly voice, give me excuses for being wayward the way she always does, or worse, she won't do that at all. She'll hawk a loogie at me and say, "Yeah? So what?" and prance into the darkness to kick up her heels.

After we got done saying our prayers, Troo was still doing an excellent imitation of an iceberg. She didn't twirl my hair and she didn't want me to rub her back or give me butterfly kisses. She drew a line down the middle of our bed that I couldn't cross without getting kicked, then rolled away from me as far away as she could and sang over and over in the coldest voice, "Every party has a pooper, that's why I invited you. Party pooper. Party pooper," until I couldn't take it for one more second and had to run out to the green bean teepee.

That's where I am now. Listening to the crickets and trying to decide if I should hop the white fence and ask great-advice-giving Ethel what she thinks I should do about thieving Troo, when I hear the first wails of the ambulance. I automatically cross myself and say a Hail Mary the way the nuns taught us to for the poor person's suffering soul and go back to figuring out how to get Troo out of dutch, but I can barely hear myself think. The siren is getting closer and closer and doesn't wind down to a whimper until it's right next door.

Knowing that can only mean one thing, I scramble out of the teepee as fast as I can and shout, "Ethel! I'm comin'."

Because of my fly-like-the-wind speed, I beat out Dave, Mother, Troo and all the other neighbors who heard the siren and have come to see what the ruckus is about. The flashing light on the ambulance parked in front of Mrs. Galecki's house is making our faces go red, then black, red, black, while we watch the men who've come to do their job. They hurry up the steps with a stretcher to hunch over Mrs. Galecki, whose head is slumped down to her baggy chest. The porch light is shining down on her face, which matches her gray hair. Ethel is swaying next to her patient and friend, wringing her hands and asking for Jesus's help.

I want to go to her, but the porch is small and there's no room for me. All I can do is call to Ethel from the bottom of the steps in my most soothing voice that I learned from her, "Everything's gonna be fine, sugar," but she either doesn't hear me or doesn't believe me because she's pleading to the heavens even louder.

The ambulance guys are the same two that always come when Mrs. Galecki's heart acts up. Like Laurel and Hardy, one of them is fat and one is skinny. When they get done poking around, they heave Mrs. Galecki onto the stretcher with "A one and a two and a three a," and struggle down the steps with her in their hands. She looks even worse close-up. Her toothless mouth is hanging open and she's only got on one of the pretty pink slippers that Ethel knit her.

Ethel is scurrying after them with the other slipper in her hand, whimpering out, "Don't you fret, Bertha, don't you fret. Ya gonna be back home eatin' berry cake in no time."

Ethel doesn't notice me when she rushes past me in the dark. I don't think she knows if she is coming or going. When I chase after her and tap her on the shoulder, she turns with a start, brings both of her hands to her chest and says, "Oh, Miss Sally. Bertha . . . she's real bad!"

"Is it her . . . ?" I place my hand across my heart the way you do for the Pledge of Allegiance.

"I . . . don't know . . . we was just sittin' there on the porch talkin' about Mr. Gary's visit and then all of a sudden . . ." Ethel goes back to taking giant steps toward where the ambulance is parked and I'm working hard to keep up. "Bertha give out a shout and went limp and . . . she didn't come back 'round the way she does mosta the time with a little jostle and the smellin' salts so I called the operator."

Down at the curb, the men slide Mrs. Galecki through the open doors of the ambulance like she's a refrigerator shelf. She clanks, and that sound . . . it gives me the shivers in the hot night.

Ethel wants to get in, too, so she can comfort Mrs. Galecki on the way to the hospital, but the skinny man with *Augie* embroidered on his white shirt puts a hand on her arm to stop her. "Family only. You know the rules."

Of course she does. This has happened so many times before. She's just not thinking straight.

"Rest easy, Bertha," Ethel calls through the door. "Your boy . . . he'll be here right quick and—"

Augie slams one door shut and then the other. "Give the hospital a buzz later on," he tells Ethel on the way to his shotgun seat beside his partner, who cranks the siren back up and off they go ripping down 52nd Street to St. Joe's.

Somebody laughs and the crowd of neighbors breaks up to go back to whatever they were doing before all the excitement except for Troo, who is hanging back, and Mother and Dave, who've come to Ethel's other side.

Dave puts his arm around Ethel's shoulders and she leans against him and for just a second I think she is gonna faint right there in the street and Mother must think that, too, because she says to her, "You look like you could use a stiff drink." To me, she puts her foot down. "You and your sister get back to bed on the double."

All there's left for me to do is watch them guide my good friend across the grass to the front of our house, propping her up between them.

"Ethel?" I call to her.

"Don't you worry, Miss Sally," she calls back over her shoulder. "Everything's gonna be fine," and as much as I want to believe that, my pounding heart is letting me know the smartest woman I know couldn't be more wrong.

I try to never disobey Mother, but I can't do what she wants me to. Go back to bed and let my thoughts chase their tails. Listen to my sister sing that party pooper song until she falls asleep and I'm left alone in the dark to toss and turn in the damp twisted sheets, watching the aquarium fish swim by the sunken pirate ship and think about Troo's half-buried feelings and what trouble she's in and how the fox-stole-wearing angelfish don't seem to care about anybody but themselves and poor Nell, just a skeleton of her former self. And how Dave is probably gonna get shot in the back by a bank robber after he marries our unlucky-in-love mother. And Daddy. All he asked me to do was pay attention to the details and keep Troo safe. He expected me to come through for him in the clinch and I'm batting 0 for 2.

I just can't face all that tonight.

I want to go sit on our backyard bench. I need to calm down. Breathing in the garden smells sometimes helps. I'm taking the alleyway home so Mother won't spot me.

Troo, who is trailing after me like it's an accident that we're both going in the same direction, finally breaks the ice when I round our garage and open the gate to our yard. "I think Mrs. G bought the farm this time," she calls to me outta the dark.

I want to charge back down the alley, push her down and shout, *If she does die, she'll never know the truth! She was right all along that somebody stole her jewelry, but it wasn't Ethel, the way she thought it was. It was you! You grabbed the necklace out of Mrs. Galecki's bedroom. I hope you're proud of yourself . . . you . . . you . . . lyin' stealin' brat! I never want to talk to you again for the rest of my life. I hate you!*

But I don't do that. I just don't have it in me. I think instead about how if Mrs. Galecki does pass on, I'll go with Ethel to the funeral, stand right by her side while she bawls into her handkerchief and moans in her black dress and hat with a veil. Even though she knows the end has been coming for a while now and that her patient has had a good long life, dear Ethel, she's not really prepared. Nobody ever is. You can never get your heart ready.

The only good thing that would come out of Mrs. Galecki's dying is that Ethel will inherit the money from her Last Will and Testament so she can start up her school and I'm overjoyed for her, I really am, but I have been dreading this day for a long, long time. Even if she wanted to stay, Ethel's gonna have to move away from the neighborhood. There are people on these blocks who have never shouted hello when she glides by on her way to the drugstore. I've heard them call her *jigaboo* and *little black Sammy* behind her back up at the Kroger. She only got to live here in the first place because she was working for Mrs. Galecki. Colored people are supposed to live with other colored people. Ethel'll have to move down to the Core.

I cannot imagine my life without her warm honey voice, her wise advice. Troo and me sleeping in her screened-in porch on nights when it's just too stuffy in our room. Listening to Ethel's jazzy music and eating her Mississippi blond brownies, smelling her violet toilet water behind her ears when she bends down to kiss my foreheard with her cool full lips. Even her bunions. Every square inch of the finest woman I know . . . her goneness is going to make me ache forever in a place I can't rub.

Chapter Twenty-five

I never did get around to telling Dave that he should take out the corn he planted in Daddy's memory. He did okay for his first try. The stalks are tall and tassled. Fireflies are flickering around the leaves and the smell of the damp dirt is almost as strong as the smell of the cookies drifting over from the factory tonight.

When Troo comes trailing after me into our yard, she doesn't sail past me like I'm part of the scenery the way she's been doing. She sits down next to me on the glider, picks up my hand off my lap and squeezes it so hard, which is something she used to do back in the olden days when she got scared of one thing or another, mostly the boogeyman, who doesn't seem to bother her in the least anymore.

With our sunburned shoulders so close together, we watch the breeze flutter the corn and remember the good old days. How I'd sit in Daddy's lap on the back porch after supper, smelling hard work on his sky-blue shirt. He'd wrap one of his hands around a cold bottle of beer and his other arm around me and we'd listen to a baseball game coming out of the Motorola radio that would light up his face the same way dawn did when he'd head out to the fields on his red tractor like a conquering hero. I know that Troo is picturing how her and Daddy made mustaches out of the tassles and that he always grew maroon Indian corn just for her because it matched the color of her hair. When August came, acres and acres of his hard work would wave outside our kitchen window like we lived on the shores of a green sea. We all looked so forward to the first of the corn. The taste of a just-picked cob, the salty butter dripping off our chins. Daddy's triumphant look when we told him it was the best we ever had.

Even with my sister by my side, I haven't felt this alone since the night I waited for his car to come down our road back from the game at County Stadium. Troo is remembering the crash, too, but she'd never admit it, even if I say to her, *It's not true what everybody says about time healing all wounds. My heart . . . it feels like it's permanently cracked, doesn't yours?*

"Sal, my gal," Troo says, twining her fingers around mine. "I got a little surprise for ya. I was gonna save it, but I think . . . yeah, wait here."

She goes to the garage and kicks two times on the door that Dave keeps trying to remember to fix. I can hear her rummaging around in there and then a long scraping sound on the cement floor and a few swear words.

After she switches off the light and the yard turns black again, she calls, "Close your eyes." I can hear her grunt as she drags something across the grass. The nearer she gets to me, that rusty smell she's had on her a couple of the times she's snuck back into bed in the middle of the night gets stronger and stronger. "Okay." Troo claps her hands just once. "Open saysme."

Right in front of me, the moon catching it just right, is something else that I thought was long gone. I reach out and run my fingers across the worn-down green seat to make sure it's not my imagination, but Daddy's and my bench from the zoo feels real.

"But . . . I went back to look for it and it was gone," I say. Those kids in Fatima who were paid the miracle visitation by the Blessed Virgin couldn't have felt any more awestruck than I do. "I . . . I thought it got destroyed by the men with the bulldozers."

"I know you did." Troo is puffed up. "Mary Lane and me . . . we went and got it. Her dad told us they were just gonna throw it out, so we carried it all the way down Lloyd Street in the middle of the night so nobody would see us and blab the surprise. *Onree* let us keep it behind the drugstore for a while and then last week all three of us brought it the rest of the way," she says. "Dave told me it was okay to keep it in the garage." When I don't get up right away because all the amazement I am feeling seems to have settled in my heinie, she shoves me on the shoulder and says, "Whatcha waitin' for?"

After I get up from the glider and ease down in the middle of the bench, leaving the spot empty where Daddy always sat, Troo quickly curls up on the other side of me and says, "Feelin' better?" She reaches up to pat me on the top of my head. "I sure am." Of course she is. There's just about nothing in the whole world that Troo adores more next to scaring the life outta somebody and bushwacks than having a plan and making it stick. "It's good you're sittin' down. I gotta tell you something really bad," she says.

She's finally gonna come clean about her cat-stealing. They're always telling us at church that confession is good for the soul so I should let her get it off her chest, but I've got Troo in one of her once-in-a-blue-moon generous moods. "Before you do that, could you do one more really nice thing for me?"

That catches her off guard. I don't usually ask her for favors because the chance of getting one is too slim.

Troo says, "But . . . I need to . . . fine. I'll go out to the new zoo to see that dumb gorilla with you, but if you start cryin' and wavin' at him, I'm warnin' you, I'll . . . I'll . . ."

I hook a chunk of her hair that's fallen in her eyes behind her ear and say, "That's really sweet, but that's not what I was gonna ask you." I have thought this through already over ten times. I let it out in a rush so Troo can't interrupt. "I want you to climb through our bedroom window, get Mrs. Galecki's emerald necklace out of your sock and stick it back under her bed. Nobody'd have to know that you stole it."

"What?!" Troo flies up off the bench, flapping her arms, legs going every which way. "What . . . what are you talkin' about? Who told you I stole it?"

"I . . . I . . ." Nobody did. I was just so sure, but now . . . the look on her face, she can't fake that one. That's her genuine, you-better-not-be-callin'-me-a-liar-or-I'll-sock-you-in-the-breadbox look. "Didn't you?"

"No, I didn't!"

"Then who did?"

"That's what I've been tryin' to tell you, if you'd shut up and listen!" She is so agitated, she can barely get out, "Father Mickey. He stole the necklace."

"Trooper," I say, shaking my head low and slow. She's mad at him, and trying to shift the blame onto somebody else the way she always does when she gets caught doing something bad. Father Mickey couldn'ta snuck into Mrs. Galecki's bedroom to take the necklace because Ethel's got eyes in back of her head. But then I remember that's not exactly true. She isn't watching every minute of every day. When Mrs. Galecki goes down for her long afternoon nap, Ethel leaves to do grocery shopping at the Kroger or over to the drugstore to get the medicines. During one of Father Mickey's visits would be another good time to get those errands done.

Still flapping, Troo says, "I thought you already knew about . . . Mary Lane bragged that she filled you in when she ran into you up near church, didn't she?"

I nod. Reluctantly. She's gonna blow a gasket when she hears me admit that.

"Goddamn it all! That bigmouth Lane, she's always trying to prove she's better than . . ." My sister is pacing fast in front of the bench, punching her fist into her hand. "I was gonna tell you all about the altar boys and Father Mickey and . . . and the rest of it over at the Latours' last night, but you never showed up and now—"

"*Shhh, shhh,* you gotta lower your voice. They're gonna hear you." I point to the house. The kitchen curtains are closed, but the light is on above the sink so we can see the outlines of Dave, Mother and Ethel sitting around the table. "Why don't you . . ." I pat the bench.

Troo takes her time, but when she sits back down, she shoots me a hurt look that you never see much on her face anymore and takes one of her L&M's from her shorts' back pocket. I almost ask her for one. Cigarettes might smell like a cat box, but they seem to round the rough edges for everyone and I think I'm going to need a little smoothing.

"I bet Mary Lane didn't tell me everything," I say. "Start at the very beginning."

Troo strikes a match, thinks about that for a minute and says,

"The first time I went up to the rectory for my extra religious instructions, the doorbell rang and when Father Mickey went to answer it, I did, ya know, what I do." She means she snooped like she always does in Mother's dressing table and my notebooks and Nell's closet and only God knows where else. "I pulled out the drawers of Father's desk and in the top two there was only notebooks, but in the bottom one, I found Mr. Livingston's fancy silver belt buckle."

I gasp. "Did he . . . did Father catch you looking through his stuff?" The thought of him coming up on her from behind the way Bobby did last summer makes the whole backyard feel like it dived underwater. I can barely breathe.

Troo shakes her head and says, "By the time he came back from paying the paper boy, I was already back in the chair memorizing the parts of the missal he gave me to learn."

"Didn't you wonder what he was doin' with Mr. Livingston's buckle?" I ask.

She shrugs. "I figured Father found it in church or something and was goin' to give it back, but then I heard that it'd been stolen and I . . . I didn't know what to think."

My sister has gone pale. I dab the sweat beads off her forehead with my fingertips. I don't want to upset her more than she already is and she can get snooty if you push her, so I'm going to try and let her unravel what she's got to tell me in her own time.

"After that first visit, Father and me never studied religion again." Troo lets out the longest exhale. "We played hangman and tic-tac-toe and he made me cherry Kool-Aid, but mostly. . . we talked."

"You talked? About what?" I ask, finding that a little hard to believe. Priests don't usually have conversations with kids. They just tell them they're going to hell if they aren't good and obey their parents and stuff like that.

Troo says, "He seemed so interested in me, Sal. He wanted to know what I thought about this and that. Like the Braves. The neighborhood. We talked about everything. Even Daddy." She takes an extra long drag off her L&M. "I told him how much I hated Dave and how mad I was at Helen and . . ." She probably cried, but she'd never tell me if she did. "He gave me a hug and promised that he'd make sure that Mother never got the annulment letter and . . . I believed him."

The heart of the matter, that's what this is.

Troo says, "That's how come when Father asked me to keep my ears open around Dave and report back to him what was goin' on in the cat burglar investigation, I told him I would."

"Didn't you think that was kinda weird?" I ask. I sure do. Usually when somebody asks her to do anything she tells them where to go.

"Kinda," Troo says, puffing away. "Until he explained to me that the reason he was so interested in the burglaries was because he studies wrongdoing. He told me it's important to know thy enemy."

I would have to agree with him.

My sister says, "I . . . I swear. I didn't know then that he had something to do with the stealing. I just wanted to return the favor, ya know, for him being so . . . oh, I don't know." I do. Father made her feel the same way Daddy used to. Number one on the hit parade. Not second fiddle like she sees herself now. "So after that, every time I went up to the rectory, I told him everything I heard Dave tell Helen about the burglaries and what I heard him talk about with Detective Riordan on the telephone. Father seemed so happy to hear that, but . . . but then he broke his promise and brought the annulment letter to Helen anyway."

Because of mental telepathy, I know she was also thinking that if she fed Father tidbits about the cat burglar case it would make it harder for Dave to solve the case. He would have to spend more time on the job and less time with Mother and that might get her steamed enough to call the wedding off.

Oh, Troo.

After letting all that sink in, I say, because I'm itchin' to know, "But what does any of this have to do with Mrs. Galecki's necklace? How did you get a hold of it?"

"I'm gettin' to that." She taps off her ash. "On the Fourth, on my way up to Granny's to get my Eiffel Tower costume, I stopped by the rectory and went through a window into Father Mickey's office. I knew he wouldn't be there, that he'd be over at the park helpin' get everything ready for the parade. I was so mad, Sal. I . . . I was gonna take the belt buckle outta the drawer—I don't know what I was gonna do with it, but when I looked for it in the desk, it was gone." I am biting my nails over how brave she is. "So I searched around for something else I could take. I couldn't believe it when I found Mrs. Galecki's necklace stuffed behind some books. I didn't know how Father got a hold of that either, but tit for tat. I took it." Troo inhales her cigarette smoke up through her nose, which is so French. "I think he stills likes her."

"Mrs. Galecki? Why wouldn't he?" Sure she can be kind of annoying, sometimes she coughs for fifteen minutes at a stretch, but she's still one of his flock.

"Not her," Troo says. "Helen."

She looks up and into the kitchen window. I hope Dave and Mother put cold water in a bucket for Ethel's bunion feet and are saying uplifting things to her. If I was in there, I would sing about the ant moving the rubber tree because it's got such high hopes.

Ethel really likes that song. She sings it to Mrs. Galecki when she's spraying her thinning hair tall with Aqua Net every morning.

"Before Mother started going out with Dave in high school, her and Father Mickey were hot and heavy," Troo says. "Aunt Betty told me during rummy."

"Yeah, she told me something like that, too."

Up at the Five and Dime the same day she surprised me with the news that Father was from the neighborhood, Aunt Betty winked at me and said, "M.P.G. could give a girl the ride of her life. Ask your mother."

I've got so many questions that I don't know which one to pick. It's like trying to decide which candy to buy outta the case at the Five and Dime. Troo looks so petered out, but I gotta know all of it if I'm gonna help her outta the jam she's gotten herself into.

"Do you know how Father's makin' the altar boys be cats?" I ask. Even though we have fate in the Catholic Church, we also got free will. I'm not sure where one starts and the other takes over, but it seems to me that the boys could have told the priest that they didn't want to steal.

Troo points up to the western sky. The stars tonight look close enough to put in my pocket and save for a rainy day. "The Big Dipper and the Little Dipper."

Daddy used to say that they reminded him of us.

I squeeze her hand harder than she's squeezing mine. "Tell me. How's Father makin' the boys steal?"

Troo says, "Artie told me down at Honey Creek on the Fourth that before he ran away, Charlie Fitch told him that Father threatened the altar boys. Told them that he'd kick 'em out of school if they didn't steal for him."

He can do that. Our pastor is the boss of everything, not only the church and the nuns, but the school, and everybody in the neighborhood.

I say, "But Charlie, he didn't have a house of his own and there's nothin' good to take out of the orphanage." When our Brownie troop went up to St. Jude's to sing Christmas carols to those poor kids, the place reminded me of the dump near the farm.

Troo says, "You know that antique railroad watch Mr. Honeywell's got? The one he's always braggin' about? Father told Charlie that the second after he got adopted he'd have to steal it and if he didn't, Father would make sure the Honeywells picked another kid from the litter."

Poor Charlie. He really was caught between a rock and a hard place. "Do you think after he ran away that he . . . um . . . got his head chopped off or eaten by a bear or—?"

"Jesus, Sal. Quit bein' so fuckin' weird," Troo says. "Fitch is fine. He's livin' in the country in this place called Fredonia. Artie got a letter from him a couple of weeks ago."

"Why'd he go there?" I ask. I never even heard of the place.

"Remember booger-eatin' Teddy Jaeger?"

I nod. He's kinda hard to forget.

"After he got adopted, him and Charlie became pen pals," Troo says. "That's where Charlie went to get away from Father Mickey. When he showed up at Teddy's new home, the mother and father told him he could stay for the rest of the summer and help them sell vegetables outta their roadside stand."

I don't doubt that for a second. If those people were charitable enough to adopt finger-up-his-nose Teddy Jaeger, Charlie Fitch musta seemed like the guy from *The Millionaire* showing up at their front door.

After I think some more about everything she's been telling me, I come up with one more question. "But why didn't the altar boys just tell their mothers or fathers or . . . or the police that Father Mickey was makin' them steal against their will?" We're not exactly big on that kind of thing around here, we're supposed to fight our own battles, but this is sort of a special situation where you might want to call in the cavalry.

"The altar boys are dumb, but they're not that stupid," Troo says, flicking her cigarette into the grass. "They knew nobody would take their word over a priest's."

She's right, of course. Even if they gave confessions signed in blood. The boys also had to know that their parents would punish them within an inch of their lives just for saying something so bad about Father. No one would believe the four of us either if we wanted to tell on him. Mary Lane is a famous no-tripper story-teller and I have a problem with flights of imagination and Troo, everybody thinks she is the next Bonnie from Bonnie and Clyde, and Artie Latour, they'd say anything he heard from Charlie Fitch about Father Mickey was wrong due to him being a half-deaf mess.

Even Dave, who is the fairest person I know, wouldn't take us seriously. He couldn't believe us over Father Mickey even if he wanted to. It's against his religion. If I got up off this bench and marched into the kitchen to tell him everything Troo just told me, he'd look helplessly across the table at Mother and she would say, "Get out the cod liver oil and a serving spoon," or she might slap me across the face. That's what she did when I told her that I hated God after Daddy died. And when Troo came home from school rubbing the back of her noggin, complaining that Sister Imelda whacked her so hard with the back of a geography book that she was still seeing the Canary Islands, Mother told her, "Take out the garbage."

They can't help it. The Lord thy God comes before all others and the same goes for anybody who works for Him.

Completely tuckered out from all this telling, Troo drops her head into my lap and stares up at the sky. I am feeling ashamed of myself as I pet the top of Daddy's and my bench. When Troo disappeared outta our bed those nights, I thought at first that she was out looking for Greasy Al. Then I was positive that she was stealing. I was so sure she was up to no good. It never crossed my mind she could be up to good.

Troo asks, "You believe me?"

"Yeah."

My sister lets out a sigh that lets me know that's a real load off her mind.

"Mary Lane told me that Mr. Fazio is a gangster and she thinks Father owes him money for gamblin'," I ask. "Do you think that's true?"

My sister says, "I know it is. I didn't understand what I was seein' when I went through Father Mickey's desk drawer, but in those notebooks I found . . . there was a long list of all these numbers with dollar signs and dates. They had to be bets. Uncle Paulie used to have a notebook just like that. Remember?"

I didn't until just now. It was blue. He always had it with him before the crash. When he was a bookie and not a pin setter. So many times, I watched him slide it in and out of his back pocket where he keeps his Popsicle sticks now.

Troo says, "I . . . we can't let Father get away with this. Not just for lyin' to me, but the altar boys and . . . everybody in the parish. He betrayed all of us, Sal. The same way Judas did Jesus."

I know where she's headed and it's not down the straight-and-narrow path. Father Mickey is who I suspected Troo was going after with a vengeance because he got Mother the annulment, but now she's got even more reasons to balance the scales.

I bring my face down to hers and use my strictest voice. "I know what he did was bad, but you can't go after him. He's a priest. What if he—"

Troo cuts me off with, "I already decided." She's got that steely glint in her eyes. "I got me a plan."

Those are the exact same words she used when she told Mary Lane and me last summer that she wanted to go after Bobby Brophy and we all know how good that turned out. Troo probably already figured out a way to cut the ropes on the heavy crucifix that hangs above the altar so it will come crashing down on Father while he's saying Mass or maybe she'll knock him over the head with an incense burner or hide a cherry bomb in the sacristy or . . .

"You with me?" she asks.

Even though I know whatever revenge scheme she's come up with to get back at Father Mickey doesn't have a snowball's chance in Miami Beach, I stroke her hair and tell her the way I always do, the way a good sister should, "Always and forever."

Chapter Twenty-six

Having our excellent friend, Mr. Gary Galecki, come all the way from California for his summer visit is a huge deal for the O'Malley sisters. That's why Troo shoved whatever plan she's cooking up to get back at Father Mickey onto a back burner for the time being. So we can spend some time with Mr. Gary. (Believe me, she has not forgotten her revenge. She's just put a temporary lid on it.)

Unlike he usually does, Mrs. Galecki's son has not come back to the neighborhood to have his usual visit with his mother during the first week of August. The two of them won't be reading the paper and eating jam and toast and talking around the kitchen table like they always do. Instead of putting her up on a pedestal, the poor man has been spending most of his time up at the hospital. His mother is not dead, but she isn't exactly alive either. Dave told me our old neighbor is in something called a *coma*, which means she's neither here nor there, which sounds an awful lot like purgatory.

Right after Mr. Gary arrived, Troo and me wanted to rush over and welcome him home, but Mother told us we could not intrude on his grief. That we had to wait until he came to us. So when he knocked on our back door tonight and asked if the two of us were available to play cards, we jumped at the chance and followed him over here.

Outta habit, I came straight into the kitchen, but Ethel isn't in here puttering around like she normally would be. Since today is her day off, she went to spend it at her Baptist church down in the Core to pray for her coma friend with Ray Buck. I wanted to go along this morning the way she lets me sometimes, but she pinned on her hat, picked up her handbag and said, "Not today, Miss Sally. Got me some things to take care a. Maybe next time." She didn't say so because she wants to spare my sensitive feelings, but the both of us know there might not be a next time. I bet she's already looking for a new place to live and somebody else to nurse just in case things turn for the worse for Mrs. Galecki, which they will, they always seem to.

Ethel left blond brownies on the kitchen counter, and in the sink there is a coffee cup rimmed in bright pink lipstick, a new shade she was excited about trying. Seeing that cup, that souvenir of her, makes me want to go into her bedroom and put my head down on her feather pillow that always smells of fresh-cut strawberries and think of the good old days. Ethel hasn't been herself lately. She's been spending her time dusting and crying over Mrs. Galecki's sickness and nothing I say to her makes any difference. Even radish sand-wiches or reading her Nancy Drew doesn't put a smile on her face.

"You better get out here. I'm dealing, Sally," Mr. Gary calls to me from the porch.

Troo and me have gotten too big for Old Maid, but Mr. Gary loves this game and we're his guests. Ethel would be ashamed of me if I didn't play along. My sister and me are the only friends this poor man's got left in the neighborhood.

The reason his name is mud around here is because when he went back to California after his visit last summer, he took our old pastor, Father Jim, with him so they could grow *flowers* together, not *fruits*, like everybody keeps saying. I really miss Father Jim. He always gave the easiest penances after confession and his finger-nails weren't shiny like Father Mickey's are. Father Jim's were always dirty. I used to help him pot plants in his gardening shed the Men's Club built for him behind the rectory. I have never seen somebody with such a green thumb. He had a lotta rosebushes growing in the backyard, but the irises were his trademark. They were just magnificently purple and that's a very popular Catholic color, especially during Lent. Even Mary Lane telling me she peeped on him up at the rectory last summer and saw him dancing around in a white dress to *Some Enchanted Evening* didn't change my opinion of him one iota, or Dave's neither. We had a long talk about Father Jim and Mr. Gary and the both of us agreed that it's kinda unusual, but if you love somebody it shouldn't matter if you both wear the pants in the family. The Bible even says so. We are all created in God's image. His own Son doesn't have a girlfriend in the Bible and he was really good pals with the Apostles who were all guys, so that kinda makes you think.

After Mr. Gary shuffles and deals and we get our cards straight, he draws the Milking Maid out of my hand with one of his beautiful ones that God musta given to him to make up for his ears, which are only somewhat smaller than Dumbo's.

He says, "I understand you were the belle of the ball at the Fourth of July party this year, Troo."

My sister, who is next to him on the little wicker couch in her baby doll pajamas, says, "See?" and points down to her neck. She's wearing her blue ribbons that she never takes off even when she's in the tub. "And that's not all." She brought over her trophy that she won at camp for being so talented. Troo lifts it out of the shopping bag and sets it down. She spent an hour yesterday trying to clean off the green color it's turning, which didn't work, so now it looks like a lucky tomahawk instead of a golden one.

Mr. Gary wolf whistles, picks up the trophy and lets his hand drop almost to the floor. He's pretending it's too heavy for him. At least I think he is. He takes his tortoiseshell glasses from his shirt pocket and reads the writing stuck to the side. "First place . . . Heap Big Talent Show . . . Camp Towering Pines 1960."

"And I'm going to be Queen of the Playground this year, too, right, Sal?"

When I say, "*Saaa*right," just like Senor Wences on the *Ed Sullivan Show*, that makes Mr. Gary crack up, which was exactly what I was trying to do. His face is longer than it usually is. I've already given him plenty of lanyards, so the next time I come over here I'm going to give him one of those leather coin purses I made at camp and a matching one to take back to Father Jim. Because they're going steady, they should match. Those purses could be the silver lining of the dark cloud that's hanging over him.

Mr. Gary says, "Ethel tells me there's going to be a wedding in September. You must be so excited. Helen will make a lovely bride. She's got such beautiful coloring." He went to high school with her so he's known Mother for a long time. They weren't friends because he wasn't popular like her. Mother told me Mr. Gary was kind of a twerp. "I always liked Dave. Great basketball player. He was smart, too, and kind. Different from the other boys." He plucks a card outta Troo's hand, but winks at me. "You know what they say, Sally, the apple doesn't fall too far from the tree."

I want to ask him to tell me more about Dave, but Troo says, "My turn," and changes the subject because she still is not thrilled about the wedding, but most of all because the sun isn't shining unless it's on her.

"How's your mother feelin'?" I ask. That's the same thing everybody always asked us when our mother was in the hospital, even more often than they do now.

"Mom . . . she's . . ." When Mr. Gary leans forward with his elbows on the knees of his nice slacks, I can see all his cards, which I will try not to use against him. "Do you understand what's going on, girls?"

I take a sip of milk out of my favorite lilac metal glass that Ethel so thoughtfully also left out on the counter next to the brownies and say, "The only thing we know is what Dave told us."

"Your mother's in a comma," Troo says. I don't want to embarrass her and Mr. Gary must not either because neither one of us corrects her. "Her heart's on its last legs."

Mr. Gary runs his fingers through his hair, which is even lighter than mine. Nell told me his comes out of a bottle. "The doctors don't think it's her heart this time."

Like she's been studying Mother's maroon medical book day and night and is quite the authority, Troo says, "Really? Huh. I thought for sure it was."

"It must be her tummy then," I say. I'm sure Ethel already told him how sour his mother's stomach has been on their every-Sunday long-distance phone calls. "It's really been botherin' her no matter how much Pepto she takes."

Mr. Gary lays down his cards, picks up his whiskey drink and gives Troo and me such a serious look. I am getting the feeling that he didn't just invite us over here to play Old Maid. "I want . . . I need to ask you two a couple of questions," he says. "Is that okay?"

The O'Malley sisters can only nod because we've got bites of Mississippi brownies in our mouths.

"Have you seen or heard anything unusual going on around here lately?"

I gotta try hard as I can *not* to see or hear anything unusual going on around here. Things are getting unusualer by the hour, the minute, the heartbeat.

Troo swallows and says, "What do you mean by unusual?"

"You know . . . have you noticed anything out of the ordinary? Especially you, Sally. You're so observant," Mr. Gary says. "For instance . . . would you say that Ethel's been doing her usual excellent job of taking care of Mom?"

"A course she has!" I say. "She never even complains about having to wipe drool or puttin' together strawberry shortcake every week or pushin' your mom for walks around the block even though her bunions are just killin' her and she can hear people call her names even though they don't think she can and . . ." I could go on and on, but listing every single one of Ethel's virtues could take days.

"The reason I ask is," Mr. Gary says, "you know I think the world of Ethel, always have, but . . . there's been some talk about her being negligent. Not giving Mom her medicines or too much of one—"

"No! No! She would never do that," I say much louder. "She's so careful!" Mrs. Galecki's bottles are lined up on the sill above the sink. Ethel takes out what she needs, puts them into a little cup and hands them to her patient every day at two o'clock with a glass of fresh-squeezed lemonade. She even stands watch until she's sure she's swallowed them down and doesn't hide them in one of her cheeks, which she has tried many times.

Mr. Gary says, "And Mom called Jim and me a few times complaining that Ethel was stealing her jewelry. I put that off to old age, but now . . . I don't know."

"That's right. I'm sorry, but you don't know. You don't see her every day the way I do. You should go look under your mother's bed," I tell him, almost frothing at the mouth. "I bet you find her emerald necklace that's been missing right off the bat." I made Troo put it back already when he was up at the hospital.

"And Father Mickey has made quite a few comments to Doc Keller," Mr. Gary says like he didn't even hear me.

At the mention of Father's name Troo and me raise our eyebrows at each other.

"Mickey's been casting aspersions on Ethel's abilities. He told Doc that during his visits he noticed that Ethel doesn't seem up to the task of caring for Mom anymore. That she's falling down on the job." And then more under his breath, he says, "Not that I'd take anything he'd say to heart."

"I don't know what aspersions are . . . but the rest of it . . . that's a doggone lie! She never falls down," I out-and-out shout. "She's tripped a couple of times on the back steps, but she's never landed hard. Ever."

Troo, who is remaining a lot calmer than me for once, says, "Why wouldn't you take anything Father Mickey says to heart?"

"I . . . uh . . ." Mr. Gary says. "Let's just say that Mickey and your uncle Paulie were quite the pair when they were kids. They used to lie in wait for me right back there." He lifts his finger and crooks it toward the alley. "Your uncle would hold me down and

Mickey would kick the sh . . . stuffing out of me." Mr. Gary tries to smile, but doesn't quite make it. "Of course, that was a long time ago. Before Mickey was called to the priesthood."

"He didn't have a true calling," I say out loud, not meaning to.

"No, he certainly didn't." Mr. Gary doesn't seem surprised that I know that, but Troo's mouth has turned down on the corners. I'm supposed to tell her when I hear gossip that I think she'd be interested in hearing, too, but I never told her what Aunt Betty told me up at the Five and Dime that afternoon. I knew she'd get mad if I did. That was back when she was still playing Scarlett to Father's Rhett. "Do you know the whole story, Sally? Why Mickey became a priest?" Mr. Gary asks. His words are getting a bit fuzzy around the edges. He's had three of those whiskey drinks.

Troo sticks her tongue out at me ever so slightly and says, "I know! Aunt Betty told me that in the old days Father got caught bettin' for a third time by the police and was supposed to go to jail, but then he got told by the judge that if he became a priest he wouldn't have to do time."

I cannot believe she didn't tell me the minute she found that out! She can be so, so secretive.

Mr. Gary says, "That's not all there was to it, but close enough."

The three of us sit for a while listening to Mr. Moriarity's dog bark down the block. Troo is twirling her hair and Mr. Gary looks like he's trying not to break out in tears. "I always forget how the smell of the chocolate chip cookies hangs over the neighborhood," he says. "When we were kids, we could go up to the factory and stand in line. You could get a bag of the broken ones for a nickel. They still do that?"

"Ethel goes up there *every* Friday afternoon because your mom loves dunkin' them in a glass of milk before bed," I say, reminding him one more time how hardworking and sacrificing Ethel is. How tender and caring. That she's thriftier even than Mrs. McDougal.

Troo says to Mr. Gary, "Your turn." She has the Old Maid. The first day we got the deck, she folded over one of the corners so she could spot it easier. She tugs it up a little higher than the rest of the cards to make it more tempting.

Falling into her trap, Mr. Gary plucks the card out of my sister's fanned-out hand and asks, "Do you girls remember when I told you last summer that Mom had left Ethel something to remember her by in her will?"

After he had too many cocktails on this very same porch, he sloshed out that secret and made Troo and me promise not to tell anybody. I kept my word. I'm not sure if my sister did.

"Yup, we remember when you told us about all that money," Troo says, pleased as all get out that she pulled a fast one on him.

"Well . . . Mom's lawyer, Mr. Cooper?" Mr. Gary says. "He called to inform me that . . . if she should . . ." He reaches for his glass on the table and gulps the rest of it down. "In the event of her passing, Mother of Good Hope will be receiving quite a tidy bundle. Mom cut Ethel out of her will."

"No! No! She can't do that! Ethel . . . she deserves . . . her dreams . . . we gotta get up to the hospital and pour cold water over your mother's head. Right away," I say, throwing down my cards. "When she comes to, we'll set her straight. Tell her that Ethel would never mix up her medicines or steal her jewelry or anything else bad."

Mr. Gary snuffles and says, "I'm sorry, Sally. I feel as bad about this as you do. But other than a few gifts for the orphanage and St. Joe's, the bulk of Mom's estate will be going to the church. Mickey has been named executor of her will and unless Doc Keller agrees that Mom's not of sound mind, which he doesn't seem willing to do, there's not a thing I can change about that."

"But Father Mickey, he's . . ." It's my duty to mention the godforsaken things we know about him. I'm sure of it. "You should know that Father Mickey—ow!" Troo gives me the hardest pinch on the back of my hand.

"I'm sure Mom had her reasons, I . . . I just can't figure out what they could be," Mr. Gary says, looking toward the alley again. "Doesn't she remember how Mick beat me over and over and . . . and . . . how the church has gone out of its way to make Jim's life a living hell since he's left?"

I don't think he expects me to answer that question, but even if I could, Troo sets her last pair down on the table and says, "I win. It was great to see you again, Mr. Gary." She stands, brushes the brownie crumbs off her legs and picks up her shopping bag. "Thanks for the refreshments. We hope your mother gets better really soon. We gotta go right away, Sally."

I don't know what her hurry is, but she's already out the door.

I don't rush right out after her. Troo stuck our host with the Old Maid. I can't leave him sitting here by himself feeling so defeated. Ethel wouldn't like that. So I say, "Don't let the bedbugs bite and if they do, beat 'em black and blue with your shoe." That's the same thing she would tell him if she was here. I'm being charitable. But I'm also reminding him one more time how Ethel has slaved over his mother for so many years, just in case he should believe for one second those terrible things Father Mickey told him about my good friend falling down on the job. "And by the way, just so you know, Doc Keller is not the end and be all. He can't even cure his own stinky breath. 'Night."

Catching up to Troo in our backyard, I get her by the arm and say, "Why didn't you let me tell him about Father Mickey doin' what he's doin'? Didn't sound like Mr. Gary's nuts about him either. He mighta believed us."

Troo yanks outta my grip. "So what if he does? What do ya think he's gonna do about it?"

"He could tell Dave. He could explain to . . . somebody would have to listen to him. He's a grown-up and—"

"A fairy who's livin' with our old pastor in the land of fruits and nuts! Nobody 'round here is gonna take anything he says seriously. You saw the way people were makin' fun of him after Mass on Sunday."

They really were. When Mr. Gary walked past the St. Francis-is-a-sissy statue sorta up on his toes, more than a couple people snickered.

As I go through the back door of our house, another reason comes to me why my sister didn't want to tell Mr. Gary about the bad stuff that Father Mickey is up to. There's always the chance Mr. Gary really *could* do something to help us. That would mean Troo wouldn't get her revenge and she wouldn't like that at all. She *needs* to do that plan.

Both of us call out "Good night" to Mother and Dave, who are on the living room davenport with their arms around each other, and head straight to our room. Troo peels off her grimy shirt and shorts, switches on the fan and swan dives into our bed. Her head hits the pillow like a brick, so she doesn't hear Mr. Gary crying from next door the way I do. I feel plenty bad for him, but his feelings are not what I'm thinking about. What's rushing around in my mind is what Mr. Gary told us about Ethel not getting Mrs. Galecki's money when she dies. How his mother is leaving it all to the church instead of to the hardworking woman who so rightly deserves it. Mr. Gary told us he doesn't know why she would do that, but I think I might.

During his many visits next door, slippery Father Mickey musta slowly but surely put a bug into Mrs. Galecki's ear. The first thing he would have to do is convince her that Ethel was the one who stole her emerald necklace after he rolled under Mrs. Galecki's bed, opened up her hatbox and helped himself. After he was sure she fell for that lie, he probably picked another rose from her bush and set it in her lap before he said so charming with his black Irish smile, "It would be very charitable if you left your money to me, I mean, the Church, dear Bertha, and not to an outsider, who is also a Negro and a thief. It's your chance to guarantee a spot for yourself in heaven."

He could use that money to pay back the gambling debts he owes Mr. Fazio before he makes him a cement overcoat and drops him in Lake Michigan. But how did Father find out that Mrs. Galecki had all that dough in her will? I know from watching movies that kind of thing is usually kept very confidential. Did she tell him what a wad she has? As much as I would love to think that, I don't. She's like Dave that way. Neither one of them is showy about how much money they got.

No, it wasn't my next-door neighbor who told him that she's rolling in it. Every time I close my eyes, all I can see is Father Mickey. And my sister. Their heads together up at the rectory. I don't have to wake snoring Troo up to tell her, *You told Father, didn't you? You promised you wouldn't, but when you were having one of those chatty visits, you bragged about what Mr. Gary told us last summer. How his mother was a huge moneybags. I know you. You were trying to impress Father with how you're friends with somebody rich, and you did. He never gave a hoot about visiting Mrs. G until recently. Ethel told me it's only been the last few months that he's been coming by. That's how long you've been getting your extra religious instruction.*

I'm getting surer by the minute that one afternoon when Ethel needed to do her grocery shopping or make a trip to the drugstore, Father Mickey told her, *Go right ahead. I'll be happy to watch Bertha until you get back.*

Ethel would be so grateful for the help. She wouldn't think twice about leaving her patient in his trusting priest hands. She'd even ask him if he'd mind giving Mrs. Galecki her special medicines if she left around two o'clock.

Father Mickey probably had joy in his heart and dollar signs in his eyes when he poured that poor old lady a tall glass of fresh-squeezed lemonade and told her, "Time for your pills. Open wide, dearie," and gave her too many of one or not enough of another or maybe some other awful poison that he brought along with him. *That's* why she's in that coma. It's not her heart and it's not her tummy and it's not my imagination. Mrs. Galecki has been tottering on the edge of death for quite some time. All it'd take is one good push from the executioner of her will to knock her off.

Chapter Twenty-seven

Mother's got on a yellow dress and her hair is pulled back in a bow that matches when she sets the laundry basket down on the backyard grass. With her pinched-in mouth, she looks like a buttercup about to bloom. Even though Dave bought her a new dryer to replace her old wringer, she still hangs sheets on the line in the summer, thank goodness. When I put my head down on them in the dark, the smell of sun and sweet-smelling clover reminds me that the night won't last long; tomorrow is another day.

Troo and me are down on our hands and knees weeding the vegetable garden, which has always been one of our chores even out on the farm.

Mother slips the last clothespin into place, glances over at Mrs. Galecki's house and says, "O'Malley sisters, I need to talk to you."

Troo gets up to her feet and grumbles to me, "She's got on her dog butt look. She's probably gonna start complainin' about the bench again."

Mother wasn't happy about Troo lugging Daddy's and my bench over here from the zoo. It's not new enough for her taste. Troo told me she almost didn't let her hide it in the garage. That's why our mother sits down on the white glider with the hearts cut out on the back. When Troo and me go to either side of her, I can tell she's been to Doc Keller's office for her checkup because not even perfume from gay Paree can cover up the stink of tongue depressors.

Mother doesn't look at either one of her girls head-on. She hardly ever does. She is twirling her diamond engagement ring round and round on her finger. "I want you to hear this from me before you hear it from somebody else." She pauses like she doesn't know where to go next and that's not like her. She is usually very sure of herself, very full-steam-ahead. "They took Ethel away early this morning to question her about Mrs. Galecki's illness."

I say, "No!"

The only reason I haven't fainted right off the glider is because I was already afraid something like this might happen. I imagined the subject around every table this morning in the neighborhood went something like—*I heard that Negro woman who was* supposed *to be taking care of Bertha Galecki mixed up the medicines and that just goes to show you, right?*

Troo, who is playing with her cat's cradle, says, "Who took her away?"

Mother yanks the bakery string outta her hand.

"Dave?" my sister asks with a sliver of a grin.

"No. It was that horse's ass, Joe Riordan," Mother says. "Couldn't he have waited until after the wedding?"

She doesn't mean she would've liked it more if Detective Riordan waited to take Ethel over to the station house to ask her questions about how Mrs. Galecki got into a coma until after the wedding. What's bothering Mother is that Detective Riordan, who was going to be Dave's best man, dumped Aunt Betty, who was supposed to be Mother's best lady, and that screwed up her marriage plans beyond belief.

I ask, "But how could they . . . what proof . . . Ethel—" I get an even worse thought. "Did Mrs. Galecki . . . did she—?"

"Kick the bucket?" Troo says.

"Watch your mouth." Mother brings up her left hand and gives what she calls a love tap to Troo's cheek. "And another thing . . . I understand you've been skipping your meetings with Father Mickey." She reaches into her big square dress pocket, takes out a cigarette and says even more disgusted, "He's been taking time to teach you enough decency that you can go back to school in September and you can't be bothered to show up." She picks a piece of tobacco off her tongue. "I wouldn't give you a second chance." No, she wouldn't. "But Mickey—I mean, Father—despite the fact that he's exhausted from sitting by Mrs. Galecki's hospital bedside, he called to tell me that he'd be willing to see you tomorrow night after the fish fry to continue your studies."

I am desperate to tell her that Father is probably not *sitting* up at St. Joe's. That he's circling Mrs. Galecki's hospital bed like a buzzard, so the second she's dead he can fly over to see Mr. Cooper the lawyer to get his hands on her inheritance to save his *own* life. I really should say that out loud, but Mother . . . well. What's the use?

My sister perks up and says, "Father wants to see me up at the rectory tomorrow night? That'd be great!"

Mother looks like she's going to give Troo another love pat

because she thinks my sister is being a wisenheimer, but I know she isn't. My sister looks excited, like she does when she drops in the last piece of a jigsaw puzzle. Getting up to the rectory must be part of the revenge plan that she's gonna finally reveal to us tonight over at the Latours'.

"If I hear back from Father Mickey that you gave him one bit of grief, mark my words, Margaret O'Malley, you won't be able to sit down until Christmas," Mother says, getting up and bustling back into the house like she just remembered something really important.

Troo laughs and says, "Goddamn Helen doesn't know her own strength." She doesn't rub her cheek where Mother smacked her to make it feel better, she never would. "You look a little peaked." That's something my good friend says to me if she thinks I look under the weather. "You okay?"

"No." Not even a little. I'm so worried. About Ethel, who is over at the precinct house getting grilled for something she didn't do, and Mrs. Galecki, who is holding on to life by her fingernails, but most of all I'm worried about Troo, who I'm supposed to be keeping safe. "You can't go over to the rectory tomorrow night," I tell her. "I'm beggin' you. That could be so dangerous."

Both of us know that Father Mickey is not having her over to give her some religious instruction the way he told Mother. I bet he's been looking and looking for Mr. Galecki's emerald necklace, wondering what the heck happened to it. He must've finally figured out that Troo had to be the one who took it from behind those books in his office.

"Are you off your rocker?" Troo tells me. "A course I'm goin' up there tomorrow night." She gives me her most blinding smile. "This is the moment I've been waitin' for. It's a sign from God."

When I don't jump up and clap my hands, she says, "You'll get why this works out so perfectly when I tell you the plan tonight."

She doesn't understand. Not really. She thinks she can beat Father Mickey at his own game, but she can't. She's just a little girl with too-big britches. I know I should try harder to talk her outta her revenge plan, but like Granny always says, stubborn runs worse in our family than a pair of cheap nylons, and that goes double for Troo. Once her mind is made up, nobody is going to stop her and that includes me.

(Like always, sorry, Daddy.)

By the time Troo and me recover from Mother's Spam-and-brussels-sprouts casserole, the sky has gone dark enough for the streetlights to come on. We are on our way to the Latours' to join up with Mary Lane and Artie so we can have the put-off powwow where *aaalll* will be revealed. The fastest way over to Vliet Street is shortcuts.

About halfway through the Hamlins' yard, I ask my sister the question that won't stop rolling over and over in my mind. "Hey, did you break your promise to Mr. Gary and tell Father Mickey about Mrs. Galecki's will during one of your talks?" I'm pretty sure she did, but I'd like to hear her admit it.

Troo reaches over, strips the leaves off a bush and throws them up in the air like confetti. "So what if I did?" she says. "You're the only one around here who makes a Federal case about breakin' promises. What's the big deal?"

I'm positive that finding out about that gigantic inheritance is what made Father Mickey come up with his plan to murder Mrs. Galecki, but I can't let Troo know that. It doesn't seem like she would, but my tough little nut would feel terrible about causing somebody else to accidentally die, the same way she feels terrible about causing Daddy's crash. That's why I tell her, "No big deal. Just wonderin'."

After coming out of the Hamlins' and crossing the alley over to the Latours', Troo jiggles open the unhinged gate. From inside the house, we can hear Mrs. Latour screaming at the kids about brushing their teeth and getting into their pj's. That sounds so good to me and Troo knows that, so she grabs me by the wrist and drags me down to where Mary Lane and Artie are already waiting for us in the bomb shelter.

Troo and me had never seen one of these things until we moved onto Vliet Street. (Daddy told us we didn't need one out on the farm because "Joe McCarthy's full of hooey. The only Reds we have to worry about, girls, are the ones from Cincinnati.")

Tonight's not the first time I've been down here. Our first day in the city, Troo and me met Artie over at the playground. He brought us over to his yard, showed us the shelter and told us how his dad is sure that we're gonna get bombed by the Russians, it's just a matter of time. Artie bragged about how his family can live down here for two weeks or more. In my opinion, that was, and still is, a harebrained idea. You stuff all the Latours into a small space like this they are going to kill each other before any radiation could.

I get the heebie-jeebies when I'm closed up, but the underground hole isn't too bad if you keep the door open. But once it's shut, like it is now, it feels like I think it would if you were buried alive with lots of canned goods and candles.

The reason Troo insisted we meet in the bomb shelter is not only because she adores it, but because she's being extra, extra careful about Father Mickey or some blabbermouth finding out what we're up to. That might sound kinda silly, but she's right, ya know. These blocks have ears and eyes. And motoring mouths. My sister wants to lay out her revenge plan in absolute, walls-of-steel secrecy.

"This meeting is called to order," Troo announces, and makes us say the Girl Scout Promise for some reason. "On my honor, I will try to serve God and my country, to help others at all times . . ."

For the next half hour, she spells out exactly what is expected of us, what parts we'll be playing in her revenge plan against Father Mickey tomorrow night. Because I can't tell her without letting her know what part *she* played in *his* plan, she thinks she's only going after a priest who got Mother an annulment and is the head of a gang of altar boy thieves. Only I know that Father Mickey is much more than that. He's an attempted murderer who is trying to frame Ethel for something he did.

When my sister's done explaining, she folds her arms across her chest and says, "Any questions?"

She taps her foot on the concrete floor. "Sally?" She's staring at my hands, where there is a whole lotta shakin' goin' on.

I answer, "No, no questions," and so does Artie.

But Mary Lane says, "Yeah, I got a couple." She fans her hand in front of her nose. "What the hell did you eat for supper tonight, Fartie? The Wisconsin Gas Company?"

Chapter Twenty-eight

I don't know if it's a sin to skip the fish fry, but everybody sure acts like it is. In the winter or when it rains, people drive their cars if they've got one. But on a clear summer night like this one, that's considered bragging. For blocks ahead and behind Troo and me, we can see the faithful heading up Lloyd Street on their way to Mother of Good Hope Church and School for our every-Friday-night supper.

Before we left the house, I went out to the garden to spend some time with Dave, who I have hardly gotten to be alone with lately. That's why I've been feeling a little shy around him. I watched him water the garden, thought how ruggedly handsome he is, a real Viking, then told him, "By the way. When we were playin' kick the can last night, I noticed the light over Mrs. Goldman's stove was on again even though I turned it off weeks ago."

He said, "It's probably a short. I can't tonight, but as soon as I get a chance, I'll take my toolbox over there and make it right."

I waited for a little bit and then asked him what I really wanted to know. "Could you please, please, please tell me how the questionin' of Ethel went?"

When he switched off the hose, his eyes looked like he wanted to tell me, but his mouth said, "I know you're worried, but it's an ongoing investigation, Sally. I wish I could, but I can't discuss it." He reached into his back pocket and took out his wallet. "Your mother and I are going to pick up your grandmother and uncle and drop them off at the church, and then we'll swing back to get Nell and the baby at the apartment." He gave me a couple of dollars. "We'll see you and Troo up there."

So, no thanks to Dave, all I know right now for sure about what's going on with my dear Ethel is that she didn't come back to Mrs. Galecki's after they were through questioning her at the station yesterday. And I only know that because I sat and watched the house all afternoon. Mr. Gary came back from the hospital looking glum.

Ethel's not in jail; Dave would've told me that. She musta gone back to the Core to be with Ray Buck, or Reverend Joe Willow, who is also good at making her feel better. She might also be at the Greyhound Bus station. Since she is the smartest woman I know, she has got to have put two and two together by now and figured out that she's going to get blamed for Mrs. Galecki's coma. She is the perfect patsy. As much as I'm going to miss her, I wouldn't blame Ethel for buying a bus ticket for far, far away, maybe all the way back home to Mississippi to go live in a swamp, which sounds like a dangerous place, but has to be a whole lot safer than staying around here. (Alligators with their huge choppers and sharp claws are attempted murderers, too, but at least a person knows to steer clear of them. Not like you-know-who with his black Irish smile and manicured fingernails.)

On the corner of 54th Street, Troo points and says, "There they are. Right on schedule," and takes off toward Mary Lane and Artie Latour, who are standing out in front of the Sheinners' waiting for us just like Troo told them to last night.

When I catch up to them, even as nervous as I am, Artie makes me smile. He's back to his old self, yo-yoing like it's going out of style. He's already started practicing for when his best friend gets back. If everything goes the way it's supposed to tonight, Artie is going to write to Charlie Fitch tomorrow morning and tell him that he can come home to be adopted by the Honeywells.

Troo can tell Artie's raring to go by how high he's bouncing on his toes, but she asks Mary Lane, "Ready, Freddy?"

Our other best friend tosses her banana peel down and says, "Ready, Betty."

Of course she is. She already went over to the rectory to set up what she needs. She found a better concrete block, one that she won't fall off of this time, and carried it to Father Mickey's office window. She also hid her Brownie camera in the bushes. Artie doesn't have anything to do tonight except be a lookout and stick close to Mary Lane to remind her to stay on point. If she starts chowing down, she might forget all about the plan. (Fish fry Friday is her favorite night of the week and she can get carried away.) Artie's much bigger part will kick in later after all is said and done.

When we round the corner of 58th Street and the church comes into sight, Mary Lane throws down a challenge. "Last one there's gotta sit next to B.O. Montanazza at church this Sunday."

Of course, I get there first, but it's my sister who holds the side door of the school open for us. She says, "Age before beauty," and gives me a goose when we head down the steps to the cafeteria, which is even louder than usual with gossip and complaints about the weather and more gossip. I hear someone say, "The radio reported there might be rain on the way. Somebody else says, "Did you hear about Jilly Wilton? She got caught in the boathouse with Joe Riordan without her blouse," and the whole place reeks of just-waxed floors and steam and so many perfumes and sweat.

When it's our turn to pry apart the sticky trays, the same lunch ladies as always slap limp fish sticks on our plates and a scoop of coleslaw that runs into the rye bread and for dessert there is always fruit cocktail. We'd usually try to find a place at the crowded cafeteria tables, but the cashier told us to go out to the playground. "The janitors set up out there tonight. The heat, ya know," she says, handing back my change.

When the four of us come out of the cafeteria doors, I can see everybody spread across the playground.

"Thally O'Malley!" Like always, Wendy spots me when we get close to the Latours' long, long table. After Artie takes a seat on the end next to his sister, she grins up at me with coleslaw lips and gives me one of her super-duper hugs around my waist. Even though I'm standing right next to her, she yells, "Hi. Hi. Hi. Thit. Now," and tries to pull me down to her lap.

"I can't, Wendy." I'm trying to balance my tray so it doesn't tip over onto her tiara-wearing head. "I gotta go be with my family the same way you're with yours."

Letting loose one of her strong arms, she points over to the set on the playground and says, "Thwing. Now. Thally."

"I'll . . . I'll push you later, okay?" I don't like to fib to her, but I'm sure she'll forget because of her bad memory and she's not so good at telling time. Sometimes she shows up in her Sunday clothes on Wednesdays and sometimes she goes to the playground in the middle of the night.

Wendy says, "Yeth, Thally, later," but Artie's got to tell her, "Tapioca," three times before she'll let the rest of me go.

From behind me, Mary Lane says, "I'll be over there," and weaves through the crowd to the table where her family's camped out.

Across the playground, tall Dave is standing up and whistling with his fingers to make sure Troo and me know that he's waiting for us with saved seats, but I don't budge. Because of our mental telepathy, Troo knows I'm petrified in place and that I want to back out of the plan the same way I do every single time I climb the steps up to the high dive over at the pool.

She says, "Geronimo," and bumps me in the back of the knees to get me unfrozen.

When we set our trays down at the table, Granny in her yellow-and-pink *muu-muu* is quibbling with Mother about something to do with the wedding, so they only give us quick nods.

Uncle Paulie doesn't lift his mouth up from his plate. He's shoveling in his food so he's not late for his job up at Jerbak's.

Smiling Peggy Sure is on her mother's hip. Nell looks a lot like the fish fry. Her hair is flat with grease and her skin looks whiter than the tartar sauce and her mind has probably gone fruitier than the dessert. Troo and me haven't been going over to her apartment much. The way it smells sour and Nell walking around like the star of a zombie movie . . . geez, it's bad. She's across the table from me, staring off into the distance like she is waiting for her ship to come in, which it won't. It already sunk.

Eddie is not here with us because he spends all his time when he's not working at the cookie factory cruising North Avenue with Melinda Urbanski in his pride and joy—his souped-up Chevy.

Keeping her eyes on the crowd, Troo digs into her food with a lot of gusto. I don't know how she can. I have no appetite at all.

If I look out at our neighbors sitting shoulder-to-shoulder on the table benches, all I see is a flock of bleating lambs that don't even know they've been fleeced.

If I look at the cross high up on the church, I think about how God has let me and everybody else in the neighborhood down.

Positively, I cannot look at Dave, who is next to me at the table with his sleeves rolled up. I know I should say something to him about Troo's plan, but if I ever tattled on my sister she'd spend the rest of our lives sucking in her breath when she passed me in the hall so her skin didn't touch mine. She'd treat me forever like I should take the next boat to Molokai, which I gladly would. I'd rather be a leper than not have my sister by my side.

And if I look at Father Mickey, all I can see is exactly what Daddy warned me about. The devil in the details.

"As always, there are a few announcements," Father says. Our pastor is standing in the middle of everything, turning slowly so all of us can hear what important thing he has to say. He doesn't have on his regular black dress. He's being sporty tonight in a short-sleeved black shirt and black pants.

"The Ladies Club has called off its meetings until mid-September," Father Mickey says, reading from a piece of paper. "Sister Raphael would like to remind all you mothers that school uniforms are available through the J.C. Penney catalog this year." When he sees what's next on his list, he puts on a sad face. "Please remember to keep our beloved parishioner, Mrs. Bertha Galecki, in your thoughts and prayers."

Hearing how concerned he sounds, so caring, so . . . he's a better actor even than Charlie Fitch. I can barely keep myself from doing the same thing that poor orphan did. I want to grab my sister and run for our lives. We could stop by the Latours' table and get the address of that family that Charlie went to stay with. Troo and me, we're farm kids. We know a lot about digging and planting and selling vegetables in a roadside stand, especially corn. We could be a real help.

"And . . . ," Father Mickey says, brightening back up again, "I've saved the best for last." He points over our heads to the big hole in the ground next to the rectory that's got the rope around it and the DANGER signs hanging off it. "As a result of your generous contributions and the discounted price we're receiving from Mr. Fazio's construction company, I'm happy to announce that bright and early tomorrow morning the foundation will be poured for the new school!"

Everyone just goes nuts, jumping off the benches and slapping each other on their backs. I think because they really are happy that their kids aren't going to be jammed into the classrooms anymore, but also because they won't have to drop so much of their paychecks into the collection plate this Sunday.

Somebody yells, "Let's hear it for Father Mickey," and starts up, "For he's a jolly good fellow . . . for he's a jolly good fellow . . . for . . ."

Next to me, Troo is singing along and just radiating. It's not the heat tonight that's making her glow. It's the revenge plan that's incubating inside of her, just dying to burst out like an about-to-hatch chick.

She leans over, pinches both of my cheeks and whispers, "You're looking a little green around the gills. You better go over it all in your head one more time to make sure you don't forget anything."

There are a lotta parts to her plan. She added them on to her THINGS TO DO THIS SUMMER list that she made me memorize:

1. ~~Figure out some more ways to torture Molinari.~~

1. Make Father Mickey lose his black Irish temper.

This part will be succesful because there is nobody in the world who is better at getting under somebody's skin. My sister could make Job blow his stack. She's going to threaten Father. Warn him that she's going to tell the police on him for stealing Mrs. Galecki's emerald necklace, which is what I told her to do in the first place, so when you get down to it, whatever happens tonight is all my fault.

2. Wear a turtleneck, take in a deep breath and get strangled.

Troo thinks that after our pastor goes crazy with fear over getting sent to prison, he's gonna wrap his hands around her throat and try to squeeze the life out of her. Only she forgot to wear the turtleneck tonight.

3. Mary Lane takes the picture.

After Father starts choking my sister, that's when Mary Lane is going to get out her camera and shout, "Big cheese," so Father will turn her way and that flashbulb will go off in his eyes and he'll be so shocked and blinded that he'll let go of Troo and she'll run outta the front door of the rectory. Troo thinks a snapshot of Father Mickey trying to strangle her will be the very proof we need. Once we show it to Dave and everybody else in the neighborhood, they will see how awful he is and will have to believe the rest of the stuff we tell them. (Priests can smack you whenever they want to, but we're all fairly sure strangling isn't allowed.)

4. Practice getting away.

I used Daddy's watch to time Troo when she stood on the rectory porch this morning while Father Mickey was saying his regular eight o'clock Mass. She ran in place to get going and then made a sharp right turn at the new school hole in five seconds and woulda been faster if she didn't keep getting tangled up in those concrete poles that surround it.

5. Sally puts the pedal to the metal.

The second Troo comes ripping outta the front door with Father Mickey in hot pursuit, I'm supposed to jump out from a nook in the school where I'll be waiting. He won't know it's me and not her because of the flashbulb spots in front of his eyes and I'll be so far ahead of him with my fly-like-the-wind speed and by that time, it should be dark.

6. ~~Randa Rhonda~~ Rendezvous

Tearing around the big school hole as fast as she can, Troo's going to run down the block to meet up with Mary Lane and Artie, who will be at the church already. The three of them are going to hide in one of the confessionals because even if the plan goes wrong and Father finds them, he can't hurt them because they are seeking sanctuary in the house of God. (We saw that in a movie with bank robbers.)

It isn't the worst plan Troo's ever come up with, the one to catch murdering and molesting Bobby Brophy was, but it still seems too much like skating on thin ice to me. Black thin ice.

Dave is saying to me, "Sally?" in a way that I know he has said it more than once.

When I turn his way, he's grinning and pointing across the street at the Piaskowskis' house. "I forgot to tell you that Betsy and her husband are moving back in tomorrow." He's done a great job of making that empty house look like a home again. The grass is cut, the porch is swept and he even gave a new coat of paint to the little blue birdhouse he made for Junie. "They're both looking forward to getting to know you better."

I'm looking forward to that, too. If I make it through the night.

Troo is swinging her legs out from beneath the table.

She calls to Mother, who has started walking with Granny toward our station wagon that is parked out on the street, "I'm goin' over to the rectory now, Helen, for my religious instruction, just like you told me to."

Mother stops and says, "Fine," and Granny says, "You little banshee," and they go right back at each other.

Dave tells me, "I talked to Father Mickey earlier. He's going to give Troo a ride over to the park after her instruction." Everybody is going straight from here to Washington Park to hear *Music Under the Stars*, they wouldn't miss it. "Paulie's already left for work, so I put the baby's buggy in the third seat of the car. You can sit on Nell's lap on the way over there."

"I'm not goin'. I'm gonna wait for Troo."

It's the first time I've said a word to him the entire fish fry. I feel so fidgety about what we're about to do that I'm afraid if I try talking my voice is going to sound like I got a Mexican jumping bean stuck in my throat. Dave's my father, but he's also a detective. Both of those jobs mean you know when a kid is up to something.

Dave places his hand on my forehead and says to me, "Are you feelin' okay?"

"Just peachy!" I say with a laugh that even to me sounds Virginia Cunningham loonie. I'm sure he's getting ready to question me further, but then Mother calls to him, "Dave! We're waiting."

"Be right there," he hollers back, but his eyes don't leave mine. "The concert starts at eight thirty like always. Ask Father to drop the two of you by the statue. We'll be in our usual spot."

"Sounds . . . sounds . . . good," I say. So good that I want to follow after him to the car, sit on Nell's lap with Peggy Sure in my arms and bury my nose in her neck all the way over to the park and forget this whole darn plan. I wish so bad I could leave with him now to go lie out on our plaid blanket and listen to the orchestra and stare up at the stars and not think for one more second how my sister is already halfway across the playground, halfway to the rectory.

Chapter Twenty-nine

By the time the church bell rings eight times, all that's left is the four of us.

We had to wait to get the plan underway until after the janitors took the tables back into the cafeteria and cleaned up the playground mess. I can hear the last of our neighbors' voices calling to each other down the block. Anybody who drove a car is already at the park staking out a good spot on the grass for the concert.

Artie and Mary Lane are at the back of the rectory. They should be crouching outside Father Mickey's office window by now and I'm where I'm supposed to be, too. In the nook of the school, dying to poke my head out and call to Troo, who is on the porch, *Pretty please with sugar on top, let's forget this whole thing and go listen to* Music Under the Stars. *I'll give you my root beer and my leather coin purses and anything else you want for the rest of our lives,* but my sister doesn't get my mental telepathy, or maybe she does and rings the rectory door-bell anyway. I can hear the chimes, that's how close I am.

From somewhere inside, a light goes on and Father Mickey calls out, "Come in, my child," and that's just what Troo does, making sure that she leaves the front door open a crack so it's easier for her to make a getaway.

I'm watching the minutes tick by on Daddy's watch and when it gets quarter past the hour, I think that Troo's been in there way too long. I'm sure the plan isn't going the way she thought it would. What if she needs my help and I'm standing here twiddling my thumbs? The only way I have of hearing what's happening inside with her and Father Mickey is by leaving my hiding spot and going to listen in. Because of the heat that feels like somebody is holding a feather pillow over my face in the shower, every single one of the rectory windows is open as far as they go. When I press my ear against the screen of the nearest one, the one next to the front door, I can make out voices, but not clearly. Artie and Mary Lane, who are on the opposite side of the building, are closer to the action and must be getting an earful and hopefully soon a good picture of Father Mickey trying to choke Troo and then we can meet up in the confessional and all of us can go over to the park.

"Thally! Thally! Hi! Hi! Hi!"

I think at first that it's my guilty conscience making me hear Wendy because I told her I'd swing with her later and didn't. But when I come away from the window and look in the direction I hear her croaky voice coming from, I can make her out in the full moonlight.

"I thee you."

Oh, Jesus, Mary and Joseph, no, no, no. I watched her leave the fish fry, throwing her Dinah Shore kisses to me all the way down the block. But Wendy, she can be an escape artist. Especially when the whole Latour family is together somewhere, she can get away from her mother so easy because she gets lost in the crowd and that's just what she's done.

"Thally! Thally! Thally!"

She's on the middle of the three school swings, pumping with all her might. I can't yell at her across the playground to hush up, Father Mickey might hear me. And what if he hears her? She could wreck Troo's whole plan. But I can't just ignore her either. Wendy doesn't understand ignoring. I know from years of experience that she'll yell louder and louder the higher and higher she goes, so I do the only thing I can think of. I peel across the blacktop and try to talk her down.

"Wendy, you gotta stop," I pant out as she swings past me. "You gotta be quiet. Please. Tapioca, tapioca, tapioca." I never know how much of what I say she really understands so this is always a shot in the dark. "You should go be with your mom. She's callin' you. She's gonna be mad if you don't." That's worked a couple of times in the past. "See? She's right over there." Wendy doesn't look where I'm pointing. She throws her head back and looks up and then so do I. The moon that was so bright just a few seconds ago is wrapped up in black clouds and the wind is picking up enough that the trees are rustling. "Uh-oh. You know what that means. A storm's comin'." Just like Troo, Wendy is not nuts about thunder and lightning. "It could even be a tornado. You don't want that. Remember what happened to Dorothy in *The Wizard of Oz*?"

"With flyin', Sally," Wendy says, pumping harder.

"Yup . . . yup, that's really good witch flying, but you . . ." I'm trying to get ahold of the swing chain and drag her to a stop, but she's really high and weighs a lot more than I do, and that's not even counting how strong she is. The last time I tried to do this over at the playground, she spun around to get away from me and when she twisted back she knocked me down.

"Be with, Thally," she yells. "With . . . with . . . with."

"Wendy . . . no . . . please, please . . . *shush* . . . *shush* . . . *shhh*." She's asking me to do my impression of the Wicked Witch of the West that makes her laugh so hard, but once I start, she'll want more . . . more . . . more! I don't have time for that. I have to get back to where I'm supposed to be over in the nook of the school. Troo is going to come charging out that rectory door any minute and if I'm not there to do my part, to be the decoy, Father is going to catch her. "All right. Okay," I tell Wendy. "You stay and swing and . . . ah . . . if you're real quiet, I'll come right back in a little while and be the witch, okay?"

When I take off, Wendy doesn't do exactly what I asked her to. She yells again, "Thally! Thally!" but I can't help that. I can't stop.

I hurry to listen in the window again. I can hear much better now. Things are really heating up inside the rectory. Troo is yelling and Father Mickey is, too, then my sister shouts even louder and something breaks and then everything goes quiet. There's a flash, which must be Mary Lane's Brownie bulb, and then Troo comes dashing out the rectory door much faster than when we practiced. She didn't give me the chance to get back to my hiding spot.

My sister whizzes past me, yelling, "Run, Sal, run!"

From inside the house, Father Mickey roars, "Fuckin' kids!" and just like Troo thought he would, he comes charging out the door, which is supposed to be my cue to run across the playground and lose him in the neighborhood, but I barely get five feet when he grabs me from behind, spins me around by my braid and slaps me across the face so hard that I feel my front tooth break on his ring. He is cursing and trying to pull me back up off the ground by my right arm. In the light of the rectory hall that's spilling out behind him, Father Mickey looks rabid. His hair is standing on end and his black Irish eyes look frantic above his mouth that's pulled back into a snarl.

"Help! Help!" I yell, hoping that Troo or Mary Lane or Artie will hear me and come back to rescue me, but they're already too far away.

But there's somebody else who isn't.

His back is to her, so Father can't see Wendy running her crazy windmill way toward us the way I can. Even the lightning that flashes right over our heads doesn't slow her down. She understands that Father Mickey is hurting me, twisting my arm so hard that I think it's going to break. She's coming fast like she did over at the Vliet Street playground the time Buddy Deitrich was bullying me.

Father Mickey barks at me, "I'm going to teach you and your snotty sister a lesson about minding your own business. Where'd she go? And the other kid . . . the kid with the camera. Get up, get up!" He yanks me again, and Wendy, she's almost right on top of us.

I try to shout, "No!" but she bowls into Father Mickey from behind like she's a ball and he's a pin up at Jerbak's. I try to reach out to break his fall, but I'm not fast enough and he goes down hard. His head bounces off the side of one of the poles that are set around the DANGER hole where the foundation is getting poured tomorrow for our new school wing.

I don't know what to do. This is nothing like Troo's plan. Father Mickey is sprawled out next to me. Out for the count.

It takes me a minute or so to get my wits about me, but when I finally get up on my knees and say, "Hello?" my tongue brushes against my front tooth that feels jaggedy and tastes like an iron railing because of the blood. "Father Mickey, ah . . . you . . . you okay?" He's lying tummy down, blending into the blacktop, but his white face is cocked my way. I'm not sure if I should be trying to wake him up. I'm scared about what he's going to do to us when he comes to. Maybe Wendy and me should just run off and leave him. When he wakes up he might have amnesia and forget all about what happened. You can get that if you hit your head as hard as he did. That's the best we can hope for. I try again. "Father?" He doesn't groan. He doesn't thrash around or move at all and once I lean down closer to him, I think that he's not ever going to again. Wendy didn't knock him out cold just for a little while. I'm pretty sure Wendy mighta knocked him out cold *forever.*

I've seen plenty of dead people. Daddy. Granny O'Malley. I saw Bobby after he fell into Sampson's pit over at the zoo. And the longer I stare at Father, the surer I'm getting that it's too late to run inside the rectory, find the telephone and call the operator so she can send one skinny and one fat ambulance man to come put Father Mickey on their stretcher and take him up to St. Joe's with the siren blaring. But I gotta be positive. It takes me three tries to put my two fingers on his neck the same way I've seen Ethel do so many times to Mrs. Galecki when she has one of her spells. His skin is warm and soft under his stubbly beard, but nothing is pounding beneath my fingertips. I think I must be doing it wrong and move down to his wrist. Not a beat. I don't see any other marks on him.

He's only bleeding a little from where his head hit the concrete post. I'm not sure why he's dead. It could have something to do with his neck. It doesn't look right.

From behind me, Wendy says, "Thwing now, Thally?"

She doesn't know what she's done. She doesn't understand death. She swats skeeters and waits for them to fly off again. That's when it really hits me that Wendy Latour has accidentally killed Father Mickey because she was protecting me and the tears come gushing. My whole body is shaking and my mind, it feels like it's spinning away from me and I can't catch up to it. I don't know if I'm grateful or scared or relieved, maybe all of them. So many feelings are whirling around inside of me and I can't tell one from the other. I don't think there's any sadness, though. Not for Father anyway. A good Catholic should be feeling sorrowful about his death, but I'm not. I'm not rejoicing, but I'm not broken up either. I feel *something* every time I look at him, I just don't know what the word for it is.

"Thally?" Wendy comes up behind me and cups her hands under my arms and lifts me up to my feet. She lays her head on my shoulder and gives me a gentle honey bear hug. I can smell fish sticks and fruit on her T-shirt when she gives me a couple of hard pats on the back. "Don' cry. Don' cry, Thally O'Malley," she says, licking the tears off my cheek. "All better now."

We stay there together, rocking back and forth like we are slow dancing under the darkening sky. The wind pushes a piece of trash across the playground and the swings are twisting and the flagpole is making a *clink . . . clink . . .* sound. It seems like we are in each other's arms forever until I realize I gotta do something and even longer before I figure out what.

"Wendy?" I whisper.

"Yeth?"

"I wanna play a game, do you?"

"Yeth, Thally," she says, unlocking her arms.

I pick up the rhinestone tiara that got knocked off when she tackled Father Mickey and set it back where it belongs on her shiny black hair. "We're gonna play hide-and-seek. You remember that one?"

She nods really fast, but she doesn't. Every single time we play a game I have to go over the rules with her.

"Go into that little nook." I point to the part of the school where I was supposed to hide and wait for Father Mickey. "I want you to put your hands over your eyes and start countin' very, very slow and I'm going to hide and then you can come find me."

"Then thwing?"

"Yup . . . then we'll swing."

"With laugh."

"And witch laugh. Go on now."

This time Wendy does exactly what I tell her to do and while she's counting around the corner with her wide face in her chubby fingers, "One . . . free . . . nine . . ." I squat down and push with everything I got. When he flips over . . . Father's face . . . he still looks so handsome.

I know what I'm about to do is against the law. You're supposed to tell the police if someone dies, even if it's an accident. I also know that according to the Church, I'm committing a sacrilege. Horrible as he was, Father Mickey deserves a proper burial. But this isn't the first time I've examined my conscience. I've spent countless sleepless nights questioning what's right and what's wrong. I finally decided that knowing bad from good isn't always so black-and-white. I mean, there *are* times when you know you're about to do something that maybe you shouldn't so you stop yourself, but there are other times when you know you're committing a sin but have no choice except to go full speed ahead. You can't always pick what's right. Sometimes you can only pick what's less wrong.

This is one of those times.

I can't leave Father Mickey here to be found in the morning by one of the old neighborhood ladies. When he doesn't show up for eight o'clock Mass, they'll come storming up to the rectory. The police will be called in and all sorts of questions will be asked. Dave will remember that after the fish fry, Troo and me stayed up here for her religious instruction. My sister will be cool, but when Dave questions me, I will put up a good fight at first, but the love I have for him will eventually win out and I'll confess everything. In nothing flat, what happened here tonight will fly through our neighborhood.

No one will believe me when I try to explain that what Wendy did was an accident. No matter how hard I try to convince our neighbors that she didn't mean to murder Father, that she was only trying to save me, I know what will happen. They will not watch Wendy's loping run or hear her funny way of talking or remember her swinging at the playground with her blouse off and smile to themselves the way they do now. Our neighbors won't even feel sorry for her. Every time they look at her, all they will see is the girl who ended the life of the best pastor we ever had. Her picture will be in the newspaper and on television. She might even have to go to jail or reform school. I can't let that happen. I won't. Mongoloids don't live as long as the rest of us and over my dead body is Wendy Latour spending whatever time she's got left on earth where there aren't any swings.

She calls over from the school corner, "Ready or no, here I go, Thally!"

I shout back, "No, stay there, Wendy! Gimme a minute."

I'm sure God wouldn't have let Wendy tackle Father Mickey hard enough to kill him if that wasn't part of His plan. Our fate is in His hands, right? Even though I'm positive that what I'm about to do really is for the best, it wouldn't hurt to get a second opinion.

I bow my head and pray:

> DEAR LORD, I KNOW THAT I HAVE NOT BEEN THAT GOOD LATELY, SO I PROBABLY DON'T DESERVE ONE, BUT YA KNOW, IF YOU COULD JUST GIVE ME A SIGN THAT WHAT I'M ABOUT TO DO IS OKAY WITH YOU, THAT'D BE GREAT. AMEN.

When I open my eyes and look to the heavens for my answer, the wind that was blowing suddenly stops and the dark clouds that were so threatening break apart to let the moon shine down on me again. That's all I need to know. This is His celestial way of giving me two thumbs-up. God is letting me know that I am in His good graces. It's not my imagination. How could it be?

Wendy calls to me again from around the corner in her croaking voice, "Now, Thally?"

"Almost," I holler back.

All it takes is a couple of strong pushes to roll Father Mickey into the deep hole, where he lands with a soft *thump*.

When I get up off my knees and scurry around the corner to hide so Wendy can seek, I think about how tomorrow bright and early, after the cement trucks come and pour their load, Father will become part of the foundation for the new school. After I call out, "Ready!" I also think how the next time somebody tells me that the Almighty works in mysterious ways, I will have to agree with them.

Chapter Thirty

Whehen I didn't show up at the church confessional the way I was supposed to according to Troo's plan, my sister came looking for me. She heard my Wicked Witch of the West cackling from down the block and the three of them followed it to the school playground. Of course, none of them are shocked to see Wendy. Just like the time she showed up in our bathroom eating a stick of butter, her appearing out of nowhere happens all the time. She really is like a mirage.

"Well?" Troo asks, coming to my side. I check her throat right away to see if Father Mickey tried to strangle her, but I don't see any marks, just a coupla skeeter bites. There's a handprint on her right cheek, though.

Mary Lane and Artie ask at the same time, "Well?" They want to know the nitty-gritty.

"After Troo came peelin' out of the rectory, Father was right behind her, but I had a big head start and got across the playground in nothin' flat." I run my tongue over my tooth. They can't see that it's broken as long as I don't smile. "I was going so fast, he didn't even bother tryin' to follow me. Probably he's halfway to Mexico already," I tell them, because a lot of times in the movies that we see at the Uptown Theatre, that's where people go when they are on the lam so that seems really believable.

Mary Lane, who's up on top of the monkey bars, points down to the ground where she left her camera for safekeeping and says excited, "I got the picture. It woulda been better if I waited until Father got his hands around Troo's throat instead of just slappin' her across the face, but Fartie here"—she cocks her head at him— "knocked my hand and the camera went off. I have to go to the zoo tomorrow with my dad, but I'll take the film to get developed at Fitzpatrick's soon as we get back."

As soon as Artie is done giving Wendy an under doggie on the swings, he comes back and asks, "Should I still talk to the altar boys tomorrow?" He's anxious to do his part of the plan. "See if I can get them to tell their parents what they did?"

Before Troo can answer, I say, "Naw. Don't bother. I'm tellin' ya, Father Mickey isn't comin' back. There's no sense gettin' the boys in trouble and everybody else in the neighborhood all worked up. I think we should leave things just like they are, don't you, Troo?" It is her plan after all.

Troo says, "Yeah . . . okay," but she's giving me her squinty sister look that means *What kind a crock is this?*

When the church bells get done ringing nine times, Mary Lane swings down from the bars and when her back is turned, I pick her Brownie up off the ground like I'm being courteous, but I'm not. I flick the switch and open up the back of the camera long enough so her picture of Father Mickey gets ruined. The last thing we need is proof of any kind of what happened up here tonight. The second we get home, I'm taking Troo's genius plan that she wrote down in her notebook and flushing it down the toilet.

Mary Lane says, "Thanks," and hangs the camera back around her neck. "I gotta get over to the park. My ma and dad are waitin'. They brought caviar and champagne." (What she really means is that they brought her a box of jujubes and a bottle of orange soda.)

"Oh, shoot," I say, slapping my forehead and doing my best to sound disappointed. "I wish we could go, too, but I just remembered. We told Granny at supper that we'd wash out Uncle Paulie's socks 'cause we missed this afternoon, so that's what we gotta do." I turn to Artie and Wendy. "You guys should also get a move on before your dad notices you're not there." (Mr. Latour uses a leather strap when you don't follow his rules.)

Of course, my sister knows what I said about going to Granny's is a big fat lie, but she says, "Yeah. Ya better get outta here *toot sweet!*" which is French for—get going!

Mary Lane and Artie right away say their good-byes, but Wendy, she gets her inscrutable face up close to mine, and says, "Thafe now," before she windmills off after them.

Watching her take off down the block, I'm thinking that I'll be wondering every time I see her or when I can't sleep and maybe for the rest of my life . . . does she understand what she did? Does she? I know she's a lot smarter than she lets on, she's proved it to me a couple of times, but . . .

"What gives?" Troo asks, exasperated.

"I gotta show you something."

I lead her over to the DANGER hole, telling her what happened along the way. What Father said, what I did after Wendy did what she did. For a little while, I'm not sure if my sister believes me because when we get to the edge of the hole, the priest is real hard to see down there in his black sporty shirt and pants, but then Troo hawks a loogie, and says, "We need a coupla shovels."

I knew she'd say that. "There should be some in the . . . shed."

She knows the one I mean. It's where Father Jim kept all his gardening supplies when he was still our pastor and growing the most beautiful irises and other gorgeous flowers that still smell wonderful tonight. He left a little part of himself behind.

"I'll go get 'em. Wait for me over at the ladder," Troo says, for once not teasing me. No matter how sure I am that Father Mickey has to get buried so the men pouring the cement won't see him tomorrow, a shed is still a shed. If my sister wasn't here to take charge, I hate to think that I'd leave Father to get found by the church ladies in the morning because I was too much of a scaredy-cat to do the right thing.

What would I do without my Troo?

When she comes back, she's got a flashlight that is running low on batteries stuck in her armpit. She's also lugging two shovels that are kinda like the ones they use over at Holy Cross Cemetery, only smaller. She throws them down into the hole, hands me the flashlight and backs down the ladder that was left there after Denny Desmond lost that walk-across-the-plank challenge and ended up breaking his collarbone.

Of course, Troo goes down first because she is so much braver than me. She shines the light on lumpy Father Mickey, who is still here, which is such a relief. When Troo left me alone with him to go to the shed, I got the creepiest feeling that he was gonna resurrect himself outta the hole, grab me around the throat and whisper into my ear, "Gotcha!"

Taking baby steps toward where he's lying, I can see that Father Mickey landed facedown, which is another real blessing. Him looking at Troo and me while we throw dirt on his face might be too much even for my sister.

Daddy had to bury dead animals out on the farm, so we know just how it's done. We don't talk at all, just breathe hard, but while we're working, even though I believe with my whole heart and soul that what we're doing is the best thing for Wendy and the rest of the neighborhood, I'm wondering if I'm going to be having nightmares over this the same way I do about Bobby carrying me over from the lagoon and Daddy's dying, but there's no turning back now.

After one final scoop, Troo says, "That should do it. Grab one a his feet." She takes the other one and we drag Father into the hole that isn't six feet deep, maybe only three. Deep enough so the man driving the cement truck tomorrow shouldn't notice anyway.

After we get done patting the last bit of dirt back into place, my sister wipes the sweat off her forehead and tells me something that surprises me. "We should say some words. You first."

Together the O'Malley sisters bow our heads and I say the only thing I can think of, it's what Daddy always said in the spring after he finished planting. "Ye shall reap what ye shall sow."

But when it's Trooper's turn to say good-bye to Father Mickey, she does me one better. She says very solemnly, "His mean justified his end," and I don't bother correcting her.

Chapter Thirty-one

By the time Dave and Mother got home from *Music Under the Stars* last night, Troo and me had already cleaned all the digging dirt off in the tub, talked some more about what happened over at the rectory and got our stories straight. When the lovebirds came in the back door, laughing like they had a great time over at the park and didn't want it to end, the O'Malley sisters were in our bed pretending to be asleep.

After Dave went upstairs to turn in, Mother slipped into our bedroom. I breathed in the smell of Blatz and her Chanel No. 5 when she bent down and gave us each a kiss, which is the only time she likes to show that she loves us—when we're asleep. (She thinks she's being tricky, but Troo and me find her lip prints on our cheeks in the morning.)

I spent most of the night going over in my mind what Wendy accidentally did to Father Mickey. And how Troo and me buried him. But when I finally fell asleep, I didn't have any nightmares, which I took as another thumbs-up from God.

Troo decided it would be best if we make ourselves scarce today, so we are up and at 'em early, even before Mr. Peterson gets here with the milk. So that Mother doesn't get sore at us, I scribble a note for her and tape it to the coffeepot before we take off:

> Good morning! Sorry. I forgot to tell you. Mary Lane invited us to go see the new zoo today. Be back later! xxxooooxxx P.S. You looked swankier than Mamie Van Doren last night at the fish fry.

My sister is riding me over to the Lanes' on her handlebars. When we pass by our neighbors' houses, I picture them snuggling together in their beds, dreaming sweet dreams. What a surprise they're in for this morning when Father Mickey doesn't show up for Mass.

When Troo pedals past the Molinaris' house, she says into my ear, "What the hell do ya think happened to him?"

I don't answer her because the reason that Greasy Al never showed back up to get his revenge against my sister for sending him to reform school even I can't imagine.

After rounding the corner of 58th Street, two houses down, I hop off and Troo dumps her bike on the Lanes' front lawn. We know which room is Mary Lane's. We've done this a million times before. After Troo gives me a boost through our friend's window, she stands on the hose faucet and slithers over the sill after me.

Troo wants to get some warm water out of the bathroom so she can stick Mary Lane's hand in it, but I stop her. I'm feeling a smidge disloyal for not telling our other best friend the truth about what happened to Father Mickey, but I guess Troo's right, we need to keep it to ourselves because it is better to be safe than sorry. She *is* Mary Lane, after all. There is no one better at keeping secrets, but she might work the story of what happened last night into a no-tripper tale with gypsy priests and wieners and blood-dripping altar boys, not even realizing she is doing it. We can't take that chance.

I gotta be careful when I shake Mary Lane awake by her bony shoulder because, I'm not kidding, it's so sharp she could use it to open tin cans. "Mary Lane. Mary Lane."

"What?" she says, sitting up straight from the waist and reminding me again of that actress in *The Bride of Frankenstein* when she's on the doctor's table right after she's brought to life. Mary Lane's permanent wave hasn't settled down at all.

Because of our mental telepathy, I know Troo's about to crack wise about her electrified hair, so I hurry and tell Mary Lane, "It's a matter of life and death. We need to go out to the zoo with you today. I can't wait anymore. I gotta see Sampson." That's not a lie I'm telling her just to get out of the neighborhood for the day. I really do need to see him bad. It's been almost three months. He must be missing me as much as I'm missing him.

Mary Lane, who smells like her pillow, which I'm sure is stuffed with potato chips, says, "Fine by me, but we gotta ask my dad."

After she pulls on her usual high-tops, T-shirt and shorts, the three of us go out to the kitchen and beg Mr. Lane to take us with him to work. Being the nice man that he is, he swigs down his cup of breakfast java and says, "Yeah, sure. The more the hairier." (He is known for these kinds of animal jokes. I think telling them is part of his job the same way shoveling poop is.)

Mary Lane was right when she told me at the beginning of summer that it would take at least three buses to get out to the new zoo on Bluemound Road. It takes almost a half hour by car. It kills me to say it, but it was worth it. It's really nice. And HUGE. There's an all-the-time pony ride and the hot dogs they sell are the Oscar Meyer wiener whistle kind and the critters have a lot more room to roam. I want to see Sampson right away, but Mary Lane wants to show us around. She is a big believer in saving the best for last.

We're her guests, so that's what we do. Spend the whole day, running here and there. The polar bears' area looks like the North Pole and Monkey Island is something straight out of a jungle. There's lots of animals that we didn't even have at the old zoo, like seals and reindeer. The Reptile House is full of snakes. The boa constrictor sticks his tongue out and makes me think of Bobby Brophy. The only out-of-place cage we come across is the one that belongs to the camel, who doesn't look like he lives in the desert of Arabia, but the dirt lot on the corner of 53rd Street.

When I ask her why, Mary Lane tells me, "That's the best Dad could do. Bringin' in all that sand costs a lot of money and camels are really stupid and they spit worse than your sister. What'd ya do to your tooth, by the way?"

I forgot all about it. "Ah . . . I . . . tripped and um . . . can we go see Sampson now?"

Troo and me follow her past the flamingoes and the penguins over to the Primate House. Mary Lane pulls open the door and says, "He's got a big yard all to himself, but he's indoors today. This way." She leads us past the chimps and the mandrills and all the other monkeys doing their shenanigans until we get to the biggest and busiest cage of all.

Mary Lane clears her throat and announces very professionally, "Zoo business. Comin' through," and we push to the front of the crowd.

Seeing him in all his glory, it makes my knees go floppy. I tenderly press my hand against the glass and wait for him to do the same, the way he always did, but Sampson stays where he is, looking at me with his fudgey brown eyes the same way he's looking at everybody else. He isn't singing *Don't Get Around Much Anymore* or *Take Me Out to the Ballgame*. He's not beating his chest because he's so happy to see me, after so much time apart. He just hangs there for a while from his ceiling rope and when he gets tired of that, he starts looking for that thing in his ear that he's still not found.

Troo says, "Doesn't look like he remembers you," and I can't get mad because it seems that way to me, too.

I think Mary Lane knows how let-down I'm feelin' because she says very kindly, "C'mon, we gotta go. Time to meet Dad in the parkin' lot."

On the ride back home, I'm wondering if Sampson acted cool toward me because he's living in a much better place than he used to. Sorta the same thing happened when Troo and me went to visit our old Vliet Street friend Louise Greely after she moved to a much bigger house near Enderis Park that had a huge yard and a swing of her own hanging off a tree. We didn't have much to say to each other anymore either.

Sampson's snub woulda cut me to the core in the olden days, but for some reason I'm going to have to think long and hard about, when Mr. Lane pulls up in front of our house I notice that my heart isn't feeling shattered into a million pieces. More like one of its wings fell off.

Chapter Thirty-two

Dave is out on our front porch steps, reading the evening newspaper. He calls out a friendly "Thanks, Phil" to Mr. Lane when he drops us off, but when Troo and me try to scoot past him, Dave sounds more like Joe Friday from *Dragnet* than Mr. Anderson from *Father Knows Best*.

"Girls, wait a minute. I need to talk to you," he says. When I slow down, Troo pokes me in the back, so Dave follows us into the house, straight through to the kitchen.

I say to Mother, who's standing in front of the stove, "We're home." Whatever she's cooking is making it stink worse in here than the lions' den up at the zoo. "Did you get my note?"

Mother says, "It's about time. Supper's in ten minutes," and goes back to stirring.

"What happened to you two last night?" Dave asks, crossing his arms over his chest and leaning against the counter in front of the sink. "Why didn't you come over to the park?"

The O'Malley sisters knew he'd ask us this.

Just like we planned it out last night under the sheets, Troo says, "Didn't Father Mickey tell you this mornin' after Mass?" Dave almost always attends the eight o'clock. "He kept me later than he usually docs and then he couldn't give us a ride over there because he forgot he had an important meeting, so Sally and me came straight home, took our baths and went to bed."

I can't wait to tell him all about the new zoo, but I ask him, "How was the concert?" because that's the polite thing to do.

Troo grins and says, "Wait, before you go into all that—after we finished up last night, guess what? Father Mickey told me I don't have to come back anymore. Isn't that great?!" Instead of being in a freak show or a drummer in Sal Mineo's band or a professional Kleenex-flower maker, my sister could be a movie actress when she grows up, that's how easy she can turn the truth off and on. "You're gonna have to order me a new school uniform, Helen. I did such a good job on my religious instructions that I'm purer than Ivory soap! I'm going back to Mother of Good Hope next month!"

See, that's Troo genius at work. I never would've thought of adding that part.

When they don't congratulate her, Troo says, "Call Father up and ask him if you don't believe me." Both Mother and Dave do look pretty stunned.

Dave says, "I'm afraid that would be . . . I have some bad news, girls. Father Mickey appears to be missing."

Troo brings her hands up to her cheeks and says, so concerned, "Oh, no! That's terrible. Really?"

"Did Father happen to mention who he had that important meeting with last night?" Dave asks.

Troo and me decided that she would be the one to answer any hard questions he had. She is very good under pressure. And even though I haven't told her that I adore Dave, she knows. She doesn't trust me not to fall into a heap and confess what we did and she shouldn't.

"The meeting? Uh . . . I can't remember if he . . . oh, yeah," Troo says, snapping her fingers. "That's right. Father told us that he was goin' to see Mr. Fazio to thank him again for startin' work on the school."

Dave is about to ask something else, but Mother says, "Wash your hands and set the table, girls," and then to her husband-to-be, "Could you join me in the bedroom for a minute?"

They're gone for a while and come back into the kitchen just as I'm filling the last glass with milk. Mother looks so pretty in her Peter Pan–collar blouse and freshened-up face that I forget and smile.

"What happened to your tooth?" she shouts, taking my chin between her fingers.

"Oh, I . . . I . . ."

Troo says, "She broke it on the swings over at the school playground when she was waitin' for me to finish up with Father Mickey. She should be more careful, shouldn't she."

"She certainly should." Mother is tilting my head this way and that to get a better look. "I'll make an appointment first thing tomorrow with Dr. Heitz. I'm not sure there's anything he can do about it, but . . . oh, damn . . . the pot's boiling over," she says when she hears the lid clatter.

During supper Dave doesn't talk much except to say, "Please pass the . . . what is this dish called again, dear?"

Mother says, like it's the best thing she's ever made, "Cow tongue in turnip sauce."

That sorta takes the spunk outta all of us except for Lizzie. But she eats shoes, too.

Neither one of them asks us anything else about Father Mickey. I think they agreed in the bedroom not to talk about it anymore because it's not suitable supper conversation. They wouldn't want to scar us for life. Only once does Dave say, like he's thinking out loud, "I'm going to have to question Tony Fazio first thing tomorrow morning."

They spend the rest of the supper discussing Dave's sister, Betsy, and her husband, Richie. Dave helped them move boxes back into their house today. Mother also tells us that she is going to look for a wedding suit like the kind Jackie Kennedy wears with a matching pillbox hat. Of course, her mentioning pills makes me think about Ethel and Mrs. Galecki's coma. I know I should, but I'm too yellow-bellied to ask what's going on with them. If it is fatal news, that will be the last straw.

Between going over and over in my mind whether Troo and me have any chance of getting caught burying Father Mickey and my worrying about what's to become of Ethel, I barely notice how disgusting the food is. Not until Dave throws his napkin down on the table and does a little lying himself. "Delicious as always, dear."

Mother says, "I'm so glad you like it. I'm thinking of entering it in the cook-off."

I have to work hard to keep myself from groaning. The cook-off is held during the celebration that marks the end of summer. In two weeks, we'll have the biggest party we have around here. The neighborhood ladies bring all the food and there is a contest for the best dishes. All I can see is bodies littered all over Vliet Street if

Mother serves her cow tongue in turnip sauce to the crowd. We'll never even make it to the crowning of the queen or hear any good rock 'n' roll from the Do Wops. I won't get to dance with Henry. It's hard to do the box step when you're throwing up.

When Mother lights her after-dinner cigarette and Troo and me get up to do the dishes, now that supper is over, Detective Dave is free to go back to interrogating us.

He asks my sister, "You sure Father Mickey was still at the rectory last night when you left?"

Thank goodness, I can always count on Troo to cover her tracks, even in an ambush. She scrapes a plate into the garbage and says, *"Absolument."*

"Sally?" he asks. "Is that how you remember it, too?"

It's my turn to wash, so I'm already at the kitchen sink filling it up. I'm so glad that I've got my back to him and he can't see my face or my goose bumps. "Yes, sir." Most sins are about doing or saying something you're not supposed to, but there are also sins that are about *not* doing something or *not* saying something you're supposed to. Those are called sins of omission. That's what I'm committing when I tell Dave, "Just like Troo said. When we headed for home last night, Father Mickey was right where we left him."

Chapter Thirty-three

After Dave and me get done watching *Peter Gunn* tonight, he tells me, "I'm going over to the Goldmans' to fix the short in the stove light. Want to come along? Buy you an ice cream afterwards."

As good as spending some time alone with Dave and seeing Henry behind the soda fountain at Fitzpatrick's sounds, school's going to start soon and I do not want to get rapped on the knuckles by Sister Raphael when I show up the first day with a half-written assignment. I also gotta finish so Troo has enough time to copy it. Summer is almost over. The block party is in three days.

I tell Dave, "Thanks, but I can't. I gotta get the rest of my charitable story written," so he goes over to Vliet Street with his toolbox alone.

Troo is in the bathroom in front of the mirror putting the finishing touches on her ventriloquist act for the Queen of the

Playground contest before she goes over to Fast Susie Fazio's for a sleepover and some *cannolis*. Mother is on the phone with Aunt Betty jabbering about this new man she is dating who is a real catch because it's Mr. Stanley Talmidge. Troo thinks Mr. Talmidge looks like Quasimodo and that he's lucky to have something else going for him. He owns the Uptown movie theatre.

So that's why I come out to my and Daddy's bench in the backyard to write more of my story with my flashlight. I need some peace and quiet, but that isn't working out either.

Mr. Moriarity's dog is barking worse than ever. I think Lizzie broke his heart and is now seeing the Johnsons' poodle. The crickets are rubbing their legs together to beat the band. I can't usually hear them, but tonight a strong warm breeze is bringing the sound of the kids at the playground trying to get in their last licks. Loudest of all are the cookie factory dads and their wives out on their steps, giving each other their two cents' worth on the mystery of Father Mickey's disappearance. "What do you think coulda happened to him? Do you think he was kidnapped? Murdered?"

Even though it's been weeks since Troo and me buried Father, the neighborhood just won't shut up. Even during Mass this Sunday, which Father Louie returned to say from his special dry retreat, I could hear people taking guesses in the Communion line. And it's not only up at church or on the stoops. No matter where you go or what you do, Father Mickey's missing is the subject of all conversations. There was even a story in both newspapers with a picture of him looking so sharp, and a quote from Mrs. Latour: "He was a saint. I don't know how we'll manage without him."

Mostly, it seems like people are leaning toward foul play. The cops especially think that. Dave and Detective Riordan have been searching the rectory for clues and when they're not doing that, they're working hard to find Father's body in the lagoon and Jack Hoyt Woods and garbage cans because you got to have a dead one to prove something like murder. Troo and me aren't worried a bit. Well, Troo isn't.

The police are also asking everybody a lotta questions about their whereabouts the night Father disappeared. They're even questioning kids. I got the jitters over that until Troo reminded me that we can count on Artie and Mary Lane. When Artie is grilled, he will keep mum about the revenge plan no matter how high-strung he is. My sister told him if he doesn't keep his mouth shut about us being up at the rectory that night he has to give back the coonskin cap. And Mary Lane, I'm especially not concerned about her spilling the beans. She's been tortured by the best in the world—nuns. So detectives asking her a couple of questions wouldn't bother her at all. (The one thing that is bothering her, though, is why the picture she took of Father up at the rectory slapping Troo that night didn't turn out. I told her it musta been bad film, but she is leaning toward evil spirits. I expect very soon to hear one heck of a blood-dripping-gypsies-with-wieners ghost story.)

Everybody has been so caught up in thinking about Father Mickey's vanishing that they've already forgotten about the other big news we've had. Mrs. Galecki has come out of her coma! Doc Keller told Mother at her visit this week that it is still nip and tuck, but he has high hopes that Mrs. G will recover—not fully, but at least she might be back to where she was in the first place. Dotty and drooly, but not dead.

Because it was all very under-the-covers, hardly anyone in the neighborhood knows the way I do why Mrs. Galecki got so sick in the first place. I was sure that Father Mickey had given her too much or too little of her medicines to try and murder her for her inheritance money, but it turns out that I was wrong. Mrs. Galecki had something running through her that wasn't supposed to be there and *that's* what made her go into the coma. A much happier Mr. Gary told me after a couple of whiskey sours and some hands of Old Maid, "The docs don't know what it was in Mom's blood, only that it was something they'd never seen before. Something foreign. It's a real mystery."

Not to me, it isn't. I mighta been mistaken about *how* Father Mickey attempted to murder her, but I'm not mistaken that he did try to. Father was the *only* person from around here who had been to someplace foreign. Aunt Betty told me the afternoon Troo and me went to the Five and Dime that he was sent to a bunch of different places after he left the seminary and one of them was the Congo, which is in the dark continent of Africa. I've seen those little Pygmy people in Tarzan movies. They're always sneaking around the jungle trying to poison somebody. That's what Father Mickey musta done. Not with a blow dart, that's stupid. I bet he mixed some poison he borrowed from the Pygmies into Mrs. Galecki's fresh-squeezed lemonade on one of those days Ethel went out to do her errands.

Of course, my good friend was let off the hook for any wrongdoing because Ethel has never been anywhere foreign. So, hurray! She has not had to pack up her things and move down to the Core. She is right where she belongs, next door with Ray Buck sitting in the screened-in porch this very minute, which is another reason why I came out in my yard besides wanting to work on my "How I Spent My Charitable Summer" story. I wanted to listen to their low talking and clinking ice cubes and jazzy music, which is such an improvement over Mr. Gary's *Oklahoma!* music, I just can't tell you. Right before he left for the airport to go back to California, I gave him the two leather coin purses to take back to Father Jim so they would steady match, but in all the excitement, I forgot to ask him if he remembered to talk to his mother about changing back her Last Will and Testament so Ethel will inherit the money she needs to open her school for children when Mrs. Galecki really does die, which I'm not too concerned about anymore. For goodness sakes, if Pygmy poison can't kill her, what can?

"Ya alright over there, Miss Sally?" Ethel calls over the fence.

"Now that you're back, I am," I holler. "I don't think I could take much more of hearin' about the wind sweepin' down the plains."

Ethel rewards me with her million-dollar laugh that I have been missing. It is so rich and there is no end to it. "Thought ya'd like to know that the doctor told me this afternoon Miss Bertha might be comin' home next week if she gets more of her strength back. Ya still got the Nancy Drew story to read to her?"

"Yes, ma'am." I checked it back out of the library last week, hoping she'd ask.

Ethel says, "That's good. Real good," and I don't know if she's talking to me or Ray Buck because she's gone quiet again, so I get back to being busy, too:

How I Spent My Charitable Summer
By Sally Elizabeth O'Malley (Part 2)

We were all so surprised to hear about the disappearance of Father Mickey. Especially my sister, Troo, (known to you as Margaret) was so broken up because Father was so kind to allow her to come back to school. She also got me a souvenir bench from the old zoo that means a lot to me, so she really went all-out this summer.

I would also like to mention that Mary Lane was also charitable, just in case she screws up and forgets to write her story again this year. She won the Billy the Book-worm prize this summer at the library and took Troo and me to the Uptown to see that movie by Alfred Hitch-cock that everybody has been talking about. Just a warn-ing to you and the other sisters. You may not want to see *Psycho* or you will never want to sit in a rocking chair or take a shower or teach a kid named Norman for as long as you live. (I don't know if nuns go to motels, but if you do, that will be out of the question, too.)

My mother and Dave will no longer be living in sin after September 24th because they're getting married. Dave took all of us to the State Fair in West Allis and we ate cream puffs. I brought two back for Ethel Jenkins, who had a pretty rough summer. She really needed some creamy filling. Troo and me rode the Tilt-a-Whirl and the roller coaster. Dave won Mother a teddy bear and also won me a couple of goldfish for my fish tank by throwing ping-pong balls that looked exactly like Gran-ny's eyeballs into little jars. Troo also got to go to the Freak Show to pay her regular visit to the fat lady named Vera from Moline, Illinois. Troo told Vera that she was looking like she had lost some weight, so that was also charitable. We also talked to the fortune-teller, Rhonda of the Seven Veils, who told us just like she does every year, "Soon *aaalll* will be revealed."

Just thinking that Rhonda might be right makes me shiver on this hottest of hot nights. Troo and me may think we are home free, but just like Granny always says, "The best laid plans of mice and men," which I take to mean that somebody could have the most genius plan in the world and you could still find yourself caught in a trap. I'm worried about Wendy Latour blowing it. She could say something after church one of these days like, "Father Mickey . . . fall down go boom," but since nobody really pays attention to her except Artie and me and her mother, who is real busy with the rest of her brood, that *should* be all right. And me, I'm worried about me. I know from experience that it's hard to keep a secret this big even if it's for the best of all reasons. I would like to tell Dave the whole kit and kaboodle about what happened to Father Mickey. Maybe someday I will. After Wendy Latour passes away. Right after her funeral, once I can walk and talk again, I could come clean as long as Dave promises on his life not to tell Troo that I told him. We'll see.

Dave opens the screen door and calls, "Sally?"

Like I'm caught doing something that I shouldn't, I jump and say, "What?"

I'm surprised he's back from Mrs. Goldman's so soon. I'm a little bit disappointed, too, when I see that he is empty-handed. I was hoping he'd stop at Fitzpatrick's and bring me back a quart of Peaches 'n Cream. He is usually very thoughtful about things like that.

"Could you come in here, please?" he says. "We have visitors."

"In a minute, okay?"

Aunt Betsy and Uncle Richie must have stopped by, which is good news. I haven't had a chance to get up to visit with them as much as I'd like to, but Nell has been spending almost every day there except for when she's cutting hair. Nell and Aunt Betsy have really hit it off. Wait, that's not exactly right. Dave told me that

Peggy Sure and Aunt Betsy have really hit it off, which makes a lot more sense. It must feel so good for the mother of dead Junie to hold a little girl in her arms again.

I close my notebook and call next door, "See ya tomorrow at the block party?" I'd love for Ray Buck to come, but it's especially important that Ethel doesn't skip it. I want her to see the fruits of our labor.

"Wouldn't miss it for all the barbeque in Mississippi," she drawls back. "Sleep tight, Miss Sally. Don't let them bedbugs bite and if they do . . ."

"I'll beat them with my shoe, Ethel. Night, you two lovebirds," I say, wishing when I tug on the back screen door that it was me and Ray Buck lazing around that porch together, only he'd be a lot younger or I'd be a lot older. I'd be a lot browner or he'd be a lot lighter. I know it's just a crush, Henry doesn't have a thing to worry about, but I got to say, that man is the answer to the *Who Wrote the Book of Love?* question. Ray Buck makes my toes curl.

When he hears the door slam shut, Dave calls out to me, "We're in the living room," and that's followed up by a baby crying, so it must be Nell and Peggy Sure paying a visit and not my aunt and uncle like I thought. That's okay with me. Troo and me bumped into Nell last week at the Five and Dime. I think she might be getting a little better from whatever she had. She didn't look like she was going to win any beauty pageants soon, but her teeth were brushed and she wasn't talking to the hot pads in aisle six or singing to herself, which is a step in the right direction. (I have been making dirty phone calls to her on a regular basis so maybe that could be what's picking up her spirits. I heard her tell Mother that she has a "secret admirer.")

I say, "Hi, Nell," as I push open the swinging kitchen door.

I can see through the dining room straight into the living room. There's a baby in there all right, only it's not Peggy Sure. This baby is chubbier with lots of dark hair and it's not sitting in Nell's lap, but is getting bounced on the knee of somebody I thought was gone forever. Somebody who I was sure escaped a dragnet and moved to Brooklyn to work in a pizza palace. Somebody who is Greasy Al Molinari!

Chapter Thirty-four

Sitting next to Greasy Al on our davenport, I'm shocked to see somebody else I thought I would never see again as long as I lived. Dottie Kenfield! So that baby . . . that's got to be the one she was supposed to leave in the unwed mother's home in Chicago!

Dave says, "Come in, Sally."

I don't. That wouldn't be safe. I'm sure fugitive-from-justice Greasy Al must have a gun on Dave's back like in that Humphrey Bogart movie when he was holding that nice man against his will, but then I think that can't be right. Mother and Dave look calm and Dottie seems content and the baby's quit crying and . . . and this is something I never saw before. This is a once-in-a-lifetime experience. Greasy Al Molinari is grinning from ear to ear!

Dave smiles and pats the seat of the red velvet wingback chair, but I don't move from the kitchen doorway. If he's not here to hold Dave hostage, the only other reason I can think of to explain why

Molinari's sitting in our living room is that's he's piping mad about the poison-pen letters Troo wrote him in reform school every Friday. He's come to get his revenge by ratting Troo out.

I'm trying to come up with a good explanation so my sister doesn't get in trouble when Mother tells me, "Stop acting like such a ninny. Get in here. You're embarassing me."

Edging closer, I don't take my eyes off of Molinari for one step. He looks so different. His hair is cut shorter and isn't even that greasy and he doesn't smell like pepperoni, more like . . . like *schnitzel*? I haven't seen Dottie in the longest time in real life, but she looks the same as she does in her picture that is hanging in the Kenfields' living room. The one she had taken in her mint-green senior-dance dress. She's not wearing that, she's got on a pair of white pedal pushers and a blue gingham blouse, but the ruby ring is still hanging around her neck on a gold chain.

What are these two doing here? Together?

Dave, who I am sure is getting mental telepathy with me the same way Troo does, says, "Sally, I'd like you to meet Mr. and Mrs. Alfred Molinari and their daughter, Sophia."

Greasy Al musta slipped something into Dave's drink that made him say something so goofy. These two *can't* be married. They don't have a thing in common the way they're supposed to. Greasy Al dropped out of high school to spend all his time stealing hubcaps and kids' bikes and siphoning gas outta cars. Dottie Kenfield was the apple of her mom's and dad's eyes and on the honor roll at school and would help out at the Five and Dime on the weekends. The two of them being married would be like . . . like the Creature from the Black Lagoon and Julie Adams getting hitched!

Greasy Al hands the baby over to Dottie and stands up when I finally make it all the way into the room. "Thanks for leavin' the

Goldmans' back door open, kid," he says, very politely. "We'll pay them back for the food."

I gotta grab on to the arm of the wing chair to steady myself. Did I do that? After I promised Mrs. Goldman that I would keep such a good watch on her house? The afternoon I fell asleep . . . ran out . . . Oh, for the love of Mike.

I say to Dave, who musta found them over there when he went to fix the stove light, "I'm really, really sorry. I went to bring Mrs. Goldman a couple of Mother's old kitty puzzles and I . . . I . . . was gonna lie down just for a minute and I guess I didn't lock her place back up again and—" I never went back inside the house after that one time, only checked it from the sidewalk.

Dave says, "Calm down, Sally," the same way he does in the middle of the night after one of my nightmares that a lot of the time feature a certain *goombah* who is sitting across from me.

Mother shoots me a look, but says to her guests like she's been reading every issue of *Good Housekeeping*, "May I offer the two of you something to drink?"

Dottie, who's patting the baby's back, says, "I'd love a glass of ginger ale if you've got it, Mrs. O'Malley. I mean . . ."

"You can call me Helen, honey. I won't be Mrs. Rasmussen for a few more weeks. And how about you, Alfred?"

Oh, if Troo was only here to see this and not over at Fast Susie's! My sister's never gonna believe me when I tell her. She's going to roll her eyes and say something mean about my lunatic imagination.

"Ginger ale sounds good," Greasy Al says. "Thank you."

Dave, who is watching me rubbing and blinking my eyes, tells me, "They've been getting some help from Alfred's youngest brother for the past few weeks. He's been bringing formula and diapers and whatever else they need over to the Goldmans' once the neighborhood settles down for the night."

Moochie Molinari is on the smallish side and sneakier than an Indian about to raid a wagon train, so I don't doubt for a second that he could creep around these blocks without getting spotted.

"But . . . but why aren't you arrestin' him?" I ask Dave. "He escaped from reform school! He's wanted! He popped a guard!"

"I didn't wanna hit Mr. Franklin," Greasy Al says, forgetting his new manners and using his old bully voice. "I only did it 'cause I had to."

Dottie places her hand on his knee and gives him a pat. That must be some sort of secret signal she gives her husband when she wants him to pipe down. Mother gives signals like that to Dave, too. She scratches her nose when she wants him to change subjects.

"The baby and I were alone in Chicago and she got sick with scarlet fever," Dottie slowly explains to me. "I needed Alfred's help."

"But once the baby got better, why didn't the both of you stay hidden down there?" I ask. That's what I woulda done if I was them. "Why'd you come back?"

Dottie's eyes go moist when she says, "I . . . my mom and daddy . . . the baby . . ."

Greasy Al puts his arm around her like she's a flower he doesn't want to crush.

"These are what are known as extenuating circumstances, Sally," Dave says. "Alfred will be returning to the reform school to deal with his problem and while he's there, Dottie is hoping to stay with her mother and father."

I catch that. "What do you mean *hoping*? Don't the Kenfields already know about . . ." I point at the three of them.

Dottie sets the baby in Greasy Al's arms and comes up to the chair to kneel down in front of me. Up close, she looks older than in her picture except for her smile, that hasn't changed. She's still got very good teeth.

She says, "We didn't know how to . . . we were just talking about the best way to break the news to them and I thought you might be able to help us out. I know what a soft spot my dad has for you," she says.

That's true. At least it used to be. I always ask his wife to say hello to him for me when I visit the Five and Dime, but I've never heard anything back. And Mr. Kenfield hasn't invited me once to swing on his porch with him the way we did last summer.

I tell Dottie, "You know . . . your dad . . . he is . . . he's . . ." I'm trying to prepare her the way you would anybody who's in for a shock. "He's different than he was when you were still here. Sometimes he has too much to drink and he chases kids if they step one foot in his yard and he fell down in the dime store and knocked over all the Christmas decorations and . . . well, I'm sorry to have to be the one to tell you this, but he's pretty much gone down the drain."

Mother and Dave don't disagree with me or remind me to mind my manners. Everybody knows what bad shape Mr. Kenfield is in. It would be wrong to pretend we don't.

Dottie takes my hands in hers and says, "If you could just pave the way . . . I'm sure that Daddy . . ." She looks like she is about to start choke-crying. "It would mean the world to us."

I think about what she is asking me to do. I'm pretty sure that Mr. Kenfield isn't furious at his daughter anymore. If he was, he wouldn't have moved that picture out of her bedroom and hung it in his living room. It might be too much to expect him to feel the same way about his new son-in-law, Greasy Al.

Molinari says, "If ya could do this for us . . . the sooner the better. If things go smooth, I can leave without havin' to worry 'bout my girls."

My girls? Did he just say that so loving? I doubted Dave, but I guess he was right when he told me at the beginning of the summer that all Greasy Al needed to straighten out was some TLC.

Dottie gives my hands a squeeze and says, "Please, Sally."

I can see what she's feeling. It's that awful missing that never seems to get better. I know what it's like waiting around for time to heal all wounds.

I look down at Daddy's watch on my wrist and make up my mind. "Let's go," I say. "He should be out on the porch by now."

Dave thought the fresh air would do us some good, so Dottie, Greasy Al and me and the baby took the alleyway. I didn't want Mr. Kenfield to see us coming down the block. Just appearing without any warning might make him have a heart attack or something. Miracles can do that. At least twenty people musta died the day Jesus turned loaves into fishes.

We're standing together back by the tipped-over garbage cans when I tell them, "Wait here." I decided on the walk over that they should stay hidden for a while. I might have to peel Mr. Kenfield off the porch swing and wouldn't want Dottie and the baby to see him sloshed to the gills. "If you hear me whistle, come to the front porch. If you don't hear me whistle, maybe you two"—I point to Dottie and the baby in her arms— "could stay in the upstairs of the

Goldmans' until"—I point at Greasy Al—"he comes back after serving his time. It's empty and I've got the key." Our old landlady won't mind one bit. She was heartbroken when Troo and me moved out. She told me she would miss hearing the pattering of little feet.

There are a couple of lights on inside the Kenfields' when I wade through the backyard where the grass is almost up to my knees and over to the side yard where the bushes still need trimming. I peek around the corner of the house real quick to make sure he's out there the way he usually is, then I stand there for a minute, waiting for my courage to kick in. "Mr. Kenfield? Sir?" I can smell his cigarette smoke and see him in the shadows.

He doesn't answer right off, but then he asks, "Is that you, Sally?" When he leans forward toward the sound of my voice, he doesn't fall off the swing and his words don't sound like they're mushing together, so that's good.

"Yessir, it's me," I say, coming a weensy bit closer. If there is one thing I've learned in life it's that there is just no telling with people. I'm mostly sure Mr. Kenfield is going to be overjoyed to have his girl back again and his wife will be happy that she can take that stick outta her butt and maybe—this is a slim chance, but just maybe—finding out Greasy Al Molinari is part of their family now won't make the two of them run out of the house screaming. But . . . Mr. Kenfield could also jump offa that swing and chase me down the block, so I gotta be prepared to run. I'm keeping my knees bent. "Can I . . . would you mind if I sit with you for a while? Ya know . . . like the old days?"

He doesn't say yes, but he doesn't say no either, so I climb the front porch steps and go to my old place on the cushion where we used to be together on hot summer nights when I still lived next door. There's enough light coming through the living room window that I can see his scruffy beard. He's got on a holey T-shirt and floppy slippers and his suspenders are around his waist. He smells a little like milk that's gone bad.

After a few back and forths on the still-creaky swing, Mr. Kenfield says in a sticky voice, "My wife tells me that you're doing well." I'm glad to hear that he's been keeping track of me the same way I've been trying to keep track of him. "I understand your mother and Detective Rasmussen are planning to get married."

"Yessir, they are."

"Dave will be good for Helen," he says, taking a drag off his cigarette. "She could use a steady influence."

We don't say anything else for a while, just rock and listen to the night sounds. Across the street they're turning the lights out at the playground and kids are calling to each other, "See ya tomorrow, same time, same station," and somewhere down the block a radio is playing a song I don't recognize and a girl laughs.

When I think enough time has gone by for Mr. Kenfield to be used to me again, I pick up his hand and say, "I like where you hung Dottie's picture."

He doesn't turn to look over his shoulder at it. He has to know it by heart.

"I been thinkin' . . . how about . . . what if . . ." I can't figure out the best way to tell him, so I just come out with it. "Wouldn't it be great if all of a sudden Dottie came walkin' around the corner of the house with her little baby in her arms? Wouldn't that be something?"

Mr. Kenfield brings his hands up to his face and makes a noise that I know so well. It's the same sound people make when they come to the cemetery to visit the graves of their dearly departed.

That's all I need to hear.

After I put my fingers between my lips and give a whistle to Dottie and Greasy Al, who are waiting in the alley, I pat Mr. Kenfield's knee and say, "I want you to know that I've really missed you, Mr. Kenfield. See ya at the end-of-the-summer party." With that, I hop down the porch steps and head toward home, knowing that I'm leaving them in good hands. Up to now, I could only *hope* that love was standing by all this time, waiting to give them a push in the right direction. I don't get sure of it until I hear their happy crying all the way down the block.

Chapter Thirty-five

Red balloons are waving off the playground fence and Christmas lights are twinkling from everybody's front porches. There was some talk of calling the block party off because of Father Mickey's disappearance, but that didn't last very long. Everybody in the neighborhood really looks forward to this night and after all we've been through the past three months, I think we need it the way you do a drink of water after you've run a long race. It's still warm and muggy tonight like it has been all summer, but the sky is clear and the moon will come up with a little orange around the edges. I know that means the leaves are getting ready to change and harvest time is not far off. I wish Daddy was here to see this. He always did like a lush party.

The end-of-the-summer shindig is always held on Vliet Street because we can all spread out at the playground after they declare the Queen and King. We really do need room to dance to the Do

Wops' music after we get done stuffing ourselves with food from the cook-off. Card tables are lined up on the sidewalk and you can just grab a plate and eat as much as you want. My stomach is going to have to wait, though. I'm in a big hurry to get to where Mother has set up. I want to make sure the surprise I planned is going the way it's supposed to.

Troo's not the only one who can come up with a plan, ya know.

Last week, so Mother wouldn't send half the neighborhood to the hospital, I fibbed to her. I told her I heard Mrs. Latour was also bringing cow tongue in turnip sauce to the cook-off. (I slipped Artie the recipe. He's supposed to talk his mom into that. I've got my fingers crossed.) I warned Mother that if she didn't want to be called a copycat behind her back, she better bring another dish that would knock everybody's socks off. "Mississippi blond brownies would be a sure blue-ribbon winner," I said, knowing that she would fall for that because this is another way her and Troo are so much alike.

After I planted that seed in Mother's brain, I ran next door and told Ethel what I wanted to do. She nodded her head and said, "Bless your heart."

She can't enter the contest because she's not one of us. She didn't say so, but I could tell by the way her eyes crinkled that she thought it was funny that we were going to pull the wool over everybody's eyes. Over the past few days, we've baked dozens and dozens of brownies in Mrs. Galecki's kitchen. On our last batch, I asked her if it bothered her that after all this hard work, she wouldn't get a lick of credit. Ethel slid the pan of blondies outta the oven with a knowing smile and said, "It'll be different someday, Miss Sally, but 'til then, it's a smart cat who knows how to use the back door."

When I get to where they've set up, Dave is standing by Mother's side at her cook-off table. She looks outstanding tonight in a pink blouse and pleated beige slacks. She wore her hair my favorite way. Long and loose, just flowing. Dave, who looks good, too, in a very Danish way, is handing out the brownies as fast as he can. I can't even get close, that's how long a line there is for Ethel's delicious something-somethings.

"*You* made these, Helen?" Mrs. Latour asks from the next table over and helps herself to three. There is not one person standing in front of her and her dish. Not even Mary Lane.

Mother gives me a wink when she says back to Mrs. Latour in her most charming voice, "So sorry that your cow tongue in turnip sauce is such a flop, Dolores. You might want to go easier on the lard."

Down the block, in front of their house, Mrs. Kenfield is set up with a ton of candy from the Five and Dime, and her face . . . it's beaming like a saint's on a holy card. Dottie is by her side and from up on the porch, little Sophia is crying on her grampa's lap, which has to be music to all their ears. Greasy Al is not here. When we were working together in the garden this morning, Dave told me Molinari was returned to the reform school yesterday. I'm not sure when he'll get out, but until he does Dottie and the baby will be staying in her old room.

Of course, every lip in the neighborhood is flapping about Greasy Al and Dottie. That news spread faster than melted butter. (I wish you coulda seen Troo's face when I first told her. She rolled her eyes into the back of her head and said, just like I knew she would, "Married? Dottie and the *goombah*? That's nothin' but a fig newton of your lunatic imagination!")

When Mr. Kenfield spots me stopping at their table to pick up Oh Henry! bars and Snirkles for Mother and B-B-Bats for Dave and wax lips for Troo, he calls down, "Load up your pockets. Take as many as you want, Sally." That is a happy ending, which I admit I am a sucker for. Since they pay a visit to you so rarely, you just gotta throw down the welcome mat when they show up, right?

The Vliet Street gang has settled into our usual spot on the O'Haras' front steps, eating until we can barely breathe. Except for Willie. He gets butterflies before he has to perform so he just drinks Kool-Aid.

From across the street at the playground, cheerful Debbie the new counselor—I really have to hand it to her, she has not lost one ounce of her pep no matter how many times Mary Lane ties her shoelaces together or sticks gum in her hair or calls her Roy—announces into a microphone from the stage that's set up especially for the party, "It's time for the further festivities to begin! Will all the contestants who are participating in the talent show please join me?"

Troo picks up the Jerry Mahoney ventriloquist doll that Dave bought her at the toy store for doing so good on her extra religious instruction. (I told him to do that. Troo likes people better when they give her things.) "Here goes nothin'," she says, and runs across Vliet Street to join the other kids.

I yell after her, "Break a leg," because that's what Willie told me you're supposed to say to a performer before their show. I think it's mean, but I also wish just a little bit that could happen. My sister would be so much easier to keep track of if she was in a cast.

Once all the kids have filed up onto the stage, Debbie announces to the crowd, "Let the talent show begin!"

For the next hour, everybody in the neighborhood gets to hang up their troubles and be entertained by seventeen kids who do all sorts of talent like baton twirling and tap dancing and card tricks. Troo is excellent with her Jerry doll. Her lips move only a couple of times. Mary Lane swings across the monkey bars four times without stopping and Mimi Latour sings *Ave Maria*. Because she has a true calling, that's extremely good holy singing on Mimi's part so it will be close between her and Troo for Queen.

I don't take part in the contest. I tell everyone I have a sore throat. I do that because my impression of a munchkin singing the *We Represent the Lollypop Guild* song, if I do say so myself, is dynamite. Real TNT. I couldn't do that to my sister. Or to myself. I don't want to wake up with worms in my bed.

When it's the boys' turn, they are good, too. Artie is excellent with his yo-yo tricks, especially that three-leaf clover one, but I think Willie O'Hara is a shoo-in for King. His jokes have us all in stitches.

This is his best one:

"Did you hear about the Polack who thought his wife was tryin' to kill him because he found a bottle of polish remover on her dressin' table?"

Now that everybody's done giving it their best shot, we can't wait to hear who the winners are.

"Attention, please," says Barbie, the old counselor. Since she is the boss of the playground, she's the one who's got the crown in her hands. It's made out of gold or something. Not like the tiara the girl is gonna get, with sparkling rhinestones. "It's time to announce this summer's King of the Playground." She unfolds a piece of paper and says, "Congratulations . . . Willie O'Hara!"

You can tell everybody thinks that's a great choice because they're hip, hip hurraying!

Troo is standing next to me in front of the stage, looking very sure of herself when Barbie says, "And the Queen this summer is . . ."

That's when my sister does something that I will never forget until my dying day. Instead of running up onto the stage to receive the tiara that I think she's sure to win, Troo cuts Barbie off by shouting, "Wen . . . dy! Wen . . . dy! Wen . . . dy!" and then I join in, too, and before you know it everybody else in the neighborhood, even the mothers and fathers and the hoods who are hanging out near the fence, are chanting along with us.

Maybe it's because another summer has slipped by and we all know Wendy doesn't have many more left. Or maybe it's because she looks so pretty in her frilly dress with her shiny hair and the new Cracker Jack ring I slipped on her finger before the party. Whatever the reason, what can Barb do? She tears up the piece of paper she has in her hand with the real Queen's name on it, throws it up in the air and announces, "For the second year in a row . . . may I present her Royal Highness Miss . . ."

Wendy Latour. You'd think she'd be shocked and shy, but she isn't. She acts like she knew all along that she was gonna be the one. After she glides up those stage steps and lets Barb take off her old rhinestone crown and put the new one on, Wendy waves and throws a load of Dinah Shore kisses to her adoring subjects.

And then the Do Wops burst into *Rock Around the Clock* and all of us grab partners and start dancing.

When Henry takes me by the hand, he calls me Peaches 'n Cream and I almost faint, that's how good it feels to dance with my pale future husband. I don't even care that Troo gives me that dumb smoochy face when she bops by with Artie doing the jack. Even though it's a fast song, Dave and Mother are waltzing next to Henry and me. (Practicing for the wedding, I think. Mother has a hard time letting Dave lead so they have to work that out.) Even Nell looks less like death warmed over. She is doing the twist with Uncle Richie

Piaskowski, who I really like. He laughed the hardest at Willie's
Polack jokes so I think we're going to get along great because just like
me, he doesn't get his nose pushed outta joint that easy. (Of course, it
runs to the large side, which Troo pointed out when she asked him,
"What do ya use for a handkerchief? A bedsheet?")

And Ethel and Ray Buck, man, oh, man. They are doing this
new dance called the boogaloo. I'm going to suggest a dance competition to the counselors for next year's party. Maybe next summer could be the "someday" Ethel mentioned to me.

Uncle Paulie is having a ball, too. He's doing a dance with
Granny in her *muu-muu*, which I think is supposed to be the kind
of hula the girls do on *Hawaiian Eye* but to me seems very voodoo-
ish because my uncle is too jerky around the hips.

But best of all—I will love Dave forever for doing this—when a
slow song starts up, he bows to Wendy Latour and takes her for a
royal spin. Watching them, I can't help but think about how she'll
be able to go on just the same way she always has giving hugs and
swinging half-naked and showing up in the oddest places without
everybody thinking bad of her for accidentally killing God's worst
employee.

Father Mickey isn't the only one not having the time of his life
tonight. Poor Aunt Betty. Mr. Stanley Talmidge, owner of the
Uptown Theatre, gave her the brush-off at the party so she won't
get into the movies free anymore. And Mrs. Latour is also sulking
because Mother won the cook-off with the blondies. Eddie, Nell's
butt of a husband, isn't having the best night either. He was breathing so hot and heavy into Melinda Urbanski's high-and-mighty
bosoms that he didn't notice right off the fire in the backseat of his
'57 Chevy that somebody near and dear to me started. It wasn't a
four alarmer or anything, just big enough that Dave, who might

have a lot more Viking in him than I originally thought, walked past me and Mary Lane *very* slowly with a bucket of water. Between the holes in the leather and the water damage, what a pity that Eddie's gonna have to pay to get it reupholstered.

The block party doesn't end until close to eleven o'clock. We all want it to go on longer, but that's the way the cookie crumbles. Tomorrow morning Troo and me will have to go to Shuster's to get our new loafers and Granny will put in shiny new pennies and then over we'll go to the Five and Dime for our school supplies. The day after that we will walk these blocks with all the other kids in our new uniforms to Mother of Good Hope School beneath trees whose leaves are thinking about turning. Before we know it, Mother and Dave's wedding bells will be ringing and Ethel will be making Troo and me warm Ovaltine instead of cold.

Not until we get back home after the party and get cozy between our sheets, once Troo has Daddy's blue shirt on and her baby doll in her arms, do I tell her, "Givin' away the tiara to Wendy . . . that was really something." The reason I waited until we were alone was because I didn't want to say anything good about her in front of everybody. She wouldn't want her reputation wrecked. "You were gonna win for sure." That's a lie. When nobody was looking, I pieced together the paper with the *real* winner's name. It wasn't Troo who was going to be crowned. Believe it or not, it was monkey-bar-swinging Mary Lane. (That's a pretty crummy talent, but I think Debbie the peppy counselor was too afraid *not* to make her Queen.)

Then we mention Lou Budette for Daddy the way we do every night, and after I butterfly-kiss my sister on her cheek, I add on, "I'm so proud of you." I don't think I've ever said that to her before.

My sister says, "Yeah, well. Ya know."

I do. On the walk home from the party I figured out why Troo did what she did for Wendy tonight. Those two have a lot more in common now than they used to. My sister accidentally killed a father, too.

I move my hand to my favorite furry baby blanket part up near Troo's neck. We haven't talked even once about what we did to Father Mickey since that night. I kept the outside of her safe this summer the way I promised Daddy I would, but what about her insides? Her half-buried feelings? More and more, they seem important to me to dig up.

I ask, "How do you feel about what happened?" She knows what I mean. "Ya know, deep down."

Troo doesn't answer right off, but when she leans in to give me my butterfly kiss, when she twines her fingers into mine, she doesn't smart-mouth me the way I thought she might. She sighs and whispers, "The Almighty works in mysterious ways, *ma cherie*," and with the sound of Ethel's saxophone music coming over the fence and the Moriaritys' dog barking up the block and the smell of the chocolate chip cookies drifting through our window, I would have to agree with her.

Acknowledgments

Heartfelt thanks to:

My editor, Ellen Edwards, for her genius insights.
Publishers Brian Tart and Kara Welsh, for believing in me.
The fabulous behind-the-scenes team at Dutton and NAL.
My wonderful agent, Kim Witherspoon.
Emily Lewis, Lenore Buss, Maddie James, Paul Sheldon and Rochelle
   Staab, my early readers.
Mike Lebow.
Madeira James for her superb work on my website.
Readers and book clubs. You've made my life sweeter in so many
   ways.
Devoted booksellers.

Acknowledgments

Milwaukee.

Pete, who still makes me laugh.

Riley and Casey, my dream team.

John-Michael, our ray of southern sunshine.

Charlie, my wonder baby, you make it all brand-new again.

About the Author

Lesley Kagen is an actress, voice-over talent, and restaurateur, as well as the author of three previous novels. Her national bestselling *Whistling in the Dark* has been translated into five languages and was a Midwest Choice Award winner. The mother of two grown children, she lives with her husband near Milwaukee, Wisconsin. Visit her at lesleykagen.com.